Fly Away
With Me

Books by Susan Fox

Blue Moon Harbor Series
Fly Away With Me

Caribou Crossing Romances
"Caribou Crossing" novella
Home on the Range
Gentle on My Mind
"Stand By Your Man" novella
Love Me Tender
Love Somebody Like You
Ring of Fire
Holiday in Your Heart

Wild Ride to Love Series
His, Unexpectedly
Love, Unexpectedly
Yours, Unexpectedly

Also by Susan Fox
Body Heat

Writing as Susan Lyons
Sex Drive
She's On Top
Touch Me
Hot in Here
Champagne Rules

Anthologies
The Naughty List
Some Like It Rough
Men on Fire
Unwrap Me
The Firefighter

Fly Away
With Me

SUSAN FOX

ZEBRA BOOKS
KENSINGTON PUBLISHING CORP.

http://www.kensingtonbooks.com

ZEBRA BOOKS are published by

Kensington Publishing Corp.
119 West 40th Street
New York, NY 10018

All Kensington titles, imprints, and distributed lines are available at special quantity discounts for bulk purchases for sales promotion, premiums, fund-raising, educational, or institutional use.

Special book excerpts or customized printings can also be created to fit specific needs. For details, write or phone the office of the Kensington Sales Manager: Attn.: Sales Department. Kensington Publishing Corp., 119 West 40th Street, New York, NY 10018. Phone: 1-800-221-2647.

Zebra and the Z logo Reg. U.S. Pat. & TM Off.

First Printing: August 2017
ISBN-13: 978-1-4201-4324-9
ISBN-10: 1-4201-4324-7

eISBN-13: 978-1-4201-4325-6
eISBN-10: 1-4201-4325-5

10 9 8 7 6 5 4 3 2 1

Printed in the United States of America

Chapter One

When Eden Blaine tugged her wheeled carry-on bag off the sloped ramp from the seaplane terminal onto the wooden dock, she almost lost her balance. The surface beneath her feet looked flat, but it moved gently, disconcertingly.

Thank heavens I left my lawyer suit and heels in Ottawa. Her jeans and loafers were much better suited to this venue, even though Vancouver Harbour Flight Centre nestled along the shore of a huge, cosmopolitan city.

For a moment, she forgot all about being rushed and frazzled. The view compelled her to stop and stare. On this sunny, early June afternoon, the harbor spread out before her in a spectacular panorama. Boats bustling along, green swaths of parkland, a cruise ship terminal, the white sails of Canada Place, commercial docks, and a whole other city on the far shore, sheltering under dramatic mountains: There was too much to take in. She breathed deeply, expecting to fill her lungs with the fresh tang of ocean air, but a nose-wrinkling underlay of fuel odor reminded her why she was here, standing on this narrow, unstable dock in the middle of all this amazing scenery. The scent, the motion, and the anticipation of the upcoming flight combined to make her jittery with nerves.

Eden hadn't done much flying but had occasionally taken a smallish jet from Ottawa to Toronto or Montreal. Compared to what she'd thought of as *smallish*, the seaplanes tied up to the dock were minuscule. Add to that the fact that she'd never taken off from or landed on water . . .

Her hand rose to her mouth and her teeth closed on a fingernail. Before she could gnaw on it, she forced her hand down and curled her fingers around the handle of the briefcase that hung over one shoulder along with her purse. Nana had broken her of the nail-biting habit when she was in fourth grade, saying that not only was it unattractive and unhygienic but it was a sure giveaway of anxiety, insecurity, and lack of control. None of which were qualities Eden wanted to reveal to the outside world.

This was going to be an adventure, and adventure was definitely *not* her middle name. Still, she'd face any peril if she could restore her mom's once-bright spirit. The seaplane flight would get her to Destiny Island a day earlier than the ferry would have, and with only a week off work to find her mother's long-lost sister, every hour was important. Her mom, fragile after a double mastectomy, followed by chemotherapy and radiation, was counting on her. Eden's parents were wonderful and she never, ever let them down.

Eden refused to let herself think for one moment that her quest might end in learning that her aunt, Lucy, was dead.

Squaring her shoulders, she tugged her wheelie along the dock toward the plane with the Blue Moon Air logo. She had to admit it looked perky with its blue-and-white paint shining in the sunlight, the wings mounted from the top of the cabin, and the pontoons holding it atop the deep, bluish-green ocean. The logo was appealing too: a blue moon with a white plane flying across it.

Half a dozen people clustered beside the plane: three sixtyish men in outdoorsy clothes, two women a decade or two younger in jeans and hoodies, and a lean but broad-shouldered guy in jeans and a blue T-shirt. His back was to her as he hoisted luggage onto the plane. One of the women spotted Eden, raised a hand in a tentative wave, and said something to the others.

The broad-shouldered guy turned, straightening, and she felt a physical sensation akin to the one she'd experienced when she first saw the horrendous taxi lineup at Vancouver International Airport. *After* her flight from Ottawa had been late arriving.

Well, not exactly akin. At the airport, the legs-stopping-moving-of-their-own-accord, air-leaving-her-lungs-in-a-whoosh sensation had been nasty, whereas this one was quite pleasant.

As she forced her legs onward, she took a visual inventory. Lean and nicely muscled; narrow hips and long legs to complement those broad shoulders. Hair so dark a brown it was almost black, longish and shaggy rather than styled. Medium brown skin. Aviator sunglasses hiding his eyes, making it difficult to assess his age, though she guessed it was close to her own twenty-nine. Ruggedly handsome features lit by a smile as he strode to meet her.

That smile warmed her in a way that made her feel special. And that was silly, because of course he merely was relieved that she'd finally shown up and the flight could depart.

"I'm Aaron Gabriel, Blue Moon Air pilot. And you'd be Eden Blaine." He reached for the long handle of her wheelie.

As he shoved the handle down and hefted the bag, she confirmed, "Yes, I would be. I'm so sorry for the delay." She hated being late, hated inconveniencing people. When she'd phoned Blue Moon Air from the airport taxi lineup, she'd said she wouldn't make the flight on time and asked if she could reschedule for the next morning. To her astonishment and delight, the man who'd answered had said they'd hold the flight for her.

"Ah, well, airlines," the pilot now said in a joking tone. "Never can rely on them being on time."

What could she possibly say to that? She firmly believed in adhering to schedules, yet the airline's flexibility had worked to her benefit today. Rather than respond, she kept quiet as she followed him to the plane.

As he loaded her carry-on into the cargo hold, she apologized to the other passengers, who all murmured variations of "No problem."

Aaron took her briefcase from her and stowed it, too, but let her keep her purse. "Climb aboard," he told her.

"But what about everyone else?" No one else had boarded.

"We have a boarding order. Your seat's first. Hop in." He offered her his hand.

Eyeing the dock, which heaved rhythmically up and

down, the plane, which also bobbed up and down but to a different beat, and the insubstantial three-step metal ladder that connected the two, she gratefully put her hand into his.

Warm, firm, secure. Touching him reminded her of just how wonderful male-female contact could be. She'd missed that since she and Ray had ended their four-year relationship. In fact, she didn't remember Ray's hands ever feeling this good. He had city hands, well-groomed but not supermasculine. Hands that were efficient in operating a computer, handling legal files, and bringing her to orgasm. Competent, yet not exactly virile.

And what was she doing, thinking about sex? Embarrassed, she clambered up the ladder and then let go of Aaron's hand. "Where do I sit?"

"Up front, right-hand seat."

"But that's the copilot's seat."

"Don't need a copilot on a plane this size. That's a passenger seat."

No copilot? Aaron Gabriel looked entirely healthy, but anyone could have a stroke, a heart attack, or an aneurysm.

He shoved his sunglasses atop his head and winked. "Don't worry. I'm one hundred percent fit." His gaze rested on her for a long moment, and there was a spark in his long-lashed, bluish-gray eyes that hinted at flirtation.

That spark sent a corresponding tingle rippling through her blood, almost strong enough to combat her jittery nerves. She'd never been a highly sensual woman, so it was unsettling to feel this purely female awareness of a sexy man. She cleared her throat. "I'm glad to hear that." Her voice came out in lawyer mode, too formal for the situation. Giving herself an internal headshake, she scrambled into the right front seat and fumbled for the seat belt as the other passengers piled in behind her.

Eden liked order and predictability, situations she could control, and this one was anything but that. Taking deep breaths, she thought ruefully that up until a year ago, her life had been happy and uncomplicated. She'd had her family, her terrific job, and Ray, her life mate. Then Nana died, Mom was diagnosed, and, two months ago, Eden and Ray broke up. Now her mom was finally finished with chemo and radiation but still feeling sick and depressed—at least until a week ago, when she'd found an out-of-the-blue clue to her sister Lucy's disappearance, and nothing would do but for Eden to follow it. Immediately. And so here she was, about to put her life in the hands of the handsome pilot and his perky miniature plane.

Aaron stowed the ladder and shut the boarding hatch from the outside, then stepped onto a float and entered through the door by the pilot's seat. He gave the passengers a safety briefing that included seat belts, turning off electronic devices, emergency procedures, life preservers, exits, and so on. He advised them to read the safety card in the seat pocket, asked if there were any questions, and then said, "Let's fly, folks."

Buckled in, with a headset on, he started the plane's engine and talked to air traffic control.

Eden concentrated on memorizing the safety card, trying not to imagine crash landings or pilot heart attacks.

Aaron signalled a man on the dock, who untied the

ropes. As they motored out into the harbor, the plane bounced over gentle waves. The motion was rather like driving over a heavily rutted road in her little Smart car. Except that the fragile plane was soon going to fling itself into the great blue yonder. She clasped her hands and squeezed them together, another defense against nail-biting.

"We'll be making three stops this afternoon," Aaron told the passengers, speaking loudly to make himself heard over the engine noise. "First, we'll fly up the Sunshine Coast to Texada Island for our Sylvan Retreat couple. Then west to Campbell River to drop off the three fishers. Then south again to Blue Moon Harbor on Destiny Island."

Eden's dad had booked the flight and she had assumed it was a direct one from Vancouver to Blue Moon Harbor. Her logical brain suggested that flying north, west, and then south wasn't the most efficient way to reach Destiny Island, but it didn't really matter. Her goals for today were to get settled at the Once in a Blue Moon B and B, confirm the rental car she'd reserved for tomorrow morning, and make inquiries of the owners of the B and B.

Normally, Eden planned everything in exquisite detail, but the past week had been crazy. She'd had to organize files and appointments at work so she could leave her assistant in charge and make copious notes for her younger sister Kelsey, who was home from university for the summer and would help Dad care for Mom. There'd been only a moment here and there to prepare for the trip. Her dad had helped, making travel arrangements and using his Internet skills to search for information on the island, but most of what he'd found was tourism-focused. He'd located only two mentions of the old commune, nothing that would help Eden track down a hippie girl named Lucy Nelson who'd come to Destiny Island in 1969. Eden hoped her hosts at the B and B could identify some of the island's longtime residents, whom she could interview.

The plane increased speed and its nose came up, the floats skimmed the tops of the waves, and then the small craft lifted into the air. Rather than the white-noise drone Eden was used to when flying, she heard a whiny engine roar and a rattling sound. The dashboard—or whatever they called it in a plane—sported a collection of confusing dials and gauges. The huge window in front of her made it impossible to ignore the scarily vast expanse of sky outside. To her right was another window, in a flimsy door. If that door snapped open, the only thing holding her in the plane would be the seat belt. The aircraft seemed so insubstantial and she felt vulnerable, which she hated. She gulped, took more deep breaths, clenched her hands more firmly, and glanced over at Aaron's comforting solidness and his strong brown hands on the steering yoke.

The man's been thoroughly trained, he knows what he's doing, and he must have regular medical exams. The plane's a commercial craft, owned by a reputable airline, and is inspected regularly. There's not a single thing to worry about.

"Nervous?" Aaron asked, shooting a pointed look at her tightly clasped hands.

Since her body'd already given her away, she admitted, "Trying not to be," speaking up to be heard over the noise.

"Relax and enjoy it." He gave her a smile full of warmth and enthusiasm. "It's the best thing in the world."

You must be kidding. But he wasn't. The sincerity of his tone and body language confirmed that he meant it. As he returned his attention to the plane's controls, she mulled over his words. To this man, the best thing in the world was flying. He had a job where he experienced joy every day, just as she did. Her work as program counsel for the Butterworth Foundation involved administrative and legal details, which she excelled at and took satisfaction in, but what she truly loved was helping provide funds for worthwhile charities and nonprofits.

Still, as much as she enjoyed her job, the best thing in her world was her family. She loved her mom, her dad, and her younger sister with all her heart. They were the center of her world, her top priority at all times. Idly, she wondered about the handsome pilot beside her. What people were special to him? A wife or girlfriend? Parents? Maybe a son or daughter? Had he considered them when he made that blithe statement about flying being the best thing in the world?

She was overanalyzing. That attribute was useful for a lawyer, but family and friends kept reminding her it wasn't the most comfortable trait to bring to bear in a personal relationship. Yet her musings had distracted her from her anxiety and she felt more relaxed.

"Lions Gate Bridge," Aaron announced to the passengers. "Also known as First Narrows. It connects Vancouver's Stanley Park to West Vancouver and the North Shore."

The view was a dramatic one of contrasts: the forest

green of the park versus the high-rises of the city; the impressive and beautiful man-made span of the bridge versus the untamed ocean below; the industrial loading docks versus the rugged mountains behind. "Ottawa seems awfully"—she searched for the right description—"sedate and old-world in comparison."

"You're from Ottawa?" Aaron said. "How about the rest of you?"

"Vancouver," one of the other women answered. "Even so, the scenery never gets old."

"We're from Edmonton," one of the men said.

Another added, "We came out here for the fishing a few years ago and now it's an annual thing. There's something about fishing for salmon on the open ocean that gets into a man's blood. Not to mention being able to take home fish you caught yourself and lord it over all the Alberta beef-eaters."

Fishing held no appeal to Eden and she'd had no experience with the ocean. But gazing down at tankers and sailboats gave her some small notion of what an important role the sea played in some people's lives.

Ever since she'd agreed to undertake this mission for her mother, she'd been focused on practicalities, but now a tingle of excitement quickened her pulse. She was in a new place, a ruggedly scenic setting, and something about the vista of ocean and mountains invigorated her. Adventure might not be her middle name, but it seemed she was on one, and right now it didn't feel half bad.

Something had drawn Lucy, the aunt Eden had never even known about until a week before, to Destiny Island. What had Lucy experienced there—and what lay in store for Eden?

Chapter Two

Aaron was multitasking. Every sense was alert to the sky and attuned to the de Havilland Beaver, the plane's nonverbal language more familiar to him than that of any human being in his life, even his complicated, frustrating, and much-loved half sister.

That didn't stop him from giving his standard tourist spiel, providing his passengers with information about Lighthouse Park, Bowen Island, and the Sunshine Coast. He was also, inevitably, very aware of the slim, brown-haired woman in the seat beside him.

His first impression of Eden Blaine had been twofold: beautiful in a sneaks-up-on-you way and stressed-out. Feeling upset and guilty over arriving late and more than a little terrified about flying in a seaplane. He'd been afraid she'd be a white-knuckle flyer or, even worse, a puker, but instead the magic had captured her. Her body had relaxed and she'd lost that strained expression, gazing bright-eyed at the scenery and joining the other passengers in asking him questions.

It made him happy when passengers related to the

allure of flying in this beautiful part of the world. He especially liked it when the passenger was a woman he was attracted to. Eden's enthusiasm made her even prettier. When she glanced at him, those bright eyes were the amber of dark maple syrup. They went perfectly with the glossy walnut-brown hair that was trying to escape the clasp that held it in a low ponytail. Her complexion was pale and creamy, the opposite of his own skin, darkened by his biological father's First Nations blood and by many hours spent outdoors. Either Eden had a heavy hand with the sunscreen or she hadn't been outside much recently.

Her ring finger was bare.

At twenty-eight, Aaron was a sworn bachelor and didn't figure his views on the subject of commitment would ever change. So he was careful about who he got involved with. He didn't want to disappoint or hurt a woman who was looking for something more than he'd ever be able to give.

Why was Eden traveling to Destiny Island? As the owner of Blue Moon Air, he reviewed the bookings regularly and knew she was scheduled to fly back in a week's time. An Ottawa woman wouldn't likely come to Destiny on holiday by herself, and her blazer, briefcase, and initial stress level conveyed a business-trip aura. What kind of business could occupy her for a week? Destiny was small and relatively undeveloped, which was a big part of its charm. Oh well; he had time to learn more about Eden before the flight ended, because she was the final passenger.

"We're five minutes out from Texada," he announced. He glanced over his shoulder at the two women who were traveling together. "Have you been to Sylvan Retreat before?"

"Yes," the older one responded, leaning forward so her voice would carry over the engine noise. "We go two or three times a year. Marg's a painter and I'm an author, and it's a wonderful place for recharging our creativity."

"Creativity?" one of the fishers said, his tone making it clear he didn't relate.

"Yes," the younger of the two women, Marg, said firmly. "In the morning, we do yoga, meditation, and creativity exercises. In the afternoon, we each work on our own projects. In the evening, everyone gathers to share what we've done and, more importantly, what we've learned."

"Meditation?" the same fisherman said. "Well, if that's what turns your crank."

Not liking the guy's disparaging tone, Aaron said, "I've heard some fishers say that fishing can be kind of a Zen thing. There's just you, the ocean, the fish."

The older woman took up his theme. "Really, it's the *possibility* of fish. You know they exist in that ocean around you, but will they take your hook? You wait, you're in the moment but part of something bigger, something timeless. And then it changes in an instant when a fish bites. Nothing else exists but that primal battle. Isn't that what it's like?"

"It is," one of the other fishers responded, sounding surprised. "That's exactly what it's like. It can be the most peaceful thing in the world, or the most exciting."

"It's not meditation," the first guy said stubbornly.

"Because real men don't meditate?" Eden asked in a pseudoinnocent tone.

Everyone but the stubborn fisher chuckled. The guy's friend said, "She's got you there, Fred."

"Real men," said Marg, "have the self-esteem to not feel threatened by terms like *meditation* and *Zen*."

Aaron agreed, but he didn't want ill will in his plane. "There's Sylvan Retreat," he announced, squinting behind his dark glasses as he flew over the small V-shaped harbor, checking the glittering ocean surface. He noted a powerboat heading out and a pair of kayakers hugging the shore, as well as a tall figure on the dock, waving. "Harold Janks is waiting for us." The white-haired man and his wife owned the retreat. Aaron had been flying in this region since he was a teen and knew many of the locals.

Choosing his approach, he set the Beaver down to skim the waves, then the plane settled into them with a gentle bump and swish. At the dock, Harold helped him tie up. Aaron assisted his two passengers down the steps to the wharf, where they hugged Harold.

"Thank you for a lovely flight," the older woman said as Aaron set their bags on the wharf. "We appreciated the information you gave and your willingness to answer questions."

"Usually," her friend Marg said, "we feel as if we're just more baggage in the back of the plane, for all the attention the pilot pays us. Are all Blue Moon Air pilots as personable as you?"

"There's only me and Jillian flying for Blue Moon." He raised his sunglasses to wink at the women. "Hate to admit it, but she's even more personable than me."

As they laughed and turned away, he untied the mooring lines. Being *personable* was something he'd had to learn. When Lionel Williams had taught him to fly—an antiestablishment, middle-aged man and a teenaged rebel doing it by themselves without giving a damn for legalities—Aaron had loved flying immediately. Sitting in that cockpit up in the sky, he'd felt like he belonged for the first time in his life. Flying was what he was born to do. Besides, it was daring, a challenge, and it let him escape from real life. Once he'd become comfortable as a pilot, it had become a Zenlike experience, and he had no problem admitting that. He was always alert, yet he and the plane felt like a single being, as much a part of the sky as the soaring gulls.

Years later, after he'd done his formal training and started Blue Moon Air, he'd realized that passengers disturbed that Zenlike feeling. So be it. If they paid him good money and enabled him to make a living doing what he loved, he would be grateful and give them as much as he could in return. Fortunately, as he'd grown up and made a good life for himself, he'd become a happier man. One who didn't carry resentment, hurt, and anger. It didn't take all that much effort for a contented guy to be friendly to folks. Especially to folks who had chosen, even if only for a visit, to be in this special corner of the world.

Back in the Beaver, he steered out of the harbor and took off, the light breeze serving as a tail wind. As they gained altitude, he set a course northwest to Campbell River on Vancouver Island. Painter's Lodge was renowned for salmon fishing; people came from all over the world. "How long are you guys staying at Painter's?" he asked.

"We booked ten days," Fred said. "We'll see how the fishing is. If they're not biting, we'll go somewhere else."

The Zen one said, "We haven't arranged our flight back because we're not sure where we'll be. Okay if we give you a call when we know?"

"You bet. You can tell me about the ones you caught and the ones that got away."

"Deal," the man said.

"Last time we were here," Fred said, "it was in the fall and we fished the Tyee Pool. You know about that? Where there's no engines and you have to use a row-boat?"

Aaron did know, but Fred was already telling him how he'd caught a forty-five pounder, making it sound like an epic battle. Aaron glanced at Eden, who gave him a hint of an eye roll, and he grinned. Fishers and their tall tales were an everyday experience in these parts.

He was looking forward to dropping the three men and having Eden alone in the cockpit. In the mean-time, as he flew across the Strait of Georgia, he saw her gaze out intently, seeming intrigued by the ocean traffic: a couple of white BC Ferries, a tug towing a log boom, tankers and container ships moving from port to port, sailboats with colorful spinnakers unfurled, and powerboats of all shapes and sizes. He guessed this was a new world for the city girl.

When he finally unloaded the men and their luggage, Fred took off along the dock, the Zen one thanked Aaron, and the man who'd never spoken gave a nod of acknowledgment.

When Aaron climbed back into the Beaver, the cockpit felt smaller. Alone with Eden, he was even more aware of her, her presence almost like a soft touch arousing his senses. "First visit to this part of the world?"

She turned to him with a smile. "Yes. I've actually never traveled outside southern Ontario and Quebec before, which is embarrassing to admit for a woman who's almost thirty."

"I've never been outside British Columbia and Washington State, so we can be embarrassed together. So, what brings you all the way over to the West Coast?"

"I'm trying to track a long-lost relative."

"Wow. Haven't heard that story before."

"Do you know much about Destiny Island?"

"I've lived there since I was sixteen."

"Really? I assumed you lived in Vancouver."

"Nope. Blue Moon Air is based on Destiny. Tell me about this relative. Maybe I can help."

"Thank you. I really hope you can. It's very important to me and my family to find her."

When he glanced her way, he saw she was dead serious. He wanted to bring a smile back to those soft lips. "Tell me about her."

"She's my mother's sister, Lucy Nelson. She came to Destiny Island in 1969 and joined a commune. She was with a boy named Barry. I don't know his last name."

"I know there used to be a commune back in hippie days. That was so long ago, no one talks much about it." He reflected. "The only Nelsons on the island are a married couple in their eighties, and her name's Jane."

"No, that wouldn't be her." She sighed. "Lucy and Barry may well have split up. She could have married and changed her surname."

"The only Lucy I can think of is Lucy Smolenski. She'd be, oh, midforties? She probably wasn't even born in '69. And I don't know any guy named Barry on the island."

"Could Ms. Smolenski be older than that? Mom's sixty and her sister was—is—five years older. She was seventeen when she ran away from home with her boyfriend and came to Destiny Island."

Aaron had been one year younger than that when he and his half sister came to Destiny, after their mom overdosed and her parents grudgingly took them in. Forcing away the bad memories, he told Eden, "I'm almost sure Lucy Smolenski isn't that old. She has a son in elementary school and I don't think he's adopted. But we can ask."

"We?" She cocked her head and studied him.

"I'd like to help." That was the truth. He'd also like to see more of her, find out if the attraction was mutual.

"That's nice of you." Eden's voice had gone formal. "But I can handle it. I'm a lawyer. I'm used to tracking people down and interviewing them."

He thought about that and then said, "In Ottawa?"

"Yes, and the surrounding area."

"What kind of people?"

"I'm program counsel with a foundation that funds charities and nonprofits. Mostly, I work with the boards and the staff of the organizations we fund, and with applicants for funding. Why?"

"Do you know anything about Destiny Island?"

"Not much. What's that got to do with anything?"

"People who live on Destiny tend to be, shall we say, a touch eccentric. They're characters. Independent, often bloody-minded. They'll bicker fiercely among themselves, then close ranks against outsiders. Tourists are tolerated more than appreciated. Even though they're responsible for a sizable chunk of the island's economy."

"What are you saying? The residents won't talk to me?"

Glancing over, he saw her forehead was scrunched up. "Some will but others likely won't." People like Lionel, an American who'd come to the island as a Vietnam War draft dodger. "It'd help if a local person smooths the way."

"You'd do that?"

"Sure."

The scrunchy knot was still there. "That's very generous, but why would you help me?"

"Why wouldn't I? We'd have to work it around my flight schedule, but I'm generally only flying five or six hours a day."

"I do appreciate the offer, but I'm on a tight schedule. I took a week off work and I can't stay longer. My assistant is good, but he's quite new. I don't want to dump too much on his shoulders. Even more important, I hate leaving my mom." She cleared her throat. "She's a breast cancer survivor. She had surgery and chemotherapy and just finished six weeks of daily radiation."

"Oh man, I'm sorry."

"Thanks. It's taken a lot out of her and she depends on Dad and me. My younger sister's home from university for the summer, but she's not, well, the most reliable person."

The more Eden spoke, the more she revealed about herself. "You have a strong sense of duty." Plus, she didn't think her assistant or her sister would do as good a job as she.

"Duty?" She sounded offended. "I love my job, I'm paid to do it, and of course I feel responsible. As for my mom, it's not *duty* to care for her, to help her find her sister. It's what I want to do. Why can't people understand that?"

That sure wasn't how things had gone in his family. Not with his cocaine-addicted mother. Not with the grandparents who'd taken in him and Miranda after their mom overdosed—and never let a day go by without making it clear how harshly or unfairly treated they felt. Even with Miranda and her two-year-old, Ariana, the only people in the world he loved, the relationship was more stressful than rewarding. But those were subjects he didn't talk about. "People?" he asked.

"My boyfriend didn't get it. He *said* he supported my close relationship with my family, but that's not how he acted. Can you believe he almost seemed jealous of my mom? He resented that I spent so much of my free time helping her rather than hanging out with him. But what could I do? Dad and I had to handle everything: getting her to medical appointments and support group meetings, doing the housework and grocery shopping. And, most important of all, giving her emotional support, encouraging her to fight, trying to help her recover her optimism."

"That sounds hard."

"On top of that, Dad and I had to sort out my grandmother's estate. She died just before Mom was diagnosed."

"Sorry to hear that." This woman had had one hell of a year. Destiny, with its lovely natural setting and laid-back vibe, would be good for her.

"And yes, all those things meant that I couldn't give

as much to my job or to Ray, and I really, really hated that, but it's not like I had a choice. He should've been more understanding, and he could've helped out more himself."

It wasn't fair to judge a relationship from the outside, but all the same, Aaron said, "He sounds kind of needy."

"I know, right? When we met in law school, I thought we were a perfect match. Everything came so easily. But over this past winter, I realized I didn't really know him." She folded her arms across her chest. "I'm glad I found out when I did." Gazing out the windshield, she said, "There are a lot of islands here. Is one of those Destiny?"

"It's farther south. And yeah, there are lots of islands. Salt Spring's the biggest, with a population of nine or ten thousand. That's the north end of Salt Spring over there." He pointed to the forested shore. "The other islands range in size from a quarter or a third the size of Salt Spring down to specks that are uninhabited."

"There's a tiny island down there with a single house on it. Do those people actually own their own island?"

"Yeah. It happens."

"I can't imagine. You'd be so cut off from the world."

"Some folks like it that way." At one time, Aaron might have chosen that life himself, before Lionel and others showed him the benefits of community.

"Not me. I need to be close to my family. And I like having colleagues to talk to."

"I gather you broke up with the needy boyfriend?"

In other words, was she available and maybe interested in blowing off some rebound steam with him?

"We certainly did. It was mutual, after a big fight brought everything to a head. He said I didn't have the time or emotional energy to be in a relationship, and I said he didn't have the commitment and generosity of spirit to be in one."

Aaron winced. "Sounds nasty. How long were you together?"

"We dated for two years and then lived together for another two." Her voice lowered so he could barely hear. "I thought we'd end up getting married and having children."

Whoa. That was major. "That's a long time." And a significant commitment. "I'm sorry it didn't work out for you." If that was the kind of relationship she was looking for, so much for any hookup potential. She wouldn't be interested in a week of casual, and he didn't have anything more than that to offer.

His experience with family had left him convinced that concepts like love, marriage, and a happy home weren't in the cards for him. He wouldn't have the faintest idea how to go about creating them. He was perfectly happy as he was, going through life with a hey-how's-it-going relationship with most of the islanders and no one expecting him to be anything more than he was. The only strings in his life were to Miranda and little Ariana. And those strings were complicated ones, with his two-years-younger half sister making stupid choices and being pigheaded about accepting help, letting her misguided notion of independence come between them.

He needed to call her again. Recently, she'd responded to his texts with brief ones saying things were fine, but she'd ignored his last voice mails. She lived in Vancouver and he flew there once or twice a day, yet it had been ages since he'd seen her and Ariana. He sure hoped everything really was okay. Refocusing on Eden, he asked, "Is that what you want? Marriage and kids?"

She glanced over, her eyebrows raised. "Eventually. I did learn something from Ray, though. Right now, I only have time for two priorities, and those are my family and my job. It's hard enough juggling them and trying to do them well. And if you commit to doing something, you need to take responsibility and do it to the best of your ability."

Eden sure had high standards. It also seemed to him that she was confirming what Ray had said: She didn't have the time or emotional energy to be in a relationship. He wasn't about to point that out to her. "How about this week? You're away from your family and your job."

"My priority is finding out what happened to Lucy. My mom . . . well, it's really important to her. She's been feeling, uh, intimations of mortality, I guess you'd call it." Her voice firmed. "Not that she's going to die. She'll be just fine. But she gets worried and depressed, and it's been nagging away at her that she hasn't seen her sister for half a century. She needs to know Lucy's okay, to reconnect their lives. She wants my aunt to know my dad and my sister and me and she wants to know Lucy's family, if she has one."

He respected that Eden wanted to help her mother. "I get it. But is there any reason you can't have some fun while you're trying to track down your aunt?"

"Fun?"

He glanced over, saw her scrunched-up forehead,

and figured she was well on her way to getting a frown line. "You sound as if you don't know the meaning of the word."

When she frowned even harder, he laughed. "Relax, Eden. Let me help you. Help you find your aunt and help you loosen up and have a good time. You've had a tough year and you could use some R and R."

"I'm not sure what you have in mind," she said stiffly.

"You're an interesting, attractive woman. I'd like to spend some time with you, show you the island, see where things go. *Things*, to clarify, meaning man-woman things. Just for this week. You don't want to invest in a *relationship*, and I am, to use that trite expression, a confirmed bachelor."

"Oh." He'd clearly taken her by surprise. "Oh, I, uh . . . I don't know what to say."

"You could say you find me interesting and attractive. That you'd like to spend time with me and see where things go."

The corners of her mouth tugged upward and a spark of awareness flamed in the amber depths of her eyes. "You don't waste time, do you, Aaron Gabriel?"

Smiling as he refocused on the sky, he said, "Think about that expression. *Waste* time. What's the point in wasting anything?"

"Hmm. You make a good argument."

"Is it a winning argument, lawyer lady?"

"Will you respect my priorities? Not try to pressure me into doing what you want instead?"

"Agreed." No pressure, but that didn't rule out efforts to tempt or persuade her. Not to be arrogant, but he'd always had a lot of success with women. "Here's the thing about Destiny Island: People come for one reason but often find something completely different." He and Miranda had been forced to live with their begrudging grandparents, but the natural setting had won him over, and flying made him happy. When his grandparents decamped to Florida, he'd realized the island was a place where he could feel at home. The islanders' quirky personalities and live-and-let-live tolerance suited him.

"There's only one thing I care about finding," Eden said, sounding lawyerlike again.

"Ah, but the island may have another destiny in store for you."

Chapter Three

Eden had to laugh. "Seriously? *Your destiny awaits you on Destiny Island?* Can you be any cheesier?" Still, she had to admit Aaron was charming as well as hot, and there was something incredibly tempting about the *fun* he was offering. He was right that she was stressed out from all that had happened this past year. Not to mention she was almost thirty and it was going on five years since she'd dated, much less had sex with any man other than Ray. Five years!

Her twenty-one-year-old sister Kelsey would say, "Go for it, girl!" Kelsey was the free-spirited, spontaneous one. Responsibility slid off her shoulders like water off a duck's back. When Eden had told her about the breakup, she'd recommended a rebound fling.

Was there, for once, some merit to Kelsey's advice? Eden weighed the pros and cons of spending time, maybe time that would lead to sex, with Aaron Gabriel. Pro: He was hot, very hot! Pro—and a major one she really should put first: He could help her meet islanders who might have known Lucy. Pro: As best she could tell, he seemed genuine about wanting to help her find her aunt and about respecting her boundaries. Pro: There should be no negative consequences for either of them.

Con: A fling wasn't Eden's style. She was a serious woman with serious goals, and when it came to relationships, the ultimate goal was a loving marriage, a home, and a family.

Counterargument to the con: She didn't have time for that kind of relationship, not until her mom's physical and emotional health had improved a lot. Aaron wouldn't make demands on her time or her emotional energy, not after this one week was finished.

Query: Was there any harm in, for one short week, acting out of character and having a meaningless flirtation, maybe leading to sex, with a hot man who seemed like a decent guy?

"There's a lot of serious thinking going on over there," Aaron said.

"That's me. Serious thinker. I need to analyze situations before I make decisions. It's the only sensible way."

"Because being sensible's so much fun," he said dryly.

"Life's about more than just fun."

"Yeah, but it's also about fun. Otherwise, what's the point?"

She firmed her jaw and stared at him. "Being a good person. Looking after the people you love and helping others who aren't as fortunate as you."

"You're pretty sexy when you get all earnest like that."

She puffed out air in exasperation. About to shoot

off a snippy retort, she stopped herself. So he wasn't the same kind of person she was. It wasn't a sin to prefer fun to living a more responsible life. She wasn't going to go all self-righteous on him. After all, it wasn't as if she were considering the man as a potential boyfriend.

Flirtation wasn't a skill of hers, but she gave it a try. "Okay, being totally earnest here, and therefore sexy, you might be interested to hear the result of all that analysis."

"I just might."

"I'm opting in. I'm grateful for your offer of assistance and I accept. I'm also open to the concept of fun and seeing where that may lead us."

He took his right hand off the steering yoke, rested it on her hand where it lay on her thigh, and squeezed gently. "Good places. It'll lead us to good places, Eden. I promise you that."

From the tingly warmth that spread up her arm, she figured he'd live up to that promise.

He lifted his hand to point out the windshield, to a rocky shore fringed with tall evergreens. "There's your first view of Destiny. I'll fly over and point out the landmarks. Blue Moon Harbor's on the south side."

"The island looks pretty rugged."

"The Pacific Northwest is like that. Nature has a rawness, which the indigenous people who lived here respected. What we think of as civilization is a fairly new thing. Destiny was first settled around 1860."

"By Europeans?"

"Mostly, but there were also Chinese, Japanese, freed slaves from the States, people from just about every country you can name. Destiny has a colorful history. I'll tell you about it if you're interested, but right now let me show you the lay of the land."

"Okay."

"The island's shaped roughly like an hourglass, with the north part a bit smaller than the south. The north end is more rocky and mountainous and less inhabited. That bay to the west—the right—with the grouping of three dozen or so houses, is Sunset Cove. Yes, it does get lovely sunsets. The pub's a great place for dinner. We'll go there one night."

"That sounds nice." After all, she had to eat. She couldn't spend every minute on her quest to find her aunt. Surprised by how sparsely settled this part of the island was, she asked, "What's the population of Destiny Island?"

"Around fifteen hundred."

"That's tiny."

"That's permanent residents, with maybe three hundred in the north part of the hourglass and the rest in the south. Lots of other people, mostly from Victoria and Vancouver, have cabins or houses they use for holidays. And we get a lot of tourists, especially in summer."

Intrigued by the scenery unfolding below them, she said, "It's lovely."

"Best place on earth." He flashed a grin. "But I guess most of us think that when it comes to the place we live."

"Yes. Ottawa is, for me. I grew up there and it's home, I love my job, but mostly it's where my parents are." Her heart would always lie with her parents.

Aaron pointed out a lake with cabins beside it and boats scattered across it, a couple of campgrounds, and a beachfront summer camp run by a church. The farther south they flew, the more development she saw. Now he was indicating the schools, a medical clinic, and a community center. "And that's Blue Moon Harbor—the village and the bay," he told her.

The bay was like a teardrop-shaped bag with a draw-string neck, but the string hadn't been pulled tight. She guessed the narrow neck reduced ocean swells to provide a calm harbor. Houses and a few apartment and town-house buildings were scattered among trees along the sides of the bay, stacked on two levels: one down close to the ocean and another above, clinging to the rocky hillside. At the head of the bay was the village, not much more than four blocks long and two blocks deep. Here there were no office towers; the tallest buildings were two stories. A green space indicated a park, with a parking lot beside it.

Below the village, docks were lined with boats, and more boats were anchored out in the harbor. On the west side of the bay was another web of wharves with boats—a marina, she guessed. On the other side was a huge dock with a parking lot that would hold thirty or more cars. "What's that big dock?"

"It's for the ferries. They run among the Gulf Islands, as well as over to Swartz Bay on Vancouver Island."

"Not to Vancouver?"

"No. You have to take the island ferry to Swartz Bay, then the big one to Vancouver. Or, of course, fly."

"If you live on an island, you can only get on and off by boat or plane." She gave a snort. "Duh, that's so obvious. It's just not something I'd really thought about. Don't you start feeling claustrophobic?"

"Not if you can fly a plane."

"Good point."

He flew over the harbor out toward the neck of the bay and spoke into his headphone, announcing their arrival to someone he called Kam. Eden recognized the name; that was the obliging man she'd spoken to earlier on the phone.

The plane banked in a graceful turn and came back, dropping altitude as it soared down a clear stretch of water between a variety of pleasure craft, some anchored and some in motion.

"I was nervous at first," she said, "but this is cool. Does it ever wear thin, like driving a bus over the same route every day?"

The plane's floats caressed the water like lips touching lightly and then sinking deeper into a familiar kiss.

"Nope. For one thing, it's never the same. The routes change depending on passengers' needs, and the weather's always a bit different. And the more experienced a pilot gets, the better he knows his plane, the whole thing kind of goes to a different level. Deeper." He gave a self-deprecatory laugh. "That Zen kind of thing."

His comment reminded her of something she'd overheard when she was a teen. Her mom had been talking to a friend who'd gotten engaged. The other woman had said she worried that, after years with one guy, their sex life would go stale. Eden's mom had said that if the couple really loved each other and was doing things right, making love went to a whole different level of intimacy. For the most part, Eden had been horrified to have heard that. Yet she was sensible enough to know that of course her parents had sex, and she was happy it was still meaningful for both of them.

She'd hoped for that with Ray. The sex had always been good but never amazing, and she'd hoped that once they married they'd find that deeper level of intimacy.

"You sighed," Aaron said as they approached a dock and she saw the Blue Moon Air logo on a small wooden building above it, up a ramp. "Sorry the flight's over or worrying about whether you'll find your aunt?"

Lying went against her moral code. "I was thinking about my breakup. I know we weren't right for each other, but every now and then I feel a moment of regret."

"Regrets are a waste of time. You gotta leave the past behind you and move on."

"You can learn from the past. But yes, I agree about moving on. I'm doing that, Aaron." A sense of optimism and a thrill of excitement made her smile. "And you're going to help me."

He returned the smile and then concentrated on jockeying the plane up to the dock behind an even smaller plane painted with the airline's colors and logo. Waiting to assist was a slender young man with black hair and light brown skin, wearing the same blue, logoed T-shirt as Aaron. When a float nudged the dock, Aaron jumped out and the two men secured the ropes. Aaron then pulled down the ladder, said, "I'll see you up in the office, Kam," and extended a hand to help Eden out.

The dock certainly wasn't solid land. It moved gently and it took her a moment to find her balance. Boats of all sizes lined the surrounding wharves, two of the larger ships looking like commercial fish boats.

Up above, the village was picturesque, the jumble of architectural styles and paint colors creating an intriguing tapestry.

Aaron had her wheelie bag in one hand and her briefcase in the other. "Where are you staying?"

"The Once in a Blue Moon B and B." Her dad had booked it for her. "They're supposed to be within walking distance."

"That's it on the hill." He nodded toward a big, old-fashioned house just past the west end of the village. "You'll like it."

"It's charming." She was no expert on architecture, but the three-story building struck her as kind of Victorian, with lots of interesting details like shutters and trim. Funky Victorian, though, with its paint in multiple shades of blue: a soothing grayish tone for the walls, indigo for the front door, robin's egg blue for the shutters, and a purplish-blue for the trim. She'd never have put those shades together herself, but the result was perfect.

"I'll help you get your luggage over there and you can get settled in. Maybe have a nap. I've got a flight to Victoria in the Cessna 180—that's the smaller plane—and then I'm done for the day. How about I pick you up just before seven? We'll have dinner, you can tell me whatever you know about your aunt, and we'll work out a strategy."

"Sounds good." Much better, in terms of fun as well as productivity, than an evening alone in her room with her laptop computer.

She followed him along the dock, so used to toting her briefcase as well as her purse that she felt unbalanced not having its weight on her left shoulder. Not that she was about to protest. Nor did she complain when Aaron mounted the skid-stripped ramp ahead of her. No woman would complain about following a world-class butt and a pair of long, lean, denim-clad legs.

He poked his head through the open door of the Blue Moon Air office, a small building made of weathered wood with bright blue trim. "Kam, I'm taking Ms. Blaine over to the Once. Back in ten for my next flight."

It seemed an informal way of checking in, but obviously, things were done differently on Destiny Island.

Aaron led her at a brisk pace down the main street of town, which a carved and painted wooden sign told her was Driftwood Road. It was lined with restaurants and an eclectic and intriguing array of stores, everything from a marine supply shop to one selling fancy soaps and lotions. A bookstore called Dreamspinner, a clothing shop, and several arts and crafts stores drew her eye, and she hoped she might have some free time to explore them.

When they arrived at the Once in a Blue Moon, which looked as appealing close-up as it had from a distance, Aaron avoided the wheelchair ramp and hefted her bags up the ten or so front steps. He wasn't the slightest bit winded when he reached the top, though Eden had trouble keeping up. "I'll leave you now," he said. "Give me your cell number and I'll give you mine."

Though she hadn't known him long, she'd noted that he had a habit of making statements and issuing orders rather than offering suggestions. Still, what he said made sense, so she didn't protest. After they'd exchanged numbers, she said, "Thanks. See you just before seven."

"Don't forget that nap." He winked. "You want to be rested up for when the fun starts."

Honestly, the man was incorrigible. How strange that, rather than being annoyed by it, she was amused and, let's face it, kind of turned on.

Inside the reception area, the air smelled of lemon and the furniture was either genuinely old or artificially distressed, but the blue-striped upholstery was fresh and the wood gleamed. There was no one behind the writing desk that was signed "Reception," but a brass bell sat alongside a computer, so she rang it.

A few seconds later, a slight woman with short, spiky salt-and-pepper hair bustled out from a back room. She wore a pretty red top and denim capris and was smiling warmly. "Hello there. How can I help you?"

"I'm Eden Blaine and I have a reservation."

"Welcome, Eden. I'm Bernie Barnes." The woman held out her hand. "My husband Jonathan and I own the Once in a Blue Moon."

Eden exchanged a firm handshake with her.

Bernie seated herself behind the desk and tapped energetically at the computer. Dangly earrings made up of wire and colored stones tinkled like miniature wind chimes. "A single room and you're with us for six nights, correct?"

"Exactly." Eden unzipped her purse. "You'll want my credit card."

"No need. I'll show you to your room and you can get comfy."

Bernie came around from behind the desk, took the handle of Eden's wheelie, and pulled it across to an elevator. "You're on the top floor, with a lovely view of the harbor. Your timing was perfect, you know. Normally, we're full up from the May twenty-fourth weekend through Labor Day weekend, but we'd just had a cancellation when you checked online."

Eden sent a mental thank-you in her dad's direction. Not only had he found her a charming place to stay but he'd done it at the height of tourist season. She hoped the B and B would also prove to be a good place to start her hunt for her aunt. Bernie looked to be in her fifties. Was it possible she might have known Lucy? As they rode up to the third floor, Eden asked, "Have you lived on Destiny Island long?"

"Roughly ten years. Jonathan and I were in Vancouver, him working as an accountant and me doing human resources at a hotel. We holidayed here two or three times and fell in love with the island and the lifestyle. We sold our house, pillaged our savings, and opened the B and B."

"That was brave of you." Eden couldn't imagine uprooting her life and taking such a risk.

Bernie gave a mischievous grin. "Ah well, when destiny calls, what can you do?" She led Eden down a narrow hall lightened by pale yellow paint and decorated with paintings and photographs, discreet labels indicating they were for sale. After unlocking a door with an old-fashioned key, she ushered Eden inside.

"It's lovely." The room was furnished with a four-poster bed with a canopy, a distressed-wood desk and a tall cabinet, and a comfy chair by the window. A vase full of mixed-color dahlias sat on the desk. Beside the window, a paned-glass door led to a small balcony with a couple of chairs and a tiny round table. Unable to resist, Eden went out and leaned on the wooden railing, gazing over the village and harbor. The tiny Blue

Moon Air Cessna was leaving the dock as a larger white-and-red seaplane approached.

Bernie joined her. "From here, I feel like a bird perched in a tree, surveying my domain. It's a lovely place to while away time with a pair of binoculars, a good book, or a glass of wine. By the way, there's a wonderful winery, Destiny Cellars. They do tours and wine tastings."

"Thank you so much. I'll be very comfortable." Eden hadn't come here to while away time, so she went back inside, and the proprietor followed. "Bernie, you've been here long enough to know a number of islanders and a bit of the island's history. I wonder if you have twenty or so minutes to spare? There's something I'd like to talk to you about."

"If it's tourist recommendations, there's a set of brochures in the desk drawer. They're quite thorough."

"No, it's something a bit more complicated than that."

"I'm so sorry, Eden, but I only have a few minutes right now. How about tomorrow morning, after breakfast?"

"Sure. I'd appreciate it." By then, Aaron would have given her some ideas as well, so her conversation with Bernie might be even more productive.

Her hostess quickly showed her the other amenities: bathroom, closet, TV inside the cabinet. "The Wi-Fi password is *once*, all lower case. If there's anything else you need, call us or ring at the front desk. Oh, will you want a rental car?"

"I've booked one to pick up tomorrow. I think I'm all set. Thanks again."

After Bernie left, Eden snapped photos of her

room and a selfie out on the balcony. She emailed her
family to let them know she'd arrived safely, show
them the place, and tell them she had met a couple of
contacts who might help with her search for Lucy.
She also sent an email to herself at the Butterworth
Foundation, attaching files she'd worked on during
the day.

Using the security app on her laptop, she signed
into her work account and saved the files using the
Foundation's document management system. She
popped off an email to update her assistant, Navdeep
Grewal. She also reminded him of what documents he
needed to take to the Monday afternoon meeting
with a prospective applicant for funding. Though she
hated to miss that meeting, Navdeep had accompanied
her to similar ones and ought to be able to provide the
applicant with the information they needed and ask
the right questions of them. When he sent her a
report, she could advise him on how to proceed.

A few years ago, she'd have had a bunch of personal
texts and emails to answer, and she'd have used social
media to update her friends and check on them. But
since she'd graduated from law school, she'd been so
busy establishing herself at work and getting involved
with Ray that she'd cut back on girlfriend time.
Then, when her mom got sick, Eden had abandoned any attempt to have a social life. She stifled a
pang of regret, reminding herself that her priorities
were valid.

Unloading her tightly packed carry-on, she fought
back a yawn. Though she had more than an hour and
a half before Aaron would pick her up, she wasn't
going to waste the time by napping. She'd see if the

tourist brochures provided any information to help in her quest.

A bottle of water sat on the desk and she poured herself a tall glassful. She'd been up before dawn and it had been a long day of travel. Her body was on Ottawa time, which meant it was past eight o'clock rather than past five. She took the water, the tourist information, and a snack bar from her purse, and settled on the decadent bed, propped up with two pillows.

She munched, drank, perused brochures, and yawned. The island newspaper, the *Destiny Gazette*, was enlightening. The news and announcements told her, as if she didn't already know, that she was a long way from Ottawa. Here, people were interested in kids winning 4-H prizes, in artisan craft fairs, and in whether the chamber of commerce would approve the addition of a second traffic light. The pace of life was certainly slower. Maybe that was why she was yawning so much.

Her brain felt so groggy she had trouble concentrating. Perhaps she did need a catnap to recharge her batteries. She set the alarm on her cell for an hour and pulled one of the pillows from behind her head. This was a wonderfully comfortable bed. Too comfortable. It almost tempted her to call Aaron to cancel tonight and settle in for a long, deep sleep. In the past year, she'd rarely slept more than five or six hours a night, staying up late to catch up on work after taking time off during the day to help her mom and dad.

A familiar guilt niggled at her. She'd come to this

island for one reason, and it wasn't to *while away time*, as Bernie put it, with a seaplane pilot.

But Aaron had offered to help her. Surely she could carry out a thorough investigation and also enjoy spending time with a man who was, objectively speaking, one of the most attractive she'd ever met. A man who had offered her fun without commitment or pressure. On the verge of sleep, she remembered Bernie joking about not being able to refuse the call of destiny.

If fun is my destiny, who am I to deny it?

Aaron wasn't exactly hot and sweaty after a day of flying, but all the same he used the bathroom at the Blue Moon Air office to shower after his last flight. He kept a change of clothes there, so he slipped on fresh jeans and a black Henley, rolling the sleeves up his forearms and knowing he'd roll them down later. Though the early June days were mostly warm, the temperature dropped in the evenings.

He walked the few blocks to the Once, as locals called it. Bernie Barnes, seated at the reception desk clicking a computer keyboard, looked up with a welcoming smile. "Hi, Aaron. What brings you here?"

"Hey, Bernie. I'm picking up one of your guests, taking her to dinner. Eden Blaine."

"Ah. I should have known."

"Because . . . ?"

"She arrived without a car, which suggests you flew her in. She's young and pretty, which means you hit on her."

It hadn't happened exactly like that, but close enough that he said, "Busted."

She shook her head, the spikes of her gray-flecked hair flicking. Sounding amused and a touch exasperated, she said, "Will you ever grow up?"

The jibe hurt a little; after all, he was a twenty-eight-year-old man who owned his own business. But he knew that wasn't what she was referring to, so he brushed it off. "If someone ever convinces me there's a good reason to. So far, no one has. Besides"—he winked—"name me a woman who doesn't find Peter Pan irresistible."

Bernie gave a snort of laughter, and at that moment Eden stepped out of the elevator looking classy and beautiful in tan-colored pants and a sleeveless black top with an abstract design in shades of tan. Her big purse hung over her shoulder and she carried a black sweater. She'd freed her hair from the confining ponytail and loose waves framed her face and caressed her shoulders. Aaron felt a compulsion to smooth those glossy strands back from her face and kiss the pulse point on her neck.

Bernie wished them a good time and Aaron ushered Eden out of the B and B. As they walked down the steps, he said, "Nice room?"

"Very. And yes, I did have a nap and a shower and I feel much more rested."

Had she showered for him or only to wash away a day of travel? "Good. Now, what do you feel like for dinner? Blue Moon Harbor is a small town, but we have some good restaurants."

"Seafood? Being by the ocean, it seems appropriate."

"Italian seafood, Cajun blackened fish, fish and

chips, sushi, or the best grilled fish and prawns you've ever tasted?"

"Wow. Who could resist the best?"

"C-Shell, then. It's near Blue Moon Air. Nice view of the harbor."

They meandered along Driftwood Road with Eden gazing into the windows of the now-closed shops and making comments. The handful of restaurants and bars were doing a lively business. So was Dreamspinner, the bookstore and coffee shop. Many of the people strolling the sidewalk were tourists, but now and then Aaron exchanged greetings with another islander. Colm, a young local man, stood in the doorway of Blowing Bubbles, the children's store, playing Celtic music on his fiddle. Aaron added a two dollar coin to the substantial collection of coins and bills in the fiddle case and Eden did the same.

Inside the entrance of C-Shell, several people sat on benches waiting for tables. Rachelle, co-owner of the restaurant and a high school classmate of Aaron's, looked up from telling a pair of tourists that there'd be a fifteen-minute wait, and grinned at him. "Hey, Aaron." Her brown-eyed gaze skimmed Eden and she said, "Reservation for two, right? Your table's being cleared. You can come in with me now."

"Appreciate it," Aaron said with a wink.

Rachelle led the way, tall and trim in flowing black pants and a black halter top that showed off her beautiful dark brown skin. Her long black hair was, as usual, braided intricately, with colorful beads interwoven.

He liked the restaurant's décor. Lots of wood, candles in pottery holders made by one of the locals, small flowering plants on each table rather than cut flowers. A few nautical touches like coiled ropes, fishing nets, old glass floats, and a rusted anchor. Local art on the walls.

Eden glanced back at him and murmured, "You made a reservation? You knew which restaurant I'd choose?"

He stepped closer, taking the excuse to rest his hand on her lower back. She gave a slight start but didn't protest, and he enjoyed the warmth and motion of her body as they kept walking.

"Nope. Rachelle's being nice to me. Locals get priority over tourists, right, Rachelle?" he said as the hostess seated them across from each other at a window table for four.

"Locals are repeat business," Rachelle said. Turning to Eden, she added, "Besides, Aaron and I were both rebels back in high school. We black sheep gotta stick together." She handed them menus. "Jonah will be by to take your drink order."

Eden thanked her and then, when she'd gone, said, "You two went to school together? Is Rachelle a native Destiny Islander?"

"Rachelle's family goes way back. Her great-great-great-whatever-grandparents on her dad's side were American freed slaves who came up to Victoria via San Francisco, and then they came over to Destiny. There are descendants of those original black settlers scattered all through the islands. Her mom was born here, too, but that side of the family doesn't go back as far."

"So her parents might—" she started.

"Be useful people for you to talk to. After dinner, when the place has quieted down, we can ask her."

Jonah, nineteen or twenty, skinny in his black shirt

and pants, came over. After he and Aaron exchanged the usual, "Hey, how's it going?" greetings, Jonah asked if they'd like a drink.

"I'm fine for the moment," Eden said, and Aaron agreed.

"You know him, too," Eden noted after the waiter had gone.

"He's Rachelle's cousin. He works for the restaurant during the summer to help pay for attending university in Victoria. By the way, Rachelle and her wife Celia own this place."

"C-Shell. Now I understand the unusual spelling."

"Celia's the chef. Not an islander. They met when Rachelle was at the University of British Columbia in Vancouver and Celia was doing culinary training."

"Are family-run businesses the norm here?"

"Pretty much. It's a small island, small population. It's also, from the beginning, been a place that attracted free-spirited people and entrepreneurs. Ones who do better going their own way rather than toeing some corporate line."

"Unlike Ottawa, where most people work for the government or for some organization, corporate or nonprofit. It's such a huge responsibility and risk, running your own business."

Yeah, especially when you employed other people, owned seaplanes, had to deal with insurance issues, and on and on. But he wouldn't have it any other way. "Yeah, but you're working for yourself, so that makes it worthwhile."

"Hmm." Her tone said she wasn't convinced. She opened her menu. "Let's decide what to order, then we can strategize about how to find my aunt."

Getting this woman to have fun was going to be a challenge, but intuition told him the result would be worth it. She sure was pretty, with candlelight warming her cheeks and the pale skin of her arms and casting highlights in her walnut hair. "Not even going to spare a moment to appreciate this great table Rachelle gave us and admire the view?"

"Oh." Eden glanced around. "Sorry. I can be pretty single-minded."

"Gee, I hadn't noticed."

She gave an amused huff. "Point taken. Yes, it's a wonderful table and the harbor looks spectacular with all the lights on the boats twinkling. As for the restaurant, I like the simple décor and how there are oceany accents, but they aren't overdone and kitschy."

"The nautical things are real, not the gimmicky stuff manufactured for the tourist trade. Rachelle's dad is a commercial fisher and he supplied them. He also provides the fresh seafood."

They studied the menu and Eden said she was torn between cedar-planked sockeye salmon and skewers of prawns and veggies.

"Let's order both and split them."

"Sounds great." She closed her menu.

"White wine?" he asked. "Or do you prefer red?"

That scrunchy knot appeared in her forehead, the one he'd learned meant she was worrying or over-analyzing. "I probably shouldn't drink, not if I want to concentrate."

"A glass of wine's going to throw off your concentration that much?"

"Well . . ."

"It'll help with part two of tonight's agenda."

Warily, she asked, "What exactly is part two?"

"Forgotten already? Having fun. Good food, great view, terrific company"—he winked—"so why not a little wine as well?"

Her lips curved slowly. "Why not?" But then the frown returned. "Wait a minute. Pilots aren't supposed to drink, are they?"

"We can't fly when we're under the influence, or have a drink within eight hours of flying. If I'm flying in the morning, I'm safe with a glass of wine or a bottle of beer with dinner."

"If you're sure . . ." she said doubtfully.

"Believe me, I am." No way would he endanger his passengers, much less risk losing his license and his business.

"Well, okay." She opened the bar menu and glanced at the wine list. "Bernie mentioned Destiny Cellars. Are their wines good?"

"They are."

"I'll try the pinot gris."

Aaron caught Jonah's eye, and he came over to take the order.

A few minutes later, he returned with their wine. He also brought warm, fresh-baked bread: a small loaf on a wooden board, together with a bread knife, a bowl of oil and balsamic vinegar, and another bowl of herbed butter.

After Aaron and Eden had each spread butter on a slice of bread, she opened her large purse and pulled out a laptop computer.

"Wait," he said. "Before we start planning, I need to hear the story. The whole story, not the bare bones you gave me before."

"That makes sense. Okay." She put the laptop aside,

took a sip of wine, and gave an approving smile. "Until a week ago, I never knew my mother had a sister. Lucy was older than Mom by five years. My grandparents were conservative, straitlaced, and strict. They set rules for their kids. Mom obeyed and Lucy didn't. Lucy challenged, rebelled, fought back."

"I'm liking Lucy."

Eden rolled her eyes. "This was the mid- to late sixties. Hippie days, and Lucy was into that whole scene. A scene that Nana and Grandpa, who were quite religious, thought was sinful. Mom says she and Lucy'd been close when they were younger, but they grew apart, and she didn't understand what was going on with Lucy."

"It's pretty normal for teenagers to rebel."

"I never did. But sure, some do. Kids need to figure out who they are, as compared to who their parents want them to be. In my case, I realized I'm a lot like my parents. My baby sister is less so. She's spontaneous rather than being a planner. But she's still a decent person. Not someone who'd hurt her parents like Lucy did Nana and Grandpa."

"Maybe they hurt her by not trying to understand her. By imposing rules that made no sense to her." No, wait. Just because his and Miranda's grandparents had been crappy to them, that didn't give him the right to judge Eden's. "Sorry, I shouldn't have said that."

Looking thoughtful, she finished chewing her bread. "My dad's parents died before I was born, then Grandpa passed away when I was five. My family spent a lot of time with Nana. She was set in her ways. Demanding and . . . well, she could be judgmental. Kelsey—my sister—and I used to say Nana must never have been a kid. She sure didn't seem to remember what it was like." Her forehead scrunched. "But all the same, we always knew she loved us and wanted what was best for us. And when we did win a word of praise, it meant a lot."

To him, the woman sounded manipulative. "She's dead now?"

"Last year. And that's what started all this. Well, that and Mom's cancer. Mom had a really awful year." She took a breath, as if she was bracing herself.

"I'm sorry. It must've been hard for you, too."

She nodded. "First, Nana died from a stroke, unexpectedly, and that was really rough on Mom. And then Mom was diagnosed with breast cancer. Dad and I handled the practical details surrounding Nana's death, like selling her house and most of her furniture, and probating her will. Mom inherited everything, so at least that was straightforward. But she was in no shape—after a double mastectomy, and then starting chemo—to think about what she wanted to do with Nana's belongings. Dad and I shoved everything into boxes and put them in the attic."

As she'd been talking, she'd sipped wine, and now her glass was almost empty. Aaron signaled Jonah to bring another as Eden went on.

"Recently, Mom finished with radiation and had enough strength to start going through those boxes. Last week she found a letter. It was addressed to Nana and Grandpa, from Lucy."

She shook her head. "No, wait, I'm getting ahead of myself. I didn't finish telling you what happened when Lucy was seventeen, in twelfth grade. The push and pull between her and her parents got worse. They fought all the time. One night, Mom heard Lucy screaming that she hated them. They said she was grounded. Lucy said they couldn't lock her in the house. They said if she went out, she shouldn't come back because she no longer had a home with them."

He groaned. "I don't know much about parenting but that doesn't sound smart."

"No. They locked her in her room, not knowing she had an escape route out her window and down a huge old maple tree. The next day, when they unlocked the door, she was gone."

"What did they do?"

"They figured it was just Lucy being Lucy and she'd be back in a couple of days. All she'd taken was her school backpack, a few clothes, and a couple of treasured possessions. But she never came back. And they didn't call the police."

"Oh man. Never? I mean, not even after weeks?"

"No. Mom's positive about that. They stopped talking about her. After a few months, they converted her room into a sewing room for Nana, and threw out everything Lucy had owned, even every picture that had her in it."

He whistled. "That's harsh." Maybe his grandparents weren't so awful after all. They'd been planning to retire to Florida when their estranged daughter, Corinne, OD'ed, and they were pissed off at having to delay their move. But they'd done it and taken in their grandkids, something they'd never been willing to do before, not when Corinne was alive and social services had put Aaron and Miranda in foster care for weeks, even months at a time. Anyhow, for whatever reason, this time they'd stepped up to the plate and provided a home, even if they made it clear they hated having to do it. They'd told Aaron and Miranda that they'd better learn useful skills in high school because they'd be on their own after that.

"It was harsh," Eden agreed. "I was stunned. I didn't think Nana could be so unforgiving. Mom managed to hide away a few mementos, photos of her and Lucy. But if she ever mentioned Lucy, her parents shut her down, saying they had no daughter by that name."

Jonah slipped the second glass of wine in front of her, but she didn't seem to notice.

"Your mom let it go?" Aaron asked.

"They didn't give her a choice. She was twelve; what could she do? She did ask Lucy's friends if they knew anything, and they said no, just that she'd been madly in love with some new guy. Some secret, hippie boyfriend named Barry none of them had met. Later, once there was the Internet, Mom and Dad both hunted for Lucy. Dad has mad computer skills. They'd try every now and then but never found anything. Mom said that thinking about her missing sister hurt, so she mostly avoided doing it. That's why she never told Kelsey and me about Lucy."

Jonah brought their meals, steaming hot and smelling so good that Aaron's stomach growled. "Okay if I split this?" he asked Eden. At her nod, he proceeded to do an even split, though she protested that she'd never be able to eat that much.

She tasted both dishes, pronounced them delicious, and for a few minutes they savored their meals in silence. Then she said, "Okay, to get back to the letter Mom found. Lucy sent her parents a letter in the fall of 1969, a few months after she ran away. She said she was on Destiny Island with her boyfriend and they'd joined a commune."

"Bet that went over well."

"Mom said, looking back, that must have been when Nana and Grandpa said they no longer had a daughter named Lucy."

At least Aaron's mom's parents hadn't been that harsh. They'd accepted responsibility for their grand-kids because there was no one else to do it. There'd never been another set of grandparents, not for him or his sister. His own father—a guy from the Musqueam First Nation his mom had been crazy about—had disappeared when she got pregnant. By the time she'd gotten pregnant with Miranda, she'd been turning tricks to pay for drug money and hadn't had a clue which man had knocked her up.

Aaron and Eden had both been eating in silence for a few minutes. He drew his mind back to her story. "So that letter gave your mom the first clue."

"Yes, and she has an urgent desire to find her sister. Cancer's had a huge impact on Mom." She swallowed and firmed her jaw. "She's fighting the disease, and we keep telling her she'll beat it and she needs to remain positive. But it's thrown her. Badly."

Moisture sheened her amber eyes and Aaron reached across the table to touch her hand. "I'm sorry." His own mom had been pretty much broken from way before he'd been old enough to realize his childhood wasn't a normal one.

"She was always so strong, physically and mentally. She's a high school teacher, she coaches the debate team, and she's made a difference in so many kids' lives. To see her so shaken, so fragile and vulnerable—" She broke off and a tear slipped down her cheek. "So afraid," she whispered.

"Aw, Eden." He knew she must be scared, too.

Helpless, he watched as she used her free hand to swipe away the tear.

She sniffed. "She'll heal and regain her strength and confidence. I'm sure of it. And finding Lucy will help immeasurably."

Aaron vowed to himself that he'd do everything in his power to locate the missing aunt. And he wouldn't mention the possibility—which Eden and her mom had to be aware of—that the search might result in the discovery that Lucy was dead.

Rachelle approached their table. "How are you two enjoying—" After a glance at Eden's face, she stopped. "Sorry; I didn't mean to intrude."

Eden waved a hand and gave a wobbly smile. "No, it's okay. Just a family thing that gets me a little emotional. On top of being run-down, stressed, and drinking too much wine. I'm so embarrassed." Her voice had firmed as she spoke and she sounded rueful as she went on. "Believe me, the interruption is welcome. Rachelle, this restaurant is great and the food's wonderful. My compliments to the chef. Aaron tells me she's your wife."

"The first time Celia cooked for me, she won my heart."

"Aw, that's so sweet. And I can understand why."

"Say, Rachelle," Aaron said, "you know pretty much everyone on Destiny. Can you think of a woman named Lucy, age sixty-five? Or a man named Barry?"

She tilted her head, reflecting. "I'm pretty sure there's no Barry on Destiny. Lucy Smolenski's a lot younger than sixty-five and Lucinda Barrie is a teenager. I think they're the only ones named Lucy. Why do you ask?"

"I'm looking for a missing relative," Eden said. "She came here in 1969, joined the commune, and, uh, the family never heard from her again."

"That's too bad. There were lots of hippies on the island and some ended up staying. Maybe one of them will know what happened to her."

"When you're not so busy," Eden said, "would you mind giving me some names? And Aaron said it's possible your parents might know something?"

"Dad didn't have much patience with the hippies. He says their idea of living off the land was expecting the land and sea to provide for them without them having to put in the hard work. Mom's eight years younger than him, so I'm not sure she even had much contact with the commune folks. But I'll ask them and let you know."

"I'd appreciate that. Could you ask them if they'd mind talking to their friends as well?"

"You bet. The wider you spread the net, as Dad says. Now, you finish up your dinner so I can tempt you with dessert." With a flick of her beaded braids, she moved on to the next table.

And with any luck, after dinner Aaron would be able to tempt Eden into a shared kiss or two in the moonlight.

Chapter Four

What was Aaron thinking that brought a smile to his sensual lips? A smile with a hint of sexy wickedness. It made her remember something Rachelle had said earlier. "So, you and Rachelle were black sheep in high school. In what way?"

He ate a bite of salmon before answering, and she sensed he was deciding what to say. "There were groups. Jocks, geeks, academics, do-gooders, party kids. Was your school like that?"

"Aren't they all? I guess I fit in with the do-gooders and academics. How about you?"

"Neither Rachelle nor I fit into a group. And we didn't want to."

"I guess you two didn't date each other?"

"No, she figured out she was gay pretty early on. We were . . . well, friends, I guess."

"High school can be complicated," she sympathized. "What kind of black sheep stuff did you do?"

He gazed out the window and she did too, enjoying how the boat and dock lights glittered against the darkening sky. This view was so different from the one of

Ottawa's city lights from her fifteenth-floor apartment. And the man across from her in the candlelight, with his dark-skinned, muscular body and his black Henley with the rolled-up sleeves, was so different from any other man in her life. The guys she knew in Ottawa, even when they wore jeans, somehow looked as if they were wearing a suit. Aaron's natural physicality was so appealing, just like the magical ocean view.

"I skipped class," he said, "didn't turn in assignments. You know."

"You sound like half the kids in my school."

"Yeah, well . . ." He paused. "That was the least of it."

"You've got me curious." Not that she'd ever been attracted to the bad-boy type. She'd thought kids who broke the rules were stupid. It never did them any good in the end.

"It was a long time ago. I'm not that guy now."

"Okay, I believe you. So why not tell me?"

"I don't talk much about those days."

She cocked her head. "You're making a big deal out of this. If I ever do find out, it's going to be an anticlimax."

"Yeah, but you're not going to find out."

As her family and coworkers knew, once Eden got an idea in her head, she wasn't about to let it go until she was satisfied. So she prompted, "I'm guessing typical teenage stuff like drinking, drugs. Street racing. Spraying graffiti."

He was gazing at her with a quizzical expression that gave nothing away.

She continued. "Or there's the ever-popular shoplifting."

Tiny muscles around his eyes flinched.

Her own eyes widened. "Shoplifting? Really?"

He shrugged. "Along with that other stuff you mentioned."

"What did you steal?"

"Junk food from stores. Loose change from houses when people weren't home."

"You broke into people's houses?" That was more serious than pinching an occasional candy bar from a grocery store.

"I was a messed-up kid." His voice grated. "God knows where I'd have ended up if I hadn't got caught."

At least he realized how stupid his behavior had been. Eden kept quiet as Jonah came to clear away their empty dinner plates. The young man with his mocha skin, close-cropped hair, and black shirt and pants was a great waiter, efficient and personable. He offered more wine, and Eden realized that somehow, without her noticing, she'd managed to empty two glasses. No wonder she'd gotten so embarrassingly emotional.

She and Aaron both refused the offer, and Jonah left dessert menus on the table.

When he'd gone, Eden said, "You were arrested?"

Aaron shook his head. "I had the amazing luck to be caught stealing from a cabin in the woods that belonged to a guy named Lionel Williams. He called himself antiestablishment. Had no fondness for authority of any kind, much less the police."

"So he caught you but didn't report you, and yet you turned your life around? I gather he played a part in that?"

"Oh yeah. Lionel didn't let me off easy." Aaron sounded grateful, even affectionate. "He made me work for him. He said he'd turn me in if I didn't, which I later realized might've been an empty threat.

Anyhow, he had me doing all sorts of hard physical labor around his place. Chopping wood, fixing the roof, painting. I whined and cussed in the beginning." He grinned wryly. "But a part of me liked it. I realized I had value. I could put in a hard day's work. I came to respect Lionel and he turned me into a better person."

"Every kid should have a mentor like that." Surely Lionel couldn't have been the only person to make Aaron face up to the consequences of his actions, to make him feel valued when he worked hard. Cautiously, she asked, "Your parents didn't push you that way? Or any of your teachers?" Her mom the teacher complained about parents who wanted to be their children's best friend rather than to take on the parental responsibility of setting rules, disciplining their kids, and encouraging and rewarding them for acting maturely. According to her mom, too many teachers also shirked that responsibility. As a result, kids were immature, spoiled, and acted out—as, it seemed, Aaron had.

He snorted. "Only Lionel. And after I'd worked for him a few weeks, he took me flying." His face lit up.

The picture was falling into place. "He was a pilot?"

"That little Cessna 180 you saw? That used to be his, before I bought it off him when his arthritis got so bad he couldn't fly any longer. He loved flying, and he used to take folks places they needed to go. Not as a business. He never set up anything formal, much less legal. He flew people; they paid him in money or goods or services. Barter's popular on the island. Don't tell Canada Revenue, okay?"

She didn't approve, but it was none of her business, so she said, "Okay. So let me guess how the story goes. Lionel taught you to fly?"

"He did, and created an addict." A shadow crossed his face. He gave his head a shake and the shadow was gone. "But in a healthy way, because it kept me active, engaged, learning. He said if I wanted to work as a pilot, no one would ever hire me if I didn't finish high school and get proper pilot training. So I did, graduating, then moving to Victoria and working at whatever jobs I could get as I paid for pilot training."

"Didn't you need to get a university degree, too?"

"If I'd wanted to be hired by one of the major airlines, but I didn't. No, it's not a requirement for licensing. Pilot training is intensive and you put in a lot of flying hours."

"That makes sense." She considered his story. "Lionel sounds like a special guy. Does he have a wife and kids?" If so, she wondered how they'd felt about him taking a stranger, a thief, under his wing.

Aaron shook his head. "He's kind of a loner. Oh, he has cronies to hang out with and a special lady, though they don't live together. He likes living on his own and so does Marlise. Not having to account to anyone or be responsible for anyone. Makes a lot of sense to me."

"Are you like that, too?" Aaron had said he wasn't interested in anything long term with her. Was that his general approach to relationships? He was certainly attractive enough that he'd have no trouble finding dates.

"Yeah, I am. I like most people, but I don't want them to get too close. That's asking for problems, seems to me."

Asking for problems? Well, sure. Problems like her mom's cancer, her dad's stressing out over her mom's health, her grandmother's death, and Kelsey's apparent inability to commit to anything. But just being alive meant facing problems, and Eden's love for her family and theirs for her was the foundation that gave her the strength and joy to face whatever came her way. "You don't want to get married and have kids?"

"Nope."

What a waste. She bit her lip. "I don't mean this as a criticism, honestly. I'm just trying to understand. Don't you think life would be kind of empty without a partner? A family?"

"More like it'd be too full if I had them." He rested his forearms on the table and leaned toward her. "Eden, I get it that some people are suited for all that. I can see you're one of them. The way you talk about your family, it's obvious you care a lot about them and would do anything for them."

"Yes. Totally."

"And when you find the right guy, a good guy who deserves you, you'll give him that same caring and commitment, and your kids as well. It's how you were raised; it's who you are. And that's great. Good for you. But that's not who I am."

It was so hard for her to believe a person would want to live his entire life alone. Especially a guy like Aaron, who was friendly and good with people. But then, it seemed as if his family hadn't been there for him, not the way Lionel had. A stranger had taken him in, a stranger who believed in helping a teenager turn his life around yet didn't believe in letting people come too close. How much had Lionel's example influenced Aaron?

"You're doing that scrunched-up forehead thing again," he commented. "Look, people are different. We want different things. That's normal."

"I guess it is." She wanted to pursue the topic, but,

clearly, he didn't. Besides, she realized she'd let this conversation, as well as the appeal of her companion, the lovely setting, and the wonderful meal, distract her from her priority. "We should get back to Lucy. Might Lionel know anything about her?"

"I doubt it. He wasn't into the whole *flower child thing*, as he called it. But we'll put him on the list. Oh, I see Jonah heading our way. Want some dessert?"

"No, thanks." She resisted opening the menu. She loved sweets but couldn't afford the calories. Except for a twenty-minute walk to and from the office, she led a sedentary life. "Just coffee for me," she told Jonah. "Decaf, please."

"A cappuccino maybe?" the young man asked.

"Twist my arm. With skim milk?"

"You got it. Aaron?"

"The real stuff, black and strong as it comes. No dessert."

Eden glanced after Jonah as he left, noting that the customers had thinned out and the restaurant was now only about a third full. She really had lost focus this evening, and it was so unlike her.

Rachelle walked over and handed a slip of paper to Aaron. "These are the names I came up with. Can you think of any to add?"

"Thank you, Rachelle," Eden said. "Do you have a moment to sit with us? I'd love to get some background on these people." She reached for her laptop. "You've lived here longer than Aaron."

The other woman caught Jonah's eye, gestured, and then slipped into the chair beside Aaron. A few minutes later, Jonah arrived with cappuccinos for the two women and Aaron's black coffee. Eden typed notes as Rachelle and Aaron gave her names and snippets of background information. They described one woman, Azalea, as "tie-dye, long white braid, a gentle soul, but her brain got so fried on drugs that she never makes a whole lot of sense." A man, Forbes, "looks like an old hippie, too, but don't let that fool you; his mind's sharp as a tack." Another man, Bart, was only in his fifties, but "his family lived beside the commune and his parents, now deceased, had some run-ins with them."

When the two islanders had completed the list, Rachelle rose. "That'll give you some starting points."

"I can't tell you how much I appreciate it." Eden bit her lip. "Normally, I'd look up phone numbers and call to make appointments. But Aaron said that might not work so well here."

"It'd work with people like Bart, the real estate guy, and Tony, the retired cop. The ones who are part of, um, the mainstream culture, I guess you'd call it. Not so much with the more colorful ones. They have their own way of doing things."

"My offer holds," Aaron said. "I'll help smooth the way for you."

Rachelle shot him a knowing glance. "Yeah, make yourself useful, flyboy."

He winked at her, and with a laugh, she left them.

"Give me that," Aaron said, reaching for the laptop.

He scrolled the screen, clicked keys, and then handed it back. "The ones I've starred, you can use your Ottawa lawyer methods to contact. We'll do the others together."

She studied the list. He'd only put asterisks beside five of the twenty names. "I'm truly grateful for the offer, but isn't your flying a full-time job?"

He shrugged. "It'll work out." He pulled out his

phone and thumb-typed a text message. "I'll need to confirm, but I think I can be free by around quarter to four tomorrow. That'll give us time to see a couple of people."

Eden would have breakfast, talk to Bernie to see if she had anything to add to the list, and then try to set up appointments with some of the asterisked people. With any luck, she'd be able to interview two or three of them before meeting up with Aaron. Feeling optimistic, she said, "That sounds perfect. Drop me a text when you know for sure."

He'd put his phone down on the table and it pulsed. He checked the screen. "I know now. I'll pick you up at the Once at three-forty-five in my Jeep. Top down, so bring a sweater."

He did like issuing orders, but again, his plans worked for her so she didn't protest. "Thank you." She pushed aside her empty coffee cup. "I guess it's time to go."

"Sure is. For a stroll along the docks."

"What?"

"Did you forget about the second part of tonight's agenda? The having fun part?"

She'd already had fun. Chatting with a handsome, interesting man, eating delicious fresh seafood, and enjoying an incredible view—those combined into an evening that was the most fun she'd had in a very long time. Even with Ray, once they'd been together for a year, the romance had given way to practicality. Both of them were busy and life had fallen into a routine—and then, after her mom's illness, Eden had had even less time to spend with him. She'd almost forgotten what it was like to read clear male appreciation in a sexy guy's eyes, to see that sparkle that hinted that the night was only beginning.

Had the woman across from him ever in her life just let loose? She was thoughtful, serious, very much his opposite. He usually didn't go for that type, yet Eden fascinated him. He could lose himself in her amber eyes and never want to look away. His fingers were tense with the desire to test the softness of her wavy hair and then explore the curves revealed by her slim-fitting yet not tight clothing.

"You've got a game plan for starting the search for your aunt," he reminded her. "There's nothing more you can do tonight."

Her mouth softened, almost forming a smile. "I'm still on Eastern Standard Time. I should probably get a good night's sleep."

"You should. But not yet, or you'll wake up before dawn. The best way to adjust to time zone changes is to pretend they don't exist." Or so he'd been told by some of the passengers he'd flown. "Act like it's the time here, not back home, and your body will adjust more quickly."

The smile appeared, a little grin with a hint of mischief. "Maybe I'm a person who always goes to bed early."

"I don't think so." Deciding to call her bluff, he said, "Of course if you don't want to take a romantic moonlight stroll, I sure won't force you. Just say the word and I'll have you back at the Once in five minutes."

Her smile softened and her eyes glowed with warmth.

"Compared to a moonlight stroll on the dock, that doesn't sound so appealing."

Appealing was the word for her right now, with her golden eyes and that gentle, sensual curve to her lips. Sometimes her mouth could look pretty strict, but right now it was eminently kissable.

Jonah arrived to check whether they wanted anything else, and Aaron told him they didn't. When Jonah put down the bill, Eden reached for it, but Aaron beat her to it.

"Give it to me," she said. "It's the least I can do, considering the assistance you've offered me."

"It's your first night on Destiny. You deserve to be treated to dinner."

Her teeth touched her bottom lip. When she gave in, he was relieved. An argument was the last thing he wanted right now.

Rachelle wasn't in sight when they left, but they both thanked Jonah for a wonderful meal and great service. As Aaron held the restaurant door for Eden, she paused a moment to pull on her sweater. Outside, he rolled down his sleeves. "It's usually coolish at night, even in the middle of summer. Especially by the ocean."

"Ottawa can be sweltering in the summer. Our best seasons are spring and fall."

"Every season's a good one here." Even in winter, when fog, rain, and clouds made it impossible to stick to their flight schedule, he loved the West Coast's moodiness.

When he reached for her hand, it slid into his without hesitation, slim and warm, feeling like it belonged there. They walked the block to the walkway between the harbor office and Blue Moon Air's, both closed now, and then down the skid-stripped ramp to the docks. The island's private marina for local boat owners was a few miles away, on the west side of the harbor. Here, at the head of the bay, the docks were working ones where seaplanes could land, charter services and whale watching businesses operated, fishers docked their boats, and visiting boaters could moor for a few hours or overnight. His Cessna and Beaver bobbed securely in their usual spots.

"This is magical," Eden said. "The sky's so clear, I've never seen so many stars. It's like an astronomy chart come to life. The scent of the ocean, the lights on the boats; it's so different from back home."

"That's Destiny Island, serving up magic for visitors." Avoiding the fingers of wharf that held the fish boats and always smelled slightly of fish, he led Eden to the area set aside for visiting boaters, who paid a sizable per foot fee to dock here rather than anchor out. Tonight, there was the usual variety, ranging from a small, beautifully restored twenty-four-foot wooden sailboat to a three-story fiberglass yacht that was well over sixty feet and, to his eyes, ugly as sin. Lights gleamed from inside several of the boats and danced in the rigging. The night sounds were distinctive: the jingle-jangle of metal rigging as boats shifted with the tide, the murmur of voices from people sitting out on their decks with nightcaps, a thread of music too low to identify.

Releasing Eden's hand and putting his arm around her shoulders, he asked quietly, "If you could have any of these boats, which would you pick?"

After a moment, her arm slipped around his waist.

Keeping her voice low too, she said, "Not the big white plasticky ones. Nor the tiny ones, because I can't imagine them being comfortable." She pointed. "That one's nice. It looks so perky."

Following her finger, he saw a thirty-four-foot trawler. "That's a Nordic tug."

"Tug? You mean a tugboat? Don't they tow things?"

"Yeah, like the ones towing log booms we saw when we flew over Georgia Strait. But Nordic tugs are a pleasure craft. I think the design was inspired by tugboats. They're a nice boat. Damned expensive, though."

"I've never gone boating."

He was happy to hear wistfulness rather than disinterest in her voice. "I'll take you."

"You have a boat?"

"No, only kayaks, which are fun, too. But I know a couple of people with boats and they're happy to loan them out."

"That sounds nice. But I doubt there'll be much spare time."

"We'll see." He'd already arranged with Jillian Summers, his other pilot, to take his late-afternoon flight tomorrow, and put her on notice that he'd likely be giving her more work over the next few days. Blue Moon Air wasn't busy enough to need both of them full-time, and he used Jillian on an as-needed basis. At the height of tourist season, he kept her busy; on slow days in winter she might not have any flights. Unless she had kid-related commitments her parents couldn't handle, the single mom, who loved flying almost as much as he did, was always happy to get more hours of flying time.

He walked Eden to the end of a dock that was sparsely

populated with boats. "Moon's almost full. Another couple of nights."

She gazed up. "It's beautiful. By the way, is there such a thing as a blue moon? Other than in songs?"

"Sure. More than one kind. Technically, where a season of the year has four full moons rather than the normal three, the third is called a blue moon."

"The third, not the fourth?"

"Yeah, for whatever reason. They happen every two or three years. The island always has a blue moon festival and tourism goes into overdrive."

As Eden studied the sky, Aaron went on. "But that's actually not how the name came about on Destiny. Ours is the other kind, which is rarer. The moon can look blue when tiny particles of smoke or dust fill the atmosphere. Like after a volcanic eruption like Mount St. Helens in Washington, which happened in 1980, or after a forest fire or dust storm. In our case, it was due to a forest fire on the mainland, back when the first explorers were charting the island."

"Even if it's not blue tonight, the moon is so clear. And the stars."

"No city pollution."

She drew a deep breath. "It's clean and bracing, the scent of the ocean."

He turned so he faced her and finally gave in to the urge to raise a hand and smooth waves of hair back from her face. Then he cupped the sides of her face in both hands and tilted it up toward him. "You're going to like it here, Eden. You might not have come here looking for a good time, but that's what Destiny and I are going to give you."

Her voice breathier than usual, she said, "I'm starting to believe you."

He leaned down slowly, giving her a chance to back away. But she stood her ground, and he touched his lips to hers. So soft they were, and he treated them gently. Caressing, coaxing until she gave a tiny sigh and kissed him back. She seemed tentative, as if she wasn't convinced this was a good thing, or maybe she was just learning the shape of a different male mouth.

After a couple of minutes, he slid his tongue against the crease between her lips, and they parted for him. He put his arms around her and she moved closer until the fronts of their bodies brushed. She felt so damned good. He wanted more, so much more, but was afraid that if he pushed too hard, he'd scare her away.

So he settled for slow, sensual kisses, not too deep or passionate, and for running his hands up and down her back, stopping just above the sweet curve of her ass.

Eden's head was back, her eyes closed, and she seemed totally focused on the kiss. Her hands didn't roam; her body didn't wriggle against his.

He heated up the kiss, probing her mouth demandingly and tugging her closer into his arms so she couldn't help but feel the thrust of his erection beneath the fly of his jeans.

She gave a soft moan, met his tongue with her own, and now her hips did swivel as she pressed herself against him needily, telegraphing her own arousal.

After a few more wonderful minutes, Eden's eyes popped open and she stepped back. Crossing her arms over her chest, she said, "Oh my. That was . . . well, it was wonderful. But I . . . I don't think we should, uh . . . I mean, I just met you today and I'm not ready to, you know."

He was disappointed but not surprised. Occasionally, he'd hooked up with a woman on the day they'd met, but Eden was different and, he suspected, worth waiting for. "It's okay. No pressure, remember?" Except behind his fly, but he could exert self-control. "I'll walk you back to the B and B."

When he reached for her hand, she put it in his with a quiet, "Thank you."

In silence, they walked back along the wharf and up to the main street. As they passed C-Shell, Eden said, "It's been a lovely evening. And afternoon as well, with that scenic flight. I didn't know what to expect when I came here, but it wasn't this."

"Today's been unexpected for me, too. In a very good way. I'm already looking forward to seeing you tomorrow."

"Me too."

Neither spoke again, but the silence between them felt easy. Aaron liked that she didn't constantly chatter, as so many women did.

The Once in a Blue Moon had artistically placed outdoor lights, making it picturesque and welcoming. Aaron walked her up the front steps and they stopped on the wraparound porch. He touched her cheek, then brushed his lips against hers. "Good night, Eden. Sleep well."

"Same to you." She gave him a smile, then turned to open the door.

Whistling softly, Aaron went down the steps. Yes,

he'd sleep well—the sound of waves outside his window was the best kind of lullaby—and he'd bet his dreams would feature Eden.

Tomorrow, maybe he'd have a chance to turn those dreams into reality.

Chapter Five

The sizable dining room at the B and B was more than half-filled with people when Eden went down for breakfast at eight, her laptop stowed in her big purse. To her surprise, instead of worrying about her mom, fretting over whether she'd be able to trace Lucy, or replaying that incredible kiss, she'd had a sound night's sleep. She hadn't woken until her alarm went off at seven. Now, showered and dressed, email dealt with, she was hungry and ready to get on with the day.

A day that would include seeing Aaron later, which meant they'd probably kiss again. Maybe this time she'd let him take the kiss a little further. She'd have known him for more than a day by then, and she was only here for a week. The man was so enticing, it would be a pity not to find out everything he had to offer.

She drew her attention back to her surroundings. The wooden dining room table seated ten and was supplemented by three tables for four, all of them set with bright place mats and vases of flowers. Half a dozen guests sat at the large table and two of the smaller tables were occupied as well, one by a hand-holding middle-aged

couple and the other by a family of four. A distressed
oak sideboard held a buffet-style meal. Bernie was
there, today in sky blue, wearing a matching pair of
wind-chime earrings. With her was a balding man with
a tidy gray beard and a friendly smile whom she introduced to Eden as her husband, Jonathan. The couple
said they'd be happy to whip up an omelet for her.

She turned them down, assuring them that the
buffet looked delicious. Her mom had always been a
big believer in the importance of a good breakfast,
so Eden rarely skipped the meal. Avoiding the more
decadent treats like bacon, sausages, pancakes, and
French toast, she chose homemade yogurt, fresh fruit
salad, and a raspberry-oat muffin.

Sociable by nature, she chose the big table and dug
into her breakfast, pleasantly surprised to discover
tiny chocolate chips scattered through her muffin.
The other diners were tourists, comparing notes on
island attractions and activities. For such a tiny place,
it seemed there was lots to do, whether you preferred
outdoor activities, visiting artists' studios, pampering
yourself at a spa, or sampling organic products.
Because no one at the table had any long-term connection with Destiny Island, she didn't share her
reason for visiting, only saying she had personal business here but also planned to play tourist.

The others scattered gradually, and Bernie and
Jonathan began clearing the sideboard. "I'm going to
pour myself a nice big mug of coffee," the woman told
Eden, "and we can have our chat. Can I get you anything else first? And what do you think of Jonathan
joining us?"

"A top up on my coffee would be great," Eden said.

"And yes, I'd welcome Jonathan's input if you can both spare the time."

"This is our feet-up break," Bernie said. "We get up early so everything's fresh for breakfast and then we're run off our feet. Once the guests leave, we give ourselves an hour or so to relax before tackling the dishes and cleaning the rooms."

The three of them settled at one of the smaller tables, which was set in a bay window overlooking a casually landscaped garden full of flowers. "Your garden reminds me of my mother's," Eden said. "She loves gardening." Or at least she used to, before cancer robbed her of her energy and, it seemed, her ability to find enjoyment in life. If only Eden could help her reconnect with her sister, surely her mom's spirits would lift. "And on the subject of my mom, that's where my story starts."

For the next few minutes, she gave them an abbreviated version, mentioning that Aaron had offered to help her. She opened her laptop and showed them the list of names she'd compiled last night. "Can you think of anyone to add?"

"I can't think of any other names," Bernie said. "Jonathan?"

"No, but I'm in a band with Forbes Blake. How about I ask him for lunch and you can talk to him?"

"That would be terrific. Thanks so much."

"We're friends with Di and Seal SkySong, too," Bernie said. "We could invite them."

Eden's notes said that couple had belonged to the old commune and now owned a serenity retreat. "Aaron said he flew them over to the mainland last week," she commented, "and they'd yet to book a return flight."

"Oh, that's right," Bernie said. "They always leave for a couple of weeks at this time of year. I doubt they'll be back while you're here. Hopefully some of the others will be able to put you on the track to finding your aunt."

They gave her a few additional snippets of information about other people on the list, and then Jonathan called Forbes and arranged a one o'clock lunch. He stood. "I'm going to walk over to the tourist center. We're running low on maps of the island." He bent to exchange a lip brush with Bernie. "See you later, Eden. Have a good morning."

After he'd gone, Bernie said, "So Aaron offered to help you? When he took you out for dinner, I thought maybe it was a, er, more personal relationship." She didn't come out and ask the question, but her curiosity was obvious.

Remembering that wonderful moonlight kiss, Eden's cheeks warmed. "It may be both."

"Oh."

She was good at reading people and saw the uncertainty that pinched her hostess's face. "Bernie, is something worrying you?"

"It's just, well . . ." She ran a hand through her spiky salt-and-pepper hair. "Aaron's a great guy. Sweet as pie, generous, a lot of fun. And eye candy, to state the obvious. But you seem like a—how to put this?—more serious kind of person. More a family-values woman than the type for a fling. And Aaron . . . well, I'm not saying he's superficial, but he's, er . . ."

Eden rescued her. "It's okay. I know what you're getting at and I appreciate your concern. If anything develops between us, it'll be purely a holiday fling. You're right that I'm normally more serious, but for the foreseeable future I don't have the time or energy for a relationship. If a man offered serious, I'd turn him down in a flash."

Bernie grinned. "I confess I'm relieved. I can be a bit of a mother hen. I want you to enjoy your time on Destiny and go away with fond memories, not a broken heart."

"Believe me, my heart's in no danger." Even the breakup with Ray, tough as it had been, hadn't exactly shattered her heart.

She mused on that as, after taking her leave of Bernie, she went back to her room. When it came to romance, some women felt so much passion—both sexually and emotionally. One of her colleagues, Liz, for example: For her, it was all about the drama of falling in love, the amazing sex, and the tragedy when it ended. For Eden, loving Ray had been more about comfort and compatibility, in bed and out. After that final argument, she'd realized they weren't so compatible after all. Though she'd felt a sense of loss, disappointment, and anger, she hadn't shed many tears. Maybe she'd used up all her tears crying in private over her mom's cancer, getting them out so she could show an optimistic face to her family. Or maybe she just wasn't a deeply emotional, passionate woman. Would that be so bad?

She opened the balcony door and went out to gaze at the village that nestled in a curve around the harbor. On one of those docks, Aaron had kissed her. Maybe it had been the romantic setting, with moonlight on the ocean, but that kiss had been special. Almost . . . passionate. More intense than any she remembered sharing with Ray.

But then, just as people were different, so were

relationships. Hers with Ray had developed slowly: law students studying together, getting a bite to eat, coming to know each other. With Aaron, things couldn't proceed too slowly or she'd be gone before . . . well, before they had sex, to be blunt. And if his kiss was anything to go by, it would be a real pity to miss out on sex with him. She had decided against a committed relationship for the time being, so why shouldn't she indulge in a few days of mindless pleasure with the hot pilot? No one would get hurt and maybe she'd discover a whole new, more passionate side to herself.

Eden pressed a hand to a flaming cheek. Here she was, doing a logical analysis of the advisability of having a fling with a man she barely knew. That was not why she'd come to Destiny Island.

Aaron had been flying steadily since the crack of dawn, barely finding five minutes to gulp down a sandwich at noon. When he landed the flight from Vancouver at three-twenty, he caught Jillian in the office as she was preparing to take a couple of tourists up in the Cessna for a sightseeing flight. The two of them, along with Kam, put their heads together over the schedule for the next few days. Kam Nguyen, an aspiring pilot, handled the office, reservations, website, and pretty much everything else that kept the business running.

Blue Moon Air's schedule was flexible. Seven days a week there were morning and afternoon return flights to Vancouver, with other stops along the way as needed. Some days, especially in holiday season and around weekends, they needed additional Vancouver flights. As well, they took whatever private travel and sightseeing flights could be fit into the schedule.

"You're sure you're okay taking on these extra flights?" he asked Jillian. It was a challenge for the single mom to juggle work and looking after her seven-year-old son. She relied on her parents' assistance because the boy's father had never, other than providing child support, been part of the picture.

"It'll be fine, and I'm glad for the extra flying time." She flicked blond curls back from her face and gazed up at him, her blue eyes narrowed. "But it's not like you to take so much time off, Aaron. Is everything okay?"

"It's good. I'm helping out a friend." He'd spent only a few hours with Eden, but he did think of her as a friend. He hoped that, before much more time passed, he'd also be thinking of her as a lover. "Okay," he told his two employees, "I'm heading out. Call me if anything important comes up."

He went back down to the dock to buy fresh crab for dinner and then, hefting a small cooler, hurried to the lot where he parked his old olive-green Jeep Wrangler. The top was down and a light breeze ruffled his hair, reminding him that he ought to make time for a haircut.

When he pulled up in front of the Once in a Blue Moon, Eden was seated in one of the painted Adirondack chairs on the front porch. She came down the steps to meet him, a rather shy smile on her face. "Hi," she said as she climbed into the passenger seat.

He leaned over, hooked his right arm around her, and tugged her close for a light kiss. "Hi." Her lips were warm and soft, and a delicate flowery scent made him want to get closer. But he figured she'd prefer to focus on her mission before allowing time for the fun stuff.

"Do I look okay?" she asked.

He'd texted her during the morning, telling her who he thought they should start with and suggesting she dress casually. Her interpretation of that was to wear slim-fitting jeans and a silky, short-sleeved top with a swirly beige-and-blue pattern that made him think of the ocean lapping against a sandy beach. Her hair was down and she carried her big purse and a navy sweater. "You look great," he said. "I like that top."

"Me too. I saw it in a shop window this morning and couldn't resist." She took a hair tie out of her bag and pulled her hair back into a ponytail.

"Supporting local business. That's a point in your favor." As he drove through the small village, he asked, "How's your day been so far?"

She told him about the conversation she'd had with the owners of the B and B, and then said, "Jonathan invited Forbes Blake over for lunch. You were right that he looks like an old hippie and that his mind's sharp. Sadly, he didn't remember Lucy or Barry. I asked him if he had any photos from the commune, but he said no, that cameras weren't a part of their lifestyle. Also, he wasn't a member for long. He didn't get along with the leader, a man named Merlin. A made-up name, Forbes figured."

"I'm sorry he wasn't more help."

They were driving through the outskirts of town now, on the two-lane road that was the main route from Blue Moon Harbor to the north end of the island. They passed the fire station, the small medical center, and the school buildings that housed kindergarten through twelfth grade. Eden gazed out the window, taking in the sights as they talked.

"He and Jonathan said their band's playing Friday night at the Quail Ridge Community Hall," she said. "They invited me."

"They're called B-B-Zee and they're good. We should go. They play a mix of music: country, folk, rock. It's good to dance to." He liked dancing, feeling the music in his blood and holding a supple, smiling woman in his arms. He would especially like dancing with Eden.

"I'm not a very good dancer. It's not something I've done much."

"We'll change that."

"Hmm. What did you say they're called?"

"B-B-Zee. That's capital *B* for Barnes, capital *B* for Blake, capital *Zed* and two small *E*s for Zabec. Christian Zabec is originally from America and wanted to make sure everyone knows it's a Zee, not a Zed."

She nodded her understanding. "This morning I went to the *Destiny Gazette* office and talked to the editor, Mr. Newall. He's not much of a people person, is he? I wondered if . . ."

As she figured out how to phrase her question, Aaron said, "He has Asperger's syndrome. He does the management and detail work and his wife and brother do most of the reporting, interviews, ad-taking, and the people end of it."

"He was very efficient about finding old copies of the newspaper. I asked about the man who was editor back then, but Mr. Newall said he died. In fact, he seemed compelled to give me the date, time, place, and cause of death."

"Yeah, that's Mr. Newall. Did you find anything useful in the old *Gazette*s?"

"Stories that—" She broke off, pointing out the

window. "Oh look, sheep! It's so peaceful and pastoral with all those cute white sheep grazing in the green meadows."

"There's a lot of agriculture on the island."

"I saw that when we flew over. And no, the *Gazette* articles and letters to the editor weren't about individual commune members. Just general comments ranging from philosophical discussions of communes and their values to complaints about the hippies. Which ties in with what I learned from Tony Iacobucci. I phoned him this morning and he was happy to talk."

"What did he have to say?" Tony was a retired Royal Canadian Mounted Police officer who'd been a rookie on Destiny during the commune days. After that, he was posted to other places, but when he retired, he and his wife came back to the island and bought a house.

"There was one overdose, a guy in his early twenties." She swallowed and then rushed on, as if thinking about hippie overdoses was too uncomfortable. "Complaints against the commune ranged from the predictable ones like too much noise, immoral behavior, and use of illegal drugs through to some less concrete but scarier ones."

"Scary?" He glanced over at her.

"A few parents contacted the police saying their kids had joined the commune and that it was a cult and Merlin was brainwashing them, using drugs to control them, and claiming sexual ownership of the girls."

"Crap. I had no idea."

"It could have been parental paranoia. Mr. Iacobucci—Superintendent Iacobucci—said that when he questioned the commune members, everyone was loyal to Merlin."

"Did he have any contact with Lucy or Barry?"

"He didn't remember them. I emailed him the couple of old, not very good photos of Lucy I have, and he didn't recognize her. He said he'd pull out his old notebooks, and this afternoon he emailed to say he had no note of either name."

"That's too bad."

"It is," she said absentmindedly, and then she shook her head. "If the commune did have a dark side, I hope Lucy would've had the sense to realize it and to leave. With or without Barry."

She raised a hand to her lips then lowered it again and clasped her hands on her lap. "So far, I'm not doing so well. Two interviews, all those newspapers, and not a hint of a lead."

He took his right hand off the steering wheel and rested it on her clasped hands, feeling her tension. "We've still got a lot of names on that list."

She took a deep breath and her hands relaxed. "Who are we going to see now?"

"Azalea. She isn't a Destiny native. She came from someplace else—I've never heard where—joined the commune, and never left the island."

"I'm curious to meet her. She's the one you and Rachelle said lives pretty much off the grid, so I'm not sure what to picture."

He grinned. "I could tell you, but it's more fun if you see for yourself."

A few minutes later, he put his hand back on the wheel and turned the Jeep down a narrower road that led off the main road. They drove past small farms, a few rather run-down old houses, and several fairly new, more ostentatious homes.

"She really doesn't have a surname?" Eden asked.

"I imagine she does, somewhere on legal records,

but she never uses it. And why should she have to if she doesn't want to?"

"I guess *because everyone else does* wouldn't seem like a sound reason to her?"

"You got that right. I also don't have a clue whether Azalea's her birth name. It could be that, like Merlin, she rechristened herself."

"Really?" Excitement sharpened her voice. "You don't think she could be Lucy, do you? My aunt might have changed her name."

"Azalea is First Nations."

"Oh," she said disappointedly. And then, tentatively, "Are you? You look like you might be."

"Yeah, on my father's side." And that was a subject he had no interest in talking about. "It's just up ahead," he told her as they passed the Hackinsaws' rambling log home. He took a rutted dirt road that was so overarched by trees and overgrown by salal and other bushes that it was almost concealed. "Azalea may own this land, or the Hackinsaws, who live next door, may have rented it to her or given her permission to use it, or she may be squatting with everyone turning a blind eye. I'm sure someone knows, but I don't think anyone cares."

He'd first met Azalea when he was in his teens, when Lionel had taken him along to help bring down a couple of dead trees and buck and chop them into firewood for her. Since then, he'd had some occasion to visit once or twice a year. As he drove through the last screen of trees to draw up in front of her home, he turned to watch Eden's reaction.

"That's an odd-looking cottage," she said. "Is it octagonal?"

"Yeah. It's a yurt, not a cottage."

"A yurt? What's that?"

"A cross between a cabin and a tent. I think they originated with nomadic people in Mongolia. One of the campgrounds has a few of them, too."

"What are the black and silver frames in the yard? I've seen them at a number of other houses as well."

"Solar panels." He glanced at the yard, a cheerfully jumbled mass of flowers, azalea bushes, and clumps of interesting grasses. "See how the panels are angled to catch the sun, where nothing will shade them? They provide her electricity. She has a well, too, so she doesn't need to use any utility services."

"Oh, come on. Phone, cable TV, Wi-Fi?"

"None of the above. She has a guitar, an old-fashioned record player and a bunch of vinyl records, she gets used books and magazines from somewhere, and that's her entertainment."

"I see what you mean about *off the grid.*"

He pointed toward an area enclosed by a tall fence made of wire mesh attached to stripped branches—a fence he'd helped repair for Azalea a year or so before. "That's a garden with vegetables, berries, and herbs. There are apple and pear trees in a meadow past the house. And see the little hut with the fenced plot beside it? That's a chicken coop. She has a pair of goats, which supply her with milk, yogurt, butter, and cheese. She's vegetarian and pretty self-sufficient when it comes to food. A few islanders swap with her: goat's milk feta or raspberry jam in exchange for flour or canning jars. That kind of thing."

"I can't imagine someone living that way in this day and age."

"Climb on out and let's see if Azalea's around."

"You didn't call and make—oh, of course you couldn't

make an appointment if she doesn't have a phone."
She opened the Jeep door.

He hopped out and came around to join her. "I
don't think she has much use for the concept of appointment schedules either." If he suggested such a
thing, Azalea would laugh her head off and refuse to
have anything to do with Eden. "Try not to act all busi-
nesslike, okay? We're her guests and we need to respect the way she likes to do things." He caught her
hand in his, where it felt so good.

She squeezed his hand, which felt even better.
"I'll try."

As he led her to the open door of the yurt, a strange
melody of tinkles, clanks, and clunks greeted them,
and they both glanced at the wind chimes made of
oddly shaped bits of glass, small rocks, and tarnished
silverware. Aaron tapped the door frame. "Azalea?"

When he received no answer, he shouted, "Azalea!
You around somewhere?" Even though she owned an
old bicycle, she rarely left her place. Of course there
was no guarantee that, even if she was here, she'd be
in the mood to speak to visitors.

After a minute, he called her name again and added,
"It's Aaron Gabriel."

The only answer came from one of the goats, somewhere in the distance. Its loud *aackgh* made Eden jump.
"Oh God, Aaron, she's hurt! We have to find her."

He laughed. "No, it's only a goat. And it's not hurt,
goats just have strange voices."

Eden looked skeptical, but then her attention shifted
and he turned to see Azalea emerge from the woods.

"Oh," Eden breathed.

In her late sixties or early seventies, the tall woman
wore a faded, tie-dyed T-shirt over an exotic-looking

embroidered skirt with tiny mirrors scattered all over it. Brown feet were thrust into tattered leather sandals. Flyaway tendrils of silvery hair escaped the thick, butt-length braid to form a halo around her nut brown, deeply wrinkled face. Long brown-and-white feathers—real ones—hung from her ears.

Deep brown eyes peered at him from behind wire-framed glasses held together with tape. "Aaron Gabriel," she said. "A fine name, the angel Gabriel, walking in space. Your mom did good there, but that was maybe the last time, though who'm I to say? A woman oughtn't criticize another one, not unless she's walked a mile in her shoes, which I'm not about to be doing, not with these damned bunions."

Eden's mouth gaped open and Aaron felt the tiniest bit guilty for not having warned her, but mostly amused.

He'd spent some time with Azalea over the years, doing work around her place, delivering her weavings to the artisan co-op that sold them, giving her a lift when she was hitchhiking somewhere farther than she wanted to bicycle. Occasionally she'd offered him a bowl of tasty vegetarian stew or curry, put on some of her old records, and they'd spent an evening together. She wasn't the easiest person to understand, but she had a gentle soul and she was never boring.

Now he said to her, "Seems to me Azalea's a good name, too. Pretty flowers, blooming so bright in the spring."

"My favorite flower." She nodded vigorously. "That's why I called myself that, though it's maybe too audacious, arrogant, outrageous, and maybe one day I'll pay the price for that, if there's such a thing as a heaven. Anywhere else than on earth, that is." Her gaze focused on Eden. "I don't know you."

Aaron answered before Eden could, figuring the older woman would be more welcoming if he made the introduction. "This is Eden, come to visit Destiny from Ottawa."

"Ottawa," Azalea echoed. "About as far away from paradise as you can get. Bureaucrats and politicians, dirty snow full of dog shit. Who'd ever want to go to Ottawa?"

Aaron wondered if she'd once lived there, or if her information came from books and magazines.

Eden gave a soft laugh. "You have a good point. But I was born there and my family's there, and we're very close."

"Huh." Azalea studied her and then walked through the open door of the yurt. After a moment, she yelled, "Well? You two coming?"

He gestured for Eden to enter, then followed her. Azalea's home had a single bed covered in a striped cotton spread and laden with colored pillows, a recliner chair with a footstool, a little round table with a single chair, and a kitchen with a fridge and propane stove. Aaron watched as Eden glanced around, her gaze touching the wood-burning fireplace, the golden-wood guitar, the turntable record player, and stacks of records, books, and magazines. The furniture was simple, but the walls were hung with abstract weavings of colored wool interwoven with feathers, silky threads, more colored glass, shells, and other odds and ends.

"The weavings are amazing," Eden said, sounding sincere. "I love them. Did you create them, Azalea?"

The older woman went into the small kitchen. "I weave, the spider weaves, threads and mazes and traps, pretty webs to catch pretty dreams and make them come true."

Eden glanced at Aaron, her eyes wide and questioning. As Azalea turned her back to take something from a drawer, Aaron bent to whisper in Eden's ear. "Just go with it. It's stream of consciousness, too much LSD when she was young, whatever."

Azalea turned back to them. "Sit. Waiting for an invitation's never going to get you anywhere in life." She let out a surprisingly youthful giggle. "Not that we all want to go the same places, do we?"

Aaron tugged Eden down on the bed couch, where they stuffed pillows behind their backs. Azalea came toward them with something in her hand, and when she struck a match he wasn't surprised to discover it was a hand-rolled joint. He knew that, among the carrots and strawberries in her garden, she also grew marijuana plants. She took a toke, closing her eyes as she inhaled. A sweetish tang seeped into the air.

When she held out the joint to Aaron, he said, "Thanks, but no." Growing up with an addict mom, he avoided drugs.

Azalea held it out to Eden, who also said, "No, thank you."

"Politician or bureaucrat, uptight Ottawa girl?"

Aaron glanced at Eden, wondering if she'd tell Azalea she was a lawyer—and, if so, how the older woman would respond.

Chapter Six

Eden had trouble following Azalea's conversational style and she'd certainly never met anyone like her before, yet she found herself liking the white-haired First Nations woman with her dangly feather earrings. Besides, she'd been brought up to respect her elders, so she told Azalea the truth, phrased in a way she hoped wouldn't alienate her. "Neither a politician nor a bureaucrat. I work with a foundation that funds some wonderful charities and nonprofit organizations. As for uptight, I guess sometimes I am." She gave a tentative smile. "Takes all kinds, doesn't it?"

A twinkle sparked in Azalea's eyes. "Guess it does, clever girl."

Clever girl was a step up from *uptight girl*, Eden figured. "But the thing with marijuana," she went on, "isn't about me being uptight but that it reminds me of my mom's cancer. She used medical marijuana during her treatment."

"Cancer, Big C, disease of modern society," Azalea said, sinking down onto a cushion on the floor with an agility that belied her age. "Cancer grows, cancer flows, terrorist cells taking a body hostage." She blinked and stared at Eden. "I'm sorry about your mother."

"Thank you. I am, too. You're right about those terrorist cells, and it's not only the body they prey on, it's also the mind. For a person who's always been strong to suddenly feel sick and have no control over what's happening . . . well, it can be devastating." She swallowed and focused on the positive. "But Mom's doing better. She's finished a bunch of nasty treatments and I'm convinced she's going to get well."

"Believe in it, make it so," Azalea commented.

Eden nodded strongly. "That's exactly what Dad and I think."

Beside her, Aaron settled back on the couch, seeming to relax. He must be relieved she hadn't come on all lawyerlike. She was a little surprised herself how comfortable she was starting to feel. This interview was so unlike the focused conversations she'd had with the B and B owners, Forbes Blake, and the retired RCMP officer.

Speaking of focused, it was time to get to the point. "Actually, it's because of Mom that I came to Destiny Island. A long time ago her older sister disappeared, and it seems she came here. Mom would really like to find her."

"Wishes aren't horses, people can fly, they can disappear into the mystic. And why not?"

Was Azalea implying that Lucy had a good reason to leave and might not want to be found? "I know that sometimes people have good reasons for leaving," Eden said. "My grandparents were strict. Too strict for an independent, free-spirited teenager like my aunt. They issued an ultimatum and she refused to knuckle under, so she ran away."

Eden leaned forward as she went on. "But after a few months, she wrote. Maybe she was hoping to reconcile or maybe she was taunting them. I have no way of knowing. Anyhow, she told them she and her boyfriend had joined the commune here. My grandparents would have seen that as immoral, not to mention disrespectful to them. It seems they never responded. From then on, they acted like she'd never existed. I loved my grandparents—who are both dead now—but I have trouble forgiving them for that."

Azalea let her breath out slowly after a long toke. Eden really didn't like that aromatic scent with its unhappy associations. She was glad the yurt door and a window were open, keeping air circulating.

"Don't expect they'd care much about forgiveness," the older woman said. "Leopards and spots and zebras and stripes." With a faraway expression in her eyes, she said, "Forgiveness is about the forgiver, anyhow. Peace in your soul, piece of your soul, hole in your soul."

Eden wondered about this woman's story and if she was relating to Lucy. "You were a member of the commune, too, weren't you, Azalea?"

"Flowers in my hair. Music, sweet music, sweet smoke in the air."

O-kay. "You may have known my aunt." She had a feeling dates wouldn't mean much to Azalea but gave them anyhow, as she took out her phone and scrolled to her photos. "She came in the spring or summer of 1969. I don't know how long she stayed at the commune."

Eden rose to show Azalea the only two pictures her mother had been able to salvage when Eden's grandparents purged the house of all traces of Lucy. One showed two brown-haired girls in shorts sitting on a flower-bordered lawn. "The one facing the camera is my mom. The one in profile is her sister." She scrolled to the second photo, a more formal one showing a teen with a rather round face, her hair almost to shoulder level and flipped up at the ends, with a line of bangs across her forehead. "This is a school photo taken three years before she left."

As the older woman studied the photos, Eden said, "My aunt's name is Lucy Nelson."

Azalea glanced up, her eyes brightening. "Lucy in the sky with diamonds, kaleidoscope eyes."

"That was a Beatles song, wasn't it?" Her father'd been a Beatles fan back in the day, and every now and then pulled out some of his old music and the turntable he'd had as a teen. Her mom wasn't a fan, saying she'd been too young to relate. Eden wondered if her aunt had liked the Beatles' music and enjoyed having her name in one of their songs.

"Beatles, Stones, sticks and stones, broken bones." Azalea shook her head and rose.

As Eden again took her seat beside Aaron, the white-haired woman wandered back toward the kitchen, muttering, "Bruises and broken bones, time to fly away."

Aaron leaned forward, his bare forearm brushing Eden's, warming her skin and making it tingle. "Bruises and broken bones at the commune, Azalea?" he said. "Merlin's, uh, magic kingdom not so magical after all? Some of the birds had to fly away? Maybe Lucy?"

Eden caught her breath. Was this what Azalea had been getting at? Would Aaron's attempt to use the woman's own kind of language get through to her, so that she'd provide some actual information?

Azalea turned, the hand holding the joint raised. "Lucy's in the sky with diamonds."

"No diamonds," Eden said patiently. "Just my aunt Lucy who came to the commune when she was seventeen along with her boyfriend. Did you know Lucy or Barry? It would mean a lot to my mom if you did."

"Lucy without diamonds? But Lucy and diamonds go together." Her eyes looked unfocused, maybe from the marijuana or because her mind was back in hippie times. "And Barry, hairy, quite contrary." She gave a snorty kind of laugh. "Bull seals barking at each other. Flower children tripping out, far out, blowing our little minds. Groovy scene, love-in, good loving, bad loving at the Enchantery."

"The Enchantery?" Eden asked. Had Azalea picked that up from Aaron's comment about Merlin's magical kingdom, or had it been the name of the commune?

"Shh," Azalea said, a finger to her lips. "Can't call it that, secret name, no one's supposed to know."

Eden didn't point out that the other woman had just said it herself.

Azalea pinched out the half-smoked joint and laid it down. "Chickens, chickadees, children, always hungry." She took a quick path to the open door of the yurt.

Caught by surprise, Eden and Aaron rose more slowly and followed her. By the time they stepped out into the sunshine, Azalea was going into the chicken coop, her long braid flicking behind her.

"Have we been dismissed?" Eden asked.

"I'd say so." Aaron put his arm around her shoulders. "Guess that wasn't so helpful."

She let herself lean against his muscled body. Why

did he feel more strong and masculine than Ray or any other man she'd ever dated—and why did that physicality appeal to her? "It's hard to tell what's real and what's a flight of fantasy. You know her better. What do you think?"

"I think maybe those parents who contacted the RCMP had it right and the commune was cultlike, called the Enchantery, with Merlin as the leader. He kept tight control over the members, using drugs and some kind of brainwashing, and they weren't supposed to talk about the Enchantery with outsiders. He abused some of the women."

"If Lucy was there . . ." God forbid her aunt had suffered abuse.

"Seems to me Azalea didn't know, or at least remember, Lucy or Barry."

"That's what I thought, too. Her only association with the name Lucy is an old song, and Barry just sends her off on one of her wordplay things." She sighed, pressed herself into his comforting warmth for a moment, and then stepped away and walked toward the Jeep. "Well, that's another name to cross off the list. Oh, I forgot to mention, Rachelle called and said she'd spoken to her parents, and neither of them ever went to the commune. Once in a while they'd see members in the village, but they didn't know any of them. They promised to ask their friends."

As Aaron opened the door for her, she asked, "Why did you choose Azalea first?"

His lips quirked. "Partly 'cause I was curious how you'd react to her. She's pretty cool in her own admittedly unique way."

"True. She's certainly different from anyone I've ever met."

"Maybe I figured if you could deal with Azalea, you'd be okay with any of the other island eccentrics I introduce you to." He went around and climbed into the driver's seat.

"I hope Lucy didn't turn out like Azalea. That would be a shock for Mom."

"Could be worse." He started the Jeep and got it turned around. "Azalea's healthy and happy, not harming a soul."

"Not helping a soul either." Both her parents, like Eden, believed strongly in trying to make the world a better place.

"You're wrong about that. She gives stuff away to people who can't pay or have nothing to barter."

Eden's teeth rattled as the Jeep jounced over the near-nonexistent road. "I'm sorry. I judged too quickly."

Aaron shot her a quick glance. "You do realize your mission for your mom may not turn out with a happy result? Lucy might not be a person your mother would want to know. And have you considered the possibility that she might be dead?"

Eden's chin came up. "I won't dwell on thoughts like that. Mom needs this. It has to come out well." His lack of response suggested that he disagreed, but she wasn't going to argue the point. "Is there anyone else we could see today?"

"We have a dinner invitation."

"Oh! Why didn't you tell me? I'd have brought something dressier to change into. Not to mention a hostess gift."

"You look great, and we can stop to pick up a bottle of wine if you want."

"Yes, please." As the Jeep turned onto an actual

paved road, she asked warily, "Is this another aging hippie like Azalea?" It took a lot of mental energy to be around someone like her.

Aaron chuckled, a rich sound that moved over her skin like a warm breeze. "Aging hippie, but not like Azalea. She's on your list: Marlise Kulik."

"Could she be my aunt?"

"No, sorry. I told her about your mission and she said her name's always been Marlise, and she and her sister, who lives in Kelowna, are in touch often. She said she'd think back to the commune days to see if she remembered anything that might help you."

"I look forward to meeting her."

"You'll meet Lionel, too. We're dining at his house."

"They're the couple who are, uh, friends with benefits, right? Who don't want to live together?"

"That's them."

And Lionel was Aaron's mentor. "I'm looking forward to meeting them. They speak like normal people, don't they?"

He threw back his head and laughed. "Yeah. And they both have sharp brains. But still, they're islanders. Don't go all lawyerlike on them."

"I'll try to refrain."

Aaron pulled into the parking area in front of a small store called We Got It. "We can buy wine here. The owner prides himself on carrying the essentials of life: food staples, a bit of fresh produce, basic bathroom stuff." Mischief tweaked his lips. "Condoms."

"If you're buying condoms, I'm not coming in with you."

He gave a snort of amusement. "You're acting like a teenager. Anyhow, I'm not buying them. I already have enough."

Enough for what? Were they really going to have sex?

She accompanied him inside. We Got It had an old-fashioned country store feel to it. While Aaron went to choose wine, she got sidetracked by a big bulletin board plastered with notices of items for sale or wanted, services offered or sought, upcoming meetings and events, even a birth announcement complete with a photo of a bald, beaming infant. She decided there'd be nothing lost, tomorrow morning, in creating a poster with the photos of Lucy and asking anyone who had information to give her a call. Hopefully, the GPS on her phone could lead her back to this store.

Aaron returned with a bottle of Destiny Cellars riesling and another of zinfandel, saying that Marlise and Lionel liked them both. The wine wasn't cheap and she insisted on paying. "The whole purpose of the dinner is so I can get information. Besides, you bought dinner last night. This is the least I can do."

From the store they drove east, past cottages with artisan signs and fields with crops, sheep, and cattle. One place even had alpacas, which Aaron told her produced wool weavers valued. The bucolic feel of the area relaxed her, and it was a surprise when the scenery changed again and they drove into a forest of tall evergreens. "For one small island, there's a lot of variety in terrain," she commented.

"Wait until you see the rest of it. Especially the beaches."

The road here was single lane and paved, though the pavement was well-worn. They passed a couple of long, dirt-track driveways that disappeared off into the woods, and then Aaron turned onto the next one. A few hundred yards along, the road ended in a gravel cul-de-sac, where he parked beside a battered old black truck and a yellow Volkswagen Beetle—one of the original ones, nicely maintained. Behind a screen of leafy green trees, she glimpsed a wooden A-frame house. A medium-sized brown dog of no discernible breed came slowly down the gravel walk from the house, tail wagging amiably. The white around its muzzle told her it was elderly.

"Hey, Chester," Aaron greeted the dog, bending to give him a good rub.

Eden leaned down, extending her hand, and when Chester sniffed it and wagged his tail, she, too, stroked him. Unless the dog was Marlise's, Lionel didn't live entirely alone.

Aaron took a small cooler out of the back of the Jeep, Eden carried the bag with the wine, and Chester followed as they walked along the gravel path to the door.

The house wasn't large and the weathered wood suggested it had been here quite a while. The yard, if it could be called that, featured only a few randomly planted rhododendrons, flowering in shades of pink, purple, and orange-yellow. A man's home, not a woman's, but attractive in its own way, like a small oasis only semicarved out of the surrounding wilderness.

The front door had a dog door in it and a tarnished brass bell hanging beside it, which Aaron rang. A male voice hollered, "We're decent. Come on in."

As they entered, with Chester choosing to stay outside, a woman came toward them. Like Azalea, she was slim, tallish, and tanned, though the wrinkles fanning from the corners of her eyes were less sharply etched. In every other way, she was Azalea's stylish opposite. Her hair, a mixture of blond, brown tones, and silvery gray, was short and fashionably layered. She wore a silk-screened blouse in shades of blue and silver over narrow-legged jeans, and her feet were in jeweled sandals. Her jewelry—dangly earrings and a pendant necklace—was silver with deep blue stones Eden thought were lapis lazuli.

Marlise and Aaron embraced, and then she held out her hand to Eden. "Hi, I'm Marlise. Welcome to Destiny Island."

"Thank you. And thanks to you and Lionel for the dinner invitation."

"It'll be casual. I hope that's okay."

"Of course." She held out the bag. "Here's my contribution."

"Wonderful. Come on through to the kitchen."

Aaron picked up the cooler again and followed Marlise. Eden trailed behind, casting a glance around. The front room was small, with a single bed shoved against one wall, a desk under the front window, and a couple of oil seascapes. On the other side of a narrow hall was a closed door, and a flight of wooden steps led to the second floor.

She entered the kitchen, which was larger than the bedroom/office. Big windows drew her, and she walked over to see the view. "Wow." The house stood near the edge of what looked like a cliff. In front of her, past a wood-slatted deck, was a weathered rock outcropping, and beyond it the intense, almost indigo bluish-green of the ocean, broken by white curls lacing the tops of waves. A stunning tree framed the view, its trunk and limbs curved in graceful, feminine lines. The bark was orange-brown, lighter than cinnamon, and the leaves were a deep, shiny green.

A male chuckle, raspier than Aaron's, broke the

spell, and the man said, "Not much I can do to compete with a view like that."

She turned, embarrassed, to see a stocky, gray-haired guy in jeans and a plaid shirt, his grin a flash of white against skin the color of black coffee. "I'm so sorry. That was rude of me. You must be Lionel." She walked toward him to shake his hand.

"And you're Eden, Aaron's new friend." Dark brown eyes studied her from behind horn-rims.

She hoped she measured up to whatever he was looking for. "Thank you for inviting me for dinner."

"Aaron says you're not the typical tourist."

Marlise chimed in. "Tourists rarely get invited to islanders' homes."

"Should I ask why?"

"We have a love-hate relationship with them," the woman said. "Destiny Islanders are possessive about this place. We figure we're the only ones who truly understand and appreciate it. Besides, we think of the stores, marinas, parks, and so on as ours. In tourist season, day-trippers flood in on each day's ferry, families come to camp, visitors fill the B and Bs and resorts, and boaters clog the marinas and harbors. In off-season, you walk down the street and recognize ninety percent of the people you see. In tourist season, it's the opposite."

"But," Aaron said, "the island's economy is based in large part on tourism. Hence the love part of the equation."

"I've only been here a couple of days, but I can see the island's appeal."

Lionel gave her that assessing gaze again. "The superficial appeal. There's a whole different appeal when you live here and a winter storm takes out your power lines."

"Or when you break your ankle and a neighbor you've been squabbling with shows up with casseroles and beer," Marlise said. "For us longtimers, our relationship with Destiny is like a marriage that's stood the test of time. Or"—she winked at Lionel—"a non-marriage that's stood the test of time. There's frustration and crankiness sometimes, but there's a bond, soul deep, connecting you." Cocking her head, she asked Eden, "Do you understand what I mean?"

"It sounds like me and my little sister," she said wryly.

Aaron gave a snort and Marlise laughed and said, "I think you've got it. Of course, not all islanders feel that way. Some hate being cut off from the world or have itchy feet or are drawn to cities or job opportunities. A number of our young people leave." She glanced at Aaron. "But a lot return. And some visitors do fall for the island's quirky lifestyle and decide to build their lives here. The population's always a bit in flux."

Eden nodded, and Marlise said briskly, "Why are we all standing here in the middle of the room? Eden, you go sit at the kitchen table and enjoy the view. Aaron, if you'd be so kind as to open that lovely wine and pour for us? Lionel and I will finish the dinner preparations."

After offering to help and being waved aside, Eden obeyed instructions. The others got to work with amiable teasing but a fair degree of efficiency. The kitchen was hardly modern, but it had the basics, along with a few relatively gourmet touches like an espresso machine.

It turned out Aaron's cooler held crabs bought fresh that afternoon at the dock, which he nonchalantly tossed in a huge pot of boiling water. Eden had a horrible feeling those crabs had been alive, but she didn't look too closely nor ask.

Lionel took place mats, napkins, and cutlery out to a table and chairs on the deck. Marlise, standing at the counter, assembled a giant salad. A delicious yeasty smell came from the oven, and when a timer went off, Marlise took out two loaves of Italian bread. In an amazingly short time they were sitting down outside to eat. It wasn't chilly yet, but the approach of evening lent a crispness to the air that had Eden and Marlise donning cardigans.

After Eden inquired about the beautiful orange-barked tree and was told it was an arbutus, they all began dismembering their crabs and dunking pieces of meat in melted butter. "This is the east side of the island, isn't it?" she asked. "So we won't see the sunset?"

"Right," Lionel said. "Except we often get a kind of echo of it. A pink glow in the sky, a reflection in the ocean."

"The sunrises are incredible, though," Aaron said. "Moonrises too."

Eden realized he'd never said where he lived. Lionel had been his mentor, so was it possible Aaron roomed with the older man? The deck was large, running past the kitchen and outside what was obviously another room. The house was big enough, just barely, to hold two people. "Do you live here, too?" she asked.

"Close enough." He pointed past one end of the deck to a trail that ran off into the trees. "That's the path that leads down to the beach, and another branch of it goes to my place."

Lionel must have had another cottage on his land or perhaps let Aaron build one. What a generous guy. The two men might call themselves loners, but in the half hour she'd been with them she'd seen the clear affection between them.

Talk over dinner was relaxed: the food, the island, places Eden should see, the climate here and in Ottawa. Eden got Lionel to tell her about teaching Aaron to fly, which he did with enthusiasm, saying Aaron was a natural. She heard about Marlise's experiences as a social worker, and how she played the cello in a chamber quintet. By the time the four crabs had been reduced to a pile of shells and both bottles of wine had been consumed, the air had cooled off enough that Eden suppressed a shiver.

Marlise rose. "We'll have dessert in the front room." She began to clear the table.

The others followed her example and then she took their requests for coffee or tea and shooed them all out of the kitchen. Eden discovered that the other room on the ocean side was a living room. It, too, had large windows, and a big fireplace made of unevenly shaped rocks, along with an overstuffed couch and a couple of chairs. Chester lay curled up in a dog bed by the fireplace.

Lionel opened a window a couple of inches. "Get a fire going, Aaron. If there's any problem with the wood, you know who to blame." As he gestured Eden to the couch and seated himself in one of the chairs, Lionel told her, "The boy cuts down the trees and chops up the wood." He held up a gnarled hand. "Damned arthritis. I can do most things, but chopping's a hard one."

Marlise entered the room holding a tray. She put it on a coffee table made from a wooden burl and handed out their drinks. "Back in a minute."

Aaron's fire had caught, and he pulled the screen across the fireplace and came to sit beside Eden, his thigh brushing hers and sending sexual awareness rippling through her.

Marlise returned, this time with bowls full of something pink and smelling of fruit, with vanilla ice cream on top. "Strawberry-rhubarb crumble, made with fruit from my garden."

Eden took a bite and sighed with pleasure. Because she so rarely ate dessert, this was a special treat. "What a wonderful meal." Glancing at her host, she asked, "Lionel, how long have you been on Destiny Island?"

"Since the end of '69." He put down his coffee, spooned up some dessert, and chewed and swallowed. "You're too young to know what it was like back then. I was an American, my country involved in that crazy war in Vietnam, boys going off and getting killed. And for what?"

"You've probably heard of the draft," Marlise said. "It was a lottery. Who'd be sent off next to be killed? Only the boys, of course. And all because of a war that many, many people considered to be immoral. There were a lot of protests. Pacifists sticking flowers in rifle barrels. Maybe you've seen some pictures."

"I learned a bit about it in school," Eden said.

"What she's leading up to," Lionel said, "is that a lot of the boys who were drafted, or might've been, didn't stick around. They left the country, and most came to Canada. Draft dodgers, they called us."

Us. So that's what had brought him here.

"Some folks called us cowards and worse," Lionel

said. "Looking back, I can't say I'm sure why I did it. I could tell myself it was the moral thing. I could espouse pacifism, which I do mostly believe in. But at that moment in time, maybe I was just scared of getting my ass blown off in some foreign country."

Marlise leaned forward to touch his hand. "If it had been a different kind of war, you would have gone. I know that, Lionel Williams, even if you don't."

"I know it, too," Aaron put in.

"Well," Lionel said, "it's the past. I came north from California, across the border, heard about the Gulf Islands, and found myself on Destiny. Stayed. Found work doing this and that, learned how to fly the same way Aaron did, from an old geezer with time on his hands. Bought myself a little Cessna, built this place. Settled in." He shot Eden a level gaze through his horn-rims. "I was never a hippie. Never set foot on that commune."

He could have said that right at the beginning, but instead he'd chosen to tell her his story. She appreciated his trust and knew it was due to Aaron's befriending her.

"But I did," Marlise said. She put down her bowl, the dessert only half-finished. "Aaron told us about Lucy. I've searched my memory, but I honestly can't remember anyone at the commune by that name."

Discouraged, Eden sighed. Had her aunt vanished into thin air?

Chapter Seven

Seeing the disappointment on Eden's face, Aaron set down his empty dessert bowl and put his arm around her slumped shoulders. "Marlise," he said, "what about Lucy's boyfriend, a guy named Barry, last name unknown?"

Eden's shoulders straightened and she shot him a grateful look. "Yes, Barry. They'd have arrived in the spring or summer of 1969. Lucy was from Ottawa, and probably Barry was, too, though I'm not positive."

"I didn't join the commune until a bit later." Marlise pressed her lips together. "Eden, you need to understand what it was like. I was a Destiny Islander, but other members of the commune came from all over the place. Many were escaping things, like war or dysfunctional families or societal mores that didn't make sense to them. Some were really just into the drugs, the free love, the seductive music. But most of us were actually seeking something better, a new, free, more natural, less judgmental way of life."

"That fits with what I know about Lucy."

"We lived in the moment," Marlise said. "We rarely

talked about the past, about homes, families, schools, old friends. Lucy and Barry might never have mentioned that they came from Ottawa. We didn't use surnames. Some of the kids didn't even use their real names. They rechristened themselves."

"Like Azalea," she said.

"Yes. And when they had babies, they gave them hippie names." Her lips curved. "I always wondered how the little boy named Blueberry Rainbow made out, and whether he changed his name when he got older."

Aaron snorted with laughter at the name, but Eden had that scrunchy frown again. "So you're saying that Lucy . . ." Her voice trailed off.

"She could've been there but called herself Sunrise or Willow."

"Show her the photos, Eden," Aaron prompted.

She rose, and his arm felt cold without her inside its curve. She went out to the kitchen, where she'd left her bag. Returning, she pulled out her phone. "My grandparents tried to destroy all trace of Lucy, but Mom managed to hang on to a few things. This is a school picture, but Lucy was three years younger than when she left."

"Ah," Marlise said, "the old Patty Duke hairstyle. She wouldn't have been wearing her hair that way at the commune. Hmm. I'm trying to imagine her older, likely with long, straight hair parted in the middle. Either that or supershort like Twiggy, the model."

Aaron didn't know the women she was talking about but did know that hairstyles could dramatically change a woman's appearance.

"And this is a picture of the two of them together,"

Eden told Marlise, "but the girl facing the camera is Mom, not Lucy. You can only see Lucy's profile."

Marlise looked at the second photo, then at Eden. "You favor your mother."

"I know. My sister looked a bit like Lucy when she was that age. Hmm . . ." She scrolled back on her phone to find another photo. "That's Kelsey now, at twenty-one."

Aaron rose so he could take a look. Eden's sister had a slim, smiling face and big blue eyes. Her hair, worn in a spiky style not unlike Bernie's, at the B and B, was light brown with exaggerated blond streaks. She was pretty enough to make a guy look twice, but he preferred Eden's looks: an intelligent, serene kind of beauty that grew the more you looked at her.

"There's something . . ." Marlise started, and then she said, "An actress, maybe, that she reminds me of. But no, I'm sorry. Do you have a picture of Barry?"

"No, I don't." She went over to Lionel and showed him the three images.

He studied them, then shook his head. "Sorry, Eden."

"It was so long ago," Marlise said, "and we were all so young."

"I know." Eden's voice was subdued as she put her phone away. "You don't happen to have any pictures from those days, do you?"

"Cameras weren't allowed in the commune."

Eden hung her head for a moment, then said, "Could you tell me a bit about the commune?"

"At the time," Marlise said, "we thought it was the ultimate in free expression. No structure, no rules. No jobs or school. But it wasn't all sex, drugs, and rock and roll. We did grow vegetables and raise animals, trying to live off the land, though we weren't very efficient."

"How did you all survive?" Aaron asked. "I mean, was there a source of money?"

"Good question," Marlise said. "Some of us arrived with money in our pockets or bank accounts we could access or relatives who were willing to wire us money. Cash went into the communal pot, which was in the custody of the leader, Merlin. Two or three of the boys went out with a local fisherman, trading labor for seafood." She frowned slightly. "Looking back, I suspect someone must have been fairly wealthy. One or more of the members, or perhaps Merlin. You had to stay on his good side because he controlled the money and most of the drugs. And oh my, were there drugs. Mary jane, hashish, acid, speed, peyote buttons, magic mushrooms. It was a psychedelic cornucopia."

"Controlled by Merlin, the leader of the Enchantery," Eden said quietly.

Marlise shot her a surprised glance. "The Enchantery. I haven't heard that in a long time. It was the name we used inside. How did you hear it?"

"Azalea let it slip but made like she hadn't and said it was a big secret. Though I don't understand why it would be such a big deal."

"Because Merlin had his own rules, and a lot of them were about building his power." Marlise gave a wry laugh. "We kids ran from one kind of structure and external control and ended up with a different one. Neither one was good."

"Tell us about Merlin," Eden said gently.

"Why do you want to know?" Marlise asked. "He left long, long ago."

"I'm just curious. It's where my aunt lived for some

period of time." Eden pressed her lips together. "Was the commune a cult?"

"A cult," the other woman said quietly. "I suppose it was. A cult with a charismatic leader who really did enchant us. Tall, dark, very attractive, with long hair and a beard. He had that *thing*, that alpha, charismatic thing that made people crave his approval. He also gave out a very sexual vibe. I swear, almost every girl got swept up under his spell."

Lionel, coffee cup in hand, snorted.

Marlise ignored him and went on. "The boys as well, but differently. Merlin made them feel as if they could become like him. Be powerful, have any woman they wanted." She swallowed. "In retrospect, there was something seriously wrong with Merlin. He may have been a sociopath or had some kind of personality disorder."

"I don't mean to get too personal," Eden said, "but did those girls go with him—I mean have sex with him—willingly, or did he force them?"

"Some were happy to have his attention. Others he manipulated, maybe drugged. Some, I'm pretty sure he forced."

This time, Lionel made a noise that sounded like a growl.

Marlise reached over and he met her hand with his. "I never got hurt," she said. "I was on the fringes of the commune, and not for very long. I realized I didn't belong there. Though I wasn't a conventional girl, I didn't like all the drugs, or the casual sex with anyone and everyone. Although Merlin fascinated me, I didn't like him. To me, he felt dangerous. Like if I stayed, I might, despite knowing better, find myself falling under his enchantment. So I left."

"Merlin didn't try to keep people from going?" Aaron asked.

"By persuasion, not by force. And then—this was after I'd left—one day, he was simply gone himself." Dryly, she added, "He did like drama. His believers said he'd turned himself into a hawk and flown away, deserting them because they didn't live up to his standards."

"No one heard from him again?" Aaron asked.

"Not that I ever heard about."

"What happened to the commune then?" Eden asked.

"They tried to keep it going. But it had gone from a dictatorship to having no leadership at all, and it disintegrated. A few of the nonislanders stayed on Destiny, building lives for themselves: Azalea, Maury, Di, and Seal. Gwendy at Severn's Reach. Forbes left the island for a number of years but came back. Then there are those of us who were islanders to start with: me, Tamsyn, Cynnie, and Darnell."

"Those names are already on my list," Eden said. "Can you think of any islanders who weren't commune members but came in contact with the Enchantery or its members?"

Marlise and Lionel brainstormed, giving her another couple of possibilities to check out. After that, the conversation turned general again. Aaron liked how well Eden got along with Lionel and Marlise. It was past nine by the time he and Eden rose to go.

Outside, the air felt cool after the warmth of Lionel's fireplace. Aaron wrapped his arm around her shoulders, glad to finally be alone with her. "Come see my place."

She glanced around. "Now? In the dark? How do you even find it at night?"

"Motion sensor lights. Powered by solar, like most things at Lionel's and my houses."

"I didn't see the panels."

"They're on the ocean side, in a clearing that gets sun most of the day. Come on." He steered her toward the path that led from the shared parking area.

Lionel had inherited some money and used it to buy a chunk of waterfront back when prices were cheap. Several years ago, he'd told Aaron he had no need for so much property, so he'd subdivided it into two lots. He'd sold the smaller one to Aaron for a very reasonable price, making for affordable mortgage payments. Aaron had paid peanuts for a beat-up little trailer, which he'd lived in on the property. With occasional help from other islanders as part of the barter network, he built a log cabin using trees from his own land. Though his home was small, it met his needs just fine. It even had a bedroom set aside for his sister and niece, in case Miranda ever accepted his invitation. The best part, though, was that he had the same view as Lionel, the sounds of the ocean and nature, and a neighbor who was his closest friend.

Lights hooked in tall trees came on, dim but sufficient to show the way. As his feet, confident with familiarity, started out on the path, the footing was soft from years of fallen leaves and pine needles, and the scent of pine and ocean filled his nostrils. A piping chorus of the ribbit variety serenaded them. The path was narrow, and Aaron hugged Eden close to his side.

"What's that strange sound?" she asked, sounding a little nervous.

"Tree frogs singing to you."

"I feel like I'm Little Red Riding Hood on the path to Grandmother's house."

"All you'll find at my cabin is me, and I'm exactly what meets the eye. No more, no less."

Her *hmm* made him wonder what she was thinking. The kind of man she'd be looking for long-term would be a city guy with an important job and a serious outlook on life. Right now, though, this wasn't about long-term, so Aaron figured that emphasizing all the opposites was a good thing. So he said, "Yup. A guy with a cabin in the woods who's lucky enough to make a living flying planes in the most beautiful place in the world. No commitments, no strings, just living day by day here in paradise." There was no need to mention the more serious aspects of his life, like his mortgage or the struggle to keep Blue Moon Air in the black during the off season, much less his always worrisome sister and her little girl.

"It smells good out here," Eden said. "There's a salty tang from the ocean and something green and earthy."

"The scent of the woods. Pine needles, arbutus bark, fallen leaves." He was glad the city girl appreciated it.

They came out in a clearing by the woodshed. Aaron had installed a switch that activated the porch light on his house, across the clearing. As he reached for that switch, he felt a moment's anxiety. He was proud of the cabin he'd built, learning as he went, gratefully accepting help from other islanders. The women he'd brought here had called it cute and cozy. But it was small, simple, rustic. What would Eden think of his home?

* * *

When Aaron said, "Okay, here it is. Home sweet home," a light came on some distance away, and it took Eden's eyes a moment to adjust.

She saw a log cottage with a porch running the width of the front and large windows on either side of the door. The logs were nowhere near as weathered as the outside of Lionel's house and there wasn't a yard. A chimney confirmed that the woodshed served a useful purpose.

"It's charming." In a rugged, outdoorsy way that was foreign to her. "I can't wait to see inside." How Aaron had furnished and decorated would tell her a lot about him. He might only be a potential holiday fling, but the man intrigued her and she wanted to know him better.

They took the steps to the porch and he opened the door and ushered her inside. "I'll give you the tour, which'll take all of a minute. It's only about fifteen hundred square feet."

The living area had an open-plan design with a big stone fireplace in the middle rather than on an outside wall. The fireplace opened on one side to a sitting area with a couch and chairs and on the other side to a dining area. The dining area was separated from the kitchen by an island. The bedroom was spacious, with a desk as well as a queen-size bed. Across the hall was a nicely designed bathroom. And down the hall was a guest room, as large as the master bedroom but sparsely furnished with a single bed and a dresser.

The walls were finished logs and the floors were hardwood. All that wood could have been overwhelming

but for the large windows and the open design. The
furniture was simple: cinnamon leather for the couch
and chairs and light oak for most of the wood furniture; beds that were basic box spring and mattress
combinations; in Aaron's bedroom, a duvet striped
in shades of blue including a navy that matched the
curtains. The guest room was done in shades of green.
There were no paintings, just a few framed photos of
ocean scenes, but then, the windows didn't leave
much wall space to hang art.

The TV wasn't very large, suggesting he didn't spend
hours watching sports or anything else. A collection
of DVDs in a basket gave her the urge to root through
them to discover his taste in movies, but she resisted.
Plain wooden shelves held a lovely pottery vase and a
bowl, some shells, rocks, and pieces of driftwood. "I
like it," she said after they returned to the living room.
"I don't know you well, but it seems to suit you."

"How so?"

"Masculine, simple rather than fussy, interesting,
comfortable. Outdoorsy." It struck her as a more airy,
modern version of Lionel's house—which suggested
to her that as a teen and younger man Aaron had felt
at home at Lionel's. She walked to a window on the
ocean side and glanced out. He, too, had a deck, and
past it she saw the gleam of moonlight reflecting on
the dark ocean. It was beautiful, mysterious, and she
shivered. "Isn't it scary, living all alone in the middle
of, well, nothing?"

"The middle of nature." He stepped up beside her
and put his arm around her shoulders.

She was getting used to that, and to how good it felt
to snuggle up against him. He managed to be warm,

solid, and reassuring at the same time as raising a sexy awareness in her.

"Seems to me," Aaron said, his voice a soft rumble above her head, "that it's safer to be surrounded by nature than by people."

That sounded pretty cynical. She wondered if he was a loner by nature or if something had happened to disillusion him about humankind. It was on the tip of her tongue to ask, but he was using those strong arms to turn her until she faced him. Without another word or any warning, he dipped his head and kissed her. His confident lips captured her surprise. "Oh!"

Last night when he'd kissed her, she'd expected the usual rather tentative first kiss, the guy checking to see if it was okay to do this, both of them finding out how mouths matched up, him not wanting to push too far. Not so with Aaron Gabriel. His sensual, knowing kiss had swept her up, banishing any possibility of awkwardness or uncertainty.

Tonight it was even better. Her lips had been created to shape and reshape themselves against his, to part for him. The moist, secret corners of her mouth had craved the intimate touch of his tongue. And her own tongue had been designed expressly to follow his lead in a dance of passion.

Aaron's arms were around her, one high on her back, the other lower, with his hand gripping her butt. Her arms rose to lock around him and her hips thrust forward to press against the hard column of his erection behind the fly of his jeans.

There might have been words to express what she felt, the surge of heat in her blood, the insistent throbbing of arousal as it pulsed through her, but the only sounds she could make were primitive ones: moans and whimpers that arose from deep within her as the kiss, the embrace, went on endlessly.

In those endless moments, she became a woman she didn't recognize—a physical, passionate, needy one who wanted nothing more than sexual gratification in this man's arms.

The intensity of her need, of her feelings, suddenly penetrated her brain and she gasped and stepped back, pulling out of his arms. She raised trembling hands to her cheeks, feeling their heat, and then touched her lips, which felt swollen and tender. Vulnerable.

She felt vulnerable, and it was never a feeling she enjoyed. "Aaron, I . . . I can't. Not now. It's too much, too soon. I have to . . ."

"Have to what?" He sounded a little frustrated but not angry. "Analyze it to death? I thought you already did that and opted in."

She was gaining control of her breathing and her thoughts. "I opted in to seeing where this goes. That kiss was . . . well, amazing. But that's as far as I'm comfortable with tonight. Tomorrow or the next day . . . maybe." She swallowed. "I don't mean to be a tease. I just need to go more slowly."

He sighed, a sound with a harsh edge. "I get it. Sorry, Eden, I didn't mean to push. That's a crappy thing to do."

"No." She shook her head. "You weren't pushing. I was totally into it until I—" *What? Came to my senses? Got scared by an intensity I'd never experienced before?* "Anyhow, when I called a stop, you stopped."

"Okay." His lips curved tentatively. "So we're good?"

"If you'll drive me back to the B and B and give me

a good-night kiss with, oh, let's say half the, um, vigor of that one, we'll be good."

"Vigor?" He chuckled. "That's a new one. But okay, let's get you back." He looped that big arm around her again and guided her to the front door. "Besides, you need a good night's sleep. I have plans for you tomorrow."

As they went out into the fresh, slightly chilly evening, she said, "Tomorrow? You mean after you finish your flights for the day?"

"Didn't you notice me having a second glass of wine? I'm taking the day off. Mondays tend to be slow after the early flight that drops weekenders back in Victoria and Vancouver. Jillian will take that one, and the couple others during the day."

They'd reached the woodshed, and the motion sensor lights along the trail came on as they walked. "I don't want you changing your schedule because of me. There are still three names on the list I can contact myself." After meeting Azalea and talking to Marlise and Lionel, Eden was understanding the value of having an islander introduce and vouch for her.

"My schedule's flexible. Jillian's happy to pick up as many flights as she can handle."

No doubt the other pilot appreciated the income—which didn't seem to be something that worried Aaron. Eden only hoped the owner of Blue Moon Air was okay with Aaron's happy-go-lucky approach to his work schedule. A thought struck her. Back in her aunt's day, would he have been a hippie? He sure seemed to enjoy a carefree, flexible lifestyle. She couldn't imagine him getting into drugs, though. He struck her as more like Marlise, in being a person who wanted to control his own life, not surrender control to drugs or to another person.

"No arguing," he said amiably.

Oh yeah, he could be amiable and laid-back when things went his way. "All right. Who do you suggest we see tomorrow?"

"I'm thinking Maury, the Hunts, maybe Sven Svenson."

She nodded. Maury'd been at the commune, the reputably reclusive Hunts had lived near it, and Svenson had been a reporter for the *Gazette*.

When they reached the Jeep, Aaron took a couple of minutes to raise the soft top and fasten it in place. "I'm not going to put the back windows in. The heater works, if you're cold."

If she got cold, remembering that kiss would heat her up.

They drove back the way they'd come in, the headlights picking out the road from the surrounding darkness. It was spooky and she was glad not to be doing this alone.

"I'll pick you up at nine," he said. "Figure on being out all day. Bring clothes like you're wearing now, but wear shorts and a tee and—"

"What? I know you don't want me to be all Ottawa formal for these interviews, but that sounds awfully casual."

"That's not for the interviews. We'll start with some play time."

"Aaron, I—"

"No arguing," he repeated. "Shorts and a tee, with a bathing suit underneath."

"A bathing suit?" She hadn't brought one with her. "I am *not* going swimming. That's the ocean out there.

It's freezing cold." Although she didn't actually know that. "Isn't it?"

"Says she who lives in the city, where the snow's piled deep all winter. But yeah, it's chilly if you're not used to it. We'll see how you feel about that after we go kayaking."

"Kayaking? Aaron, I'm no athlete. Besides, you know my priority is finding my aunt. Kayaking isn't going to help in the least."

He heaved an exaggerated sigh. "Eden, I respect that priority. I get how important it is to you to do this for your mom. But I have to wonder, does your conscience whack you upside the head every time you contemplate taking a little time to just enjoy life?"

Her mouth opened in a silent *oh*. Now that she thought about it . . . "I guess it kind of does," she admitted.

"A balanced life is a healthier one."

Her lips quirked. "That's your fancy way of saying 'all work and no play makes Eden a dull girl'?"

"I didn't say dull."

Not in actual words, no. And he did have a point about balance. "Okay, I'll try to relax a bit more. As long as I get to interview every single person on that list and any other relevant names that come up."

"I wouldn't have it any other way."

She rolled her eyes.

"As for not being an athlete," he said, "kayaking's a snap. You'll love it."

Had there ever been a physical activity she'd loved or been any good at? She'd always been the scholarly type. Neither of her parents were in to sports or the outdoorsy type, unless you counted her mom's garden.

But maybe it was time to stick a toe out of her rut and try something different.

Kissing Aaron had certainly been different. The strength of her passion had caught her off guard and scared her. But tomorrow was a new day. An entire day she'd spend with him. A day to get to know him, a day to come to terms with the attraction she felt. A day to decide exactly how far she wanted to go with him.

Even though Jillian was piloting the early morning flight on Monday, it was habit for Aaron to rise when the birds began to chatter and sing. He was enjoying a mug of steaming coffee out on the deck, his bare feet up on the railing, letting the rising sun dazzle him with all its shades of yellow and gold, when his cell phone rang.

He went inside to scoop it out of the battery charger in the kitchen, hoping Jillian wasn't calling in sick. Instead, it was his sister.

As usual, that simple, "Hey, Aaron," tied a knot in his gut. Much as he loved Miranda and was always glad to hear from her, they so often butted heads.

"Hey, Sis," he said.

"Is it okay I called now? You're not leaving on a flight right away?"

"No, it's fine. How are you? How's Ariana?"

"We're good. She's sleeping. I'm in the bathroom so I won't wake her." Miranda had a studio apartment with a pullout couch that made up into a bed and a crib he'd bought for Ariana. "When she's awake, she babbles away like she thinks she's making real sentences." He heard the smile, the love in his sister's voice, and it made him smile, too. "Except some of the words aren't real ones."

His niece was almost two. "You did that, too, when you were her age. Couldn't shut you up." He'd been four and had already realized he needed to look after his sister. Much of the time their mom wasn't around or capable of looking after anyone.

He took the phone back out to the deck and resumed his seat. "I haven't seen you guys for over a month. Let's find a time next week when I'm in Vancouver and you're not working."

"Well . . ." Now her voice was strained. "Uh, here's the thing, Aaron."

Warily, he asked, "What is it?"

"You know I've had two waitressing jobs, right? And Mrs. Sharma down the hall has looked after Ariana when I'm working nights?"

"Yeah."

"Well, poor old Mrs. Sharma broke her hip, and she's staying with her daughter's family until she gets better. Or forever, if her daughter has her way. So I had to give up my night job and it earned the best tips and so, well . . ."

He swallowed a mouthful of coffee. "You need money."

"I'm overdue on the June rent."

"Jesus, Miranda. You should've called me earlier. The landlord could evict you."

"I thought I could work it out. You know I hate asking. You shouldn't have to support me." She sounded exhausted, and he guessed she'd been up most of the night trying to come up with an alternative. He pictured her now, sitting slump-shouldered on the closed toilet seat, wearing her old purple bathrobe, her honey-blond hair pulled up into a messy knot, shadows tinting the pale skin under her bluish-gray eyes. Those eyes were the only thing they had in common, the one physical attribute inherited from their mom. Miranda's dad had clearly been a white guy. Ariana's, on the other hand, was black. Aaron's niece, with her dark hair and mocha skin, looked more like Aaron, with his First Nations blood, than like her mother.

"Ariana's father should be paying child support." How many times had he said that?

"I loved him, but he made it clear he didn't want me or our child."

"I know." Why couldn't Miranda be sensible about relationships? Instead, she took after their mom, searching constantly for that one true love—and searching in all the wrong places. At least his sister had the sense not to use drugs—and, he really hoped, never to sell her body.

"Even if he offered, I wouldn't take money from him. I don't want anything to do with him."

She had pride. Not much in the way of education or common sense, but she did have pride. "It's the law, Sis. A father is supposed to provide financial support for his child." If his own father'd done that, maybe his mom could have made a better life for her and her kids.

"And you and I've always had so much respect for the law."

Her retort gave him his second smile, though it was a wry one. When your parent didn't put food in the cupboards or buy school supplies, much less candy, you figured out how to survive. He and Miranda had been damned good shoplifters, pickpockets, and experts at finding unlocked windows. Those habits were ingrained, so that even when they moved to Destiny Island they'd continued to steal. In Aaron's case, until Lionel took him under his wing.

Aaron watched two hummingbirds yammer and posture at each other, squabbling over the favored perch on the feeder that hung from the eave. Cautiously, he asked, "You're not still shoplifting, are you?"

There was a long pause and then she said defensively, "I can't let Ariana go hungry."

Of course she couldn't. Whatever his sister's flaws, she loved her daughter deeply and tried to be a good mom. He just wished she wouldn't let pride get in her way. "Jesus. What if you got caught? If you go to jail . . ."

That had happened to their drug addict mother more than once. Then social services would come around, the same as when a neighbor reported that their mom had abandoned her kids for days on end or when the family was homeless. Because their mother's parents had washed their hands of her and her kids—at least until the day she finally OD'ed on cocaine in an alley in the Downtown Eastside—Aaron and Miranda had been sent to foster homes. Occasionally those homes were nice; more often the foster parents were callous and sometimes they were abusive. Even worse, the siblings sometimes got sent to different homes, which drove him crazy. Who was going to look after his kid sister if he wasn't there?

"I won't get caught," she asserted.

Knowing he was wasting his breath, he still had to say it. "Come back to Destiny. Live with me. You know I built the spare room with you and Ariana in mind. I'll look after the two of you while you take some courses online. You can get your GED and some training so you can find a real job." She'd dropped out of high school in eleventh grade, and Aaron blamed himself. After he graduated, his passion for flying took him to Victoria for training, leaving Miranda alone with their grandparents. She'd soon followed her own passion: chasing love in the arms of bad boys. On a visit to Vancouver, she'd fallen for a musician in a small-time band and a few weeks later she'd left Destiny to be with him. Their grandparents hadn't even tried to get her to return. They'd jumped at the opportunity to be free of both their unwanted grandchildren and move to Florida.

"You're sweet, but I can't impose. Besides, you know I hated that island from day one."

"Like the Downtown Eastside was better?"

"It was because it's part of Vancouver, and Vancouver's interesting, exciting. Destiny's the boonies, the sticks, the people are hicks—hey, that rhymes—and I wouldn't fit in any better there now than I did then. I still don't get why you like it so much."

The sunrise over the ocean, unique every morning. The whir of hummingbird wings, the flash of their emerald backs and ruby throats in the sun. The scent of pine, arbutus, and ocean. The endless fascination of the ocean. How could she hate it here? He suspected it wasn't so much about the island itself as the circumstances of their arrival as teens. When their grandparents cold-shouldered them, they broke Miranda's too-soft heart. She went all tough girl and never gave the place, or the kids at school, a chance. She seemed determined to hate everything about Destiny and had never changed her mind. Unlike him, who had, despite their grandparents, found peace and acceptance here.

"I like the outdoors," he said, "and I like that people here have that whole live-and-let-live philosophy."

"Oh yeah, our grandparents were so live and let live," she said mockingly.

"Okay, aside from them. And they're out of our lives. It's nice here, Miranda. Honestly."

"Look," his sister said huffily, "if you won't loan me the money, just say so. I'll figure out some other way."

He sighed. If only Miranda'd had a Lionel in her life at a critical time to talk some sense into her. Sadly, her big brother's advice seemed to count for less than nothing with her.

"Yes, I'll send you the money." He refused to say *loan* because there was no way she'd be able to pay him back. "I'll transfer it right now. How much do you need? And make sure you include enough to feed you and Ariana without having to resort to petty crime."

"Five hundred will get us through. I hate this. You know I do."

He did, too. He hated everything about it except for one thing. At least Miranda still loved and trusted him enough to come to him when she was in trouble. If they ever lost that closeness—or if anything ever happened to her or Ariana—it would kill him. If he could have one wish in the world, it would be for his niece to have the happy, secure, loving childhood that was denied to him and his sister. But Miranda was Ariana's mom and she got the final say. All he could do was help in whatever ways she allowed. "Any chance my niece is awake now?"

"No. Want me to wake her?"

He'd love to hear that innocent childish babble but wouldn't be so selfish. "No, but call me sometime when she's awake, okay? And I mean it about getting together next week."

"I'd like that. Now that I've come clean and told you the truth."

After they hung up, he went online and sent an e-Transfer of funds, including a couple hundred dollars more than she'd requested.

And then he shoved aside his concern and looked forward to the day with Eden.

Chapter Eight

Eden felt the gentle pull and slide of the blade through the water as she paddled more or less rhythmically, alternating right and left sides. "My family and friends won't believe me when I tell them about this."

They had climbed into the two kayaks from a big rock near shore, with Aaron holding hers steady until she was settled. He'd slipped easily into his and demonstrated the simple motion of the paddle strokes. Telling her not to work too hard at it, he'd had her paddle around, getting a feel for it. Now they cruised parallel to the rocky shore, about ten feet out, her on the shore side and Aaron on the ocean side. He'd joked that he would protect her from rogue waves—which, of course, had her imagining what on earth a rogue wave might be.

"Will you take a picture of me?" she asked.

"Sure. Stop a minute." He took her phone from the bright orange waterproof bag where he'd stowed their belongings.

She rested the paddle on the kayak while she tidied

her ponytail and shifted her sunglasses to the top of her head. Then she lifted the paddle again, smiling for the camera. She hoped she didn't look too silly in the orange life vest she wore over a long T-shirt and the blue bikini she'd bought that morning. Aaron had made her put her shorts in the bag, warning her she'd get wet. Sure enough, she'd splashed a fair bit of water on herself.

He wasn't wearing a vest, and she believed him when he said he had no need of one. He'd told her that her likelihood of tipping was minuscule, and that even if she did, they'd be close to shore and he'd rescue her well before she got hypothermia. Mere mention of the word *hypothermia* had made her insist on wearing the vest. It felt awkward and she was sure it looked worse, but she wasn't going to worry about either thing when there was so much to relish about this experience.

First, there was the sight of Aaron, tanned and fit in board shorts—still dry, of course—and a navy tee with the sleeves ripped out. He was the kind of man who'd look good in anything, from a tux to overalls, and probably best in nothing at all—a thought that had persisted in springing to mind since she'd first viewed his tanned, muscled limbs. He seemed as at home on the ocean as in the sky, gracefully maneuvering his yellow kayak as they got underway again.

Her red kayak looked like his but was nowhere near as obedient to her attempts to command it. Still, it pleased her a great deal when she did make forward progress, the slim-lined craft gliding through the calm ocean. She was so close to the water, almost as if she were a sea creature swimming along. Her paddle misfired again, splashing icy water onto her sunscreened thigh. Fortunately, the air was warm enough to counteract the occasional minidrenching.

"What's this greenish-brown stuff with the tendrils and bulbs?" she asked, nodding toward the tangled mess he was paddling around.

"Bull kelp. It's a kind of seaweed. And see that?" He pointed to an orangey-red blob with dozens of hanging tentacles moving lazily through the water between them. "That's a jellyfish. A lion's mane. If you're swimming and see a jellyfish, avoid it. They sting."

She imagined entering the icy water and having kelp twine around her legs, trapping her as a horde of jellyfish stung her to death. No way was she leaving the security of the red kayak.

"Stop paddling for a minute," Aaron said.

Gratefully, she obeyed. Her wrists and shoulders were feeling the unaccustomed exercise. "I could use the break."

"Shh," he said quietly. "Look around and wait."

For what? But then a head popped out of the water ahead of them. It was sleek, with soulful brown eyes and white whiskers bristling around a snub nose. The creature looked rather like a wise old man. "Oh," she breathed, gazing back at the eyes that studied her. Another head popped up, and another.

In a hushed voice, Aaron said, "Paddle slowly away from shore."

Glancing away from the creatures, she realized the ocean's gentle swells had carried her close to the rocky shore. She turned the kayak away, trying to paddle so that the blades disturbed the water as little as possible. "Are those seals?"

"Yes, harbor seals. They like kelp forests because they eat the fish that hang out there."

With Aaron in the lead, their kayaks glided slowly through the water, heading toward a rocky point. Heads popped up to chart their progress. Some went down again, and Eden saw a couple of seals swimming underwater in a sinuous motion. Several of the creatures had pulled themselves out of the ocean onto the rocks, sunning themselves. As she and Aaron got closer, a few gave a barking call and most lumbered, using their flippers to drag themselves, back to the water. "They're so graceful when they swim," she whispered, "and so awkward on land."

She and Aaron paddled around the point, close enough to the rocks that she saw strange purple creatures clustered in crevices, some humped up shapelessly and others spread into a star shape. "Are those starfish?"

"They sure are. It's great to see them. A disease has decimated their numbers in the past years."

"That's too bad." The creatures were utterly foreign to her and yet they were so bizarrely beautiful and fit this place so perfectly. "I hope the species survives."

She followed Aaron into a small cove with a sandy beach and a dock with a wooden sailboat tied to it. The land above had been semicleared, the trees thinned but not razed, and flowering bushes and beds of flowers dotted the property. A picturesque two-story wooden building sat in the center, with half a dozen or so cottages scattered among the trees. Behind a high, wire-mesh fence, she saw what looked like a vegetable garden, and noted the now-familiar bank of solar panels.

"This is Kingfisher Cove and that's SkySong," Aaron said.

"SkySong, like the couple on my list?"

"Yes. It's a retreat, kind of like the one those women on your flight were going to. It operates year-round and does quite well, but it's shut down now while they're away. Di and Seal wouldn't mind us using their beach."

Seeing the harbor seals made her speculate. "He gave himself that name, didn't he?"

"Maybe. He's Mi'kmaq from Nova Scotia, so it might be a traditional First Nations name."

Aaron paddled more quickly, heading to shore. She didn't try to match his pace. In the bay, the water was even calmer, the surface like deep, bluish-green glass. She almost hated to disturb it with the dip of her paddle, and after each stroke she paused to watch a crystal cascade of droplets tip off the end of the blade and splash onto the ocean's surface, creating rings of ripples. The sun warmed her back and the top of her head; gulls soared and cried overhead. She stopped paddling, closing her eyes for a moment to simply drift with the tide. Utter serenity. Had she ever experienced anything like this before?

By the time she arrived at the shore, Aaron had pulled his kayak up on the beach and was waiting to guide hers into shore and help her out. She caught his arm for balance, raised herself, and then gingerly stepped out into the water. "Brrr." The soles of her feet met a strange surface, and as she splashed ashore she studied the grayish-white particles that made up the beach. "It's not sand."

"Shells, mostly. Pounded by waves."

The beach felt coarse underfoot but pleasantly so,

like an exfoliating massage, if such a thing existed. She'd never had time to spare for massage or mani-pedis. Nor did she have much occasion to wear a bathing suit, and she felt exposed, even though her tee was long enough to cover her bikini bottom. It would be silly to put on shorts, though, because that bottom was damp.

She freed herself from her life jacket and wandered down the beach, picking up a pebble here, a shell there, a colored bit of weathered glass. If she were back in Ottawa, she'd be busy at her desk, dressed in a suit and low-heeled pumps.

Several battered logs littered the beach, perhaps washed up in a storm. She plunked down on one. "This is a lovely spot. The SkySongs have done well for themselves, for two former hippies."

Aaron walked over, carrying the waterproof bag. "They're good people. Smart. Value-driven, if you know what I mean."

"I think I do. My parents are like that, and I try to be, too."

He pulled out a large towel and spread it on the crushed-shell sand. When he sat down on it, took off his sunglasses, and extended a hand to her, she took his hand and joined him. She tugged the damp hem of her tee down over the tops of her thighs and re-moved her sunglasses because the sun was behind them.

"Tell me about your work," he said, taking two bottles of water from the bag and handing her one. "You said you're with a foundation that funds charities? How did you get into that?"

She had a long, refreshing drink. "I think I told you that Mom's a high school teacher—on sick leave this past year—and she's a great one, really caring about the kids. Dad studied business admin and went to work for a charity that provides assistance to amputees."

She stretched, feeling the pull of well-used arm and shoulder muscles. "His father lost an arm in the Korean War. You should see the photos all over Dad's office walls, of amputees enjoying life thanks to help from his organization. He's the executive director now."

"Sounds like a real good guy."

"The best." And he, like Eden, had had a tough year, trying to give his best to a demanding job while also dealing with Nana's estate and helping his wife with all the cancer-related appointments and care.

She went on. "I learned as I grew up that I, too, wanted to make a difference in the world. Law appealed to me, but I hadn't decided what I'd do with the degree. Then, just before I was admitted to the Bar, I saw a job posting for assistant to the program counsel with the Butterworth Foundation. I researched what the Foundation did and was impressed, and I guess that came through during my interview because I got the job. I learned from the program counsel and then, when she left, I got her job." It didn't pay nearly as much as a law firm would, but she loved it.

"What exactly do you do?"

When he raised his bottle, she was very aware of his bare arm only inches from her own. Though a large part of her would rather touch than talk, he'd chosen a subject dear to her heart and she was pleased by his interest.

"I handle contracts, liaise with the boards and staffs

of funded organizations and applicants, and help with our own grant applications and fund-raising drives. We've funded so many worthwhile groups, Aaron. From programs to keep teens in school to ones that assist seniors in staying physically and mentally healthy and as independent as they possibly can be." She was so excited about the various programs, she wanted to rush on and list all of them, but she didn't want to bore him.

"It must be hard to decide which groups to support."

"Very. My assistant and I work with some of the prospective applicants to help them develop strong proposals, we do in-depth analyses of those proposals, and we present our findings and recommendations to our own board. The board makes the decisions. We get more worthy applications than we can afford to fund. That's why I get so involved in the Foundation's own fund-raising."

She settled more comfortably against the log. "I know you'll think I'm crazy, but I do feel kind of guilty for being here, relaxing and enjoying a beautiful morning."

"You can't save the whole world, Eden. I bet even your parents took some time off to relax." He winked. "You and your sister had to come from somewhere."

She gave a surprised splutter of laughter. "I refuse to think about that." But she couldn't stop herself from noticing how the sunshine had turned Aaron's eyes a deeper blue with glints of light, not unlike the ocean that lapped at the beach.

"I got the deli to pack a picnic lunch," he said.

"Great idea. Thanks."

"But it's not noon yet. We really shouldn't eat until noon."

She raised an eyebrow. "I never took you for the conventional type."

"I know how you like to keep to a schedule," he teased.

She might be slow on the uptake when it came to male-female flirtation, but she was getting a clue where this might be going. "Then how do you suggest we fill the time until noon?"

"We could always go for a swim." Humor glinted in his eyes.

"I felt that water. My feet are still in shock."

"Okay. Rather than cold, we could try a little heat."

When he leaned toward her, intent clear on his face, she didn't point out that the sun was providing more than a little heat already. Instead, she moved forward to meet him. After all, if today she would decide whether to sleep with Aaron, she needed to do her research.

That morning, after she'd had a few posters made at the village pharmacy, Aaron had driven her to We Got It to stick one on the bulletin board. Then he'd taken her for a thorough, if unproductive, interview with an old hippie named Maury, who lived in a decades-old trailer up the side of a mountain and probably hadn't shaved since the day he'd first tried it and discovered he didn't like it. Then Aaron had offered kayaking with seals, to the prettiest beach she'd ever seen. Not only that but he seemed genuinely interested in her work. So far, he'd earned a lot of points in the pro column. Now, if the previous two kisses hadn't been a fluke, fueled by wine and moonlight . . .

They hadn't. Or maybe the combination of ocean, seals, crushed seashells, and sunlight was an even stronger aphrodisiac. Or perhaps she had sunstroke, because as soon as their mouths fused together, her brain turned to mush. All thoughts of pro-con lists disappeared. She closed her eyes and fire burned behind the lids, vibrant shades of red and orange. Heat blazed through her, the blood in her veins molten, her body throbbing with arousal like one huge, beating heart.

Somehow, she and Aaron had moved from sitting against the log to lying on the towel, her on her back, his body half-covering her as they kissed. The hair on his legs tickled her bare skin. Her hands were under his loose tee, caressing the smooth skin that stretched tautly over firm muscles. Through his shorts, his erection pressed insistently against her thigh.

He tugged up her T-shirt and ran his hand over her rib cage to cup her breast through her bikini top. As he brushed his fingers over her nipple, the small bud tightened almost painfully hard against the thin fabric.

"Take off your shirt," he said.

She sat up and freed her hair from its ponytail, then pulled her T-shirt over her head slowly and, she hoped, in a seductively teasing way, revealing her blue bikini. The warm sunshine felt good on her skin, skin that had rarely been exposed before. "I'm going to need sunscreen. Why don't you apply it for me?"

* * *

Aaron gaped at the beautiful, pale-skinned woman who lay back down on the towel. He'd seen bikinis skimpier than her blue one, but she sure did look sexy, and when she'd invited him to apply sunscreen, there'd been distinct flirtation in her tone. Just what did she mean by it?

This was Eden, the city girl who was unsure of herself in his world, yet who was finding her way. The serious woman who kept questioning whether she really wanted to be with him, the one who felt guilty for having a moment's fun.

The one who kissed him as if it was the one thing in the world she most wanted to do—which was exactly how he felt about kissing her.

What was she opting in to? A little harmless sunbathing? More fondling and foreplay? Or maybe, if he was really lucky, sex on the beach with the sound of the ocean for music? Earlier, she'd said she wanted to take things slow, so he would do exactly that. There was nothing wrong with slow, particularly if the journey ended up at the right destination.

He took her sunscreen from the waterproof bag. Before opening the tube, he tugged off his ripped-sleeve tee. He was a hiker, a runner, a kayaker. He had a good body, muscled and dark-skinned, and he was quite willing to use it to his own advantage.

Warm sun on his bare back, the familiar scent of the ocean fresh and clean on the air, the squawk of gulls wheeling high above them. Eden's gaze on his torso, appreciation in her eyes.

He wondered about that ex-boyfriend of hers. Was he a fit guy, a physical one? She'd said they met in law school, so Aaron imagined someone who was more her intellectual match. But maybe not so physical, and right now he wanted Eden to get out of her mind and enjoy that healthy, lovely body of hers. He squirted sunscreen onto his hands. "This stuff doesn't last all that long and you got splashed when we were kayaking. Best to be safe and apply it all over, even the places you sunscreened before."

"That makes sense." Her voice had slid a notch deeper, warm and sultry as the sunshine.

He started with the more neutral areas, applying lotion to her shoulders and arms and then to her legs, working upward to midthigh. Stroking her supple skin was a temptation that made him impatient for more.

Next, he smoothed lotion onto her face with a careful touch. He worked down her neck and then her upper chest, and then he was caressing the top curves of her breasts above the cups of her bathing suit. Her nipples pressed against the fabric, taut and aroused.

His cock was in the same state, hard with need inside his board shorts.

She'd asked for sunscreen and that was exactly what he was giving her. For now, at least. He started again at the bottom band of her bikini top, applying lotion to her rib cage, the dip at her waist, the flare of her hips, and the flat belly above her bikini bottom, making sure not to ignore her cute navel. The woman was flawless—in a city-girl, indoorsy way. He might've preferred a tan and the kind of muscles built by outdoor exercise, but he already knew he and Eden were opposites in many ways. That actually made their short-term encounter even more intriguing. He could introduce her to adventures she'd never experienced before.

Maybe even sexual ones. What had that long-term

boyfriend of hers, and the men who came before, been like in the sack?

As his lotion-slick fingers traced a line along the top band of her bikini bottom, Eden's tummy fluttered with quick, shallow breaths. Her hips twisted a little. Pure physical desire urged him to rip off that flimsy garment, yank off his shorts, and give them both the satisfaction their bodies craved. But he wasn't a lust-crazed kid. He could control his urges.

He returned to her upper legs, where he'd left off around midthigh. He stroked up the outside of her legs, her hips, stopping again when he reached fabric. And then, finally, he tracked the tender skin of her inner thighs, making his touch as sensual as he could.

She parted her legs slightly, giving him better access, and as he leaned closer he smelled something new on the ocean air: a hint of delicate feminine musk, the scent of her arousal.

He caressed the sensitive flesh that bordered the leg band, moving from the outside into the center. She gave a soft moan and her pelvis tightened and lifted, as if she was offering herself to him, begging him for more. That was when he stopped touching her.

Her eyes were closed, cheeks flushed, lips parted. She looked aroused and expectant. He sat down beside her, his back against the log. "Guess you've managed to avoid swimming. You don't want to wash off that lotion now that I've gone to the work of apply-ing it."

Her eyes flared open. "What?" She turned her head to stare up at him in surprise, clearly having antici-pated that he'd continue seducing her. Her gaze moved from his face, down his bare torso, and her eyes widened again when she saw the erection that tented his shorts. A smug smile curved her lips. "Work? So that was work, was it? You're saying you don't enjoy touching me?"

He laughed. "I'd never get away with such a bald-faced lie. I just wanted to check whether you were paying attention or if you'd fallen asleep."

She raised her arms and stretched, slowly and sensually, her hips shifting, her back arching, her breasts thrusting upward. She stacked her hands behind her head. "I'm not actually feeling sleepy." She stretched again, a shimmy that rippled down through her body.

A word popped into his head, an old-fashioned one he'd heard Marlise use: *fetching*. Eden looked fetching. The way he understood it, the word meant pretty and tempting. Something that made you want to go after it, the way a thrown ball compelled a dog to run and fetch it. "So what do you feel like doing, Eden? Maybe a brisk hike through the woods?"

Her lips twitched, but she straightened them. "Hmm, that does sound invigorating. Sure, why not?" She sat up, made as if she were going to rise, and then stopped. "Or we could be lazy and stay here. Why don't you lie down beside me and see if we can come up with any way to pass the time until lunch?"

"I kind of liked what we were doing before. I'd like it even better now that we're wearing fewer clothes."

"Hmm, I'm not sure I recall . . ." She gave a sexy grin.

"Then I'll have to remind you."

He kissed that grin right off her lips, turning it into a gasp that was raw and sexual. That gasp did him in, along with the memory of the musky scent of her arousal. They were two healthy adults, alone on a beach on a warm June day.

From her mouth he moved to her breasts, sucking and laving her nipples through her top, and then pulling up the fabric and savoring the softness of her breasts and the pebbly hardness of her nipples. Eden clamped her hands around his head, holding him there as she arched forward to press herself against his greedy mouth. He reached behind her to undo the clasp of her top and her body jerked.

Her hands freed his head and grabbed the front of her bikini top. "Aaron, wait. We're outside."

She was just now thinking of that? "We're alone. There's no one else for miles. And the seals won't care."

"But . . ." She glanced around. "What if someone comes?"

"Sounds carry. A car, a boat engine, even the splash of a kayak paddle. We'll hear them." Although when he kissed Eden, he was pretty much oblivious to everything else. Of course for him, the idea that someone just might happen upon them only added to the thrill.

Either she felt the same way or she bought his story about sounds carrying because she let out a long breath and then peeled off her bikini top and tossed it aside.

Aaron took a moment to enjoy the sight of her, topless in the sunshine, flushed, with tousled hair. He slid down on the towel to palm her mound through her bikini bottom. She gasped again as he cupped her firmly, his fingers sliding between her legs. The fabric crotch was wet, the insides of her thighs warm and damp. He fondled her until she writhed and then he hooked his fingers in both sides of her single remaining garment.

She'd asked for slow, but her body telegraphed

urgency. Needing to be sure, he said, "Eden? Are you good with this?"

"Yes! Oh yes. Please, Aaron."

Relieved, grateful, curious, and aroused, he drew the blue bikini bottom down her hips and the long line of her legs. She had a neat patch of curly brown hair, so sexy and womanly. Her thighs pressed together in an instinctive gesture of modesty or shyness. With both hands, he gently coaxed them apart and then slipped his fingers between them to learn her most intimate secrets. He stroked the glistening, rosy folds, teased them apart, and eased two fingers deep inside as she whimpered and rubbed against him in a clear demand.

His body was making its own demand clear, too. He let her go to pull off his shorts, take a condom from the waterproof bag, and sheathe himself. When he was ready, he turned back to her and found her wide eyes staring at him.

"Aaron," she breathed. "I want you so much."

"Not as much as I want you." The words came out rough with need.

He hooked his hands under her thighs and lifted her to him, then set his mouth between her legs, drinking her essence, tasting her passion. His tongue circled the tiny bud where her need centered, faster and faster, then flicked over it. When he sensed she was on the edge, he withdrew, shifted to lean over her body, and eased into her in a long, achingly slow thrust.

She moaned as he did it, and again when he withdrew almost all the way. When he returned in a harder, faster plunge into her center, she cried out, her body clutching and spasming as she climaxed.

It took every ounce of his self-control to hold steady, to not follow her into orgasm. But he managed it, and when her spasms slowed, he began to thrust again. In and out, changing pace, varying the angle, driving her higher again.

She raised her legs and hooked them around his hips, meeting his thrusts. Her hands were on his back, gripping, urging him on. Their bodies twined, hers slippery with lotion. Her breath came in soft pants between swollen pink lips. His own rasped with the pure physical joy of sharing this moment with this woman.

When she began to toss her head back and forth, her eyes glazing, he knew she was close again. Now he could let himself go, no more forcing himself to hold back. He let his body drive mindlessly toward the goal of release, confident that Eden would be there with him.

And she was, the two of them breaking together, their cries mingling.

Chapter Nine

Tuesday morning, Eden woke in her bed at the Once in a Blue Moon, stretched, and felt a host of unusual sensations. Her skin, especially over her cheeks and nose, was taut, a little dry. Despite sunscreen, several hours of sunshine combined with a slight ocean breeze had taken their toll. Muscles unused to exercise ached but not unpleasantly—through her shoulders from kayaking and also her thighs. She pressed her thighs together, feeling the pull of muscles and the tenderness between her legs. Not from kayaking but from sex. Sex on the beach with her handsome lover and then, later, in the rosy reflected glow of the sunset, in Aaron's bed.

What an incredible day. She'd been out on the ocean for the first time in her life, paddling a tiny craft, both vulnerable and powerful at the same time. She'd felt the hint of a oneness with the seals around her. Maybe she'd also begun to understand why Aaron was so bonded to this special place.

She had also made love in an uninhibited, passionate, yet also teasing and tender way. In the past, sex had been more of a . . . *routine* wasn't exactly the right word, but it came close. Routines were often pleasant, like savoring that first cup of coffee in the morning and feeling energy tingle through her veins. Sex had been like that: enjoyable but not mind-blowing. Yesterday had been mind-blowing.

"Mind-blowing," she said, and laughed. The aging hippies were having an influence on her. The word had never been in Eden's vocabulary, and until yesterday, she hadn't experienced anything that merited that description.

It had been a lot, too much to process. After a simple dinner of barbecued burgers and salad on Aaron's deck as they watched the full moon rise, she had turned down his invitation to spend the night and asked him to drive her back to the B and B. There, she'd taken a long shower, smoothed lotion into her parched skin, and slipped into her cotton pajamas. Refocusing on her mission, she'd typed notes from the day's unproductive interviews: Maury, Mr. and Mrs. Hunt, and Sven Svenson. She'd reread those notes, looking for possible clues and additional questions she might have asked, feeling frustrated that she was no further ahead in her quest.

She also couldn't help but wonder whether Merlin had been a cultlike and abusive leader, and why he'd suddenly disappeared. Might those questions be relevant to her search for Lucy? Even if not, Eden's practical, analytical mind didn't like unanswered questions. Oh well, today was a fresh day. She had set up a couple of interviews for this morning, and this afternoon Aaron was taking her to another.

The alarm on her cell phone went off, telling her it was seven. After silencing it, she propped herself up on pillows and phoned the family home. It was ten in Ottawa, so her mom should be up and dressed.

It was Kelsey who answered, with a bright, "Hey, Sis."

"Hi, Kelsey. How's everything going there?"

"Not bad. Hang on a minute."

Eden waited, and then Kelsey said, "I'm in my room and wanted to close the door so Mom can't overhear if she comes upstairs. Eden, it's so hard seeing her like this. She used to be so upbeat, you know? Now she barely even smiles."

"I know. Was she any better after the cancer support group meeting yesterday?"

"We didn't go."

"What? Kels, I know she may say she's too tired to go, but don't let her manipulate you."

"It wasn't that. I got a call from a university friend who was in town for the day and—"

"You ditched Mom's cancer group to go out with a friend? I don't believe it." When Kelsey had said she'd stay home for the summer to help out rather than get a summer job, Eden and her dad had hoped she'd finally grown up. It didn't look as if that was true.

Her sister's tone was hostile when she said, "Whatever."

"Are you at least making sure she takes her meds?" Eden climbed out of bed and went over to pull back the curtains. Aaron had told her he had an early flight.

"Meds? Oh, are you talking about all those little colored pills you set out in that seven-day plastic container thingy? I seem to recall seeing it somewhere around the place."

Eden was almost sure her sister was kidding, so she

didn't press the point. Gazing out at the still-quiet village of Blue Moon Harbor, she asked, "Is Dad around?"

"He left early for work. Since Mom doesn't get up until nine or so and I'm here and can help her, he goes in at some godawful hour. That way, he can put in a crazy-long day and still be home for supper and spend the evening with Mom. He tries to be all cheery, but he looks tired."

"I worry about him. He's sixty-six. The past year's been really hard on him."

"They're both looking a lot older, aren't they?"

"Yeah, they are." Eden and her sister were both quiet for a moment, and she felt the warmth of the bond between them. They might often rub each other the wrong way, but underneath the bickering was a solid core of love. "I'm glad you're there with them," Eden said. Watching a few people head toward the coffee shop at Dreamspinner bookstore and looking forward to her own B and B breakfast and day on Destiny Island, she felt sympathy for her sister. "I'm sure it's not the most fun way to spend your summer."

"Despite what you may think of me," Kelsey said huffily, "I'm not just about having fun. I did offer to skip university this past year and stay home to help out."

"I know." Eden and her parents had been afraid that, because discipline wasn't Kelsey's forte, she might simply drop out of school and never return. "I'm sorry, that's not what I meant. Just that it's tough looking after a sick person when you could be going to an interesting job or taking holiday time."

"She isn't just a sick person, she's Mom." The huffiness had gone, replaced by sadness.

"Yes. And in many ways that makes it tougher, doesn't it?"

"Yeah, it does." Kelsey sniffled. "Remember when we were little, how much fun the summers were?"

Because their mom was a teacher, she'd had the same summer vacation as her daughters. She'd made the days interesting, fun, even educational. There'd been lots of laughter. "I do." Eden cleared the huskiness of emotion from her throat. "Mom's going to get better. Things will get back to normal."

"You bet she will. Nothing's going to get the better of our mom." Kelsey sounded upbeat again. Just as Eden tried to be whenever she thought about her mother's future. The power of positive thinking.

A seaplane—the same one she'd flown in on—was leaving the dock and motoring across the harbor. It looked so bright and pretty with its white-and-blue paint job, and she thought of Aaron's skilled hands on the steering yoke. She respected how he'd turned away from the juvenile delinquent path to finish school and become a pilot. She also had to give him points for having created a way of life that suited him perfectly—even if her ideal kind of man was quite different: responsible rather than carefree, committed to relationships rather than a loner whose only relationships were casual and short-term.

Even though she was benefitting from the latter fact. Who better to tell than her sister? For once she'd done something Kelsey was likely to approve of. Her sister might even have a useful perspective to offer. "So, Kels, you know that rebound-fling advice you gave me?"

There was a pause, then an ear-shattering whoop. "You're screwing someone!"

Eden winced. "I wouldn't put it quite that crudely, but yes, I've met someone. Totally casual, just for this week, no strings attached."

"Excellent! OMG, I never thought you had it in you, Sis."

"Nor did I," Eden confessed. "But then I met Aaron." The seaplane was lifting up from the ocean's surface and Eden held her breath, thinking how amazing it was to defy gravity.

"Eden and Aaron, sitting in a tree—"

"Oh, shut up," Eden said, laughing. "And it wasn't a tree, it was a beach, if you must know. A deserted beach." The plane had gained altitude and was rapidly turning into a mere dot in the sky.

"Wow. I like this guy."

"I like him, too." He was charming, considerate, and wonderful company, as well as being an amazing lover. If she'd met him back home in Ottawa, at a time when her life wasn't so stressed with commitments . . . No, what was she thinking? Quickly, she clarified, "As a hookup. He has zero long-term potential, which is *exactly* what I'm looking for." Had she been too emphatic? Surely she wasn't trying to persuade herself.

Her life *was* full and stressed, and her priorities left no room for a romantic relationship. Besides, the very thought of Aaron in Ottawa, in a suit striding down Wellington Street, was absurd. He belonged on Destiny Island, just like Lionel and Marlise, Azalea, and the various other residents she'd met.

And then there was the fact that he insisted he didn't want a serious relationship—not ever. It wasn't just that he said so; his obvious self-sufficiency and contentment with his single life reinforced the point. As far as she could see, Aaron didn't want to be serious about much of anything. That would certainly rule him out as boyfriend material, had she been in the market for a boyfriend. She needed a man with a strong sense of responsibility, one who wanted more out of life than to coast through it one day at a time.

"So Aaron's perfect."

"Pretty much." For fling purposes. "He's a seaplane pilot, working for the little local airline, he's super-fit, really gorgeous. Lots of fun to be with." And that was pretty much all she knew about him. The only really personal thing he'd told her was about his delinquent teens and how Lionel had helped him turn his life around. Since then, whenever she asked him about anything that went deeper than superficial, he somehow managed to deflect and change the subject. Last night, she'd succumbed to temptation and searched the Internet, but he seemed to have zero social media presence.

"Smart? You only like smart guys."

Eden hadn't really thought about that, but Kelsey was right. If Aaron had come across as less than smart, she would have been turned off. "Smart enough to learn all the stuff required to be a pilot. That's got to be as complicated as law school."

"And sexy goes without saying," Kelsey said. "Except, hey, let's say it anyway. Aaron is . . ." She paused dramatically.

Eden, smothering a laugh, finished in tandem with her. "Sexy!"

"He's good for you," Kelsey said.

"You know, I think he is. I feel . . . lighter. Younger." Eden turned away from the window and sat at the desk. "Don't tell Mom, okay?"

"Don't want her to know you're a slut like me?" her

sister joked. Kelsey was as casual about relationships as she was about school, part-time jobs, and everything else—bouncing from one to the next on whim.

"Yeah, that's it," Eden teased back. "More like I don't want her to worry."

"I hear you. No problem."

"Thanks. Is she around? Can I talk to her?"

"She was downstairs finishing breakfast. Hang on, I'll go find her."

Eden heard the sound of bare feet thumping down the stairs, and then, "Hey, Mom, it's Eden." And then her mother's voice said, "Eden. Good morning, dear."

"Hi, Mom. How are you?"

"Pretty good on the whole."

Her voice was stronger than usual, which made Eden smile. "That's great." She was about to gently remind her mom that missing cancer support group wasn't a good idea, but her mother spoke first.

"How are things going? Have you found anyone who remembers Lucy?"

Eden had dreaded this part of the conversation. "I've talked to a number of people, including members of the old commune. But so far, no one remembers Lucy or Barry." She didn't mention that each time she went to interview a woman who'd once belonged to the commune, she felt a flutter of anticipation, wondering if the woman might be her aunt—and each time, her hopes were dashed.

"Oh, Eden. I'm so disappointed."

"I'm sorry." She rotated her shoulders, which had tightened up. "A lot of people at the commune were pretty stoned back then, and it was a long time ago. Memories are foggy. Also, it seems some of the kids changed their names, choosing hippie ones. Do you think that's something Lucy might have done?"

After a moment's silence, her mother said, "She might have. If she was mad enough at our parents and wanted to leave the past behind and become a new person . . . Oh my, this isn't at all encouraging, is it?" Her voice had lost its energy now and sounded thin and tired.

"I still have more people to see. Don't give up hope, Mom."

"Of course not. If my Eden's on the job, I know it'll get done as thoroughly as possible."

"I'll do my best." She always had. Eight years older than Kelsey, Eden had carried the weight of her parents' expectations—maybe even more so after her sister was born and proved to be so happy-go-lucky.

"If there's anything to find, you'll find it, dear."

Eden was determined to do exactly that and not let her mother down. But what if there truly was nothing to find? Her mom would be devastated. But at least that news would be better than learning Lucy had died.

After hanging up, Eden signed into her Butterworth Foundation account. She scanned through her emails and frowned. Navdeep hadn't reported on his meeting yesterday with the prospective applicant. She needed that information to advise him on the next steps to take. She fired off an email requesting an update and also reminding him to start pulling together figures for the board meeting next week.

She might not be able to fix her mom's illness or state of mind, or maybe even track down Lucy, but at least with her job she could be competent and in control.

Midmorning, Eden stepped into Dreamspinner. She had an appointment for an interview in the coffee shop in half an hour and had come early, planning to browse the bookshelves. She'd always loved reading—legal suspense and mysteries in particular—though in the past year her reading time hadn't amounted to much more than fifteen minutes in bed at night.

The store wasn't huge like the chain bookstores in Ottawa, but it was a true bookstore: shelves of hardcovers, paperbacks, audiobooks, and magazines; comfy chairs dotted here and there; and not a sign of fancy housewares, toys, candles, or candy. Eden breathed a sigh of anticipation.

Inside the door, a table with a "Local Authors" sign caught her attention. It held a dozen or more books. Three hardcovers by an author named Kellan Hawke had the gritty covers that denoted thrillers. She was about to reach for one when her gaze caught on several paperbacks, the kind her mom typically enjoyed. The covers had attractive scenes, each with a man and woman holding hands or embracing. She had just picked one up when a soft female voice said, "Looking for a good romance?"

Eden looked up to see an attractive woman in her midtwenties with long, sleek black hair framing an oval face with fine features. She wore a short-sleeved green blouse over tan capris and had a lovely silk-screened scarf around her neck. On her pocket was a name tag with the store name and "Iris Yakimura."

"In fiction or in real life?" Eden joked.

A smile quirked perfect, untinted lips. "I'm afraid fiction is all we have to offer. You're a fan of romance novels, too?"

"Actually, I'm not. The few I've read just made my own relationships look pale in comparison." She'd also thought the sex scenes were overdone, but that was before Aaron.

"Ah. That's too bad, though I understand. I like these books because they give me hope. I want to believe that women who have their own flaws and problems still deserve love and have a chance of finding it."

"That's an interesting perspective." Eden tilted her head, studying the other woman. It seemed this lovely Japanese-Canadian woman had been no more successful in the dating world than she had.

"So, if not a romance, what can I help you find today?" the bookseller asked.

"Actually, I think I will get one of these. My mom loves them." She smiled at Iris. "My parents did find love and it's lasted more than thirty years."

"I'm so happy for them."

"So am I." Iris had an aura of serenity and genuineness that led Eden to go on. "Without Dad and their love, I don't know how Mom would have survived the past year. She had breast cancer and it's been a rough time."

The other woman's dark eyes softened with compassion. "I'm so sorry. An illness like that is so hard on everyone. When my grandmother had ALS, I would have done anything to help her feel better. I felt so powerless."

"Yes." *Oh, yes!* Eden felt the ridiculous urge to cry on this stranger's shoulder. She did feel powerless. She could give her mom rides to appointments, make sure she took her meds, do chores for her, and try to keep her spirits up, but she couldn't heal her. "I hate feeling powerless," she admitted.

Iris pressed her lips together and then said slowly, "Mostly, we find the areas in life where we can have at least some control, where we feel more comfortable. When we're unable to do that, when we're forced into situations where we feel powerless, it's hard to cope."

Feeling as if she'd met an unexpected soul mate, Eden asked, "Your grandmother. Is she . . . ?"

Iris's long lashes lowered. "I'm afraid she passed away."

"I'm sorry."

Iris nodded. "Death comes. It's inevitable, after all. And when it claimed my grandmother, it was a blessing because she was in such distress."

Not wanting to think about death, Eden asked the question she'd been tossing out in every place of business she entered. "Are you and your family Destiny Island natives?"

"On my father's side, from the very beginning of settlement. They were fishers, and later farmers. Dad and my aunt opened this bookstore and Mom later added the coffee shop."

"This is your family's store? It's wonderful."

She nodded proudly. "Thank you."

"Iris," Eden started, then broke off. "By the way, my name's Eden. I'm from Ottawa and I'm trying to track down my missing aunt. She joined the commune back in 1969. Do you think your parents or aunt might have any knowledge of her?"

The young woman laughed quickly. "I doubt it. My family is quite conventional. Very industrious. Communes and hippies are definitely not their thing. But I'll ask, if you like, just to be sure. How can I get in touch with you?"

"I'd appreciate it." Eden gave her a business card. "I'll probably be back in the store again if I have any spare time. I'd love to browse some more." She gazed at Iris and found herself saying, "And perhaps to chat some more as well." If the bookseller lived in Ottawa, Eden had a feeling they might turn into friends.

Iris's smile touched her dark eyes. "I'd like that."

"But now I'd better choose a book and pay for it. I'm meeting someone for coffee."

"Here." Iris handed her a book titled *Island Magic*. "This is the first in the series."

After they completed the transaction, Eden asked if it would be all right to put up a poster on the notice board in the coffee shop. Iris readily agreed, taking the one Eden pulled from a folder in her bag and saying she'd do it herself.

Together, they went into the coffee shop area. It was an attractive place, with plants, artwork, racks of magazines and newspapers, and the bulletin board Eden had noticed on a previous visit. Every one of the eight or so tables was full and a lineup waited at the counter.

As Iris went to pin up the poster, Eden glanced around at the customers and recognized Bart Jelinek from his photo on the Destiny Island Realty ads. From the *Gazette*, she'd learned he owned one of the two real estate agencies and was also president of the Rotary. He was seated at a table by the window, a coffee mug in front of him, engaged in animated conversation with a man who stood beside him, takeout cup and paper bag in hand. Jelinek was a tallish man with graying blond hair. A pair of tortoise-shell-rimmed glasses gave him a rather distinguished air, while his short-sleeved, blue-and-white-striped shirt and slightly askew blue tie made him look approachable.

On the phone, he had confirmed that his family had lived beside the commune. His parents were deceased and he was an only child, so he was the only person she could talk to.

Not wanting to interrupt his conversation, Eden joined the lineup. A few minutes later, she claimed a low-fat cappuccino. Mr. Jelinek was now talking to a pair of middle-aged women. Tentatively, she approached his table.

He glanced up, smiled, and said, "Eden Blaine?"

"That's me. I hope I'm not interrupting."

"No, no." He rose, a hand extended. "Eden, I'm Bart Jelinek."

His handshake was hearty but not overpowering, and she got the impression he was probably a pretty successful salesman.

He turned to the two women. "Ladies, I'm afraid I have an appointment. But I do appreciate your kind words. I admit I'm seriously tempted to run when Walter Franklin's term ends."

"You'd be the perfect representative for Destiny," one of the women gushed. "You do so much for this island."

The other nodded enthusiastically, and the two of them went to join the coffee lineup.

"Sorry, Eden," Jelinek said. "Island politics."

"You're considering running for office?"

"In a manner of speaking. We have a unique kind of governance here: federal, provincial, the Capital Regional District, and the Islands Trust. But I won't bore you with that. You said you're looking for information about the old commune?"

She repeated the story she'd told so many times in the past few days.

"I was just a little kid," he said as Eden sipped her coffee, which was delicious. "It was fascinating to me, all those long-haired boys and girls in their hippie clothes, the loud music, the drugs. My parents hated having the commune there and tried to get them kicked off the land but never had any luck."

"Someone had given them permission to be there? They weren't squatters?"

"Maybe; maybe not. When I got into real estate, I checked it out. Originally, the land was owned by an elderly man from Germany who was quite a hermit. He died intestate, unmarried, childless, and without siblings. The leader of the commune, who called himself Merlin, claimed to be related. If his legal name was Otto Kruger, that claim was true. Kruger, a fairly distant relative of the deceased, turned out to be the next of kin. But by the time that was determined, Merlin had moved on and the commune had shut down. Another relative was located, Kruger was eventually presumed dead, and that relative inherited. Unfortunately, she put the land into a trust for her kids."

"Unfortunately?"

He leaned forward, his eyes bright. "That's a great piece of land. Subdivided into large, nicely landscaped lots, in keeping with the ambience of the island, it'd be worth a fortune."

"Of course." The Realtor would no doubt love to

get his hands on it. "You said Merlin was legally presumed dead. Was his actual death ever confirmed, or did anyone find out where he'd gone after leaving Destiny Island?"

"No. It seems he was another one like your aunt." He frowned. "I'm sorry, but . . ."

When he paused, Eden guessed he was thinking that Lucy, like Merlin, was most probably dead.

But he didn't say that. Instead, he finished, "You do realize how difficult it is to find someone who's been off the radar for half a century?"

She firmed her jaw. "I do. But I'll keep trying. What do you remember about the commune, Mr. Jelinek?"

"Please, it's Bart. Nothing that will help, I'm afraid. I admit I defied my parents and snuck over there to spy on the hippies. That was sure an education for an impressionable boy, I'll tell you." He gave a hearty laugh. "But I didn't know the names of any of the members."

"Might you recognize a face?"

"No, I wasn't close enough."

So much for that. Eden sighed. "Did you get any impression that something was off?"

"Off?"

She was about to clarify when a smartly dressed young man stopped at the table to ask Bart a question about a meeting the next night. After he'd gone, Eden said, "Sexual abuse."

"Abuse?" Bart's voice croaked, and behind the horn-rims, his pale gray eyes widened.

"By Merlin. Of the women."

He blinked. "No. But as I said, I was a child. Less than ten years old. I saw . . ." He swallowed. "I saw sex in all forms. Including, uh, rough sex. But I imagine it was consensual. Weren't the hippies all about free love? Love, not . . ." Another swallow. "Abuse." It seemed the congenial Realtor had delicate sensibilities.

"Maybe Merlin used some women's love for him to manipulate and abuse them."

He picked up his mug. "Well, that would be awful, of course." His brows pulled together. "Are you saying your aunt might have been abused and so she ran away again?"

"I have no idea," she admitted, discouraged.

He gave her a sympathetic smile as he put his mug down again. "It sounds like a disheartening mission you're on. I do wish you luck."

"Thank you."

"I hope you're liking Destiny Island, though."

"Very much. It's lovely."

He beamed. "It's our own little corner of paradise. And you know, there's always work for a lawyer."

Her spirits lifted a little. "You're trying to sell me a house, aren't you?"

"And here I thought I was being subtle."

Chapter Ten

Aaron had fueled the four-seater Cessna 180 and checked the floats and water rudders. Now, standing on the dock Tuesday afternoon, he checked his watch again. It wasn't yet one-thirty, the time he'd asked Eden to meet him, but he was impatient to see her. During his morning flights, his mind had kept turning to her. Yesterday had been one fine day. His only regret was that she hadn't slept over. They had only a few days together and he wanted to make the most of them.

When he looked up, she was standing at the top of the ramp, pretty in navy cotton capris and a short-sleeved blue blouse. Though she was mostly covered up, he remembered what she'd looked like naked on the beach, flushed from lovemaking.

She waved and he waved back, gesturing her to come down to the dock. Battling an erection, he went to meet her. "Hey you," he said, putting his hands on her shoulders and dropping a kiss on her lips.

She returned the kiss. "Hey back." Her hair, pulled

into a low ponytail, framed her face, and a hint of tan colored her skin.

He opened the Cessna's door. "Hop in."

"We're flying? I didn't realize that."

"We're going to see Gwendy, the former commune member. She lives on her own island along with—"

"Island?" she broke in. "Didn't you say she lives at a place called Severn's Reach?"

"Which is an island."

"I didn't realize." She eyed the plane doubtfully. "Is it far?"

"A hop, a skip, and a jump in the Cessna."

"That's a really small plane."

"And a really safe one. Jillian and I fly it two or three times a day."

"Oh. Well . . ." She gave a soft laugh. "Sorry, it's not that I don't trust your pilot skills. I guess if I can go kayaking, I can fly in a miniature plane." Glancing toward the Blue Moon Air office, she said, "Should I go up and pay for the flight now or wait until we get back?"

"You're not paying." He helped her into the plane. "The Cessna wasn't booked. It was just going to sit here doing nothing."

"But the fuel," she protested as she belted herself in. "And there must be maintenance costs and whatever else is included in the cost of a flight."

"Don't worry about it."

She frowned but kept quiet.

Five minutes later, they were up in the air. "How was your morning?" he asked.

"Frustrating, except for a nice chat with Iris Yakimura at Dreamspinner. I met with Bart Jelinek, but he didn't know anything. I phoned Cynnie Smithson, who refused to meet with me. She said her stint at the commune was a misguided little adventure and she remembered nothing about it. It was like she wanted to brush it all under the carpet and pretend it never happened."

He pictured the woman, with her neatly styled and dyed hair and boring clothes. "Yeah, Cynnie and her husband aren't exactly free spirits. He's a retired accountant and she was a stay-at-home mom."

"And a grandmother now, she told me proudly."

"Guess she doesn't tell her kids and grandkids about her days of long hair, tie-dye, and joint smoking."

She laughed. "Guess not." Then she went on. "I also talked to the friend of Rachelle's father, the man who took a few of the commune boys out fishing occasionally. They told him they wanted to learn and to catch food for the commune, and that they'd haul nets and so on for him in exchange. He said most of them were useless, but there were a couple of decent ones. He's actually still friends with one of them, Seal SkySong. He doesn't remember anyone named Barry. And he said that whenever he asked questions about the commune, the boys would giggle and say they were sworn to secrecy. He thought it was all pretty adolescent."

"I'm sorry you haven't had more luck with your hunt for your aunt."

"Me too." She sighed. "I spoke to my mom this morning. At first she sounded good, but when I told her there was no news, she got discouraged. She's always been able to count on me. I hate that I'm letting her down."

He reached over to briefly touch her arm. "Eden, you're doing everything you can. Don't beat yourself up."

She gave him a flicker of a smile. "Thanks." The smile widened. "Hey, I told my sister about us. She said you're good for me. I think she's right."

"That's nice to hear." It gave him a warm feeling that went all the way through him.

For a few minutes, they were both quiet, and then Eden said, "I see the shadow of the plane slipping across the ocean." She glanced his way. "It seems as if it should be totally silent up here and yet the engine's so noisy."

"I know." He'd gotten used to engine noise, so attuned to it that he barely noticed unless there was a strange sound that might signal a problem.

"You said this plane used to be Lionel's? How old is it?"

"Built in 1970."

Her hands gripped her seat belt. "That's really old."

"Planes have a long life if they're well maintained. This baby has always been cared for. Give her a try." The plane had dual steering yokes, and he gestured to the one in front of Eden.

She raised her hands in a gesture of protest. "I can't fly a plane."

"Just rest your hands there, see what it feels like."

Gingerly, she obeyed. "It doesn't feel so different from a car steering wheel. Okay, what do I do?"

He took his hands off his own yoke. "Gently pull straight back and we'll gain altitude. Shove down a little and that's where we'll go. And like with a car, the plane will go left or right if you turn the yoke that way. Keep all your motions slow and easy."

With excruciating slowness, she experimented. "Wow. But there's more to it than this."

"One or two things. See this dial?" He pointed to the instrument panel. "That's the altimeter. We're eight hundred feet above sea level. See how the needle responds when you pull up or push down on the yoke?"

Trying it out, she nodded.

"This is the compass, which comes in handy when you're flying over open ocean with no landmarks below to guide you."

She watched the instrument panel as she moved the yoke this way and that.

"There are other things a pilot pays attention to," he said. "I won't overwhelm you with all of them. There's just one more thing you need to think about right now."

"What's that?"

"Other air traffic."

"Oh my gosh!" She jerked her gaze to the windows. "I'd completely forgotten that there could be other planes out there."

"And birds. A flock of gulls . . . well, let's just say that's best avoided. We fly VFR, Visual Flight Rules. That means you need sufficient visibility—you can't fly in heavy fog, for example—and you rely on your eyes rather than on instruments."

She gripped the yoke tighter, peering out the windshield. "I was right. Flying is scary."

"So's driving a car. It's a matter of learning how to do it and putting in many, many hours of practice until it becomes almost instinctive."

"I suppose."

"Drop altitude slowly," he said. "Just keep taking her down."

"Why?"

"Because that's Severn's Reach down below."

She jerked her hands off the yoke. "No way am I landing this."

Laughing, he put his hands on his own steering yoke. "No, you're not. Sit back and relax." Then he said casually, "There's something I didn't mention about Gwendy. She lives with her partners, Sandra and Peter."

Eden glanced at him, blinked, and said, "But Sandra and Peter weren't at the commune?"

"No. They all got together later." He waited a moment, and when she didn't say anything else, he asked, "It doesn't bother you? Them being a threesome?"

She shrugged. "Why should it? Do you think I'm naïve or prejudiced or something?" She stiffened. "Does their relationship bother you?"

"God no. That's the joy of Destiny. You can be yourself."

"I wish the whole world was like that. If people aren't hurting anyone, why should it matter how they live their lives? If Gwendy, Sandra, and Peter have found love together, then they're lucky."

Luckier than he'd ever be, he figured.

Aaron barely watched the sunset, though it was a spectacular one viewed from the rustic deck at the Sunset Cove pub. Every shade of red, orange, and gold lit the sky, cast reflections in the still ocean, and painted ever-changing patterns over the half-dozen boats at the small dock below. But his attention was on Eden's face. It was there he tracked the progress of the setting sun, from subtle to fiery and then fading to mellow. The colors stroked her face, but even better was the fascination in her eyes and the soft curve of her lips.

She was too caught up in the experience to speak, though she occasionally reached out and absentmindedly had a sip of wine or snagged one of the tempura zucchini and yam rounds from the appetizer plate in the center of the table. When their waitress brought a thick candle in a wind-resistant holder, Eden didn't notice. Aaron wondered if she was ever like this in Ottawa, totally in the moment and at peace.

For the twenty minutes, it took for the sun to drop into the ocean, he sipped his craft beer from Blue Moonshine, munched on tempura, and reveled in her enjoyment.

Finally, she turned to him with a sigh and glazed eyes. "That was incredible. I've never seen anything like it." Her eyes widened and she groaned. "Why didn't I take a picture? Why didn't I think to pull out my phone?"

"Because you were living in the moment."

"That's not like me," she said, sounding puzzled and a little displeased.

He fought back a grin. *Wait for it . . . Yeah, there's that scrunchy forehead.*

She frowned at her empty wineglass. "I finished my wine and didn't even notice." Her forehead scrunched tighter as she gazed across at him. "Aaron, I'm organized. I don't live in the moment, I plan for the future. I'm a lawyer, right? It's all about analyzing the goal, the tasks required to complete it, and the time frame and resources that are available. Like, even with this glass of wine, I'd normally have made it last through dinner. And we haven't even ordered yet."

She sounded so puzzled and grumpy that he had to laugh. "There's more wine where that came from."

"But then I'll end up drinking too much."

"I'm driving, so don't worry about it."

Seeing she was about to argue the point, he quickly said, "And you'll have more photo ops tonight. Sometimes the sky's even prettier after the sun has sunk below the horizon."

She took her phone from her bag and put it on the table. "Don't let me forget this time."

"You could always set the alarm for ten minutes," he teased.

When she reached for it again, he groaned. "I was joking."

"It's a good idea." She fiddled with the phone and then put it down again.

She wore her hair loose tonight and her earrings sparkled in the candlelight, making him think of sunlight or starlight bouncing off waves. "Those earrings suit you." Until today, she'd worn little gold thingies that were barely noticeable. Her new ones, made by Tamsyn, a jeweler who'd once belonged to the Enchantery, were abstract silver ones with sparkly stones that looked like diamonds but couldn't be since the earrings had cost only thirty-five dollars.

After the pleasant but unproductive visit to Severn's Reach, he and Eden had driven to Tamsyn's place, talking to her in the studio that adjoined her house. As with most of the local artists, the studio also served as a storefront showcasing her work. The jeweler had

been closemouthed about her commune days but
happy to talk about her craft. She portrayed natural
subjects and tried to capture their essence. Aaron and
Eden had both admired her work.

Eden gave her head a flick, making the earrings
dance. "They're not my usual style, but they spoke
to me. I hope Mom and Kelsey like the ones I
bought for them."

For her mother, she'd chosen hummingbirds with
red-jeweled heads, saying her mom had two hummingbird feeders hanging outside the kitchen window. Her
sister was getting feather-and-bead earrings, Eden
commenting wryly that Kelsey was like a bird that
never settled in one place for long.

Eden spoke often of her family. She was straightforward, which he respected, and it made it easy to
get to know her. It was clear she was passionate about
not only her family but her job. She had strong values
and beliefs, set her goals based on them, then used
her considerable energy and organizational ability to
pursue those goals. He'd learned she was a bit of a
control freak and liked to do things her way, though
she could be flexible when necessary.

In that way—both the taking-charge part and the
flexibility—they were similar. Other than that, they
were pretty much opposites.

He had learned early on not to share information
about his personal life, much less his feelings. Now he
never talked about his shitty past or his troubled sister.
That stuff was no one's business but his.

Eden organized her life in terms of achieving
goals. He'd only had three goals as an adult. Two,
he'd already achieved: to live on Destiny and fly in this
scenic area. The third—to ensure his sister and

niece's safety and security—wasn't within his control. Other than that, he was a laid-back guy, content to enjoy his small corner of the world with the wonders of nature and the entertaining eccentricities of neighbors who accepted him just as he was.

Eden had been toying with an earring, looking reflective. "I'll be taking home souvenirs from this trip, and memories. But Aaron, I'm halfway through my time here, and so far, I don't have a single lead that will help me find Lucy."

He'd hoped she wouldn't think about that tonight. He wanted Eden to be happy. For some reason that mattered more to him each day. He knew all the sunset dinners and kayaking-with-seals adventures in the world couldn't give her the same happiness as being able to tell her mom she'd located her long-lost sister, and that Lucy was well and happy.

Aaron was doing all he could, yet he felt frustrated and inadequate because he hadn't been able to produce the results Eden wanted. Trying to encourage both of them, he put his hand over hers where it rested next to her empty glass. "There are still several names on the list. Don't give up hope. I don't think that's like you, right? I see you as a power-of-positive-thinking person."

She turned her hand over and wrapped her fingers around his. "True. Okay, I'll remain positive. And right now, I have a goal I'm very positive about. I'm hungry. Let's order dinner."

Their waitress was going around the deck lighting outdoor heaters because the air had cooled off with the sun's setting. Aaron beckoned her over just as the cell phone alarm went off. Eden clicked photos of the mellow afterglow of the sunset, all pinks, golds, and purples this evening. Aaron gave the waitress their order: a lamb burger for him, a blackened tuna salad for Eden, a Coke for him, and another glass of wine for her.

When the colors in the sky faded, Eden put her phone away. "That was beautiful." She touched one of the bright flowers in the small vase on the table. "So are these. Everything here seems so natural."

"How d'you mean?"

"The flowers came from a garden, not a florist. The fish came out of that very ocean."

"And the lamb—"

"No!" She held up a hand, stopping him. "I refuse to think that the lamb came from one of those cute, fluffy little creatures we saw in the fields we drove past. I'm going to believe it originated in a grocery store, covered in plastic wrap."

He grinned at her. "Whatever makes you happy." It didn't make sense to him that she'd happily eat fish from the ocean yet be squeamish about grass-fed lamb. But women could be weird that way.

The waiter delivered the second round of drinks and Eden took a small sip of her pinot gris. "Even if the old commune members haven't been able to help me in my search, it's been interesting talking to them."

"I'm glad you don't feel like it's been a waste of time."

She cocked her head. "Well, in terms of achieving my goal, it has. But you know, talking to these people makes me think of Mom. Of how she used to be, anyhow. Before the cancer."

"How so?"

"She's all about personal growth. As a teacher, it

fascinates her how people change from their teen years to adulthood. She tries to help her students figure out whether their dreams are pure fantasy or may be achievable, and to develop concrete ways of achieving their goals, which may be through education, travel, apprenticeships, or whatever."

He nodded, thinking of how Lionel and flying had changed a sullen, rebellious teen into a responsible adult.

"What I've been seeing here is a special group of people," Eden mused. "Who at a unique time in history had their own individual reasons for joining the Enchantery. They were hippie kids and now they're in their sixties and seventies. The bulk of their lives is behind them, and it's fascinating to see what they've done with those lives. And how the commune influenced them."

He'd never thought about it in such an analytical way. Intrigued, he said, "Go on."

"Admittedly, it's a small sample, and they're all people who chose to live on Destiny, but it seems to me they've found happy lives. Less conventional lives—well, except for Cynnie—than many people their age. Their lives suit them, whether they live a marginal existence like Azalea or they're fairly well off like Marlise and Cynnie. They're being true to themselves: raising chickens and marijuana, being a social worker, making jewelry, enjoying grandkids, and so on. Married, single, partnered, or friends with benefits—as it suits them, not because of what society tells them to do."

"Maybe what the commune—and the times— taught them was to think for themselves."

"That's not what Merlin wanted. He wanted them

to obey him. And I'm sure a number of them did, at least for a time. But somehow, sometime, they did learn to think for themselves." She smiled across the table at him. "My mom would approve."

What a concept: a mom's approval. Not something he or Miranda had ever known. He swallowed the last mouthful of beer, wishing his second drink was another beer rather than a Coke.

"Aaron, are you okay?"

"Sure. Why?"

"You just looked . . . sad or something for a moment."

He'd be a hell of a lot sadder if he told her the story of his childhood and teens—and she'd get depressed, maybe feel sorry for him. He forced a smile. "Yeah, I'm sad that dinner hasn't arrived. My stomach's growling. I hope they didn't have to go catch my lamb."

"Stop it!" She raised her hands to her ears, laughing. "I don't hear a word you're saying."

With relief, Aaron saw their waitress approaching with their meals. "Ah, in answer to my prayers." In more ways than Eden knew.

As they started to eat, he asked her to tell him about a few of the programs her Foundation had funded. Not only did that shift attention from him but he enjoyed hearing about her work and the pride she took in it. When she turned the focus back on him, he managed, as usual, to stick to topics like his favorite places to fly and stories about the island's colorful history and quirky residents.

When they'd finished eating, Aaron reached across the table for her hand. She looked so lovely, her face lit by the candle on the table and the silvery moon.

Her amber eyes sparkled, as did her earrings. "Dessert here or at my place?" He hoped she was ready for some private time.

Her lips curved knowingly. "What's on the menu for dessert at your place?"

"Because you watch calories"—he winked—"we could go with something tasty and fat-free."

"Do tell." She leaned forward, her elbow on the table and her chin cupped in her hand.

"Your lips would be a good start, followed by perhaps a nibble of an earlobe. Then I'd like to spend some time savoring your breasts and—"

"Shh," she said quickly. A smile bloomed and she said, so quietly he could barely hear it, "That's *your* dessert. What do I get?"

He gave her his best wicked grin. "Anything your little heart desires."

A strange expression crossed her face, or maybe it was just a flicker of candlelight, because it was gone in a second. "How can I turn down an offer like that?"

Chapter Eleven

Two days later, on Thursday afternoon, Eden was following Aaron's eminently watchable butt and legs, clad in shorts, as he hiked up a narrow trail ahead of her. They were at Spirit Bluff, the island's largest park. Aaron said it hadn't been developed except for picnic areas along the beach near the parking lot, but trails crisscrossed it. He'd led her along one of those trails, through heavily treed forest, rocky stretches, and fields with wild grasses. She'd stopped more than once to snap photos, stroke the smooth orange curves of arbutus trees, or gasp as an eagle soared overhead, its white head and tail gleaming in the sun.

The first half hour had been relatively easy walking, but for the last ten or fifteen minutes they'd pretty much been going up. The incline wasn't all that steep. A pair of women with gray hair, small backpacks, and hiking staffs had passed them a few minutes earlier. Still, Eden and her gray Skechers were used to flat, paved ground and walks lasting no longer than half an hour.

Aaron, with his own large backpack, had obviously

slowed his natural stride to accommodate her, but all the same she was puffing. When she got back to Ottawa, she should find a way to fit regular exercise into her weekly routine. Sadly, working out in a fitness club wouldn't be the same as kayaking or hiking in a spectacular wilderness setting.

She was about to fake another I-want-to-take-a-picture stop when the trail widened and stopped climbing. Aaron waited for her to catch up and took her hand. "How are you doing?"

Trying not to wheeze, she said, "Just fine."

Voices sounded from lower down on the trail, and they stepped aside as a group of six or seven teens rushed past them.

"This is a popular spot," Eden commented.

"Yeah. With locals and with tourists." Aaron tugged her hand. "Come on, if you've caught your breath. I know a private spot for our picnic."

"How can there be a private spot in this park?"

"Pilots know all the best places. We see what people can't from the ground."

As they resumed their hike, she tried to match her stride to his. Her shorts-clad legs were so pale and thin compared to his strong brown ones. Her size-six feet looked like city feet in her Skechers and no-show socks; his were so masculine and outdoorsy in the heavy, Velcro-strapped sandals he called Tevas.

How many other women had he brought here? Probably every single one had been more fit than she was—and that was her own damned fault. As for how many other lovers he'd had, why should she care? What was wrong with her? Was she starting to have feelings for Aaron?

He let go of her hand as he branched off onto an

even narrower, rougher trail. The green-leafed shrub he'd identified as salal almost obscured the path and scratched at her bare legs. Where on earth was this man leading her?

In more ways than just on this hike. Where was their relationship headed?

Last night, when they'd been joking about *dessert* at his place, he'd said she could have anything her heart desired. And for one moment, her heart had desired him. Not just his sexy body and skilled lovemaking but Aaron himself. His heart. His love.

And that was ridiculous. It wasn't what she really wanted and it wasn't what he was offering. Maybe she truly was incapable of relaxing and having a fling.

Or maybe . . . was it possible this really might be something more? She hadn't intended it to be, nor had he. But she was experiencing disconcerting emotions, like maybe she could really care for Aaron—*if* he had a deeper, more serious side. He must, mustn't he, even if it sometimes seemed he diverted her more probing questions? And if he did have hidden depths, might it be possible he had feelings for her?

She clambered over roots and rocks, trying to match her footsteps to where Aaron, with his longer stride, had walked. Panting, she struggled to suck in enough air.

Reality check: Time for the con side of the list. Even if they did come to care for each other, surely there was no future in it. She couldn't leave her parents, and her job was very important to her, too. Aaron was a pilot and presumably could find a job anywhere, but it was hard to imagine him ever leaving Destiny. He seemed as tied to the island as Azalea,

Lionel, Marlise, Tamsyn, and the others she'd talked to. He belonged here, like the seals and the eagles.

"This way," Aaron said. He ducked through some bushes. As far as she could see, there was no trail. Or if there was, it belonged to woodland creatures like deer, not to humans. But she followed gamely, trying to ignore the scratch of foliage against her bare legs and arms.

Ten minutes later, after dodging and ducking branches and prickles, stubbing her toes on rocks, tripping over an arbutus root, and getting increasingly sweaty, she was losing patience. But then, on Aaron's heels, she came out at a clearing. Daisies and clover sprinkled the shaggy grass. Gazing around, she saw the disintegrating ruins of what looked to have been a wooden cabin, several rambling old apple trees, and a stream. "Someone lived here once?"

"Must have done. Probably more than a century ago, before this land was made into a park. Running water. Land to grow fruit and vegetables. Likely had a cow or two, chickens, maybe sheep. Horses for transportation."

Such an isolated life. "I wonder what happened to them."

"I could probably find out if I asked around, but I haven't mentioned this place to anyone. If folks have forgotten about it, that works fine for me."

She walked over to a cluster of bushes with simple but lovely pink flowers and leaned in to sniff a blossom. The scent was heady and familiar. "It's some kind of rose."

"Wild rose."

She was enjoying another long sniff when Aaron

stepped up behind her. He put his hands on her waist and turned her to face him. "Was the climb worth it?"

Muscles she hadn't even known she possessed were protesting. But there were wild roses and daisies and, glancing past him, she saw he'd spread a big striped towel over a patch of grass. "The jury's still out," she teased.

"You're a tough sell."

Laughing softly, she wrapped her arms around his neck and swayed against him. "Ah, but I happen to know you can be persuasive."

He dipped his head and kissed her, long and slow, as lazy as the hum of bees exploring the clover. Her body was doing some humming of its own, and she murmured approval.

Aaron put his arm around her and led her over to stand beside the towel. He knelt and removed her shoes and socks. Careful to avoid bees, she plunged her feet into the rough grass and wriggled her toes among the warm, springy blades.

He rose and, starting at the top, button by button, undid her short-sleeved blouse. He tugged the tails free from the belted waistband of her walking shorts and then slid the blouse off her shoulders and arms.

She fought the impulse to cross her arms over her chest as he undid her shorts and pushed them to the ground, leaving her clad in only a white lace-trimmed bra and matching bikini panties. He stepped back and gazed at her.

She had two options. If she worried about someone coming along, she'd ruin what promised to be an-other special time with Aaron. And so, as she'd done on the beach at SkySong, she chose to believe him that this spot was private. That decision, coupled with the gleam of attraction in his eyes, gave her the confidence to straighten her shoulders and stand tall, letting him look his fill.

"You're so beautiful," he said.

Ray had said the same words, but they'd never made her skin tingle. In four whole years with her ex, she'd never felt as sexy and uninhibited as she did now. Part of it might be the grass under her toes, the sunny air on her skin, and the scent of roses that drifted from the blossom-laden bushes, but mostly it was Aaron.

Reaching behind herself, she undid the clasp of her bra and then pulled off the flimsy garment, flaunting her firm breasts with the arousal-tightened nipples. Aaron was the sexiest man she'd ever met and, while she knew he'd had many lovers before her, she was the one with him now and she had power. A feminine power she'd never truly tapped into before.

She cupped her breasts, plumping them up like an offering, and slid her thumbs over the pebbled buds of her nipples. Arousal rippled through her, but it was less from her own touch than from the naked desire in Aaron's eyes.

Keeping one hand on her breast, she slid the other slowly down her body, appreciating as never before the silkiness of her skin, the firmness of her ribs, the curving line of her waist. Realizing on a whole new level that her body had been designed to give and take pleasure. As had Aaron's, which was still clad in a faded black tank top and khaki shorts. Her sex pulsed at the thought of stripping him naked, here in the middle of nature, where he was in his element.

But first she'd finish her own striptease. Still fondling one breast, she hooked her fingers into the narrow sideband of her bikini panties and slowly peeled the thin fabric down her hips. Aaron didn't move, but his gaze followed the motion as if she'd hypnotized him. When gravity took over and her panties slid down her legs, she stroked her belly and let her hand slip down to cover her neatly trimmed vee of brown hair. How far did she dare go? Aaron made her want to do things she'd never imagined doing in front of a man.

She dipped her index finger lower to stroke the dampness between her legs, and then she lifted her hand, finger raised and gleaming with moisture.

That broke Aaron out of his trance. He closed the small distance between them and caught her raised hand. Staring into her eyes, he lifted her hand to his mouth and closed his lips around her finger.

When the wet heat of his mouth enveloped her damp finger and he began to suck, Eden's sex clenched. Her internal muscles pulsed with need and her clit tightened, craving the same attention he was giving her finger. "Aaron." It came out as a pleading, breathy moan.

The expression in those bluish-gray eyes was a little smug. He kept making love to her finger and she closed her eyes, breathing faster as arousal tightened inside her. Could she come from that potent combination of his mouth on her finger, her caress on her breast, and her vivid imagination? No, she needed one more thing. Boldly, she thrust her pelvis forward, hooked one naked leg around Aaron, and rubbed her crotch against the thick, hard bulge in his shorts.

His teeth closed on her finger, an involuntary reaction that, thank heavens, he controlled before he bit off that digit. His free arm came around her and gripped her butt, his strong hand pressing her into him and giving her support.

She threw back her head, reveling in the sensations, blissfully aware of being naked outdoors, of being sexy and wanton, of listening to her body and taking what she needed from this man who seemed entirely happy to provide it.

Finding exactly the right angle, she ground herself against him as everything inside her tightened and coiled. She imagined his naked cock, knowing that, once she took her satisfaction this way, she'd strip him bare and they'd make love again, and maybe again. He'd thrust into her deep and hard, his swollen, heated flesh probing her slick folds, and . . . "Oh yes!" That coil inside her shattered, splintered, and pleasure surged in waves.

Eden sagged against him as her climax ebbed and then faded in slow ripples. When she finally regained her senses, she saw the barely banked fire in Aaron's eyes. Was she ready for round two? Most definitely.

She reached for the fastenings of his shorts, and in less than a minute they were naked together on the towel with him inside her, rolling in a mock battle to determine who'd be on top. They resolved it by taking turns as he did exactly as she'd imagined but even better, pumping slowly, then fast, then slowly again, bringing her to the edge and then easing off. Until she lost patience, claimed top again, and rode him unrelentingly until they both shattered together, sweaty and breathless.

Eventually, she found the strength to climb off and collapse beside him, her lungs still laboring for breath.

Aaron, once again proving himself more fit than she, sat up, barely breathing hard. He removed the condom and tied off the top. "Having satisfied one appetite, I'm ready to satisfy another." He hooked a hand in the strap of his backpack and pulled it toward him. "Let's have lunch."

Lunch? He had the energy to think about food? But now that he mentioned it, her tummy was awfully empty. It had been a long time—and a lot of exertion—since breakfast. She forced her body up to a sitting position. "Sounds good." She found her panties, wriggled into them, and reached for her bra.

"Spoilsport," Aaron said. Still naked, he made no move toward his scattered clothing.

Earlier, she'd been carried away by passion and had reveled in being uninhibited. Now, though, the old Eden had returned. "I'm sorry. I know you said no one knows about this spot, but I just can't eat lunch naked in a public park."

He raised his eyebrows. "But you can have sex?"

She pressed her hands to her heated cheeks. "I know, it doesn't make sense. I was caught up in the moment."

"Those were a lot of moments, and they were mighty fine ones. But okay, whatever you want, city girl."

"Thank you. And, uh, as much as I enjoy the sight of your body, I'd appreciate it if you'd put something on."

"Or you'll get crazed by lust again?" But he reached for his boxers. "Yeah, it probably wouldn't be good if Jillian flew over with a planeload of people."

"Oh!" Eden clasped her bra against her breasts and cast an eye at the clear sky. In fact, they did have a winged audience. "There's another eagle."

He gazed up. "Bald eagles are pretty impressive, aren't they?"

"That's a good word." The huge bird, soaring with its wings spread, had a wild kind of dignity and grace.

"He commands the skies."

"Like you, when you're flying."

Aaron gave a quick laugh and pulled on his shorts. "Now can we eat?"

"Yes, please. What have we got this time?" She slipped into her bra.

"Courtesy of the deli, there's shrimp salad on a croissant and a roast beef and roasted veggies panini."

"Yum." She finished putting on her clothing. "I'll take the shrimp salad, if that's okay."

"I kind of figured." He handed her a wrapped sandwich and took out a couple of bottles of sparkling fruit-flavored drinks. "I'd have brought wine or beer, but alcohol doesn't always combine that well with sunshine and exercise."

She swallowed a bite of the delicious croissantwich, enjoying the combination of fresh shrimp, dill, celery, and mayonnaise. "No, I wouldn't have thought so. Besides, I almost never drink during the day."

"Of course you don't." He winked at her.

"Am I really so predictable?" She sighed and answered her own question. "I guess being a rational, organized person does pretty much rule out any truly spontaneous, unpredictable, or eccentric behavior." Except for when she was, as he'd said, crazed with lust. "But what can I say? My parents raised me to be responsible."

A shadow darkened his eyes and then was gone. "I guess that's stood you in good stead in your job."

"In my entire life. I'm grateful to them." Hoping

that this time he wouldn't deflect, she said, "You never talk about your family."

"Nope."

She processed that flat refusal, combined with previous conversations, and didn't like the result she came up with. "You're really quite charming and fun to be with."

"I'd say thank you, but you've got that forehead scrunch happening."

"Charming yes, but you never talk about yourself. Not beyond a superficial level. Do you ever let anyone really get to know you?"

Aaron tried not to wince. She was right about him not spilling his guts all over the place, so why should he be insulted? He summoned a carefree grin. "Hate to disappoint you, but that's all there is. What you see is what you get. I like to fly, I like Destiny, I'm an outdoorsy guy, and I avoid commitments."

"Oh, come on, I bet you have hidden depths."

"Only in your imagination."

Her frown told him she wasn't amused.

"Why do you need me to have hidden depths?" he asked, a little annoyed. "This is a one-week relationship." That was the truth, and many of his other *relationships* lasted only a night or two, yet he felt an odd pang when he thought of Eden leaving in a couple of days.

Her frown deepened. "I know it is. But I like you, Aaron. You seem to be a nice guy."

"*Seem to be.* Gee, thanks. I like you, too."

"You can't just skate through life on the surface, not really caring about any person or cause. Can you?"

He ground his teeth, holding back an angry retort. Why should her opinion matter? After another swallow of juice, he said evenly, "You're being awfully judgmental. Not everyone wants as complicated a life as yours. There's nothing wrong with living life as it comes."

And yet there was something special about Eden, even though she sometimes got on his nerves. She was so involved and intense, setting her priorities and living life with total commitment. She was brave enough to love people and causes, to devote herself to them. He admired that quality, maybe even envied it.

He shrugged sudden tension from his shoulders. Why was he thinking this way? His past had taught him that love led only to disappointment and hurt, and he'd long ago learned to guard his heart. He wasn't going to change just because his latest *hookup* found him superficial.

"No," she said. "There's nothing wrong with that. If it makes you feel fulfilled." She turned her gaze from his face, picked up her drink bottle, and twisted off the cap. It felt like a deliberate dismissal.

Fine. He raised his own bottle again. Here he was at one of his favorite spots, having just made love with a beautiful woman, enjoying a tasty lunch, and yet he felt kind of . . . depressed? Lonely? Well, aloneness was the choice he'd made. No, it was the only way he knew how to be. So perhaps it wasn't as much choice as necessity.

As a little kid, he'd hoped in vain for a loving mom and a happy home life, until he'd finally learned to stop hoping. He'd tried to teach Miranda that lesson, but her heart wasn't as tough as his, and their mother had broken it over and over. As a teen, coming to

Destiny, he'd been stupid enough to listen to Miranda when she'd said that maybe it would be different with their grandparents, and they'd finally find a home. He'd maybe let himself hope, just a little. But both their hopes had been dashed by the icy welcome they'd received. Aaron had added a couple of layers to the shell around his heart.

The only people who had access to that rarely used organ were his sister and his niece. He wished Miranda would learn from experience, too, rather than persist in chasing after some dream of love the way their mom had. Love hadn't been their mother's destiny. Nor was it his or Miranda's.

Eden would find it, he figured. Things might not have worked out with her ex, and she might not be at the right place in her life now, but when she was ready she'd come up with some plan and meet a guy who gave her what she wanted. She'd have an organized life, the kind of life that would drive Aaron freaking nuts.

Seeking to restore a pleasant mood, he said, "We're seeing Darnell Lucas this afternoon." After that, there was only one more name on Eden's list, an elderly woman they'd visit the next morning. "Want to go someplace for dinner tonight or have it at my place?" He would keep her talking about her family and her work, and afterward they'd have sex, and things would go back to being easy between them.

"Thank you, but I'll have to pass on dinner. Things at the Foundation have been piling up and I need to do some work."

He wouldn't ask why her assistant couldn't handle this stuff. Eden had trouble delegating, not trusting anyone else to get things right. Or maybe work was an excuse and she'd written Aaron off. Testing, he said, "Tomorrow night's the dance at Quail Ridge Community Hall, with B-B-Zee playing."

"Oh, that's right. I really don't dance, so it's better if I don't go."

He didn't want her to be mad at him. He did want to teach her a few dance steps, or even just cling and shuffle around the dance floor. He wanted to see her reaction to the band and its eclectic selection of music and wanted her to be part of a foot-stomping Destiny Island Friday night. "Jonathan and Forbes invited you. You don't want to offend them, do you?"

"They probably don't even remember inviting me."

He heard doubt in her voice and shamelessly exploited it. "See, now you're acting like an outsider again. Islanders don't invite just anyone to their get-togethers. It's a sign of acceptance, and it'd be rude not to come." While it was true that islanders were chary with their invitations, it was also a fact that the Friday night dances were open to anyone who wanted to attend. In summer, half the crowd was tourists. "Your mom didn't bring you up to be rude."

"Of course not." She rubbed her temple, and he wondered if the sun and exertion, or their semiargument, had given her a headache. "Okay, I'll go. But only for a little while. I'll need to get packed and organized for Saturday."

She was booked on the Saturday morning Blue Moon Air flight to Vancouver, from which she'd fly to Ottawa. Back to her normal life.

Away from Destiny Island, and from him.

Chapter Twelve

When Aaron pulled up in his Jeep in front of the Once in a Blue Moon at 8:45 on Friday morning, Eden felt a surge of happiness at seeing him. She also felt relieved that as of tomorrow, she'd be on her way out of his life.

She hopped into the passenger seat and he leaned across to greet her with a quick kiss. "Get all your work done last night?" he asked.

"I did." It was true she'd caught up on Foundation business. What she didn't tell him, as he pulled away, was that she'd also done some serious thinking. Over the course of their time together, she'd started to develop feelings for Aaron. She'd begun to build up an image of him in her mind that was more fantasy than reality: that underneath his easygoing charm there was a deeper, more serious man. If that had been true, God knows what she'd have done, because he clearly belonged on Destiny Island just as she belonged in Ottawa with her family and her job. Not to mention, as she'd decided after the breakup with Ray, she didn't have time for a relationship anyhow.

But, thank heavens, she didn't have to deal with any of that. The conversation at yesterday's picnic had told her the truth. While it was possible there was more to Aaron than met the eye, he wasn't about to admit to it—at least not to her. He was fun company, but he either lacked the depth and the desire to commit or he had no interest in a commitment to her. She was disappointed, she had to admit, but mostly relieved.

She shot a glance at the attractive man beside her, looking so relaxed and non-Ottawa in his slightly rumpled cargo shorts and a sage T-shirt. He was like the eagle in the sky, the seals swimming in the ocean: lovely to enjoy in the moment and sweet memories to take home. But that was it.

Tomorrow she'd return to Ottawa and give her all to her family and job, until her mom's health and state of mind improved. When she was ready to date again, she'd have an even clearer idea of what she was looking for. The collapse of her relationship with Ray had taught her that she wanted a man who valued family and respected her commitment to hers. Being with Aaron had shown her that, though she didn't require a man who was a total do-gooder, she could only love a man with strong values and commitments of his own.

If a relationship led to insights, it was a good thing. Aaron had taught her another thing or two about herself—like the importance of flexibility and taking an occasional break from work, and the value and pleasure of physical exercise. It would be interesting to see her family's reaction to this new version of herself. A pang of homesickness struck. But she reminded herself she'd be back tomorrow, in time for a family dinner.

At which she'd have to confess that she'd failed dismally at finding Lucy.

Aaron said all she could do was her best, and she knew her parents would echo that sentiment. Kelsey, of course, would hoot over the fact that her *perfect* big sister had failed to deliver. Unless, of course, this morning's interview bore fruit. Eden didn't have high hopes. Marlise had given her Gertie Montgomery's name, saying that the former public health nurse had once mentioned treating a girl from the commune. But, Marlise had warned, Mrs. Montgomery, who was now in her eighties, suffered from Alzheimer's.

"Still thinking about last night's work?" Aaron asked. "What was it anyhow?"

She changed mental gears. "The most important was reviewing my assistant's notes about a meeting with a prospective applicant for funding." Navdeep hadn't sent her his notes until two and a half days after the meeting, but it turned out he'd had a good reason. He'd taken the initiative to do considerable background research on the organization, a charity located not far from Ottawa that provided equine therapy for wounded veterans. His report had been comprehensive, including the group's composition, history, financial statements, and past and current activities. He'd concluded with his recommendation that he and Eden move ahead to the next step: working with the organization to put together a strong application that the Butterworth Foundation's board was likely to approve.

Eden had reviewed every detail and had only a few suggestions to offer, additional details to check into.

If Navdeep followed through on those today and the results were positive, next week they could contact the organization, give them the good news, and begin the in-depth work with them. She loved that stage and knew that together, this applicant and the Foundation could do some very worthwhile work.

Often, she got so enthused about some of the funded programs that she wished she could get more intensively involved. More than one had offered her a job, but she'd turned them down because there were so many other worthwhile projects that might not get funded without her efforts. Like the equine therapy one. She had a really good feeling about it.

She turned to Aaron, eager to share her excitement, and then thought better of it and gazed out the window. The road was one she hadn't been on before, running along the west shore of Blue Moon Harbor. Houses were scattered along each side of the road. The ones on the ocean side were set back behind trees on sizable lots; on the other side, modest houses sat on smaller properties, most with nice gardens. Aaron pointed out one of those houses as being the home of Jillian, the other pilot, whom she'd met briefly. An occasional gardener, dog walker, or cyclist raised a hand in greeting as they drove by. Ottawa was going to seem very formal and fast-paced after this.

"You don't want to talk about it?" Aaron asked.

"Talk about what?"

"The applicant?"

"Oh." She shrugged. "They look like a good possibility." Previously, she'd gushed on and on about her work. Last night, thinking about all her chats with Aaron, she realized she'd talked to him with few filters, sharing information and feelings about her family and her job. She'd always been outgoing rather than reticent, but with Aaron it felt so disproportionate, the way she'd shared and he'd tried to keep things light. They'd agreed on a fun, no-strings relationship, and though he kept teasing her about being so serious, she'd persisted in doing it. He'd been a good listener, seeming to be interested, asking good questions, even offering a few insights, but likely he'd been bored out of his mind and just being polite. Last night she'd told herself to lighten up in both her emotions and her behavior.

"This place we're going," she said, "Arbutus Lodge. Is it a nice seniors' home? My grandmother—" She broke off, stopping herself from blurting out another rambling family story.

"Did she go to one?"

"No, she died at home, the way she wanted it." Nana had flatly refused to consider any kind of residential or care facility. She'd said those places were filled with decrepit, senile old people, and while she might be in her eighties, she was nowhere near being decrepit nor senile. She'd been correct on both counts. Fortunately, she'd had Eden's family to help her out, and the money to hire a housekeeper who also prepared dinners. Nana had been able to stay in her own town house until she died unexpectedly from a massive stroke.

"Good for her. Sadly, Mrs. Montgomery doesn't have that option. She did live with her daughter's family up at Sunset Cove for a couple of years, but they couldn't keep an eye on her 24/7. She wandered off, almost set fire to the house. The family doesn't have the money for full-time, live-in care, so Arbutus Lodge was the next best option."

"You know a lot about her."

"Most islanders fly with Blue Moon Air now and then. They talk, I listen. As for the lodge, from what I've heard, it's a nice place and the staff are competent and friendly."

They were quiet then, until he pulled into the parking lot of an attractive two-story structure painted a sunny pale yellow with bright blue trim. Its wings spread across a grassy area with trees, flower beds, walkways, and benches. Ten or so people were outside, wandering lazily or seated on benches or in wheelchairs. A moderately high wooden fence marked off the property, but any sense of imprisonment was softened by vines of clematis and Virginia creeper.

When Eden and Aaron walked through the front door, the inside was equally bright and appealing and the air smelled of pine needles. Behind a reception desk sat a pretty young woman with delicate Asian features and short black hair in a flattering pixie cut. She looked up and smiled brightly. "Aaron! Hi, it's been a while." A name tag pinned to her pink blouse identified her, in large type, as Glory.

"Hey, Glory," Aaron said. "Yeah, it has. You coming to the B-B-Zee dance tonight?"

"You bet."

"Save me a dance, okay?"

Oh, great. Eden was leaving tomorrow and Aaron was already lining up his next fling.

But then Glory said, "Definitely. Brent's always glad to sit one out. He says I have to stop wearing him out on the dance floor or he won't have enough energy for anything else, once we get home." She giggled. "If you know what I mean." And then she turned to Eden. "I'm sorry. Old friends catching up."

Aaron snorted. "Old friends?"

"Okay," Glory told Eden, "we weren't exactly friends in school. I got to know Aaron after Blue Moon Air started offering free flights to our residents who have medical appointments in Victoria or Vancouver and can't afford the fare."

How nice of the airline's owner. "Hello, Glory. I'm Eden Blaine and I'm—"

"Here to talk to Mrs. Montgomery," the other woman said. "Yes, I was the one who talked to Aaron when he set it up."

"Thanks for suggesting that we come in the morning, when she's at her sharpest."

"You'll enjoy her. Gertie's delightful, and she's always glad to have company. Her memory's erratic, but Aaron said you wanted to ask her some questions about the past, and that's what she does best with."

"Will she be in her room?" Eden asked.

"Probably," Glory answered. "She likes a sit-down with the morning paper after breakfast. She doesn't read books anymore because she can't remember what she's read, but with newspapers she says it's all fresh every day anyhow. She's in 403, which is on the ground floor of wing four, just through that door." She pointed. "If you don't find her there, let me know and I'll have one of the staff hunt her down."

Eden thanked her, and she and Aaron headed in the direction Glory had indicated. Artwork lined the walls, some of it excellent and some pretty awful, but each piece was framed and had a card beside it with the title of the painting, the artist's name, and a date.

Walking past a charming watercolor of a cottage surrounded by roses in bloom, with a couple of kids' old-fashioned bicycles in the yard, she said, "Oh, look."

She caught Aaron's arm, stopping him. "See this? It was done by Gertrude Montgomery."

He gazed at the painting, seeming almost captivated. "It looks like a home, a family home," he murmured under his breath in a tone that sounded rather like envy.

"It does." She linked her arm through his and they continued on to suite 403.

When Aaron tapped on the door, a female voice called, "Come in."

They stepped through to see a cozy sitting room, the furniture upholstered in flowered fabric and more paintings on the wall. A woman with short, curly white hair and glasses, clad in a purple-and-white-striped top and mom jeans, looked up from her seat in a chair by the window and folded the newspaper she'd been holding. A walker sat beside the chair. The room smelled faintly of lavender.

"I do apologize," the woman said. "I thought it was one of the staff, so I didn't get up and come to the door." She made as if to rise.

Eden and Aaron hurried over. "No, please don't get up, Mrs. Montgomery," he said.

Gray eyes with a hint of violet focused on him. "You're Aaron Gabriel. You flew me over to Victoria when I needed those tests at the hospital."

"Yes, ma'am."

"My memory isn't what it used to be, but I certainly remember a handsome, well-mannered boy like you. And now you've come to visit me. How lovely."

"It's my pleasure. Mrs. Montgomery, I'd like you to meet—"

"Gertie. Call me Gertie."

"Okay, Gertie. And this is Eden Blaine, who's—"

Again she interrupted him, shifting her gaze to Eden. "I don't know you, do I? You're not an islander?"

"No, Mrs. Montgomery. Uh, Gertie?" She wasn't sure whether the first-name invitation extended to her. "I'm from Ottawa, visiting the island."

"Are you one of the ones who'll stay? Some stay, you know."

"I've heard that. But no, I'm not. My family and my job are back in Ottawa."

"Family is what matters," the elderly lady said firmly. "For heaven's sake, sit down, you two."

Eden and Aaron seated themselves side by side on the couch.

"I agree totally about the importance of family," Eden said. "It's my family that's brought me here." She had struck it lucky, with Gertie Montgomery seeming entirely lucid. But that state might not last, so she skipped the backstory and got straight to the point. "My mom wants to track down her long-lost sister, Lucy Nelson. She came here and joined the commune in 1969, when she was seventeen. I wondered if you might have run into her."

"I was, hmm, thirty-five in 1969. Married, with two children under ten. A public health nurse. The medical clinic consisted of two rooms off the fire station. A visiting doctor came twice a week, and so did a dentist. There was a midwife and there was me."

What a lot of responsibility this woman must have had. "Did you have dealings with any of the members of the commune?" Eden asked.

"They kept to themselves and didn't come to the clinic. One of the members had some first aid training."

"How do you know that?" Aaron asked.

"Di told me."

"Di SkySong?" he said.

The elusive Di, who, along with her husband, Seal, were the two people on Eden's list who she hadn't been able to interview because they hadn't yet returned to the island.

"Yes. When she brought that other girl to the clinic."

"When was that?" Eden asked.

"Let me see . . . I think it would have been 1970 or '71."

Was there any chance . . . ? Voice trembling, Eden asked, "Do you remember the other girl's name? Or what she looked like?"

"Oh my. It was one of those hippie names. Ah yes, Starshine, like in the musical, *Hair*. 'Good Morning Starshine,' that was a song from *Hair*. Pretty song."

Lucy could have taken a hippie name. "Did the girl have brown hair?"

"No, blond. Almost white-blond. Long, beautiful hair." She gave a girlish laugh. "That's from the musical, too, you know."

Disappointment clogged Eden's throat.

Aaron spoke again. "Why did they come, Gertie, if it was so rare for commune members to visit the clinic?"

"Starshine had miscarried and was bleeding badly," the former nurse said. "Di had a brain or two in her head, young as she was, and realized that the girl might die without proper medical attention. They'd already had one death at the commune, a boy who overdosed, and she didn't want another."

Her curiosity engaged, Eden asked, "Were you or the doctor able to help Starshine?"

"It wasn't one of Dr. Miles's days, and the midwife

was off island. I got the bleeding stopped, but Starshine was badly bruised and I worried about internal injuries."

Eden caught her breath. Had the girl been abused?

Gertie went on. "I told Di to bring her back in two days, when Dr. Miles would be in, or earlier if her condition worsened. We could have taken her to the hospital in Victoria. But they never returned. I hoped that meant the girl was okay." Her eyes, sharp until then, went dreamy. She began to sing, mumbling the words. Eden caught the word *starshine*, and something about twinkling below, and then there was just a string of nonsense syllables.

Compassion filled Eden. How tragic that a woman who'd been so accomplished could have her mind slowly taken over by dementia. She was reminded of her mother's situation, though at least with breast cancer there was a strong chance of defeating the disease—which her mom was definitely going to do. "Mrs. Montgomery? Gertie?"

"I was too old. Too old to be a hippie." At least these words made sense, but she sounded vague. "Kind of a pity. Bells and flowers."

"Bells and flowers are lovely, aren't they?" Eden feared they'd lost her, and it didn't really matter. Yet the woman's comments had reawakened Eden's curiosity about the Enchantery. If Starshine had been abused, the same might have happened to Lucy. "Gertie," she said gently, "you mentioned that Starshine was bruised. You mean she'd fallen?"

"Fallen," the older woman echoed, as if she wasn't sure what the word meant. Then her gaze and tone sharpened. "That girl fell on a boot."

Eden caught her breath. "You mean someone kicked her? Kicked her in the belly when she was pregnant?"

"Boots," Gertie said, dreamy again. "I have the prettiest red cowgirl boots. I wonder where I put them?" She smiled at Eden. "Do you like to dance, dear?"

Eden smiled back, her heart going out to the other woman. "As a matter of fact, I'm going dancing tonight. With Aaron."

"Aaron? Who's Aaron?"

Eden glanced at him and he shook his head slightly. They both rose and Aaron said, "It's been a pleasure talking to you, Gertie."

The woman looked at him blankly, as if she had no recollection of their conversation. And maybe she didn't.

Eden touched her age-spotted hand. "May I take a quick look at your paintings before we go?" She gestured around the room.

Gertie's face brightened. "Yes, yes. I do love to paint."

Eden walked around the room, recognizing that the watercolors and pencil sketches of places and people were unskilled, yet the artist had a knack for capturing the character of her subjects. "These are wonderful," she said sincerely. "I envy you your talent."

She and Aaron said their good-byes and left the room, closing the door quietly. As they walked down the hall, Eden sighed. "What a lovely woman and what a terrible disease."

"It doesn't seem like she's unhappy."

"I hope not. But I bet she was plenty unhappy when she was diagnosed. As a former nurse, she'd have been very aware of what was in store for her."

They continued on in silence, pausing only to say, "See you at the dance," to Glory.

Once they were in the Jeep, Eden said, "I haven't seen it. The commune. I've been talking to all these people about it, but I've never actually seen it."

"There isn't much to see now. The buildings weren't well constructed and they collapsed over time."

She felt the rare urge to cry. She must be PMSing, because suddenly it was all too much. She had failed her mom. She was sad about Gertie Montgomery's Alzheimer's and about her mom's cancer. Sad for her aunt, who seemed to have disappeared without anyone in the family even noticing. Sad that after to-morrow morning's flight, she'd never see Aaron again. Even the idea that the old commune—once a place that carried the hopes and dreams of a group of young people—was now just a bunch of fallen-down shacks made her sad.

So much for lightening up. She took a deep breath, fighting for control, determined not to inflict her melancholy on Aaron. "Could you tell me how to get there? I think I'll take my rental car and go see it."

"You'll never find it." He touched her shoulder. "Are you okay?"

"Sure." She strove for cheerfulness. "Looking forward to that dance tonight, though I'll no doubt step all over your toes."

"Uh-huh. Look, I've got a couple of flights today, but how about I pick you up around five and we'll go out to the commune, then grab a snack before the dance?"

She couldn't hold on to the forced smile. Instead, she gazed into his bluish-gray eyes and said, "I already owe you so much, Aaron. You've spent a good part of your week chauffeuring me around and introducing me to islanders. You could have been flying or"—or hanging out with a woman who'd show him a much better time—"or doing way more fun things. I must be the worst fling you've ever had."

"Don't be silly." His smile seemed warm and genuine. "You're good company and it's been interesting, talking to all those people and learning about the commune."

"You're a nice man."

He rolled his eyes. "I'm a selfish guy. I do what I want." He turned the key in the ignition and backed the Jeep out of the parking spot. "I'll pick you up at five. No arguing."

Chapter Thirteen

Aaron leaned against the front of the Jeep, watching Eden wander across the grassy meadow. She lingered by the ruins of a couple of shacks, the weathered gray boards nearly swallowed up by salal and blackberry bushes. She stooped to pick a daisy and twirled it between her fingers, then paused by a gnarled apple tree to stroke its bark.

She could almost have been one of the hippies from the old days, the way she looked right now. For the first time, she wore a skirt. Not a tailored, lawyer-type one but the kind sold in the shops on Driftwood Road: light cotton, down to the ankles, soft and floaty. So gauzy that, in certain lighting, he saw the slender lines of her legs through the swirly yellow- and orange-patterned fabric. On her feet were flat sandals with multicolored straps. Her top was close-fitting and sleeveless, a warm yellow he guessed would bring out the gold flecks in her amber eyes. He hadn't been able to test his theory because she had yet to take off her sunglasses.

When he had picked her up, she'd been chatty,

asking him more about island history and saying she was sorry they'd never had a chance to go out sailing. She'd seemed upbeat and yet it hadn't rung true. This morning, when they'd talked to Gertie Montgomery, he'd seen how Eden respected the woman and tried to relate to her. He'd sensed Eden's emotions and her openness, things he'd liked about her from the beginning. But since then, with him, she'd kept things on a superficial level.

He missed the real Eden. Was she upset with him? Pulling away? It was logical that she might, because she was leaving tomorrow. So why should it bother him?

When he'd bumped the Jeep over the almost nonexistent dirt-and-grass track to the commune, she'd fallen silent. He'd sensed she wanted to experience this place on her own, to perhaps imagine her aunt dancing on the grass with a chain of daisies in her hair, or eating an apple she'd just picked, warm from the sun, sweet and juicy.

Now Eden made her way toward him, walking slowly across the rough grass. "I'm ready to go," she said quietly.

Her hair was loose and wavy on her shoulders. He touched a strand, warm and silky between his fingers. "What do you think of the place?"

"It's peaceful. It's hard to imagine all the sex, drugs, and rock and roll people keep talking about." She glanced around, her hair slipping from his fingers. "But I can imagine unhappy or troubled young people wanting to escape to a place like this. I can imagine dreamers and idealists bringing their dreams here."

"Dreams. Yeah, I guess." As a child, he'd had dreams. Not ones of a utopian sex-and-drugs-for-all commune but far more conventional: of a happy, loving home.

Those dreams sure hadn't been realized in Vancouver's Downtown Eastside, nor with any foster family, and nor when he and Miranda had moved in with their grand-parents. At the age of sixteen, he'd realized it was stupid to have dreams that depended on other people. You should only dream about things within your control: like living on Destiny Island and being a pilot. He never *dreamed* about things going better for Miranda and Ariana; he only tried to be a good brother.

"We should go," Eden said, her tone brisk now.

"Take off your sunglasses," he said, needing to see her eyes, their expression. To find out if he'd been right about the gold flecks.

"Why?" But she didn't wait for his answer, just took them off and held them in one hand.

Her beautiful eyes sparkled up at him, brighter than the stones in her new earrings.

"You dazzle me," he said, the words jumping out of his mouth. The kind of compliment he'd never before given.

Her eyes widened and then her lips made a tentative curve. "You kind of dazzle me, too, Aaron Gabriel."

"Then why are you acting different today? It feels like you're pulling away." Oh God, he was mouthing girlie, needy shit. Still, he didn't take it back.

"I . . . Pulling away? What do you mean?"

She'd given him a chance to retreat, but he didn't take it. "You're acting different. Not sharing stuff the way you usually do."

She blinked, gazed down for a long moment, and then looked back up at him. "You're right." Another blink, but then she held his gaze. "The truth is, I realized I was coming to . . . well, maybe more than just like you. Even though that's not what we agreed, or what either of us want. I guess it's the danger of a rebound relationship." She pressed her lips together.

So he was just a *rebound relationship*. She'd have felt the same for any guy she hooked up with. Again, why should that bother him?

Because for him she wasn't just another fun hookup. Eden was special. Clearly, she didn't feel the same way about him.

She unpressed her lips. "But then I realized I was being silly. You're a great guy, but not the type of man I'd be looking for if I wanted a serious relationship."

Hurt and pissed off, he was about to ask what the hell was wrong with him, and then he remembered he had zero interest in a serious relationship. That must be what she meant. "No, I guess not, eh?" He managed a small laugh.

"I want a man who sees life in more of a serious, responsible way, rather than being all about having a good time. One who's passionate about things other than the outdoors, flying, and, well, sex. A man who does have depths and is willing to share them with me."

"Yeah, that's not me."

She blinked again and said quietly, almost sadly, "You kept telling me that, and I finally realized I should listen." Another blink, and she spoke more briskly. "Anyhow, I also thought about how you told me I needed to lighten up and have fun. That's what this week was supposed to be about. You've taken time off work and gone to all the effort of helping me look for my aunt, which I truly appreciate. In return, did I give you fun?"

Being with her had been different. Not as frivolous as times he'd spent with other women, but in truth more fun. He was trying to figure out how to respond when she went on.

"Not so much, right? I was forever dumping family stories and work ones on you. Just as I'd do if I were seriously dating someone. I guess I don't know how else to act. So I've decided to take my cue from you and lighten up on the heavy stuff. I'm not great at it, but I'm trying."

I liked you the old way. She might say *lighten up*, but he felt as if she'd erected a barrier between them.

Just as he did, between him and the rest of the world.

"I get it," he told her. "But don't stress out over it, okay? I'm not changing for you and I don't want you changing for me. Relax and be yourself and we'll have a nice evening."

A smile bloomed, and again he was dazzled as she said, "Sounds good to me."

"Then let's go get a burger. There's a bistro at the Blue Heron Marina, not too far from here." He'd noticed she rarely ate red meat, so he added, "They also make terrific crab rolls and popcorn shrimp."

"I'm hungry already."

He gave her a light kiss and they headed off to get dinner.

Over the meal—with her choosing a crab roll and them sharing an order of French fries—they speculated about what it would have been like to be a teenager in 1969 and about the good and bad features of communes.

After they'd argued over the bill and he'd finally agreed to splitting it down the middle, Aaron said, "The SkySongs should be coming back next week.

How about you email me the photos of Lucy, and I'll show them to Di and Seal."

"Thank you. With no one else providing any useful information, I'm not optimistic, but I want to know I've exhausted all avenues." She pulled out her phone, asked for his email address, and tapped away.

"I'll let you know what they say." He wasn't optimistic either, though he'd sure like to be able to help Eden find her aunt.

"Would you ask about Starshine, too? Hopefully, Di SkySong will know how things turned out for her." She wrinkled her nose. "Call me crazy, but I hate not knowing how a story ends."

"Sure. I'm curious, too." If the story ending was an unhappy one, would he tell Eden? Even though she was strong and capable, for some reason she made him feel protective. It was odd; until now he'd only ever felt protective of Miranda and Ariana.

Eden made him feel things. Respect, maybe even some envy. Annoyance sometimes. Frustration. Tenderness. The shell around his heart had never been endangered by any other lover, yet now it had developed a hairline crack and a weird mix of emotions was trickling out. The experience was confusing and disturbing. It was a good thing she was leaving tomorrow.

"Let's go to the community hall and I'll teach you the two-step," he said.

As they left the Blue Heron Bistro, Eden asked, "Am I dressed all right? The woman at the store said it was either a long skirt or jeans, and she suggested fancy cowgirl boots. I couldn't imagine buying cowgirl boots and besides, I don't want to do any permanent damage when I stomp all over your feet."

He chuckled. "You look great, Eden. And hopefully I'm a good enough teacher that there'll be no stomping."

On the way to the parking lot, with his arm around her slender waist, he asked, "You ever gonna wear that skirt again when you get back to Ottawa? Or those pretty earrings?"

She reached up to set an earring swinging. "The skirt will be nice for relaxing after work or at my parents' house. And the earrings if I go out for dinner."

Who would she be going out with? She'd said her priorities didn't include dating. He mulled that over as he drove the short distance to the Quail Ridge Community Hall. Music was already throbbing out the open doors of the steepled wooden building, a pioneer church that had been repurposed and expanded after the congregation built a fancier one.

"That's country music, isn't it?" Eden asked as they went up the stairs. "I don't know much about it, but I recognize the twang."

"Yeah, that one's country, but B-B-Zee plays a mix. Country, pop, rock, folk songs. Not much hip hop, rap, or that kind of stuff. A few numbers they wrote themselves." As he spoke, one song ended and another began, an edgier one, as if to illustrate his point. He cocked his ear. "They sound different tonight. I'm guessing . . ." As he and Eden walked through the door, he gazed toward the stage. "Yeah, they've got a third B tonight."

On stage were three sixtysomething men dressed in faded jeans and casual shirts or, in Forbes's case, a tie-dyed T-shirt. The fourth man, much younger, wore ripped black jeans and a black tee with a hole in it. A tattoo snaked down one arm. "You know Jonathan Barnes and Forbes Blake," Aaron said. "The other older guy with the big mustache is Christian Zabec. The younger one with the guitar is Forbes's son, Julian. He's a professional musician, making a bit of a name for himself. In Canada, anyhow." Julian, a couple of years younger than Aaron, had, like him, been a loner in school. And, like Miranda, he'd dropped out and left the island. Now he came back once or twice a year to visit his parents and half brother.

Aaron walked into the room, looking for space at one of the tables edging the dance floor, and then realized Eden hadn't budged. Turning back, he saw her staring at the stage. "Eden?"

"He looks like a tarnished angel. The tattered black, the tattoo, and that golden hair."

He stared again at Julian. A tarnished angel? What the hell did that mean? And then it sank in, leaving a bitter taste in his mouth. Jealousy was such an unaccustomed emotion that at first he didn't recognize it. "You think he's hot."

"Every woman who's still breathing would think he's hot." Eden glanced up at him, mischief dancing in her eyes. "The same as with you, Mr. Gabriel. Though in a different way."

"The same but in a different way? I'm lost."

She huffed out air, as if the concept was entirely obvious and he was a dunce for not understanding. "You're charming, laid-back hot. He's intense, playing-with-fire hot. Do you know what I mean?"

Julian was the type of man Miranda and their mom went for. "Got it." Frowning, he said, "I wouldn't have thought he was your type."

Her eyes widened. "Of course he's not. Not in the least. Me, with a musician like that? I don't think so."

Her lips quirked. "That doesn't mean I can't look and enjoy, though."

More at ease now, Aaron joked, "When men look at pretty women, they get dumped on. How come women are allowed to look?"

"Because on occasion the double standard needs to work in our favor," she shot back.

Laughing, he laced his fingers through hers and they walked across the big room. Aaron exchanged waves and hellos with a number of islanders and chatted with a few. He introduced Eden to Sonia Russo, Forbes Blake's wife and stepmother to Julian. She was sitting with her son, Luke Chandler, who'd been a year behind Aaron in high school. The island veterinarian and a widower raising young twin boys, Luke had a life that was pretty much the opposite of Julian's unattached, on-the-road musician existence.

A tarnished angel. Honestly. Women.

Glory waved from a small table, and he steered Eden in her direction. "Want to sit with us?" Glory asked. "Pull up a couple of chairs. Brent went to get beers."

"Thanks," Eden said, as Aaron found chairs and squeezed them in around the table.

"What would you like to drink?" he asked Eden, and then went to the crowded bar to get a glass of wine for her and a light beer for himself.

Waiting for the drinks, he watched the dance floor. Busy already, it held a mix of residents and tourists dressed in everything from shorts and flip-flops to cowboy boots and hats. Ages ranged from twenties to the eightysomething Nelsons, him deftly maneuvering his wheelchair while his petite wife perched in his lap with her arms around his shoulders.

And there it was: the dream. Oh, not being confined to a chair, of course. But that happily-ever-after dream. Someone who loved you, who gave you a home, who stuck by you through thick and thin, who put up with your bad habits just as you put up with theirs.

His mom hadn't given him that, nor had his grandparents. He and Miranda would always love each other, but she had her own life and wasn't about to return to Destiny with Ariana and nest build so Uncle Aaron had a ready-made family. In his teens, Aaron had hardened his heart to the idea of ever finding what the Nelsons shared. He'd convinced himself he didn't want it. So why, now, was he watching them with envy?

The bartender handed him the bottle of beer and glass of wine. Across the room, through the shifting patterns of dancers, Aaron saw Eden with Glory. Brent hadn't made it back to the table yet and the two women were deep in conversation. The soft smile on Eden's lips made him guess they were discussing Gertie Montgomery.

The patterns of people and colors shifted and grew hazy, like he'd had too much to drink even though he hadn't yet touched a drop. Or like he was dreaming. He saw one couple who looked familiar: a tall, dark-haired man and a brown-haired woman, their arms wrapped around each other with long-time familiarity and love. They looked like him and Eden, except both heads were streaked with gray.

A vision of the future? A dream?

He squeezed his eyes shut, raised the bottle to his mouth for a long swallow of beer, and looked again. The room was back to normal. So was his stupid brain. He wasn't a dreamer. He wasn't falling in love with a woman who'd made her priorities crystal clear—and they didn't include him. To wish for a future with Eden would be to set himself up for heartbreak.

As he wove through the crowded tables that lined the dance floor, he realized something. From what Eden had said out at the old commune, she'd gone through this same thought process. She'd thought she might be developing feelings for him but quickly understood that it would be crazy to do so. She had concluded that he wasn't the kind of man she could ever love.

He figured she was right about that. He also knew he wasn't the kind of man who could ever allow himself to love.

"Have a drink." He thrust the wineglass at her. "Then let's dance the night away."

She and Glory both stared at him in surprise. That soft, revealing look left Eden's face and she gave him a bright smile. "Prepare to have your feet stomped on."

Saturday morning, Eden woke in her bed at the B and B to the alarm's insistent beep. Despite the need to shower, dress, and throw the last items in her carry-on, she lay under the covers for one more moment.

Her feet and legs ached. She and Aaron had danced until late, some fast numbers but also some slow, poignant ones during which she'd nestled close to him and felt their bodies move as one. At one point, she'd buried her face against his shoulder to hide the tears in her eyes. The band had been singing a song called "Fly Away With Me," which they said was written by Matteo Brancaleoni. The lyrics, about honoring your feelings and giving your heart, about flying away together like eagles, touched a chord in her heart.

How foolish to long for a dream that was impossible for so many reasons.

She'd pulled away before the song ended, using the excuse that it was almost eleven. "It's late, and my flight's early tomorrow. As you well know, because you're the pilot."

"I'd better take you back to the Once," Aaron had said, "so you can get a decent sleep."

He hadn't invited her to his place and she hadn't suggested it. If they'd made love one last time, she'd have ended up sobbing. Her brain knew it would be crazy to care for him, but her heart seemed to have a mind of its own.

They'd driven without exchanging more than a few words, the top up on his Jeep. After a night of booming music, the comparative silence—just a few rattly vehicle sounds—made her ears ring. When he pulled up in front of the B and B, he'd climbed out and walked her up the steps. At the front door, he put his hands on her shoulders and placed a kiss on the top of her head, then her nose, and finally her lips. Light kisses, yet she felt each one with an intensity he no doubt didn't intend.

After their lips brushed, they'd murmured, "Good night," and she'd gone inside, again battling tears. She'd walked through the lobby, remembering how Bernie had warned her about Aaron that very first morning—and how Eden had blithely asserted that her heart was in no danger.

Upstairs in bed, she'd refused to let the tears fall.

Fortunately, she'd slept soundly until the alarm went off. But now, as she forced herself out of bed, depression slowed her movements. The taste of failure was sour in her mouth. She'd failed to find her aunt and hated to think how disappointed her mom would be. She'd let irrational feelings spoil her enjoyment of her rebound fling and now her memories of lovely times on Destiny would be tinged with sadness.

In the shower, she scrubbed vigorously, trying to rub energy into her body. Tonight, she'd be home in Ottawa. Dad or Kelsey would pick her up at the airport, and then they'd all be sitting around the table at her parents' house. Even if she wasn't returning with good news, the people she loved would welcome her with open hearts.

She dressed in comfortable travel clothes and threw the last odds and ends into her bag. The carry-on was lighter than when she'd come because she'd made enough purchases that she had packed a box and shipped it home the day before.

In the breakfast room, she picked up a takeout cup of coffee along with one of Bernie's delicious raspberry-oat muffins, which she'd eat in Vancouver International Airport while she waited for her flight.

Bernie and Jonathan came into the lobby to say good-bye. Bernie, who hadn't been at the dance last night, was perky. Jonathan, who'd still been playing the fiddle when Eden and Aaron left, looked worn-out but content. "You've been perfect hosts," Eden told them, "and your B and B is wonderful."

"I hope we'll see you back one day," Bernie said.

"Thanks, but I'm afraid that's not likely." Eden didn't envision holiday time in her future. And if she did take time off work, the last place she'd go was an island filled with memories of Aaron—not to mention the possibility of seeing him with his latest hookup.

Jonathan pulled her bag down the wheelchair ramp and she walked behind him, to where Aaron waited with his Jeep. Initially, she'd booked a 7:00 a.m. flight, but last night Aaron had said the departure time had changed to 7:30. Though she'd turned in her rental car yesterday, she'd told him she could get her bags to the dock, figuring he'd have preflight things to do. However, he'd insisted on picking her up.

"Seeing your family this weekend?" he asked once she'd climbed into the Jeep.

"Dinner tonight. I'll spend part of the day there tomorrow, too, as well as going into the office for a couple of hours." She gave a humorless laugh. "Yes, despite your best efforts to lighten me up, I'm the same woman who arrived here a week ago."

"I like that woman," he said quietly as he steered the Jeep into the village parking lot.

After taking her luggage out of the back, he led her directly down to the dock, not stopping in the office. She'd expected to check in, then join a group of passengers waiting to board the de Havilland Beaver. Instead, there were no people on the dock, and the only plane tied up was the blue-and-white Cessna four-seater. "Where's the other plane?"

He opened the door and stowed her bags. "Jillian took the seven o'clock flight, with stops in Victoria and on Mayne Island."

"That's the flight I booked."

"I changed things so I could take you. Rather than fly into Vancouver Harbour Flight Centre, I'm taking you to a seaplane dock on the Fraser River. There'll be a taxi waiting and it's a five-minute ride to the main terminal of the airport. Climb in."

She obeyed, wondering why he'd made the change. Did he want to be alone with her? Or did he think she might go all girlie and make some kind of emotional scene in front of other passengers? She could have asked, but he'd only give her a flip answer, so she didn't bother.

They remained silent until they were in the air, flying out of Blue Moon Harbor. Eden sighed. "I came here with such high hopes. I hate letting Mom down. I've always been the one my parents could count on. It's Kelsey who often disappoints them."

Aaron glanced over, then out the windshield, and then back at her, like he was debating whether to say something.

"What?" she asked.

"I've heard you say that before, and I've told you that all you can do is your best. As for your sister . . . well, maybe you're being kind of judgmental. You *and* your parents. Seems to me you need to respect your sister's independence and her right to make mistakes, even when you think she should do things differently."

"What?" Here she was, feeling emotionally fragile, and he had to go and criticize her? Hurt and annoyed, she said, "I didn't ask for your opinion. Especially on a subject you clearly know nothing about."

"Hey, I was just trying to be helpful." He sounded a little ticked off, too. "And yeah, I do know something about it. I have a younger sister, too. An independent one with a daughter and a pretty fucked-up life, who resists most of my efforts to help her. But that's her right and I have to respect that. I mean, it's her life."

He had a sister? A niece? All week he'd kept his mouth shut about his family while Eden went on and on about hers. They'd been lovers and she thought they'd become friends, but he hadn't even shared these significant details? In fact, he'd led her to believe there was no one in his life he cared deeply about. Stunned, she said, "You have a sister and a niece? And you're only now telling me? That's . . . it's rude, shutting me out like that."

"Shutting you out?" He shot her a nasty glance. "Just because you share all your personal shit with everyone you meet, that doesn't mean it's a good thing."

And they were back to that. She connected on a serious level with people, shared with them, cared about them. Maybe he did that with his sister and niece—perhaps with his parents and whatever other family he had—but he sure wasn't going to share anything meaningful with a random female he picked up for a week's fling. "Whatever," she muttered.

For the rest of the trip, she kept her mouth shut and her hands clasped tightly in her lap. This past week, she'd barely once felt the urge to bite her nails, but this morning it was back.

She noted the scenery below but didn't ask what she was looking at, and Aaron didn't tell her. Twenty minutes after takeoff, he flew along the mouth of a large, muddy river—the Fraser, she assumed—and took the plane down. He motored it to a wooden dock with a ramp and a small, open-sided roofed shelter with a Canadian flag flying from the top. Up on the road, she saw a parked yellow taxi.

Though she was still upset, she didn't want to leave things like this. And so, after Aaron helped her clamber from the plane to the dock, she said, "Let's not part on bad terms. We know we're different kinds of people and there's no point getting mad about it."

He gave a curt nod. "Agreed. Sorry. I wanted this to be a nice flight for you, something special you'd remember once you were home." He gave a tentative smile. "Now I'm hoping you'll forget all about it."

She smiled, too, relieved but sad. "I have a lot of wonderful memories of Destiny Island, most of them thanks to you." It wasn't his fault she'd proved incapable of a casual fling.

"I can leave the Cessna here for a few minutes. I'll take your bags up to the taxi."

"Thanks."

Side by side, they walked up the ramp and along a wharf to shore. A woman popped out of the taxi, waved, and opened the trunk as they approached.

Aaron hoisted the wheeled bag into it and the driver returned to her seat.

He turned to Eden. "Have a good trip home. I'll be in touch."

She nodded. "Thanks again. For everything." Even, perhaps, for the confusion and hurt, because they'd helped her clarify what kind of man and relationship she was looking for.

"You too."

She wasn't sure which one of them moved first, or maybe they did it at the same time, but they closed the foot of distance between them and were in each other's arms. Not kissing, just holding. She wanted to tighten her grip, to cling, in some futile wish that things between them might be different. Instead, she managed to step back. "Bye, Aaron," she said softly.

"Bye, Eden."

Tears burned behind her eyes—how stupid to cry for something that had never really had a chance—and she quickly got into the taxi before he could see them fall.

Chapter Fourteen

Aaron's Thursday morning flight from Vancouver was full, with drop-offs at two locations before he flew on to Destiny Island with Di and Seal SkySong and a tourist couple from Japan. He gave his usual spiel for the visitors, but even though they peppered him with questions, his mind wandered.

It had done a lot of that in the five days since Eden had left, and always in her direction. In the past, when he and a lover had parted ways, he might have an occasional affectionate thought or remember a particularly fun time together, but this was more like an obsession. He craved the sight of Eden's smile and that cute scrunched-forehead thing she did when she was deep in thought. He listened for the distinctive sound of her laugh. His skin itched with a restlessness that only her touch could soothe.

This was damned annoying.

Thank heavens the SkySongs had finally returned. He could talk to them, send a brief email to Eden summarizing what they said, and then surely he could get her out of his mind and move on with his life.

After Kam had assisted in docking the Beaver, the young man took the tourists up to the office to call their B and B for a pickup. Aaron put the SkySongs' luggage—colorful woven packs—on the dock.

The couple, in their midsixties, both attractive in a natural way, looked tired but, as usual, had an aura of serenity. Their hippie roots showed not only in their choice of luggage but in Seal's gray ponytail, the length of Di's silver and brown hair, and the embroidered top she wore.

"Can you two spare me a moment of your time?" Aaron asked.

Di studied him quizzically with her bright blue eyes as Seal shoved his wire-framed glasses up his nose and said, "Sure. What's up?"

"You both belonged to the old commune back in the late sixties, early seventies, didn't you?"

Di glanced at Seal, then back to Aaron. "Yes. Why do you ask?"

"While you were off-island, a woman came to visit, trying to track down her long-lost aunt. She talked to a number of people who'd belonged to or had contact with the commune, but no one could help her out. I wondered if by any chance you might remember the girl. Her name was Lucy Nelson."

Di gasped, her tanned face growing pale, and she grabbed onto Seal's arm as if she were going to faint.

"Lucy?" Seal echoed in a choked voice.

Aaron studied them with growing hope. "Yes. She was from Ottawa, would have been seventeen in 1969, and came with her boyfriend, Barry. I have pictures of Lucy." He reached into his jeans pocket for his phone, found the old school photo, and handed his phone to Seal.

Seal took it but didn't glance at the picture.

"Who is this woman who came looking?" Di asked in a thin voice.

"Lucy's sister's daughter, Eden Blaine. Her mother's been ill and really wants to find her sister and reconnect."

"Helen's sick?" Di asked, looking stricken.

Aaron hadn't mentioned Eden's mother's name. "Di? What do you know about this?"

She didn't answer. Seal put his arm around her shoulders as, with graceful but trembling hands, she took the phone from him and gazed at the screen.

"That's Lucy as a girl," Aaron said, "and if you scroll on, there's one of her and Helen."

Di stared at the two pictures for a long time. And then she said, "I'm her. Lucy."

Seal cleared his throat. "I'm Barry."

Aaron gaped at the pair of them until Di said, "I need to sit down. We have some talking to do, Aaron."

Eden tapped her fingers on her neatly organized desk at the Butterworth Foundation. It was five o'clock on Thursday and she was actually caught up with work. What a rare feeling, especially after having taken last week off.

Navdeep had really stepped up, proving to Eden that she wasn't as indispensable as she'd thought. It was tough to get her head around that, and maybe it hurt her pride, but it was also a relief to be able to delegate to someone she could trust, and to have a capable person to brainstorm with.

So what should she do now? Stop in at ByWard Market for groceries and cook dinner for herself for a change, rather than stick something in the microwave? Pour a glass of wine and sift through the small collection of shells and pebbles she'd collected on Destiny Island? Indulge in a memory-lane trip through the photos she'd taken of the island and of Aaron and sniffle into her wine?

Aaron Gabriel. The man who had shared his love of flying and of Destiny Island but hadn't really let her into his life. Not only hadn't he mentioned having a sister and a niece until that fact slipped out in the course of an argument but neither had he told her that he owned Blue Moon Air. He'd let her think he was just a pilot, and one so careless about responsibility that he'd take chunks of time off whenever the whim struck him.

On Sunday, when Eden had checked her email, she'd found a message from Kam, stating that the price of her flight from Destiny Island to Vancouver had been refunded as per Aaron's instructions. She'd been about to email back and ask for clarification, but an impulse had led her to first check the airline's website. It was the first time she'd visited the website, because it was her dad who'd made her travel arrangements. Last week, when she'd been checking Aaron's nonexistent social media presence, it hadn't occurred to her to take a closer look at the Blue Moon Air website.

The site was professionally done and included lots of pictures of destinations on Blue Moon Air's schedule, as well as the kinds of things tourists would see on sightseeing trips. It also included pictures of the planes, with their histories and specifications. And there were photos and profiles. Kam, the office manager, web designer, and aspiring pilot. Jillian, the pilot. And Aaron. Pilot, founder, and owner of Blue Moon Air. Which also made him the man who'd not only given her a couple of free flights but also given complimentary flights to seniors who couldn't afford the fare to fly to medical appointments.

Maybe she should've clued in when Glory mentioned that fact. But damn Aaron. Why had he let her think—no, *made* her think—he didn't take anything in life seriously?

The answer was obvious. As he'd said up front, he only wanted a casual relationship. He'd probably guessed, as Bernie had, that Eden was a woman who'd seek a serious relationship with a responsible man, so he'd made sure she didn't see him that way. He convinced her he was a commitment-free guy, when in fact he owned a business and was significantly involved in his sister and niece's lives. No wonder she'd suspected he had hidden depths.

He should have trusted and respected her enough to be honest with her. She wasn't insane enough to fall in love with a man who didn't want her. Sure, she might be mildly obsessed with him, but that would soon pass.

Her phone—the direct work line—rang, startling her. "Eden Blaine."

"Eden, it's Ray."

"Ray. Oh. Uh, this is a surprise." She and her ex hadn't spoken, texted, or emailed since he'd moved his stuff out of the apartment two months earlier.

"How are you? And how's your mom?"

"I'm fine and Mom's doing okay. Thanks for asking." This was all very polite, but why was he calling?

"Could I buy you a drink?"

Her mouth opened, but she didn't say anything. What was going on?

"You're wondering why."

"Yes."

"I'd like to talk. We were friends, more than friends, for a long time. I miss you and . . . well, yeah, I'd like to talk."

She frowned. She missed him sometimes, too, though not as much as she'd expected to. Which proved she had speedy powers of recovery and would soon get over Aaron, too.

"Are you still mad at me?" he asked.

Examining her emotions, she said with some surprise, "No. I was, but it faded away."

"Then let me buy you a drink. How late do you have to work tonight?"

She pressed her lips together. Oh, why not? As he said, they'd been friends for a long time. "I'm finished now."

"Meet you at Zoé's?"

Zoé's was the elegant lounge at the Fairmont Château Laurier hotel—one of Eden's favorite places, as Ray well knew. "I'll see you there." If nothing else, this should be interesting. He would never have chosen Zoé's if he intended to pick a fight, so she needn't stress out.

She gathered her things, turning off the ringer on her cell phone as she put it in her purse. In the ladies' room, she freed her hair from its low ponytail and ran a brush through it, then deliberated. Not wanting Ray to think she was trying to look attractive for him, she pulled her hair back again.

Even so, objectively speaking she looked pretty darned good. The light tan suited her, especially against the coral blouse she wore with tailored charcoal pants and low-heeled black pumps. Her earrings weren't the fanciful ones she'd bought on Destiny but her usual gold twists.

Outside her office building, a ten-story gray concrete one with reasonable rents, she didn't don the suit jacket she carried draped over one arm. The temperature was probably about the same as it had been on Destiny Island, but without the ocean breeze it felt hotter.

As she walked the five or six blocks to the Château Laurier, she passed a couple of bars and restaurants with tables set out on the sidewalk. The tables were filling with people meeting up after work, as well as shoppers and tourists relaxing at the end of the afternoon. She wouldn't have minded rolling up her shirtsleeves, putting on sunglasses, and having a drink outside, but these weren't Ray's kind of place.

Besides, she'd adored the Château Laurier ever since she first saw it at the age of six, when Nana had taken her and her mom there for tea. On the sidewalk in front of the huge limestone hotel, Eden had stared in fascination at what seemed to her to be a castle straight out of a Disney princess movie, with its turrets and flags. Since then, it had remained her ideal place to celebrate a special occasion.

Kelsey thought it was too stuffy, but their mom loved it as much as Eden did. Eden smiled, thinking about what her sister had done the week before. When Kelsey had told her on the phone about not taking their mother to cancer support group, Eden hadn't given her a chance to explain. It turned out, Kelsey and her university friend had taken Mom for high tea at the Château Laurier, finishing up with a trip to the hotel's gift shop, where they'd bought fancy tea and jam. Mom had loved the outing, and it had no doubt lifted her spirits more than the cancer support group meeting would have. Not that those meetings weren't important, but as Eden had been forced to admit, sometimes spontaneity and fun were beneficial, too.

She had been judgmental about her sister; Aaron was right. If he'd been in touch, she might have admitted it to him, but she hadn't heard a word from him. Surely the SkySongs must have returned by now. If he didn't get in touch by Sunday night, she'd text him to inquire.

Eden stepped into the hotel lobby. Although she'd never want this kind of elegant, traditional décor in her apartment, it was just right for this place. The dignified, classy ambience made her feel special.

She entered the lounge, so cool and quiet with its ivory walls and big urns filled with tropical greenery, so soothing after the hot, crowded streets. Ray was already there, seated in one of two upholstered chairs at a round coffee table. He stood as she crossed toward him and a warm sense of pleasure filled her. He wasn't a monster, just a man she'd known and cared for—but perhaps not as well as she might have on either count.

He reached for her hands and she let him take them, laughing as her suit jacket almost fell to the floor and they both let go to reach for it. "Hello, Ray."

"It's good to see you, Eden. You look terrific."

"Thanks. You do, too." There was comfort in seeing

the familiar navy suit, white shirt, and burgundy tie; the chestnut hair that, despite a good haircut and styling products, always flopped over his forehead; the gray eyes behind gold-framed glasses.

He held her chair as she took a seat, and then he sat down across from her. "A glass of wine?" he offered.

Maybe she should stick to a nonalcoholic drink. She wasn't driving and it was only a short walk home, but perhaps it was unwise to drink alcohol with Ray. But then she reminded herself that, even though he hadn't been as understanding as she'd have liked when it came to her family commitments, he was still the same man. Decent, trustworthy. "Thanks. I will."

She glanced at the menu. If she'd been outside, she'd have chosen something white and summery, but instead she picked a glass of cabernet sauvignon from an Ontario winery. And, because she'd cooled off since coming inside, she also put on her suit jacket.

Ray flagged a server and placed an order for two glasses of the cabernet, adding, "And kettle chips to share." He hadn't asked, but he knew Eden couldn't resist them.

"So," he said awkwardly, "you said your mother's doing all right? I thought about calling her or your dad but wasn't sure it was a good idea."

It was nice of him to ask and to have been thinking of her mom—but then, he'd spent a lot of time with her family over the years. "They don't hate you," she said wryly. "I just told them we realized we weren't as compatible as we'd thought and agreed to split up." There'd been a time or two when she'd had the urge to curse or sniffle on her mom's shoulder, but she'd pulled herself together. Eden and her dad needed to be strong for Mom, not give her more to worry about. Fortunately, the sniffly stage had passed quickly. Now, gazing at Ray, she felt only a twinge of the old hurt and anger. Mostly, it was just nice to see him again.

"Thanks for that." He shoved the floppy hair off his forehead. "Is your mom still in treatment?"

"She recently finished the last of the radiation, thank heavens. She hated it, and of course the chemo, too. Now she does seem to be feeling better, both physically and emotionally." At times, Eden had almost worried more about her mom's mental health than her physical illness. If only Eden had come back from Destiny with the news that Lucy was healthy and happy, it would have given her mother a huge morale boost. Instead, Eden had seen how disappointed she was.

She deliberated a moment, but why shouldn't she tell Ray about Lucy? He was smart and insightful. Maybe he'd come up with a new idea to pursue. As their wine arrived and they took the first sips, she gave him a concise summary, omitting any mention of Aaron. "There's one couple, former commune members, who were away when I was there, but an islander promised to talk to them and let me know what they said. I'm not optimistic." She hadn't told her mom about the SkySongs, not wanting to give her false hope.

Ray, who had listened attentively, said, "It sounds as if your dad's online search and your in-person one on Destiny Island were thorough. Of course it's always possible the people you spoke to were lying for some reason, or failed to remember. It was a long time ago and, as you said, drugs may have messed up people's memories. Something might occur to someone later. You left your contact information with all of them?"

"I did. And posters up on a few community bulletin boards."

"Maybe it's time to bring in a professional. You could hire a private investigator."

"Dad and I are amateurs, aren't we?"

"Sorry, I didn't mean it as an insult, but—"

"No, I know. I didn't take it that way." She appreciated how Ray was trying to be on his best behavior. "And you're right. That's a good suggestion. Any idea where to find a good PI?"

"Among all the lawyers we both know, someone must work with a PI. Maybe the family lawyers or civil litigators."

She cocked her head. "You'd help me with this?"

"Of course." He gazed at her, blinked, and then said, "I'd help you with anything. I've missed you and I've done a lot of thinking." He gulped, then blurted out, "I love you, Eden."

"Oh!" It came out as a surprised squeak. This was the last thing she'd expected when he invited her for a drink.

He started to reach for her hand and then stopped himself. "I'm sorry I got upset that you weren't spending much time with me. You had so much to worry about, and I should have supported you rather than been selfish."

"I would have liked that." She glanced away, thinking back to how it had been. Despite what she'd told her parents, in her own mind she had laid the blame for the breakup on Ray, but now she realized that some of the fault lay with her. Slowly, she said, "But

maybe that was unfair. I had my priorities: my mom
and my job. Yes, you and our relationship were important to me, but I shoved them to the bottom of the
priority list."

He nodded. "That's how it felt."

"I expected a lot of you."

"And I didn't live up to your expectations."

"No." She gave a rueful smile. "But nor did I live up
to yours. We were living together. You had a right to
expect me to devote some time and attention to you."

He winced. "Not like it was another task on your
list, though. Because you wanted to. Because you
loved me. Like how it was with your mother."

She bit her lip. "Mom always told me that even the
best relationship takes work. She said you put in that
work, even when it's tough, because of how much you
love the other person. You have to hold on to the
long-term goal even when you're frustrated or mad
about day-to-day stuff."

"Sounds like good advice. I'm sorry I didn't put in
the work."

"I'm sorry I didn't, as well."

He reached out again and this time didn't change
his mind. He cradled her hand in his, his touch so
warm and familiar. "Can we try again? Older and wiser?"

"Oh," she breathed. "I . . . need to think." Gently,
she tugged her hand free, picked up her wineglass,
and sipped slowly as her heart and mind raced.

Not long ago, she'd believed her future lay with this
man. She had loved him. She'd figured they would
marry and have children, support each other, build a
rewarding life together. He was exactly the kind of
man she wanted, long-term. Now that they'd cleared

the air and both admitted to their share of the blame, they likely wouldn't make the same mistakes again.

Ray hadn't changed. Or, rather, he'd changed for the better.

She'd changed for the better, too. Her visit to Destiny Island had given her a different perspective. She was more flexible, less judgmental, and willing to admit she wasn't perfect.

Objectively speaking, she and Ray now stood an even better chance of achieving that rewarding, happy, loving future.

Except . . . something was missing. Perhaps she didn't truly love him because that *objectively speaking* picture didn't resonate in her heart. What about passion? Excitement? Fun? Ray was a good man, handsome, smart, successful, with strong values. Yet he now seemed kind of pale and flat.

In comparison with Aaron. Being with Aaron had taught her that she wanted something more than what Ray had to offer. She wanted a man who combined the best qualities of both men. Did he exist? If not . . .

No, she wouldn't *settle*. That would be an insult to Ray, who deserved a woman who loved him fully and passionately.

"You don't want to," he said sadly.

The man did know her well. This time it was Eden who reached out to take his hand. She held it as if it was something precious, which it truly was. "I'm sorry. I've done some thinking, too. As much as I care for you and respect you, I don't think we're right together. I think that somewhere down the road, we're each going to find an even better match."

He pressed his lips together and finally said, in a

grudging tone, "You may be right." He squeezed her hand. "But I don't want to lose you. I enjoy your company. You're great to talk to. Can we stay friends?"

Relief and warmth flooded her and to her surprise, she realized her eyes were damp. "I'd like that, Ray." She let go of his hand and reached for her purse, fumbling inside for a tissue. Her hand brushed her cell phone, which was pulsing. Habit had her casting a glance at the display screen, to see the word *Mom* before the phone stopped throbbing.

"What's wrong?" Ray asked.

"I just missed a call from my mom. Would you mind if . . ." She quickly scrolled to see that she'd missed more than one call and a couple of texts from her family. She checked a text from her mother, which said, "Where are you? Eden, call home as soon as you get this."

"I'm sorry," she told Ray, her heart racing. "I wouldn't do this except that there've been a bunch of messages from home. Something's going on."

"Of course. Go ahead."

She returned her mother's call, to have the phone picked up immediately.

"Mom, what's wrong?"

"Where are you? I called your office, your cell. No, never mind, that doesn't matter. Just come home. Now."

Anxiety turned to panic. "What's wrong? Are you okay?"

"I'm fine, we're all fine. We're all here. Just get home now." Her mother hung up.

"I have to go," Eden said, rising.

Ray jerked to his feet. "Do you need a ride? My car's in the parking lot."

"Thank you so much. I don't know what's going on, but it sounds important."

He was tossing money on the table. "Has your mom had a bad spell?"

As they hurried across the room, she said, "She says she's fine. She sounded excited, really. With a big sense of urgency."

Ray was a good driver. He didn't speak as he negotiated the light traffic, leaving Eden to wonder what on earth was going on at her parents' house. Her sense of panic had subsided after hearing her mother's reassurance that she was fine. Dad and Kelsey were, too, and they were at the house to hand-hold her mom through whatever was going on.

Being away for a week had taught Eden that she wasn't indispensable at home any more than she was at work. Kelsey was still a little scattered, but she brought something positive to the healing process, ensuring their mother's life included some fun and spontaneity, and wasn't only about disease and its aftermath.

Kelsey was only twenty-one. At that age, Eden had been superresponsible, but now she could admit she likely wasn't the norm. That would be Kelsey, casual and unfocused but well-meaning. Her sister benefitted more from support and encouragement than from orders and criticism. That realization had made Eden wonder if Lucy had been the same. If Nana and Grandpa had treated her with more patience and understanding, would she have run away?

"Worried?" Ray's voice broke into her thoughts.

They were in the neighborhood known as the Glebe, where she'd grown up. "More curious than worried," she said as he turned onto the street where the family home was located. "Thanks so much for the ride."

"Call me if you need anything." He pulled into the driveway of the three-story house. The warm early evening lighting made the red brick facade with its white trim look even more homey and appealing. "And I won't forget about looking for a PI. We'll talk soon. Okay?"

"We will." She was even looking forward to it. But for now, she was eager to get inside and find out what was going on.

She jumped out of the car and, as she hurried up the front walk, saw her sister's face at the living room window. The door opened as she reached it. "Kelsey?"

Her sister was beaming and her bright blue eyes danced. "You're not going to believe this, Sis." She grabbed Eden's hand and pulled her toward the kitchen.

In the spacious room with the old red Formica table where the family had shared so many meals, Eden's mom and dad were sitting in their usual places across from each other. Her mother jumped to her feet. "There you are! Finally!" Except for the short skim of silver hair she didn't bother covering with a wig when she was at home, she looked like her old self, pink-cheeked and vibrant.

"Mom, what's going on?"

Her mother caught Eden's hands and gripped them tightly. Voice trembling with excitement, she said, "Lucy called!"

Eden gaped at her. "Lucy? Your sister Lucy? She phoned?"

Her mother nodded vigorously.

Eden sank onto the red vinyl chair that had always been hers. "How? Where is she?"

"On Destiny Island!" Mom cried.

Dad rested his hand on Eden's, his eyes serious behind his rimless glasses. "It's thanks to you this happened."

Kelsey sat down across from Eden. "Mom, sit. Tell Eden the story."

Their mother perched on the edge of her chair and clasped her hands on the table in front of her. "I'm almost too excited to talk about it."

"Mom!" Eden protested.

"I answered the phone," Kelsey said. "Mom and I were in the kitchen, preparing dinner. Dad hadn't come home yet. So this woman asks for Helen, and I pass the phone to Mom."

"Lucy's lived on Destiny Island all this time," their mom said. "Can you believe it? And Barry, too."

"But I talked to—" Eden started, and then she realized. "Not the SkySongs?"

Her mom nodded. "After they ran away from home and reached the West Coast, they changed their names. Lucy always liked the Beatles' song, 'Lucy in the Sky with Diamonds.' She took it personally, the way you do if your name's in a special song. She liked the whole mood of the song and decided to be Diamond."

"No one told me Di SkySong's name was Diamond or I might have guessed." Eden pressed a hand to her temple, remembering how Azalea had mentioned that song. Had the old hippie been telling Eden in her own unique way and Eden had completely missed it?

"Lucy—Di—told me that after she and Barry—

Seal—left the commune, she decided Diamond wasn't a name she wanted to live with. She didn't want Lucy either, the name our parents gave her. She liked the new person she'd become, and most people called her Di anyhow, so she kept it at that."

"Wow. I'm . . . wow. Stunned." Eden shook her head. "If they'd been on the island when I was there, I'd have met them. She'd have told me. At least I hope she would."

Her mom nodded. "She would. She said that when they flew home and the pilot mentioned you visiting the island and looking for Lucy, she was so shocked she almost fainted."

Aaron. Aaron had brought this amazing gift to her mother. Eden had told her parents that the pilot who'd flown her to Destiny had been very helpful and had also shown her some of the island's sights. She hadn't mentioned their relationship, nor that Aaron was young, handsome, and charming. Her parents hadn't guessed that she and Aaron had been more than friends—and why would they, considering how slowly her relationships had moved in the past? Fortunately, Kelsey had kept her secret. Eden didn't want her mom and dad thinking she was as free and easy about her sex life as Kelsey seemed to be.

Her mother gripped Eden's hand. "After our parents kicked her out and then never wrote back to her, Lucy tried to forget she ever had a family. She knew that if she got in touch with me, it'd make trouble for me with them. She said she knew I was a strong, capable girl and that I'd do okay, but she said she'd thought of me so often over the years." She gave a tremulous smile. "She even still remembers my birthday. After almost fifty years."

Eden glanced at Kelsey and her sister gave her a small smile, suggesting they were thinking the same thing. No matter how much they might squabble, it was inconceivable that the two of them would be out of touch for a week, much less fifty years.

"The pilot told her that our parents had died," Mom went on, "and mentioned that I'd been ill. He told her I was Helen Blaine now, and still living in Ottawa. Lucy—Di—said that as soon as she got home, she and Seal found my phone number online and she called."

Her dad rose. "Have you had dinner, Eden? We had ours while we were waiting for you to call back."

"I haven't. Do you have leftovers?" She started to get up.

"Sit. Listen to your mother's story and I'll fix you a plate."

"Thanks, Dad." She turned back to her mom. "What else did she say?"

"Seal never got in touch with his family either. They were in Nova Scotia, on a Mi'kmaq First Nation reserve. He didn't get along with them." She shook her head. "Our parents' two biggest prejudices were against hippies and Indians—so wasn't it just like Lucy to take up with a boy who was both?"

"Thank God you and Dad aren't like that," Kelsey said in a heartfelt tone.

"Anyhow," Mom went on, "he and Lucy—Di—were both happy to make a fresh start on Destiny Island. They married because, she said, they didn't want either the church's or the state's approval of their union. But they both took the name SkySong to symbolize their commitment to each other. They raised a daughter and a son, both of whom have left

Destiny Island but often come back to visit. They have three grandchildren, two boys and a girl." Helen gave a tremulous smile. "Relatives! All these new relatives. I hope I get a chance to know them."

"Of course you will," Eden and Kelsey said simultaneously.

Their dad rested his hand on his wife's shoulder from behind and then came around to put a plate of steaming-hot veggie lasagna in front of Eden before sitting down again.

"They have a retreat center, don't they?" Eden asked, forking up a bite.

"Yes," Mom responded, "though I'm afraid I don't remember all the details. Stupid brain." She pressed her fingers to her flushed cheeks. "I've never before in my life been this scattered." She complained frequently that since she'd started undergoing treatment, her brain hadn't been as sharp as before.

"Mom," Kelsey said, "the two of you were covering, like, fifty years in fifty minutes." She glanced at Eden. "They were talking about everything all at once. Their guys, you and me, Aunt Di's family, Mom's work. The cancer of course." She turned back to their mother. "No wonder you don't remember it all."

"I came home partway through," Dad said, "and Kelsey's description is apt. So don't worry about it, Helen. You and your sister will have lots more opportunities to talk. You'll get everything filled in."

"They talked about the commune," Kelsey said, running her fingers through her short, blond-streaked hair. "I just can't imagine a relative of Mom's being into all that hippie stuff."

"Lucy—Di—I'll have to get used to calling her that," their mother said, "told me the commune was interesting. Not perfect, but the setting was beautiful and most of the other kids were really nice." She reached over, picked up the fork that lay by Eden's plate, and helped herself to a mouthful of lasagna. "You don't mind, do you?"

"Of course not." Her mother's appetite had been poor ever since the surgery and it was great to see her eat voluntarily rather than look like she was forcing down the bites. Eden rose, got another fork, and pushed the plate over so it rested between the two of them. "We'll share."

Her mother chewed and swallowed before saying, "But yes, Kelsey, I know what you mean. Di said it was a good place to mellow out and enjoy life. Which isn't my idea of paradise. I'm so active and goal-oriented."

She'd used the present tense, which was another good sign. It seemed Di's phone call had worked a kind of magic that no number of pep talks from Eden, her dad, and her sister, or cancer support group meetings, could achieve.

"Did she say anything about the leader of the commune, a guy who called himself Merlin?" Eden asked. She hadn't told her family about the rumors of abuse at the Enchantery.

"Not that I remember. Oh, wait, I think she said the leader left and the rest of them tried to hold things together, but it didn't really work and the commune dissolved. She and Seal loved the island, so they stayed, got jobs, made a life for themselves there." She yawned and put down her fork. "Gosh, suddenly I'm worn out. So much excitement."

"You go to bed, Mom," Eden said. "You'll be talking to Di again soon, right?"

"Oh, yes. Tomorrow." Her mother smiled. "We're

not going to lose each other again." She turned to her husband. "I could use an escort up to bed, Jim."

"My pleasure." He helped her up and put his arm around her as they headed off.

Eden and Kelsey stacked the dishwasher and tidied the kitchen, and then Kelsey said, "Want to stay for a cup of tea or something?"

Eden hugged her. "Thanks for the offer, but there's something I need to do."

"More work?" Her sister made a face.

"Actually, no." She wanted to call Aaron to thank him.

She hoped that, as had happened with Ray, she'd discover that distance had dimmed her feelings for the charismatic pilot.

Chapter Fifteen

On Thursday, Aaron got home around six-thirty. Some days, he cooked for himself; sometimes he got takeout or went out for dinner. Tonight, he loaded a bunch of snacks onto a wooden cutting board: taco chips, salsa, a couple of kinds of cheese, a bag of snack carrots. He took those, a beer, and his e-reader out to the deck.

It was peaceful, just the way he liked it. Yeah, he was alone, but he'd always been good with that. Or at least he'd convinced himself that he was. Now, he missed Eden. He hated the awkward way they'd parted after that squabble. He owed her an apology, which he figured on delivering when he reported what he learned from the SkySongs—and Di had asked him to hold off on calling until she had time to process what he'd told her this afternoon.

He'd almost finished dinner when his cell phone rang. At the sound of Eden's voice, a quick burst of happiness had him grinning. "Hey there," he said.

"Hi, Aaron. Guess what? Di SkySong called Mom this afternoon."

"Good. I'm glad."

"You talked to her and Seal. Were you going to tell me?" She sounded a little miffed.

"I wanted to, but Di was pretty shaken. She asked me to give her a chance to collect her thoughts. I hoped she'd call you or your mom. If she didn't in a couple days, I'd have told you. I promise."

"Thanks." Her tone softened. "I appreciate that. And thank you so much for asking them about Lucy."

"You're welcome. How did it go? Did the two sisters get along after all this time?"

"I wasn't there, but from what Mom says, yes, they did. She's really happy. More upbeat than I've seen her since her diagnosis."

"That's great." He was happy, too. For Eden and for her mom. "They'll stay in touch?"

"Yes. It'll take a while for them to get to know each other again. Di mentioned that she and Seal had children and grandchildren, and I don't know if she plans to tell them. I guess we'll all take it slowly and see how it goes."

"Sounds wise." He sipped from his beer bottle and watched a couple of kayakers paddle by. Sunset gazers. If Eden were here, he'd suggest they do that one evening.

"Isn't it amazing that Lucy and Barry have been together since their teens?"

"Yeah, it's quite a story. They're a great couple, Eden. Each very much their own person, but the bond between them is obvious." The SkySongs could almost make a guy believe in love.

"Di told Mom they never married."

"No. They once told me they had a commitment ritual on the beach, chose the surname SkySong, and filed the paperwork to make it official. That's what they're like: part hippie forever, yet practical enough to live as a part of society and do it on their own terms. You'll like them."

"I'm sure I will." She paused. "Aaron, it doesn't sound like Di said much to Mom about the commune or Merlin, and she didn't mention Starshine. Did she say anything to you?"

"Can't let that go, eh?"

"What can I say? I'm intrigued."

He chuckled. "Yeah, me too. I did ask about Merlin. Di tensed up, glanced at Seal, and then said she didn't feel well and needed to go home."

"Evasive."

"Well, she'd had a shock and she did look pale and strained. That's when she asked me not to get in touch with you, and to give her time to get her head around all this." A great blue heron flew past: elongated body, huge wings, croaky prehistoric call. "But yeah, I got a feeling she and Seal didn't want to talk about Merlin."

"I don't understand why there's such a big secret about the Enchantery. It sounds as if Merlin was abusive and he's been gone for decades, presumed dead, yet people are still protecting him. It doesn't make sense."

"I know. But you'll get to know Di now, and Seal, too. Once they're more comfortable with you, maybe they'll open up."

"I hope so." She sighed. "I really, really hope Di wasn't abused."

"If she was, that's her secret to keep or reveal. I will say that if something did happen, I think she's gotten past it. I don't know a more whole, healthy person."

"I'm glad. Thank you, Aaron. That's what counts. That, and her reunion with Mom."

"But you're still curious." He'd learned Eden had a sharp mind and liked questions to be answered.

"I am." She gave a soft laugh. "Dad says I can be like a dog with a bone. Once I've gotten my teeth into something, I won't let go. He says that mostly it's an admirable quality because it makes me goal-directed, tenacious, and successful. It's certainly helped me in my career."

Aaron agreed that those were good qualities, but so were flexibility and the ability to relax. He wouldn't say that, though.

"Aaron, you've done me and my family a huge favor."

He was about to say he was happy to do it, but Eden was still talking.

"And here I am," she said, "taking up a bunch more of your time on a Thursday night. I hope I didn't catch you at a bad time."

"Just eating dinner on the deck."

"Oh. Uh, alone or . . . ?"

"Alone. Except for a couple of kayakers, a great blue heron, and some hummingbirds getting their sunset snack."

"It sounds lovely."

"Yeah, it's nice. So nice that I think I'm going to get another beer." He dropped his bare feet to the wooden deck.

"You're not flying tomorrow?"

"Jillian's taking the morning flight and a couple of afternoon ones as well. She wants the weekend off because her son has stuff going on." He took another bottle from the fridge and made his way back out to the deck. "So where are you? At home?"

"Yes, after visiting my family, hearing the news, and being fed veggie lasagna. Now I'm curled up on the couch in my living room with a glass of chardonnay. Just me. No kayakers, no wildlife. One purple and white orchid plant I bought a few days ago, just to have something growing in my house."

The sound of her voice was doing things to him. Good things. Sexy ones, but also warm, comfy ones. She sounded like she'd gotten over being mad at him, but he still owed her an apology. "Eden, I'm sorry for being rude about your sister. I had no right to try to give advice."

"Well, I'm sorry I overreacted. I was hurt that you hadn't told me about your sister and niece. But you're right that not everyone wants to share their personal life with everyone they meet. I shouldn't have taken it, uh, personally."

Maybe not, but he found himself taking her words personally and they stung—on her behalf and on his own. "You're not just everyone, Eden." Maybe he should have stopped there, but he didn't. "You're special."

Eden, wineglass raised halfway to her mouth, caught her breath. Had he really said that?

When she'd phoned Aaron, a part of her had hoped she could listen to his voice and think of him as a friend and only a friend. It hadn't worked that way. She could imagine him on his deck as he sipped beer and watched the ocean. The craving to be with him, to reach for his hand and share the evening, then to make love in his cozy bedroom, was a physical and an emotional one. When he said she was special, did that mean he had feelings for her, too?

She put the glass down on the side table and queried softly, "I'm special?"

"Yeah, and I didn't mean to hurt you. To deceive you or shut you out. But I've had a bunch of shit in my life and no one else needs to hear about it."

So he wasn't the carefree man he tried to portray. He had secrets, and they were painful ones. Ones that it seemed he hadn't trusted to anyone. Her heart went out to him. "It's rough having to handle everything on your own," she said tentatively. "Sometimes it can help if you share with someone who cares about you. I don't want to pry or to pressure you, Aaron, but I'm here if you want to talk."

"I'm not a big talker."

"Liar," she teased. "You can be downright garrulous when it comes to talking about flying or telling me Destiny Island history."

"Those are more interesting stories."

"You mean they're not personal ones. I think the personal ones are always more interesting." She lifted her glass again and had a sip of chardonnay. Once, this had been her favorite wine, but now it seemed a little thin in comparison with the Destiny Cellars pinot gris and riesling.

"Even the crappy ones?"

If some part of him didn't want to share, he'd have shut her down already. So she coaxed, "You could start with your sister. You obviously care about her."

"Miranda's the closest person in the world to me.

We've always been tight, even if we disagree on almost everything."

"Like Kelsey and me. Tell me about Miranda."

After a long pause, he said, "She's two years younger than me. And she's my half sister. Different fathers, neither of whom were in the picture."

"Oh," she breathed. How wrong she'd been to assume he'd had parents who'd been too permissive and that was why he'd acted out as a teen.

"Mom was . . ."

She waited and then asked, "Your mom was what?"

He sighed. "A woman who chased after love in all the wrong places. An addict—to love, I guess, and definitely to drugs. A part-time prostitute when waitressing didn't earn her enough money to buy cocaine."

"Oh my God." She curled her legs under her and listened, horrified, as, with some prompting, Aaron told her about the nasty boyfriends. His mother's arrests. The times she deserted him and his sister. Foster homes. He told of the strong bond between himself and Miranda, and how he'd always tried to protect her. He said the two of them had turned into thieves out of necessity because there was never enough food in the house. And then he talked about their mother dying of an overdose, and of the teens being taken in by grandparents who made it clear they weren't wanted.

Her heart broke for him. "I'm amazed at how you turned out. You had so many strikes against you."

"I owe it all to Lionel."

"You owe a lot to Lionel. But it was you who had the strength to turn your life around."

"It didn't take a lot of strength to run away from something shitty toward something better." His tone turned bitter when he said, "And in going over to Victoria for flight school, I deserted Miranda. I should've waited until she finished high school, then we could have moved away together."

He told her about his sister dropping out and running away to be with a boyfriend, and how her life had been a constant struggle since that time. "She's like Mom in believing that there's some great love out there waiting for her, but she always falls for the wrong guy. At least she's smart enough to stay away from drugs, and she loves Ariana more than anything. But she's too damned proud."

"On the flight to Vancouver, you said she won't let you help her."

"A little money now and then, but she hates asking. I'm always worried about her and Ariana, but Miranda's determined to look after herself and her daughter. I've told her there's a bedroom for them here and I'll look after them while she gets herself some training that'll let her get a decent job with a proper income. But she always refuses." He heaved a sigh. "This week we were supposed to get together in Vancouver, but she put me off and I'm worried about what's going on with her."

Aaron was anything but the superficial guy he presented to the world. He wasn't an uncommitted, uncaring man. He was capable of caring deeply, and Eden was sure he'd do anything for someone he loved. She could hear how much it tore him up when his sister shut him out. "I'm so sorry. It sounds like you're doing everything you possibly can."

"I'm afraid it won't be enough."

"I know. Like me with Mom's cancer. I can take her to appointments, make sure she takes her medications, and be positive, but . . ." But her mother could die.

Eden almost never allowed that thought into her mind, but somehow Aaron's story about his family had loosened her defenses.

"It sucks, doesn't it?" he said sympathetically. "Things that are out of our control."

She sniffed back tears and gave a shaky laugh. "Yes. Big-time."

"Are you okay? I dumped some heavy stuff on you and then got you thinking about your mom's cancer."

"I'm okay, Aaron." She rose and wandered over to the window. "And I appreciate you trusting me with the truth about your family. How about you? I wish I had some great advice to give about how to deal with Miranda, but it sounds like you're already doing all she'll let you. She knows you're there for her and I'm sure that's really important to her."

Outside, fifteen stories down, a man and woman walked arm in arm down the walkway that ran along Eden's side of the building. Envying their physical closeness, she asked, "Did talking help at all?" She opened the balcony door and went outside. The June air was pleasant, but it didn't have the freshness or the tang of the ocean she'd enjoyed on Destiny Island.

"Maybe. It's kind of nice to have someone know, and understand."

"I'm glad." Glad for him, though she wasn't so sure this conversation had been a good idea for her. Yes, she felt as if she understood him a lot better—and that made her care even more for him. But it also told her that caring too much would only lead to pain. Aaron had told her from the beginning that he avoided serious relationships and now she knew he had a good reason. He'd been so emotionally damaged by his mom's dysfunction, his grandparents' rejection, and even Miranda's risky lifestyle and refusal to let him help. He likely didn't believe he'd ever find a love that was stable, that he could trust in.

He deserved love—but maybe he was too damaged to ever find it.

She couldn't give it to him. He wasn't ready and she wasn't strong enough. Besides, it could only end in disaster. He was firmly bound to his sister and niece, to his business and Destiny Island, and Eden was equally committed to her family and her career in Ottawa.

If only things were different . . . She blinked back another rush of tears. What was going on with her these days, letting her feelings get the better of her?

She wanted to say that she'd like to stay in touch, that Aaron should feel free to call her, as a friend. But with her emotions in turmoil, her heart so drawn to a man she couldn't have, she wasn't sure she was strong enough even to just be friends.

"I should let you go now," he said. "I know it's three hours later there."

She heard tiredness in his voice and felt exhausted herself, physically and emotionally. "Yes." Maybe there was one thing she could say that might help him move forward. "Aaron, you try to pretend you're all *what you see is what you get.* But you do have depth." A nip in the air made her shiver and head back inside. "You're responsible and successful, but even more than that, you're capable of caring deeply for someone and committing to them. You've proven it all your life with Miranda. You don't have to live alone. You have so much to offer."

"I, uh . . ."

"Good night, Aaron."

Chapter Sixteen

There was flying and then there was flying, Aaron thought as the Airbus touched down on the runway at Ottawa's Macdonald-Cartier International Airport. Being a passenger in a cramped seat in a sardine-can jet for the four and a half hours from Vancouver to Ottawa was a very different experience from piloting a single-engine seaplane in the scenic Pacific North-west.

Everything was so much simpler and cleaner in his world. No hustle and bustle of a jam-packed, climate-controlled huge airport. No waiting among hundreds of other passengers for luggage to arrive on a con-veyor belt.

Finally, his battered duffel came around—a bag that weighed only twenty pounds but had turned out to be two inches too long for a carry-on. He'd resented paying the checked-luggage fee on top of all the other expenses he was incurring. The last-minute flight booking, the hotel, the taxi rides.

He stood in the taxi lineup. Was he crazy to be doing this?

When his turn came, he tossed his duffel in the

trunk and climbed into the backseat. He gave the name of the hotel and started to provide the address, but the driver cut him off with an impatient, "Yeah, I know," as he swung out to join the flow of traffic.

Aaron did up his seat belt and tried not to be impatient himself. He couldn't wait to see Eden, yet he wasn't sure she'd be happy he had come. They hadn't spoken in over a week, since that one phone call that might have changed his life.

First, there'd been the sheer joy of hearing her voice and feeling connected to her. As they'd continued to talk, it had dawned on him that he'd never felt that kind of closeness with another human being. Well, other than his sister, but that was a completely different kind of closeness. With Eden, he felt desire. Lust, yes, but also the desire to have her sitting beside him holding his hand as they talked. The desire to go to bed with her and to wake and see her lovely face on the pillow next to his.

Even the desire to spill his guts, to share crappy stories from his past that he'd never spoken about before. The truth had been sinking in—that when it came to Eden, his defenses were down—when she had finished the call by saying he was a good guy with a lot to offer and he didn't have to live his life alone. And then she'd hung up before he could protest.

His first reaction had certainly been to protest, because the past had taught him it was stupid to dream about sharing his life, about loving and being loved. His mom and then his grandparents had smashed that dream, and even his sister preferred to be independent and poor than to bring Ariana and live with him. But Eden was right that he could care and commit.

Miranda might reject his efforts and hurt his feelings, but he would never, ever give up on her.

Damn Eden anyway; her words had sparked thoughts, desires, that were insidious. They wound their way through his mind and heart like blackberry vines; once they'd started to grow, they were virtually impossible to rip out. They bore prickles but also the promise of juicy, flavorful fruit. There was nothing like those ripe blackberries picked off the vine in August, warm from the sun.

He'd even screwed up his courage one night on Lionel's deck, when it was just the two of them and they'd both had a couple beers, to break the guy code of not talking about emotions. "So I guess I have feelings for Eden," he'd said. "But I can't see any way it'd work out."

Lionel, after a few minutes' rumination, had said, "You liked flying. You went after it, over to Victoria to qualify for your license."

Wincing, Aaron had replied, "And look how that turned out. If I hadn't gone, I could've stopped Miranda from dropping out of school and running away to that loser in Vancouver."

Another couple of minutes, and then Lionel had said, "If she hadn't run, she'd never have met Ariana's dad."

And there'd be no Ariana, which was unthinkable. "So you're saying there's no telling how things'll work out?"

"Don't know exactly what I'm saying," Lionel admitted. "Just, sometimes, you know you have to do something. Like me leaving California ahead of the draft."

Yeah, sometimes you knew you had to do something. So here Aaron was, in late June, chasing the promise of—No, Eden had made no promises. Not even hinted that she might like to pursue a relationship with him. Aaron, the man who'd locked his heart against everyone but Miranda and Ariana, had cracked open that lock based on not even a hint, just a friendly comment offered by a woman who was as firmly tied to her family and life in Ottawa as he was to his on the West Coast.

"Certifiably insane," he muttered under his breath. The taxi driver cast him a wary look but didn't speak.

Insane or not, Aaron didn't want to be a guy who gave up without even trying. He'd taken a week off work during their busiest season. Jillian would handle the majority of the flights, which her seven-year-old son wouldn't be happy about, and Aaron had brought in their backup pilot: an older, semiretired guy from Victoria who was happy to spend a week on Destiny.

"Here's your hotel," the driver said.

Aaron glanced out at the yellow-fronted chain hotel he'd chosen for its price and its location close to Eden's address. He'd been too occupied with his thoughts to get any impression of Ottawa as they'd driven in. He paid the driver, went inside and checked in, then went upstairs to a room decorated for functionality.

He'd traveled across the country without being sure of his welcome, afraid if he'd called first, Eden would have told him not to come. It was midafternoon. Likely she'd be at her office. He'd try her cell first, and if she didn't answer, he'd call the Butterworth Foundation.

But she did answer, on a breathy note of surprise. "Aaron?"

"Hi, Eden. How are you?"

"Uh, I'm fine. Good." She sounded flustered. "How are you?"

"That's kind of a long story. Do you have plans for the evening?" He held his breath.

"Plans? Tonight? You mean you want to arrange a time to talk on the phone?"

"I was hoping for in person. Over dinner."

There was a lengthy pause and then she said hesitantly, "You're not in Ottawa?"

"I just checked into a hotel around the corner from your apartment."

"You're kidding!" Now he could hear excitement, and it gave him hope. "You're really here? I thought you never left Destiny Island? Well, I mean except for all the flights you take, but . . . oh, you know what I mean."

"I know. And yes, I'm here. Are you free for dinner?"

"I, uh . . ." He heard her take a breath and he held his own again until she said, "Yes, I am."

He did a fist pump. "What would you say to eating in, at your place? I'll bring a bottle of wine and we could order delivery from wherever you like."

"Eating in? Ottawa has a lot of good restaurants."

"I'm sure it does." But he wanted to have a private conversation. Besides, he was curious to see her apartment. Fudging a little, he said, "It's been a long day of travel. I'd kind of like a quiet evening in relaxed surroundings."

"Oh, of course. We can do that. Uh, do you like Thai?"

"Sure do." Before she could change her mind, he suggested a time and told her he'd see her then. Hanging up, he sighed with relief. One hurdle had been crossed.

With a couple of hours before it was time to shower

and dress, he headed out to explore Eden's hometown. He decided to start with the downtown core, not much more than a kilometer away, and set out on foot.

Ottawa was gray. Some of the architecture was interesting, the historic buildings were impressive, and the Rideau Canal was appealing. It was definitely an old, well-established city compared to vibrant Vancouver and picturesque Victoria. It struck him as big and bland, with little personality and few touches of color. Even the sunny sky was a uniform washed-out grayish-blue rather than the vivid color he was used to.

"Give it a fair shot," he muttered to himself when he was back at the hotel, showering. He was being unreasonable, almost like he'd made up his mind to dislike Ottawa, when maybe he should be convincing himself to fall in love with Eden's city. It wasn't like Destiny was perfect. After all, over the course of a year there were more rainy, gray skies than bright blue ones. And Ottawa had provided him with everything he needed this afternoon. He had a bouquet of multicolored flowers from a florist and a bottle of Ontario riesling from a wineshop. He'd bought a decent shirt and a pair of pants because he figured his usual jeans and tee wouldn't convey the right message.

Whatever that message might be. He'd spent some time trying to figure out exactly what he wanted to say to Eden. It would go something along the lines of: *I care for you and I think it might be serious. Is there any chance you feel the same way? If so, can we give it a chance and see where it might go?*

But then what? Could he see Eden leaving her fragile mom, her stressed-out dad, the job she loved, the city that had always been her home? Could he imagine leaving Destiny, moving more than four thousand kilometers away from his sister and niece, and giving up the business he'd built and loved so much?

First steps, he reminded himself. There were too many unknowns to think beyond tonight. Maybe Eden would tell him to get lost. She'd reiterate that he'd been fine for a fling but wasn't her type of man at all. It was true that in some ways he wasn't. But in other ways he was pretty sure he was.

He studied his reflection in the mirror. The slim-fitting charcoal pants looked okay with his one pair of black shoes, but the white shirt with denim-blue stripes looked unfinished without a tie—and no way was he wearing a tie. He undid the cuffs and rolled them up his forearms, feeling more himself. Probably he should have had a haircut, but it was too late now. As he gathered up the wine and flowers, he wondered if Eden was primping for him.

Walking the short distance to her building, he thought he liked this area better than the downtown. There was an interesting combination of old buildings and new, of offices, shops, restaurants, and residential space. She lived in a sand-colored, modern high-rise made of stone, brick, and glass. It had commercial space on the ground floor and apartments above. She was renting, he knew. She'd told him that she and her ex had shared this two-bedroom condo and she'd stayed on when Ray moved out, but that she planned to look for a smaller, cheaper apartment when she had some spare time.

At the front door, he punched in her code and she buzzed him in.

He took the elevator to the fifteenth floor, and when he strode down the hall toward her apartment, she opened the door. If she wore a suit to work, she'd changed out of it and was now wearing a short-sleeved top in a brown, white, and black pattern over leg-hugging black capris. Her hair was loose on her shoulders and she wore the earrings she'd bought on Destiny.

"You look beautiful," he said, just as she said, "Aaron, this is such a surprise."

They both laughed awkwardly as he stepped past her, into the apartment. "It's good to see you," he said, handing her the bouquet and leaning down to kiss her.

Her lips met his in a quick, warm press, and then she stepped back. "I'll put the flowers in water." She hurried to the small kitchen.

He walked into the large room, gazing around. It was open plan: a sitting area with lots of windows and a balcony off it; a dining area with a four-seater glass-topped table; and a small kitchen set off by a granite-topped island with two barstools. The design lent an air of spaciousness, as did the windows, the off-white paint on the walls, and the hardwood floors. Her furniture was attractive and comfortable-looking. There were a few nice paintings on the wall, a couple of potted plants, and a bookcase, but no clutter. "I like your place."

"Thanks," she said, her back to him as she snipped the stems of the flowers. "It's just your basic Ikea." She came around the island carrying the flowers in a simple glass vase, which she put on the coffee table. "These are pretty. Thank you." She twisted her hands together and said, in a bright, artificial tone, "So, what brings you to Ottawa?"

"You."

Her eyes flared wide. Panic? Wonder? He couldn't

tell. "Me?" It was more a squeak than a word, and her hands stopped twisting and locked together.

"Maybe we should open this." He held up the wine bag.

She swallowed. "Maybe we should. Oh, I phoned in an order for Thai food." She grabbed the bag from him and again scurried for the kitchen.

"Sounds good."

"You're probably hungry." Stuff clattered as she yanked open a drawer and pulled out a corkscrew. "I'm sure you've had lots of hours of travel. It must be strange for you being a passenger." As she spoke, she opened the wine, took down two glasses, and filled them generously. Her actions were jerky, matching with the babbly flow of words.

Aaron stepped up to the other side of the island and took a glass.

Eden didn't touch hers but instead, standing across from him separated by an expanse of granite, raised her gaze to meet his eyes. "You came because of me?" Her amber eyes held a touch of softness, maybe vulnerability.

"Take this." He gave her the wineglass he was holding and picked up the other one. "Come sit down." When he walked over to the couch, she followed and they sat side by side, close but not touching. He raised his glass in a toast. "It's good to see you."

Her eyelashes flicked down and then up. "Yes." She touched her glass to his and then drank. "Aaron, why are you here?"

Eden couldn't stand it any longer. She'd been in a state of shock since she'd learned Aaron was in

Ottawa. What was going on? Her emotions were in turmoil. How could she know how to feel until she knew why he'd come?

She'd asked, and his response was to take a long, slow drink of wine. She had a can't-breathe, every-nerve-trembling sensation, waiting for his answer. What did she want him to say? Her free hand rose to her lips to nail-bite, and she forced it down and tucked it under her thigh.

He put his glass on the coffee table and turned toward her. "After you left"—he spoke as slowly and deliberately as he'd drunk the wine—"and especially after we talked on the phone, I realized how I feel about you is different. It's something I've never felt, not for any other woman. I care, Eden."

Breath sucked into her lungs, and to her astonishment, moisture filled her eyes. He cared. Enough that he'd come here to say it in person. She blinked back the tears. When they'd spoken on the phone, she'd figured he wasn't ready for love; she'd been sure a relationship between them could never work. She shouldn't want him to care. She shouldn't have feelings for him.

But she couldn't lie to him. Knowing she was taking a huge, risky, maybe stupid step, she admitted, "I care, too."

Only then did she realize how tensely he'd been holding himself. He let out a breath and his face relaxed, a smile bloomed. "Good. That's very good." He took her glass from her hand and put it down, and then he caught her face between both his hands and kissed her.

She kissed him back with joy and abandon, moving closer to him, putting her arms around him, running her hands down his back. Reveling in the warmth and power of his body, in the fact of being with him like this after thinking she'd never see him again. But then another reality sank in, and she pulled back, ending the kiss. "But what good can come of it?" she asked. "There are so many issues and obstacles. We can never—"

The buzz of the intercom made her break off.

"Don't say never," Aaron told her as she buzzed in the delivery person.

They went to the door together and he insisted on paying. Eden had already set the dining room table and now put the takeout containers on trivets. Aaron said, "I'll get the wine."

Sitting, she watched him walk the few steps, his familiar muscular body clad in the kind of clothing she'd never seen him wear before. It was disconcerting, having him here. Aaron in Ottawa; Aaron in the apartment she'd shared with Ray. She was glad for the redecorating she'd done after the breakup. Kelsey had told her to throw out all the old stuff and start fresh, but no way would Eden's practicality or her budget allow for that. Instead, she'd bought a few new pieces to replace things Ray had taken and rearranged the rooms to give the place a new look. It was hers now, a sanctuary that no man other than her dad had visited until tonight.

Aaron put the wine bottle and glasses on the table and sat down across from her. "Don't say never," he repeated, taking them back to their conversation before they'd been interrupted.

"All right. At least not until we've talked it through."

He made a rueful face. "Guess we can't just go with the flow and enjoy it?"

Despite her anxiety, her lips twitched. "Maybe you

can, but I can't." She huffed out a breath. "Which is only one of the complications. We're such different people."

He opened containers and dished food onto their plates. "Different doesn't mean incompatible. You learn from me, I learn from you. It worked fine when you were on Destiny."

"A week isn't . . ." What? A lifetime? What were they talking about here?

"If it worked short-term, why wouldn't it work long-term?" He gestured to her plate, where he'd spooned jasmine rice, chicken vegetable curry with coconut milk, spicy prawns, and ginger beef with green beans. "Eat. I'm starving."

Obediently, she chose a prawn.

After they'd both eaten a few bites, he said, "I admit I've been a loner. It's hard to think in terms of, uh, coupledom—is that the word?—rather than being on my own."

"I did coupledom with Ray and wasn't so great at it. I had unreasonable expectations, didn't make him enough of a priority, and didn't work at the relationship."

Aaron paused with his fork halfway to his mouth. "Huh. When you talked about him before, I got the impression you thought he was the one at fault."

She grimaced. "I did, but we were both at fault. We talked about it last week."

"You talked to your ex?" There was more than a touch of jealousy in his voice.

"He invited me for a drink. We had a civilized talk about what went wrong." She didn't have to tell Aaron the rest of what Ray had said but to omit it felt deceptive. "He suggested we consider getting back together. But I knew that wasn't a good idea." She smiled across the table. "Yes, because of you. Not that I thought I'd see you again. But because being with you showed me that my feelings for Ray weren't enough, or the right kind, for us to be happy."

"Good."

His expression of smug male satisfaction made her smile. But only momentarily. She sipped the wine—a delicious, fruity riesling that went well with the Thai food—and said, "So, anyhow, lesson learned. Relationships take work. Not just ones with sisters, but with, uh, lovers, too. Caring for each other is a great start, but it's no guarantee things will work out. I know some things I'd do differently." She put down her glass. "How about you? You said you've never had a serious relationship with a girlfriend."

"No." He rested his elbows on the table. "I'm pretty messed up when it comes to relationships. I have zero role models other than casual friends on Destiny who've managed to make things work. You're the one who said I was capable of having a loving relationship. Until then, I didn't think I was." His lips twisted. "So you have yourself to blame for all this."

"I don't regret what I said. I don't regret you being here. Even if we can't make it work, I'm so happy you told me you have feelings for me."

"See, that's it. That's the thing. My feelings for you. They wouldn't quit. I'd always told myself I wasn't a relationship kind of guy, that I didn't want to share my life. Even now, I admit that a part of me is skeptical that I could ever make it work. The same with Miranda. We're both pretty screwed up, thanks to the way we grew up."

"Adults are capable of overcoming what happened in childhood."

"If I didn't think it was possible, I wouldn't be here." He stared her straight in the eyes. "Eden, I know I'm a risk. And you like things to be more predictable than risky. If you tell me to get out of your life, I'll do it. But if you're willing to take a mighty big chance on a damaged piece of goods like me, and explore what we might have together, I promise I'll try my best to be a man who deserves you."

What could she possibly say to that, with him laying his soul on the line? Haltingly, she started out. "This is all new to me, too. When Ray and I got together, we seemed so compatible and things were easy. Not passionate, not intense, not complicated. But with you, right from the beginning, even with our differences and squabbles, and the fact that it was only supposed to be a fling, I was drawn to you in a whole different way. I tried to keep things light and easy, but my heart wasn't getting the message."

He nodded, obviously identifying.

She went on. "I wanted more from you, but you made it clear you wouldn't or couldn't give it, so I tried to convince myself it was just a rebound thing. That I wasn't really falling for you, that once we were apart I'd get over you. But then we talked on the phone and I learned more about the kind of man you are. How could I not care for that man? And now here you are, telling me that you care for me."

"Complicating your life even more," he said ruefully.

"Yes. Yes, you are. As you said, I like things to be organized, predictable, comfortable. And this isn't. A future with you wouldn't be." But now she knew he had feelings for her, could she imagine a future without him?

He pressed his fingers to his temples. "I can't lie. No, it wouldn't be."

"This has been a tough year for me," she said softly. "Losing Nana hit hard, and Mom's illness was horrible. I was—still am—scared. Trying to stay positive takes a toll. Then there was the breakup with Ray. I truly believed I didn't have the time or energy for a relationship. Even if I did, shouldn't it be a comfortable, supportive one, not one that presents so many challenges?"

"I'm supportive. I helped you find your aunt."

"That's true." Did that mean he'd be supportive in other areas, like if she canceled a date because her mom needed her?

"You're comfortable with me. Comfortable enough to try things you'd never done before."

"Hmm. I hadn't thought of it that way. I was thinking more of just normal life. Not kayaking and picnics but day-to-day living. Like, do you ever just sit back in a comfy chair and read a book?"

"I've always been a reader, ever since I taught myself, then Miranda, to read when we were little. But how about you? You're the one who's wound tight, always with something you need to be doing."

"The past year has been like that," she admitted. "But even so, I've found some quiet time for myself. A bath before bed or fifteen minutes of reading before I turn out the light."

"See, I have you beat. I'm the laid-back one, remember? I can spend an hour on the deck reading, or even just watching the birds and the ocean. When it comes to books, my favorites are mysteries. I like trying to figure it out before the detective does. What do you read?"

"Mysteries too, and legal thrillers. Which is silly,

because that's so far away from the kind of law I practice. All the same, they intrigue me." And now she could imagine herself and Aaron reading companionably in the evening. Before going to bed and making multiorgasmic love. "Okay, so we have more in common than I thought. But there's still one huge obstacle. I can't imagine leaving my parents and Ottawa's their home. I'm guessing you feel the same way about Destiny Island and your sister and niece."

"People move all the time," he said tentatively.

"People who have as strong ties to their homes as we do?" She knew it happened, but she honestly couldn't imagine either of them doing it.

"You're the one who said relationships take work. There need to be compromises."

She crossed her arms. "Is that your way of saying I'd need to move to Destiny Island?"

"No. Though that would be wonderful. I mean, if things worked out with us. But no, I'm saying we'd both need to think seriously about it. You've seen Destiny. There are things you like about it. Now I'm here in your city for a week. Show it to me, Eden. Show me what you love about it."

A week? He'd taken a week off work during his busiest season? "It's a great city, but mostly what I love is my family. Are you willing to meet them?"

"Of course. I want to."

But did she want him to meet them? What could she tell her folks? If she said Aaron was an acquaintance, she'd be deceiving her parents. But if she told her family that she and Aaron had feelings for each other, her parents would worry that she might move to Destiny Island to be with him.

"You're overanalyzing again," Aaron said.

"That's because it's complicated. I don't know the right thing to do."

"Feelings like ours might only come around once in a lifetime. Isn't it worth facing all those complications and challenges?"

Eden's heart said yes. She wanted to be with Aaron. But her common sense said it couldn't possibly work. And yet, what if it could? How amazing would that be? On the other hand, if it didn't work . . . Well, she'd been there already with Ray and survived. She and Aaron had known each other only a short time. Maybe they'd find their feelings for each other really weren't that strong and it'd be relatively easy to walk away.

"Maybe it is worth it," she finally agreed. "You're here in Ottawa. So let's spend time together and see where things go."

Before she'd finished speaking, he was on his feet, coming around the table and bending down to hug her. "Thank you."

His touch felt so right. She smiled at him. "Thank you, too."

A twinkle ignited in his eyes. "As for where things might go, I have an idea where we should start."

"Where?"

"Your bedroom."

Oh yes. She wanted to be naked with him, to make love, but she couldn't resist a moment's teasing. "You've barely touched your dinner and I thought you were starving."

"Right now, I'm starving for you. After that . . . well, you've got a microwave, right?"

"I have a microwave." She rose, a quick motion that caught him off guard as she more or less launched herself into his arms. In that moment, she banished all her concerns—or at least deferred them—and vowed to wholeheartedly enjoy this reunion with Aaron. Her lover, and just possibly her future love.

He held her close, tighter than he'd ever held her, like he never wanted to let her go. Her head was tucked under his chin, her cheek against his chest, and his arms were strong bands around her back. She didn't feel confined, though. More like cherished.

Everything about this was different from before. They were on her turf, even if she felt as off-balance as she had on Destiny Island. They'd confessed feelings, had a serious discussion, and made a commitment of sorts. Rather than setting a time limit on their relationship, as they'd done when they'd first gotten together, they were braving a future.

She took a deep breath, pushed back against his encircling arms, and raised her head to his. "Let's make love."

Never would she grow tired of seeing Aaron's smile or take it for granted. He freed her except to hold her hand, their fingers firmly entwined. Joined only in that way, they walked down the hallway. The apartment had two bedrooms. When she and Ray had lived here, they'd used the large one as a shared office and the smaller as their bedroom. After he'd gone, she'd reversed things. Now she had a spacious bedroom with a queen-size bed, a long, low bureau with a mirror above it, and a reading chair by the window.

Even though she and Aaron had made love several times before, her nerves fluttered.

He took her by the shoulders, turning her so she faced him. Gently, he brushed her hair back from her face. She went up on her toes as he leaned down and their lips met. It was almost like a first kiss. Sweet and pure, just lips to lips, conveying greeting and appreciation. Even so, arousal sparked inside her.

His tongue teased the crease between her lips and she opened a tiny bit, a soft sigh of breath escaping. She let him woo her, persuade her, their mouths repeating the story of how they'd first come together. Then she took control herself, catching the tip of his tongue between her teeth and nipping, not hard enough to hurt but enough that he'd feel it.

He moaned and ground his hips against her, showing her how turned on he was.

She twisted against him, her own body taut with sexual tension, yet at the same time soft and liquid as it readied itself for him. Impatient now, she stepped away, reaching for the hem of her leopard-print top. She pulled the top over her head and ran her fingers through her tousled hair, wanting to look good for him even though she knew that once they hit the bed, her hair would be hopelessly messed.

When she undid the front clasp of her lacy black bra, Aaron's hands were there to peel off the garment and then cup her breasts. Her nipples were already hard, but when he teased them they tightened further, to the point of pain.

With a soft moan, she attacked the buttons of his shirt. A nice shirt, white with stripes that brought out the blue in his eyes. But it had to go. And so did the tailored trousers, because she wanted what was trapped behind that bulging fly.

Somehow, with hands getting in each other's way, with muffled curses and breathy laughs, they managed to get each other stripped naked. And then they were on her bed, still tangled, legs twining, hands stroking greedily, kissing and smiling. They rolled, facing each other, then her on top, then him. At some point he'd had the foresight to find a condom, and when he picked up the packet she took it from him, ripped it open, and rolled the sheath onto him in a long caress that had him cursing again.

And then he lowered himself as she raised her open legs to wrap them around his waist. He entered her in one slow, steady thrust that took him straight into her core, and she let out a sigh of relief and satisfaction. Her man, here and now, their bodies merged.

As he thrust in and out, she met his movements, tilting her pelvis up, twisting so he hit every pleasure spot. The only sounds were wordless ones: sighs, whimpers, moans. All the words had been said and now their bodies took over, communicating in a language more primitive and straightforward. Speaking of lust, yes, but also of trust, affection, and commitment.

As tension peaked in her body, Eden wondered if the day would come when, at the point of climax, she would cry out, "I love you, Aaron." Right now, it seemed entirely likely.

Even if she wasn't ready for those words, she couldn't keep quiet. "Oh yes, Aaron," she whispered against his cheek as he pumped harder and faster, stroking every humming nerve to fever pitch. And then, as her body clenched around him and burst apart, she cried, "Oh, yes!"

Chapter Seventeen

"It's pretty out here, isn't it?" Eden sounded a little surprised as she glanced up at him.

"It is," Aaron agreed. It was Sunday, late morning, and they were walking in Gatineau Park, a wilderness park covering more than 350 square kilometers. "I can't believe you never came here and it's less than half an hour's drive from downtown."

"I've never hung out with outdoorsy people. I'm glad Kelsey knew about this place."

Eden had told him she'd asked her sister to recommend activities Aaron might enjoy. That was after spending all of Saturday downtown, with Eden giving him a city tour. He'd been interested to see Parliament Hill and the Supreme Court of Canada and had admired the old-world architecture of the Château Laurier and the artwork at the National Gallery. He'd been intrigued to learn that the Rideau Canal froze over in winter and people skated on it, including some who commuted to work that way. But it was all so *city*, and he'd had his fill of cities by the time he was sixteen.

Today, it was nice to smell country air as he and Eden walked along a well-used trail through a grove of maple trees. The park reminded him of Destiny's in summer, being overrun by people. It was nice that so many folks were outside enjoying themselves this way rather than hunkered inside staring at video games, but he preferred more solitude. He thought with nostalgia of the secret spot he'd shared with Eden, and how they'd made love in the sunshine. Somehow, he doubted they'd find a secluded spot today. But maybe if he lived in Ottawa and explored the more remote areas of Gatineau Park—or, even better, rented a small plane and flew over it—he'd come across one.

He was doing his best to remain open-minded about Ottawa.

He and Eden passed a family group who were meandering slowly to accommodate a white-haired woman with a cane and a dad pushing a baby in a stroller. Okay, that was a nice sight, seeing three generations spending the day together.

His cell, tucked in his jeans pocket, buzzed. He extracted it, hoping there wasn't an emergency at Blue Moon Air. No, it was his sister's name on the screen. "Sorry," he told Eden, "I need to take this." He stepped off the trail and she came with him, standing a few feet away with her back to him, giving him at least the illusion of privacy.

"Miranda? Is everything okay?"

"I'm being evicted." She sounded discouraged.

"What? But I sent you money for the rent."

"I know. But I didn't ask you until it was already overdue, and it isn't the first time I've been late. The bottom line is, the landlord's girlfriend wants the apartment, so he used the late rent as an excuse to evict me. Without a month's notice. Ariana and I have a day to pack up and get out."

"That can't be legal." He kept his voice low as the three-generation group wandered past.

She huffed. "And what, I'm going to go hire a lawyer?"

"I could help you with that."

"No, Aaron. For God's sake!"

"So you're calling to ask if I can front you the rent for a new apartment?"

When she didn't respond, he said, "Miranda? Are you still there?"

"Yes. So, uh, I'm not looking for more money."

"What, then?" Pride was, in general, a good attribute—but Miranda's stubborn pride was hurting her and her daughter. As if to reinforce that thought, a young couple walked down the path with a little blond girl between them. The kid was dressed in shades of purple and her hair was neatly braided. Aaron wanted his niece to have the same opportunities in life as this child. The girl noticed him watching and gave a shy smile and a finger wiggle. He forced a smile and waved back as he waited for his sister to answer.

Finally, in a subdued voice, Miranda said, "Is the offer still open? To stay with you on Destiny?"

Really? She was actually considering it?

"If it's not, no problem," she said quickly, making him realize that, in his shock, he'd gone silent.

"No, of course you're welcome. There's a big bedroom for you and Ariana, with lots of light. I remember how you hate small, dark rooms." They both did. There'd been too many of those when they were growing up. Cramped, dark, noisy, smelly. With cockroaches and sometimes rats.

"I do," she said in a small voice, sounding quite different from her normal breezy self.

He moved a couple of steps farther, facing away from the trail and from Eden. Leaning against the trunk of a tall maple, he breathed in pure country air and watched the shifting patterns of light and shadow as the sun beamed through a canopy of leaves. On Destiny, his sister and niece could have all the light and fresh air they could imagine. But from the day he and Miranda had arrived on the island and faced their grandparents' unconcealed resentment, she had hated the place. "Why now? Every time I've offered, you've said no. What's different this time?"

He heard a sniffle, and when she answered her voice quavered. "I've reached the end of my rope. I need to give Ariana a better life and I can't do it on my own."

Feeling a huge sense of relief, he said, "You don't have to."

She gave a louder sniff. "You know I hate this, right? Hate being dependent."

"I'm your brother. It's not about whether you're dependent or independent. It's about us being family and looking out for each other."

"Yeah, like I can ever look out for you."

"Remember back in school, when I was dumb enough to ask Chrissie Patterson out and all I could afford was to buy her fries at Mickey D's? And she told everyone I was cheap?" He'd been fourteen.

She gave a choky snort. "I put a dead rat in her backpack. Real subtle."

"You were twelve. You were getting back at her for being mean to me. Look, Miranda, it's not about keeping score of who did what for the other person. Damn it, you ought to know that by now."

"I know. But you've done so well, all by yourself, and I'm so . . . *pathetic.*" At least she wasn't crying anymore. The last word came out with a sneer rather than a sniffle.

"You're not pathetic." Just misguided, sometimes. "You're a single mom who's trying her best, and that counts for a lot. And no, I sure didn't do it all by myself. Without Lionel, God knows what would've become of me."

"Huh. I guess that's actually true. You'd probably be as messed up as me."

"Thanks for that."

She gave a soft laugh. "So I guess I'll do it, then. We don't have much stuff. We've always rented furnished places, so it's mostly just clothes, Ariana's toys, and the crib you bought for her. But she's outgrowing it anyhow."

"Leave it. We'll get something new for her. Do you have money for a taxi down to the Harbour Flight Centre?"

"I do. Do you have room for us on your morning flight tomorrow?"

"Uh . . ."

"If you don't"—that I-can-handle-it edge was back in her voice—"we can find somewhere to stay for another night or two."

"It's not that. Even if that flight's full, we can

arrange something else. The thing is, I'm not actually on Destiny right now."

"Oh, yeah? Having a raunchy weekend somewhere?"

"Not exactly." Her question was a reminder that Eden could likely overhear his part of the conversation. "I'm in Ottawa this week."

"Ottawa? Like, Ottawa in Ontario? You're kidding. What on earth are you doing there?"

"Long story. I'll tell you when I get back." Once he had a better idea how the Aaron-and-Eden story was going to go. "But there are two pilots handling Blue Moon Air. I'll check with them and call you back to let you know which flight you and Ariana will be on. Let's see, you'll need wheels. My Jeep's parked in the village lot and Kam has spare keys at the office. The house is locked, but Lionel's got a key. I'll set everything up and let you know."

"Thanks." She sounded subdued again.

"There's only a single bed in the bedroom. The kids' store in the village, Blowing Bubbles, has furniture for toddlers, so pick out whatever works for Ariana." There'd been no point buying anything because he'd never actually believed his sister would come. "And anything else you need. I'll call the store to give them my credit card info."

"We can make do with what you've got."

"Damn it, Miranda. She's my niece. I want her to have nice stuff while she's staying at my house. Oh, there are plug covers on the outlets, but you may need to move a few things to make it more child-safe."

"Okay." She was so quiet he could barely hear her.

"It'll be fine. Everything's going to work out."

"I guess. I just can't believe you won't be there." She made an odd sound, like she was catching her breath or forcing back a sniffle. "Aaron, you're my touchstone. I know I'm an unappreciative bitch, but sometimes the only thing that keeps me going is knowing you're there. I picture you up in the sky, in one of those planes you love. Or sitting on your deck watching the ocean." She made the sound again, definitely a sniffle. "It st-steadies me. But now, I feel kind of like I've lost you. I'm going to your house, but you won't be there, and I don't know how to picture you in Ottawa."

He wasn't sure either, but he gave it a shot. "Picture me out in a forest of maple trees, leaning against one of the trees and gazing up through light green leaves at the sky."

"Really? In Ottawa? I thought it was just, you know, a bunch of gloomy old buildings."

"It kind of is, but outside the city there's some pretty countryside."

"Good. Because, while I'm a city girl, you're definitely a country boy. You're coming back, right? I mean, this is just some . . . well, I have no idea why you'd go to Ottawa. You really don't want to tell me now?"

"It's not a good time. We'll talk when I'm home. And yeah, I'm definitely coming back. I'm booked on a red-eye Thursday night, and I'll be on the morning flight back to Destiny. Then we'll catch up on what's going on in both our lives."

"I can't wait to see you. Love you, big brother. And thank you."

"You're welcome. Love you, too, little sister."

As he put his phone back in his pocket, he heaved a long sigh. When he stepped back onto the trail, Eden joined him, taking his hand. "Your sister?" she said as they continued their stroll. "I couldn't help but overhear some of that."

He told her what was going on with Miranda.

"You're giving her a fresh start. It sounds like that's what she needs."

"I'm trying to get her to take some courses, get some kind of training so she can get a better job than waitressing or retail. She could study online and live rent-free for as long as she wants."

"Will her pride let her do that?"

He scowled. "Probably not. I guess she could get a part-time job and study part-time, that way she could contribute to the expenses. Help me pay down that mortgage."

"Mortgage? I thought you rented from Lionel?"

"No. He sold me a piece of his land. At a very reasonable price, especially for waterfront. But he said it was so cheap back when he bought it, he'd feel guilty charging me market value." He grinned. "There's no arguing with Lionel when he gets his mind set."

"I get the feeling you're the son he never had."

That thought warmed Aaron's heart. "Maybe I am, and he's the dad I never had. Though we're both too manly and macho to ever say stuff like that."

She laughed. "Right."

They walked in silence for a few minutes. The place had a nice vibe, even though he'd have wished for fewer people, but nature wasn't having its normal calming effect on him. His mind was spinning, thinking about how complicated life had suddenly become. Eden was here in Ottawa and they were starting some kind of relationship, one that he figured might be pretty serious. But now his sister had finally admitted she needed his help and she'd be on Destiny. How could a guy who avoided relationships end up with such a conundrum?

"What did she do to Chrissie?" Eden asked.

"What? Oh." He chuckled. "Snuck a dead rat into the backpack she took to school."

"Ew! Where on earth did she find a dead rat?"

"Probably in the building where we lived. Or the alley behind."

Eden shuddered. "I can't imagine."

"Good. Don't even try." He squeezed her hand. "Come on, let's speed up the pace. This picnic lunch I'm toting around is getting heavier and heavier."

As they both lengthened their strides, she said, "And we don't want to eat too late and spoil our appetites for dinner."

Great. She had to go and remind him that they were dining at her family home. Of course he wanted to meet her parents and sister, but they'd be assessing him. Was there any possible way they'd think a sea-plane pilot from the West Coast might be a good match for Eden? Much less if they knew he was the product of a deadbeat indigenous dad and a part-time whore who'd OD'ed. Hopefully, they never needed to know his life story. "I'm kind of nervous about that dinner," he admitted, hoping Eden would find a way of reassuring him.

Instead, she clutched his hand tighter and said, "Me too."

Eden glanced around the dining room table on Sunday night, thinking how odd this was. Mom was in her usual place at one end, wearing a pretty blue dress, the Destiny Island earrings Eden had given her, and her stylish walnut-brown wig. Dad, at the opposite end, wore his typical Sunday golf shirt and khakis. Kelsey was on one side, looking cute in white denim capris and a pink-and-white tee, with her spiky, blond-streaked hair. Eden, wearing the casual long skirt and gold top she'd bought on Destiny, sat on the other side. Beside her, in the spot Ray had occupied for four years, was Aaron, dressed as she'd suggested, in nice jeans and the striped shirt he'd worn to her place on Friday night, freshly laundered at her apartment.

The first time Ray had come for dinner, Eden's parents had subjected him to the standard grilling. They'd taken to him, approved of the relationship as it developed over the years. When Eden had announced that she and Ray were moving in together, her dad had questioned why they weren't getting married. Her mom, though, had said it made sense to try things out before making a lifetime commitment.

Eden wasn't optimistic that they'd be as positive about Aaron, not because he was less in any way than Ray, but because he made his home so far away.

Dinner started with neutral chitchat as they passed around platters of baked ham, scalloped potatoes, and baby peas. Eden had driven over early to help with dinner while Aaron, back at her place, had made arrangements for his sister's trip to Destiny. He'd then walked the four kilometers to her family home, buying flowers and a bottle of pinot gris along the way.

As they dug into the meal, the conversation focused on Blue Moon Air. Eden's dad didn't come right out and ask how much Aaron made, but he elicited the information that business was decent but somewhat seasonal, and that to date Aaron had fed a fairly high percentage of his net profit back into the business.

"You're young and you're building the business," Dad said. "It's a sensible approach."

Score one for Aaron. Her parents weren't into wealth; they were suspicious of anyone who accumulated too much of it. To their minds—and to Eden's—there were better uses for money than lining one's own pockets. But they did value responsibility and a solid work ethic.

"Aaron's also paying the mortgage on a lovely piece of waterfront property," she said. "It's not in a fancy development, it's out in the forest. Beside his mentor and best friend's place."

"Yes," Aaron said, "it's undeveloped land except for Lionel's and my houses."

"He built his own home," Eden said. "It's all wood and fits beautifully into the surroundings."

"Building it myself really means I had a lot of help from Lionel and a bunch of other neighbors and friends," he clarified.

"That's nice, having people help out," her mom said. "You can't place too high a value on friends and family." She smiled at her husband and daughters and then fixed Aaron with a steady gaze. "Do you have a large family?"

"No, there's just me, my younger sister Miranda, and her two-year-old, Ariana." He paused. "We do have maternal grandparents, but they live in Florida and aren't in touch."

"Losing touch with family is sad," Mom said. "And that reminds me: I haven't thanked you for helping me find Di. That's such a blessing and I'm eternally grateful."

For the first time tonight, Aaron seemed almost relaxed, and the smile he gave her was full wattage. "I'm glad I could help. A sister's a special person." He gave Kelsey a wink.

Eden's sister grinned. "Yeah, they can be a pain in the ass, but they're special."

He grinned back. "That's it exactly."

"So Aaron," Dad said, putting down his fork, "what do you think of Ottawa so far?"

"It's interesting, Mr. Blaine."

"No need for formality. Call me Jim."

"Thanks. Well, Jim, Ottawa's pretty much the opposite of Blue Moon Harbor village on Destiny Island. A big city, formal architecture, you feel the weight of things. History, the federal government, the Supreme Court of Canada. The exhibit of the indigenous artists at the National Gallery." He gave a quick laugh. "Not that Destiny doesn't have a century and a half of history itself, not to mention indigenous people before that. But our history is kind of, uh, quirky."

"Hey, it sounds like my kind of place," Kelsey said.

"I bet you'd like it," he responded. "Eden seemed to enjoy her time there."

Eden almost choked on the wine she was sipping and wanted to jab him in the ribs for that suggestive comment.

Fortunately, her mother either didn't get it or chose to ignore it. She said, "Ottawa is a wonderful city. Don't you think so, Aaron?"

"It certainly seems so. And Gatineau Park, where Eden and I went hiking this morning, is beautiful. I noticed there's cross-country skiing there in winter. And Eden told me about how people skate on the Rideau Canal when it freezes, which sounds cool."

He was saying good things, as he had when she'd toured him around her city. Eden suspected, though, that he figured Ottawa was an interesting place to visit but he wouldn't want to live there. But he'd only just arrived. It could take a while to warm to a place. She'd spent a week on Destiny Island and certainly admired the natural beauty and many other features of the island, but she wouldn't say she'd felt at home there. It was too much to expect that Aaron would fall in love at first sight with Ottawa.

"Eden says you like outdoorsy stuff, right?" Kelsey asked. "You should go kayaking or canoeing."

"Where?" His eyes brightened as he turned to her.

"There are a number of lakes not far away. Some have big resorts, but others are less developed. Loads of people have cottages there where they go on weekends and for summer holidays. But there's public access, too. I've gone out there a few times and it's cool. Except for the mosquitoes. But I guess you get them too, on your island?"

"Not really," he said. "In a couple of swampy areas, but otherwise the ocean breeze keeps them away."

"I'm sure Destiny Island is lovely," Mom said. "If you don't mind being away from the amenities of a city. Arts, culture, fine restaurants . . ."

Eden glanced at Kelsey and they both rolled their eyes. Even when their mom had been healthy, their parents rarely ate in restaurants, and they went to the theater or to an art gallery at most twice a year. "Actually," Eden said, "Destiny has some great restaurants, and it's known for its artistic community. Tourists come there to see the galleries, craft shops, and studios. Like Tamsyn's, where I bought those earrings you're wearing."

Her mother touched an earring and looked rather shamefaced.

Eden went on. "The bookstore is wonderful—that's where I bought the novel you loved, by the author who lives on Destiny. And there's music as well as arts and crafts. We went to hear a local band that was great, and a friend of Aaron's plays the cello in a chamber quintet."

Aaron chipped in. "A lot of islanders hop over to Victoria or Vancouver to go to the theater, symphony, or sports events. They can take their cars on the ferry, walk on and use public transit at the other end, or fly with Blue Moon Air. Most of us figure it's the best of both worlds: a peaceful life out in nature with lots of interesting and talented neighbors, plus easy access to a couple of great cities."

"I suppose that could be appealing," Mom said, sounding unhappy.

Eden noticed her mother had eaten only a small portion of her dinner. Leaning over, she whispered, "Mom, you need to eat more than that."

"How can I eat when I'm so worried?" She started out whispering, but the last words came out louder.

Eden pressed her lips together, not sure what to say.

Dad said, "Eden, you know we're always happy to meet your friends. Aaron, you seem like a fine man and I hope you don't think we're unwelcoming. But here's the truth of it: Our daughter was away for a week and when she came back, she mentioned you only casually. Then suddenly you arrive in Ottawa. As I gather, you came for the sole purpose of seeing Eden." His eyebrows quirked inquisitorially above the lenses of his rimless glasses.

"Yes, sir," Aaron said.

"That suggests a degree of seriousness," Dad continued.

Eden's cheeks heated as Aaron again said, "Yes, sir. I care about your daughter."

Across the table from Eden, her sister did a fist pump and mouthed, *Yes!*

Dad's face set in his I'm-about-to-lecture expression. "You met two weeks ago and have spent a portion of what, seven or so days together? Eden was until recently in a serious relationship with another man, so for her this is a rebound thing. You can understand that we have some concerns about the speed of all this."

"I understand," Aaron said. "But consider this: If we lived in the same place, we'd date a few times a week and see how things went. We can't do that, so I came here to see if Eden felt the same way I did. If she didn't, then we'd say good-bye."

"But I do." Eden reached for his hand, which rested on the table beside his plate. "So we're going to spend time together this week to see how things go."

"But then what?" Mom leaned forward, her face flushed. "I see this kind of thing all the time with my high-school students. They think they're madly in love and yet one of them plans to join the Armed Forces and the other has a scholarship to study ballet. They need to be practical and realize that it's highly unlikely their lives will be compatible."

"We're not teenagers," Eden said sharply. She took a breath and softened her voice, not wanting to upset her mother any more than she already had. "Mom, what do you tell those kids? To be practical but not to give up on dreams that may be achievable. Aaron and I are aware of the issues we'd have to deal with. We know it wouldn't be easy. This is just the beginning of our relationship and we're pursuing it, uh, consciously. We're paying attention, not rushing blindly ahead."

She'd meant her words to be reassuring, yet tears formed in her mother's eyes. Mom cried so easily these days, her emotions thrown out of whack by her disease and its ramifications.

With quiet dignity despite a tear that slipped free and tracked down her cheek, her mother turned to Aaron. "We're afraid you'll take her away from us. I don't know how we'd survive without Eden."

Kelsey made a sound and Eden glimpsed hurt in her eyes before her sister said, "Mom, kids grow up and leave the nest. You can't tie Eden to you forever."

Aaron spoke up. "Mrs. Blaine, Eden loves you. She's made it clear that her family is her top priority. Please don't worry."

Her mom lifted her napkin to blot the tear. "Easier said than done, I'm afraid."

"Aaron's right," Eden said. "The last thing we want is to add to your worries. I could have kept our relationship a secret, but that didn't feel right. Aaron's important to me and I want all of you to get to know one another. I don't want you to condemn him and our relationship just because he's not from Ottawa." She thought of mentioning that he would consider moving here but didn't want to pressure him. "Can't we relax and have a good time?"

"Helen," Dad said quietly, "that sounds like good advice."

Her mother took a long, audible breath. "You're right. All of you are right." She sent a wobbly smile in Aaron's direction. "I apologize for the melodrama. I never used to be like this. Please forgive me for my lack of hospitality."

"There's nothing to forgive, Mrs. Blaine." He sounded sincere. "You should never have to apologize for being honest about your feelings."

Mom's smile strengthened. "Thank you for that. And please call me Helen."

Eden let out her own breath in a sigh of relief. For now at least, it seemed things would go smoothly. But in the back of her mind lurked the knowledge that her mom would never willingly see her daughter move across the country. Kelsey was right about adults flying the nest, but their mother's illness had made her uncharacteristically insecure. Hopefully, as her health improved, so would her confidence. She'd realize that it wouldn't be such an awful thing if Eden lived somewhere other than Ottawa—though Eden felt a major pang at the idea of substituting Skype calls and quarterly visits for seeing her parents at least a couple of times a week.

Of course Aaron might develop a love for this city and decide he wanted to move here.

Or their initial attraction might fizzle and they'd go their separate ways.

Life was so much simpler when there wasn't a man in it.

Chapter Eighteen

Late Tuesday afternoon, Aaron was trying his hand in Eden's kitchen. He'd spent an hour shopping in ByWard Market, not far from Eden's apartment. He figured he could make an interesting dish out of handmade fettucine, shrimp, fresh porcini mushrooms, shallots, and heavy cream. An Ontario white zinfandel should match it, and a salad of mixed greens, feta cheese, strawberries, and fancy balsamic vinegar. He'd been throwing together meals since he was a kid and wasn't half bad at it, especially now that he could afford decent ingredients. He wasn't much of a dessert guy, though, so he'd cheated and bought tarte tatin, an apple tart, from a French bakery.

Eden had said she could try to take time off from work, but he knew that would be problematic for her so soon after her week off. He said no, he was happy to explore on his own. Yesterday, he'd borrowed her Smart car and spent the day hiking in Gatineau Park. Today, he'd roamed the city on foot. The Ottawa area was growing on him, but he missed the ocean.

When he heard the door open at six o'clock, Eden

arriving right on time, he went to meet her. She wore tailored gray pants and a sleeveless white blouse and carried the gray suit jacket over her arm. The office garb made her look professional and surprisingly sexy.

After a lengthy hug and kiss, she said, "It smells good in here."

"Told you I'd take care of dinner." Yesterday, he'd walked over to her office to meet her after work and they'd gone to a French bistro. He hoped tonight's meal wouldn't be a major letdown after that gourmet meal.

With her arms looped around his neck, she leaned back and gazed up at him. "I thought you meant you'd buy ingredients. You didn't have to cook."

"It's the least I could do. You've given me a place to stay." They hadn't told her parents that he'd moved from his hotel to Eden's condo. He put his hands on her waist and regretfully eased her away from him. "Come eat. This meal's time sensitive."

She kicked off her shoes, dropped her purse on the small table by the door, and followed him into the kitchen, pulling off the twister thingy that held her hair back in a ponytail. As he plated the pasta dish, she oohed and aahed, making him feel like he was an Iron Chef, and then they went to the dining area where he'd already set the table.

He was happy with how the shrimp and mushroom pasta had turned out and Eden proclaimed it delicious. As they ate and sipped wine, he asked about her day and, with a glowing face, she told him about the hours she and Navdeep had spent with a funding applicant, a charitable organization that provided equine therapy for wounded veterans.

Even as Aaron thought how great this was, talking

over dinner, a part of him was saying he couldn't ask her to give up a job she so clearly loved.

Eden helped herself to more salad. "This food is amazing. Where did you find all the ingredients?"

"ByWard Market. Your sister and I had lunch there and I shopped after."

Her fork stopped halfway to her mouth. "You had lunch with Kelsey?"

"Yeah, she called me. We went to Lowertown Brewery and had craft beer and rotisserie chicken." He'd been happy for the opportunity to get to know Kelsey, who was more approving of him than were Eden's parents.

"Did you have a good time? What did you talk about?"

"Stuff. This and that. You." He winked. "It was fun. I like her."

Eden smiled. "It's hard not to like Kelsey."

"I know you think she's too directionless, but I think she's doing okay for her age. At least she hasn't made any major mistakes, the way Miranda always seems to."

"That's true. And I really think she's growing up. Maybe it happened when she was away at university, or maybe when she started looking after Mom. But she is being more responsible."

"I told her I'd seen her paintings." He gestured toward one of the walls. Eden had some interesting art scattered throughout her place. Nothing expensive, mostly prints by local artists. There were a couple of colorful abstracts of flowers. When he'd mentioned liking them, she'd said Kelsey had painted them in high school, taking inspiration from their mother's garden. Eden said it had been one of her sister's phases, before she got bored and went on to something else. *Story of her life*, Eden had commented. "I told her I thought she had talent," Aaron said.

"She did. Art was one of the things she was best at. Painting would be a hard way to make a living, but if she used her talent in advertising, graphic design, computer animation . . ." She shook her head. "But she didn't want to hear any of that."

"Maybe none of it resonated with her."

"That's the trouble." Eden pushed her empty plate aside. "Nothing resonates with her, at least not for long."

"At least she tries things, and she's getting an education. I gather she's willing to let your parents help with that?"

"Actually, she'd rather have gone traveling, picking up jobs along the way. But Mom and Dad were horrified at that idea. They place so much value on a university education. Kelsey said she'd try it out, as long as she could at least live somewhere interesting rather than go to the University of Ottawa like I did." Her mouth twisted. "When she talks about McGill, it's more about her friends, exploring Montreal, having fun, than her studies."

As compared to him, who'd been so single-focused. For him, learning to fly was all the fun he'd wanted. Maybe he'd missed out on some things, yet he wasn't envious of Kelsey. "I feel kind of sorry for people who haven't found that one thing they really want to do."

"Hmm. Maybe that's what she's waiting for. I just always thought she should pick something and commit to it."

"Hard to do if you're not passionate about it."

"I suppose. Maybe she should see a career counselor."

"Maybe. I admit I'd like to see Miranda settled on a career path. But she's twenty-six and she has a kid. Kelsey still has time. If she tries different things, she may stumble across the one that's special for her. And then she'll be motivated to work for it."

"I hope so. I want her to find something that'll make her happy and financially secure."

As they went to the kitchen to make coffee to accompany dessert, Eden said, "What did Kelsey say about you and me?"

He let her deal with the coffee machine and took the tarte tatin from the fridge. "That I'm good for you because I got you to lighten up." He cut two slices of dessert. "I just wish your parents felt the same way."

"You know it's not personal. They're afraid I might move away."

"Yeah. And yet they didn't have a problem with Kelsey going to Montreal for school."

"They protested but gave in when they realized it was the only way she'd agree to go to university. Besides, I'm the older one, the reliable one. They've always counted on me and I've always been there for them. Even though they complained about Kelsey being flighty, they kind of let her get away with it. Each parent-child dynamic is different, I think."

Probably Eden had liked being the good child, the mature one, the one her parents relied on. Was there any way that pattern could now be broken, so that she'd seriously consider moving away from Ottawa?

He sighed, wishing he and Eden could have a

normal relationship where they could just see how things developed rather than being haunted by life-changing issues.

"We'd better eat our dessert," he said. "You've got that call with Di at eight."

Helen Blaine and Di SkySong had been Skyping almost every day, and introductions had been made so that now Helen's husband, her daughters, and Seal SkySong had all spoken to each other. Di had said she so badly wished she could fly to Ottawa for a visit, but their SkySong retreat was fully booked and she couldn't leave until into the fall.

Eden hadn't had a chance to talk to Di privately and she wanted to do that. And so, after finishing dessert, she took a second cup of coffee to her office to Skype Di. Aaron did the dishes and tidied up the kitchen, then went into Eden's living room.

Her apartment was comfortable. Relatively spacious. Large windows. Of course the view was of condominiums and town houses. No ocean. No forest. No hummingbirds, but maybe they'd come if he hung a feeder. They did to the feeders outside her parents' kitchen window, but then that house had a garden.

He picked up the book he'd started, giving one of Eden's legal thrillers a try, and sat on the couch. Though he'd tried the balcony once, the sound of traffic got on his nerves.

Damn, he was being picky and negative. He had found a number of positive things about Ottawa and should focus on those. Of course the one huge draw was Eden.

"Aaron?" she called from down the hall. "Come say hi to Di."

Eager to escape his thoughts, he went, pulling up a chair to sit beside Eden at her desk. Di smiled at him from the screen of Eden's laptop, her slender face, bright blue eyes, and long brown-and-silver hair familiar and yet distorted a little by technology.

"Hey, Di," he said. "This is weird, eh?"

"I know. It's like a parallel universe, seeing you somewhere other than Destiny. Or in the air, like you're a bird."

He grinned at her. She might co-manage a moderately successful business, but a good part of her was still a hippie, the same as Seal. "Yeah, a bird. That's me."

"So, you and my niece. Tiny, bitty universe, isn't it?"

"Maybe." If it were, there wouldn't be so many kilometers between his home and Eden's.

"Aunt Di," Eden said, "when I was trying to track you down, I talked to a lot of people who'd been members of the commune, or had contact with it."

"Uh-huh."

"It sounded like Merlin wasn't the greatest guy. Like maybe he abused some of the women."

Di blinked and didn't speak for a moment. "Why do you want to know about Merlin?"

Eden sighed and exchanged a glance with Aaron, who leaned over to put his arm around her shoulders. "At first, I was concerned that something might have happened to you," Eden said.

When Di didn't respond, Eden went on. "Now, I admit it's just curiosity. Once I see a puzzle, I want to figure out the answer."

Aaron, the reader of mysteries, added his voice. "Me too."

Di shook her head. "It was a long time ago. Best to let it be."

"Why?" Eden asked. "If it was so long ago, what does it matter now?"

Di glanced away from the screen, making Aaron wonder if Seal was in the room. She sighed. "I suppose it doesn't. Okay, then. In the beginning, I found Merlin charismatic."

A male snort sounded, she glanced away, and then turned back to the screen. "Seal always figured the guy was a poser and it was all about power and feeding his own ego. Seal butted heads with Merlin a time or two."

"Oh!" Eden gasped.

"What?" Di asked.

Eden turned to Aaron. "Azalea gave us the clues whether she intended to or not. Not just the song, 'Lucy in the Sky with Diamonds,' but she also said something about 'Barry, hairy, quite contrary,' and bull seals barking at each other. Remember?"

"Now that you mention it," Aaron agreed. "Damn, I should've picked up on that."

"Did Azalea say anything else?" Di asked, her voice strained.

"Not that made sense," Eden replied. "But please go on, Aunt Di. I'm sorry I interrupted."

"As I said, Seal always had his doubts about Merlin. I was more wide-eyed in the beginning, but then I came to agree with Seal. We were in the minority. Lots of the boys emulated Merlin and lots of the girls wanted to be his lover."

Eden must have wrinkled her nose or made some other expression of distaste because Di said, "You don't know the times, Eden. We had mind-altering drugs. The Pill was brand-new and we'd never heard of AIDS. Free love wasn't just available, it was almost a commandment we lived by." She turned her head, an affectionate, mischievous smile on her lips, confirming that indeed Seal was beside her. "Seal and me as well. We weren't into fidelity. But in the end, it was always us. Soul mates."

"I'm happy for you," Eden said. "But did Merlin abuse some of the women?"

Di's jaw tightened. When she spoke, her words came more slowly. "He abused his power. There was a lot of sexual experimentation. Some rough sex. Some dom-sub stuff. Not just with Merlin, but other men and women, too. Some people liked it, some didn't. People who didn't like it generally left the commune." Di paused. "Then Merlin himself left."

"Why would he do that, when he was the wizard who ruled the Enchantery?" Eden asked.

Di started slightly at the mention of that secret name. "Who knows? Maybe he was bored with us. We were kind of a mess. After he left, we tried to carry on. We didn't want a leader and said decisions should be consensual. Except everyone had different ideas and values." She was speaking more freely now. "Some wanted to be more organized, to get efficient at growing food and homeschooling their kids. Others just wanted the 'sex, drugs, and rock and roll.'"

"Not us, of course," Seal said from out of sight.

"Aunt Di," Eden said, "do you remember a girl named Starshine?"

Maybe it was due to the technology, but it seemed to Aaron that Di's facial muscles froze before she said, "No. There were lots of hippie names and it was so long ago."

"Seal?" Eden said.

"Me either," came his answer.

Eden continued. "I spoke to Gertie Montgomery. She told me you brought Starshine to the medical clinic, Aunt Di."

Di gave a smile that looked forced. "Ah, Gertie. So sad about the Alzheimer's. You can't trust anything she says."

"We talked to her in the morning," Aaron put in. "She seemed pretty lucid to me."

"And to me," Eden said. "She said the hippies from the commune almost never came to the clinic, so this was memorable. Gertie said the girl's name was Starshine and she had long, whitish-blond hair. She'd miscarried and was bleeding badly."

As Eden spoke, it seemed to Aaron that Di's blue eyes grew wider, her expression tenser.

Eden continued. "Gertie thought she might have been abused, maybe kicked. She was afraid there might be internal injuries and she advised you to bring Starshine back in a day or two. But neither of you came back. Was the baby Merlin's, Aunt Di? Did he beat Starshine and was that why she miscarried?"

"How would I know who she was sleeping with?" Di snapped. "Like I said, everyone slept with everyone." Aaron noticed she no longer denied knowing Starshine.

"Weren't you concerned about her? You took her to the clinic, yet you let her go back to someone who may have abused her."

Di closed her eyes and rubbed her forehead. When she dropped her hand and opened her eyes, she said, "I talked to her after we went to the clinic. I said if someone had abused her, she should report him. She said she loved the guy and he loved her. In those days, we weren't so savvy about sexual abuse. Even now, you know perfectly well that it's rough on the victim. How does she convince anyone that she didn't consent to sex, to rough sex, to whatever?"

Aaron's jaw clenched. He hated that abusers so often got away with it.

"I know," Eden said. "It's a terrible situation. So, what did happen to Starshine? Was she okay?"

"She healed after the miscarriage. And she left the commune. I think it was fairly soon after that, wasn't it, Seal?" She glanced away.

Seal said, "Yeah, I think."

"Do you know where she went?" Eden asked.

Aaron stifled a smile. She really was tenacious when she wanted answers.

Di shrugged and said impatiently, "People came and went, who knows where? She's definitely not on Destiny, that's for sure."

"And she might have gone back to her real name," Eden said thoughtfully. "Do you happen to know what that was?"

"Haven't a clue," Di said quickly. "Eden, I'm afraid your curiosity is going to have to go unsatisfied this time. Can't you be content with having found me and Seal?"

Eden gave a small laugh. "I suppose I'll have to be, won't I?"

Aaron's expression was faraway, kind of wistful. Eden, sitting on a picnic rug beside him at Hog's Back Park, felt distanced by it.

It was late Thursday afternoon. He had spent the day at the Aviation and Space Museum, and then he'd picked her up and driven to this scenic park, bringing along a sushi dinner. They had avoided the neat lawns and picnic tables with noisy families and instead found a more wildernessy area. It was lovely and peaceful here on the big rocks by a river, under the shade of a leafy tree.

But Eden's mind wasn't at peace. Tomorrow, Aaron would be back on Destiny Island. That had to be weighing on his mind, as it was on hers. What would happen to the two of them? She put down the plastic box of takeout sushi she'd been nibbling from. "What's wrong?" she asked.

He blinked, as if he was bringing himself back to her. "Nothing."

"Aaron, I saw it on your face."

He leaned forward to wrap his arms around his knees. "It's nothing big. Just that I miss the smell of the ocean. It's not that I was even so conscious of it on Destiny."

"I was. I guess because it was foreign to me."

"Now that you say that, I remember noticing it when I first moved to the island. In Vancouver, the ocean was right there, too, but on Destiny there are no city smells to interfere with it. It's fresh and pure. But anyhow, I guess over the years it just . . . became part of me. It's the air I breathe. So I stopped noticing it. Until it wasn't there anymore."

She copied his posture, dropping her head to rest on her bent knees. "What's going to become of us?"

He turned his head sideways toward her. "Guess we do have to talk about that?"

She met his gaze. "I do."

"Okay," he said resignedly. "I get it. You don't want

to waste time in a relationship that might not have a future."

She grimaced. "That sounds so harsh."

"Tell me it's not true," he challenged.

"I suppose," she admitted reluctantly. "Especially not a relationship that's so difficult."

"I really do get it. I mean, if we carry on, what do we do? Skype. Have phone sex and—"

"Seriously?"

"Well, yeah. We're lovers. No need to go without sex, right?"

"Uh, I suppose not." Phone sex? Was she capable of being that uninhibited? Probably. She'd learned all sorts of things about herself since she'd met Aaron. But she couldn't believe phone sex would be anywhere near as satisfying as actual physical intimacy. She imagined curling up in her bed afterward, the phone to her ear as they talked. No warm body spooning her, no soft breath brushing her neck.

He'd resumed eating his sushi and she forced herself to do the same. Between bites, he said, "I'm glad I came. This week's been good. I saw you on your turf, learned a lot more about your job and your city. Met your family."

"Which wasn't an unmixed blessing."

"Yeah, well, Miranda isn't happy about you either."

His sister was upset that he was here with Eden rather than back home. No doubt Miranda felt as threatened by her as Eden's parents felt by Aaron. "Family approval would sure be nice," she grumbled.

"We're adults. We don't need family approval."

"I know. It's not like moving away from them equals abandonment. There's Skype, texts, email, flights."

He put down his empty sushi container. "Which one of us are you thinking of?"

"Moving?" She handed her own half-finished sushi to him. "Either, right now. I mean, I'm trying to imagine different futures. If I moved . . . Well, Mom's doing well. Her health's improving and so's her state of mind since she and Aunt Di have reunited. I like Destiny Island and I think I could feel at home there. I'm sure I could find work, something that uses my law degree and feels worthwhile to me. Maybe with a charity or nonprofit."

He touched her arm, his fingers warm and firm. "That's terrific that you're considering it."

"Only considering," she warned. "It would be hard. How about you? Are you considering moving?"

"Only all the time," he said wryly. "Sure, there are things to like about Ottawa and the area around it. I did some checking and I could probably get a job flying. Bush pilot stuff and tourist scenic flights."

"What about Blue Moon Air?"

His shoulders tensed. "I'd hate to give it up. I built it, Eden. When I was a messed-up teen, it never occurred to me that I could build a business of my own, doing something I loved."

"Maybe you could sell it and use the money to start something similar, based here." But could she really imagine him doing that? It struck her that asking Aaron to live here would be like caging an eagle in a zoo. It might survive, but it wouldn't thrive and be happy.

"Maybe." He gave her a tired smile. "Lots of maybes, eh?"

She nodded. "I know it's way too early to make decisions, but I don't do well with uncertainty."

He gave a soft laugh. "Tell me something I don't know."

When he put his arm around her shoulders, she leaned into him. "Even if the problems seem . . . well, not insurmountable but big," she said, "I can't imagine saying good-bye."

"Me either. So we won't. I can take more time off work every now and then, come out and visit you."

"If I took an extra day when there are long weekends, I could fly to Destiny."

"Good. Seeing each other would be good. In addition to the Skyping and, you know"—he squeezed her—"the phone sex."

Friday evening, Aaron smoothed dark curls from his niece's forehead and planted a kiss on her soft mocha skin. "Sleep tight, Fairy-ana." That had been his nickname for Ariana since she'd become obsessed with stories about fairies. He'd often wondered if that fascination tied in with a subconscious desire to have wings and magic so she could fly away from some of the not-so-nice apartments she and her mom had lived in. Now, though, she was safely tucked up in a toddler bed in the middle of a forest that, while it might not be enchanted, was full of beauty.

Too bad his sister didn't feel the same way. Miranda pulled the curtains with a brisk swish. "All the trees and the darkness and the freaking silence out there creeps me out. I don't know how you can live out here."

"All the city lights, traffic, sirens, and drunks on the street would drive me nuts," he shot back.

"Whatever."

They returned to the kitchen and, working together with the ease of long practice, cleared the table and did the dishes. When he'd arrived home late that afternoon, he'd been greeted by his T-shirt–clad sister, his adorable niece, a house that had never been so clean, and the aroma of tuna casserole. It had been one of his and Miranda's standbys as kids. They'd been able to stretch one tin of bargain tuna, another of cheap cream of mushroom soup, and a mess of bulk pasta into two dinners for both of them.

He'd told Miranda to help herself to the stash of cash in his bedroom drawer and he didn't like it that his sister was still eating this way. But at least she'd used more tuna, as well as some chopped mushrooms and onions, and she'd grated cheddar cheese on top, as well as adding a side of steamed broccoli.

After the dishes were done, she made a pot of tea and they went into the living room. Aaron took a chair and Miranda curled into one end of the couch, tucking her legs up. She was pale and thin, her body almost disappearing inside the oversized gray T-shirt that she tugged down over loose shorts. Her blond hair straggled past her shoulders, limp and dull. Her bluish-gray eyes, always a shade bluer than his, had mauve shadows beneath them. Despite the dragon tattooed on her arm, the symbol of her strength, she looked miserable.

"You're settling in okay?" he asked. "Despite hating the trees and all."

She nodded. "Lionel helped me with a few things. He's a good guy. He and his girlfriend had us over for dinner a couple of nights ago." She fiddled with the hem of her tee. "She's nice, too, Marlise. She told me about a couple of part-time jobs where I could take Ariana with me."

"I told you, you don't have to get a job. I'd rather you took some courses."

"Yeah, I will. I have to, right? I mean, I'm sucking at the whole motherhood thing." She sounded uncharacteristically fragile.

"You're a good mother. But you'd give Ariana a better life if you could get a decent job."

"I know."

Much as it annoyed him when she was snippy with him, it felt weird to hear resignation rather than her usual sassy tone.

"Anyhow," she said, "I can do both. A part-time job and some courses. One of the jobs Marlise mentioned is at a day care."

"Aside from being a mom, you don't have any training for that."

"I know. But I love kids, and that might be a good job for me in the future. There are loads of day cares in Vancouver and it's perfect work for a mom with a little kid. Some are unlicensed, but I'd want to get proper training. I mean, looking after kids is important, right?"

"For sure." They exchanged a meaningful look. Too bad neither their mom nor their grandparents had believed that.

She went on. "I can do some research and find out what kind of courses I'd need to take. They're sure to be available online. I mean, everything is."

"Great plan," he enthused.

A tentative smile flickered. "I have a plan. How about that?"

"What's the other job?"

"It's at Blowing Bubbles, the cool store where I got the toddler bed. They sell stuff like that, and kids' clothes and toys. The owner and the other woman who works there both bring their little ones to work, but the employee's going on maternity leave. Marlise phoned me today to say she'd talked to the owner and I can go in for an interview tomorrow. With Ariana."

"Go to the hairdresser first, okay?"

She perked up enough to glare at him, but then the energy faded from her face. "I don't know if I can take a job in the village. Seeing as your house is out here in the boonies, where the bus only comes by a couple times a day."

"We'll get you a car."

The old Miranda roared back with a vengeance. "Jesus H, Aaron! I'm trying to pay you rent, not have you buy me a freaking car!"

He rolled his eyes. "Gimme a break, Sis. I wasn't going to buy you a new Ferrari. There's a bunch of used cars around. I'm sure we can find something that's cheap and in decent shape."

"It might be cheaper for me to rent a room near the village." She dipped her head like it was too heavy to hold up.

Something stopped him from uttering another protest.

She raised her head again and said softly, "But I don't want to. Aaron, this is really hard for me to say, but I need you. I feel like I'm . . . foundering. Floundering? What's the word?" Not waiting for an answer, she went on. "I've been trying to hold it together for so long and I've run out of energy. Confidence. Pride, I guess. I need you."

"You've got me. Always. You know that."

Her head dipped again so he couldn't see her expression. "But you're dating this woman in Ottawa. You went to see her, so it must be serious."

"It's . . . new, but yeah, it feels like it could be serious."

"Wow. I've never heard you say that before."

"I've never felt it before," he admitted.

She nibbled a cuticle. "So I guess I'm happy for you. Maybe you'll have better luck than I've ever had."

"You don't sound so happy. What's wrong?"

She hunched her shoulders and dropped her head, not meeting his eyes.

"If you're worried she'll come between us," he said, "it's not going to happen. It's a whole different thing. Girlfriend. Sister. Different relationships." He wasn't explaining it well, but hopefully she knew what he meant. "Eden has a sister, too. She gets it."

"Would she move here?"

"It's a possibility. If, you know, we get really serious about each other."

In a voice that was barely more than a mumble, she said, "What about you moving there?"

He would never lie to his sister. "That's another possibility."

She said something he didn't catch.

"Miranda? What did you say?"

Her head lifted and he saw tears on her cheeks. "I'm a horrible sister. You're so nice to me and I'm so mean to you, but I don't know how Ariana and I would survive without you."

What had happened to his ballsy little sister? He hadn't seen her so vulnerable since she was thirteen and cutting her arm with a razor blade—not, she'd assured him when he caught her, as a suicide attempt but so she could feel in control of one tiny part of her life. He went over and gathered her into an awkward hug. "No matter where I live, you'll always have me."

She kind of burrowed into him, her face buried against his chest, sobbing. He felt the heat of her skin, the fragility of the bones in her back, the dampness of her tears soaking into his T-shirt. "Hey, Sis, it's going to be okay."

They'd been tough kids and they'd turned into tough adults. This depression and insecurity she was going through wouldn't last. Miranda the dragon girl would recover her spirit and things would be back to normal. She'd leave Destiny, the place she'd always hated, and reassert her independence. She'd cheer him on in his relationship with Eden.

Yeah, it'd happen. Even if right now she was crying so hard it felt like her frail body was about to shake apart.

Chapter Nineteen

It was Sunday afternoon of the first weekend in August, the British Columbia Day long weekend, and Eden was on a sailboat for the first time in her life. Ontario had a holiday on Monday too, and she'd taken Friday off as well and come to Destiny.

It was the second time she'd visited Aaron since his trip to Ottawa. She'd also come for the Canada Day long weekend at the beginning of July, sharing his bedroom while Miranda and Ariana slept down the hall. He had planned to come to Ottawa in midmonth, but, unfortunately, Jillian got the flu and wasn't able to fly, so he'd had to stay on Destiny.

It had been a long month. They had spoken almost every day, talking about their families, her work projects, his colleagues and passengers, books, TV, memories from childhood, anything and everything. And sex, of course. She'd discovered that phone sex could be surprisingly erotic, though it sure didn't measure up to true physical intimacy.

None of it was as good as being together. Especially being alone together. That time alone was a rare commodity. Even when she was on Destiny, sometimes Blue Moon Air was so busy that Aaron needed to fly. Then Eden would visit SkySong and spend time with Aunt Di and Uncle Seal, or go for coffee and a chat with Marlise, Iris at Dreamspinner, or old Gertie Montgomery, all of whom were turning into friends.

At Aaron's house, the prickly Miranda and the delightful but demanding Ariana were often around. Miranda kept apologizing for being there and Eden kept saying it was Miranda's home and of course she should be there. The two of them hadn't exactly clicked. Eden knew Miranda felt threatened by her, just as Eden's mom felt threatened by Aaron.

So far, this weekend was working out pretty well. Yesterday, Jillian and the other relief pilot had covered all the Blue Moon Air flights. Miranda had driven to town with Ariana after breakfast to spend the day working at Blowing Bubbles. Eden and Aaron had gone back to bed, where they'd spent the rest of the morning making love and talking. They'd roused themselves to pack a lunch and take it down the zigzag wooden staircase to the pebbly, driftwood-strewn beach below his place.

After eating, they again made love—and barely managed to grab their T-shirts when a couple of whale-watching boats zipped around the point. They'd then driven into town to visit the Saturday market in the village park. They admired arts and crafts and clapped along to the catchy tunes played by a three-person ensemble. Eden bought wild rose soap for her mom and they picked up cheeses, fancy bread, and fresh pasta for a family dinner.

Today, Miranda was at home, working on the online courses to get her GED, the first step toward becoming certified as an early childhood educator. Iris Yakimura had offered Eden and Aaron the loan of her family's thirty-two-foot sailboat, the *Windspinner*. Aaron said the wooden boat was a classic, and it had clearly been well maintained and loved.

It came as no surprise that he was a proficient sailor. She loved watching him as, clad only in shorts and Teva sandals, he maneuvered the sails and handled the tiller.

The day was perfect for sailing, the sun's heat tempered by a breeze that kept the sails filled and the boat skimming along. Eden, wearing a filmy, long-sleeved cover-up over her blue bikini, lazed on one of the seats in the cockpit and lifted her sunglassed, sunscreened face to the sky. When a small plane flew overhead, she waved, as people on boats had done when she'd flown over. "It's a decadent life you lead, Aaron Gabriel."

He laughed and leaned over from the tiller to run his hand along her bare leg. "Only when you're around. Other days, I'm flying from dawn until dusk." He circled her ankle with his fingers. "Have I told you how glad I am that you're here?"

"So you have an excuse to take a couple of days off?"

"Yeah sure. That's it."

"Well, I'm glad you're glad. I only wish Miranda was."

"You know it isn't that she dislikes you."

"Could've fooled me," she grumbled. But then she said, "No, I know. She and Mom are a lot alike. They were both so strong and self-sufficient, and then something happened to knock them for a loop. Mom's cancer was obviously a bigger, scarier thing, but I can see it was very tough for Miranda to finally concede that she couldn't look after Ariana by herself."

"She loves Fairy-ana so much and hates feeling like a crappy mom. She's depressed and pissed off at herself."

"I can see that. Also, she's conflicted because she hates taking what she sees as your charity, yet she knows that the best plan, long-term, is for her to get a proper education. Which means working only part-time now and continuing her dependency on you."

Eden was quiet while Aaron took down the two sails and anchored the boat in a sheltered bay off a small, uninhabited island.

When he came back to the cockpit, he leaned against the wooden frame of the open door that led down into the cabin. "I'm sorry Miranda's getting in the way of our relationship."

"Aaron, she's family. Just like my mom, she's going through a rough time. It's good that our loved ones turn to us, and it's good we can help. Seeing how great you are with her has only made me love you more."

Oops. She hadn't meant to say the words, or at least not that way, but they'd slid naturally from her lips. They were words she'd said before, to Ray, after she'd known him for a year and a half. Though it was less than two months since she'd met Aaron, the words were real and conveyed emotions she'd never felt for Ray—deeper and, due to the complicated circumstances, more confusing ones.

Yes, her love was real, and she knew Aaron had strong feelings for her, but maybe it was too soon to speak those words.

The smile widening his mouth told her it wasn't.

He came over and reached down to clasp her hands. "You mean that? You love me?"

"I do. Though I could have said it at a more romantic moment. More of a statement, not a passing reference."

"I don't give a damn how or where you say it. Hearing the words is amazing. Eden, I . . . I love you, too." He threw back his head and laughed up at the sky, the sound harmonizing with the cries of wheeling gulls.

Relief and a feeling of rightness seeped through her. He loved her.

"I never believed I'd say those words," he said. "My mom and sister were always *falling in love* and look where it got them. But this is different. It's not a misguided crush, it's real."

She nodded. "I know."

He laughed again. "Oh man! I never believed I'd feel this way. Never believed a wonderful woman like you could love me. Come here, you." When he tugged her hands, she rose and stepped into his arms. They hugged tight and kissed as the breeze ruffled their hair.

They loved each other. Everything would work out. Somehow.

"We need to make love to seal the deal," he declared.

His phrasing made her grin. "We need to," she agreed with pretended solemnity.

"On deck or below?"

She glanced at the sky. Now there were only gulls, but so far this morning she'd counted four small planes flying overhead or nearby. "Below. So I can concentrate on us and not worry about providing X-rated entertainment for people in planes."

They went into the cabin, with its miniature kitchen

and bathroom, small dinette and couch, and V-berth in the bow. The wood gleamed and everything was ship-shape.

It took only a few seconds to strip off their few items of clothing and spread a large beach towel over the V-shaped bed. The space intrigued Eden: so wide at the head yet tapering to a point at the foot; low-ceilinged so you couldn't sit up; and dim because there were only two small portholes, one on each side. "It looks cozy but restrictive of movement."

"Yeah." He winked. "But on the plus side, there's no one out here to hear you scream."

She laughed. At his house, they had to muffle the sounds of their lovemaking so the noise didn't carry down the hall to Miranda and Ariana's room. "How liberating."

There was more laughter from both of them as they climbed awkwardly through the rectangular opening at the head of the bed and got their bodies turned around. They curled on their sides facing each other and with tender hands explored each other's bodies, almost as if it were the first time.

And then Eden rolled a condom onto Aaron's hard length and, in classic missionary position, they made love slowly as the sailboat rocked gently from side to side. And with each motion, she thought, *We love each other.* This was the deep, special sense of intimacy that she'd always hoped to one day experience.

After they both climaxed and then held each other for long, wordless minutes, hunger claimed them. They managed, with a bumped elbow and knee and some chuckles, to extricate themselves from the V-berth and dressed again. Eden reapplied sunscreen as Aaron took their lunch from the fridge, and then they went to sit on the front deck of the boat.

As they ate, they talked about this and that: the news of the day, Destiny Island politics, whether shy Iris would ever find a boyfriend. After they finished eating, they stretched out in the sun and Aaron said, "Over the past couple of months we've discussed politics and religion, books and movies, and the pros and cons of both Destiny and Ottawa."

"We have." They'd found that in the important areas they were compatible, if not always of identical mind. Their differences were the good kind, stimulating rather than troubling. Eden was confident they were a good match.

"There's one thing we haven't discussed, though," he said. "Children."

"Wow, that's a big subject, isn't it? How many, when, philosophies on child-rearing, things like—"

"Whoa." He sat up. "Uh, I actually meant . . . well, do you want to have kids?"

She blinked, and sat up, too, her heart suddenly racing. "Of course I do." Didn't he? Why had it never occurred to her, even once, to ask? "Aaron, you know that family's the most important thing in the world to me. Tell me you want children."

He gazed out toward the islet, where small waves splashed white froth against the rocky shore. "To be honest, the idea scares me. I think the worst thing you can do is have a child and be a bad parent. My mom was, and I figure her parents must have been, too, given how she turned out and how they treated Miranda and me. And then there's Miranda, who loves her daughter and tries her best but keeps screwing up. That's what family looks like to me. Why would I do better than any of them?"

She took a breath, her pounding heart slowing again. This wasn't so bad. It wasn't that he hated the idea of having children; he just lacked confidence. "Because you're not an addict like your mom. You don't have that kind of personality. And you're not cold and selfish like your grandparents. You're already established, settled, unlike Miranda. But look at her now. She's working to improve things. I bet she doesn't screw it up this time. And you wouldn't either."

"D'you realize how much pressure that puts on me? Like you think I'd be a perfect dad, and I can't even imagine that." He rubbed the heels of his hands against his temples. "I'd never measure up to your father."

"Dad's wonderful, but he's not perfect. Nor is Mom. And nor am I. We're human, which means we can't be perfect, and neither can our relationships. Not ones like yours and mine, and not parent-child relationships. But that doesn't mean they can't be loving and wonderful and worth investing your heart in. Look at you and Miranda. As much as you argue and get frustrated with each other, neither of you could imagine life without the other one."

"I guess that's true." He leaned closer and bumped his shoulder against hers. "So how many do you want?"

Relief made her beam. "Two or three. How does that sound?"

"Scary as hell."

"But I'm in no hurry. I think a couple should spend a lot of time together and really know each other before they bring children into the world."

"Sounds right to me."

Yes, she and Aaron were compatible. They'd make a wonderful couple and wonderful parents. If Eden moved to Destiny, Miranda would come to accept her and the two of them would become close.

The decision was still a long way in the future. Eden wasn't about to uproot her life and stress out her mom over a man she'd known for two months. Yet the more time she spent with Aaron—and the more time apart—the more she was coming to believe they did have a future together.

There was a month until the end of summer. Eden's mom was doing a lot better and becoming more self-sufficient every week. She was optimistic that she'd be able to return to teaching in September. Kelsey would go back to McGill and life would pretty much return to normal. Eden would be released from caregiver obligations.

She and Aaron would continue to talk every day, to visit whenever they could, and maybe by Christmas they'd be ready to make a decision. It was seeming more and more possible that by next spring Eden might be living with Aaron on Destiny Island.

Eden sat at the desk in her home office checking texts and emails. The August night was hot and humid, oppressive outside, and she had the window closed and the air conditioner going.

A few nights ago, she'd complained about the heat to Marlise in an email. Tonight, Marlise had sent her a recipe for chilled gazpacho soup, saying it was perfect for hot summer days or nights. She added, "Come for a visit and I'll make it for you. BTW, it's not humid here. Just warm and sunny, with that lovely ocean breeze." She'd added a smiley-face emoticon and also attached a photo of a gorgeous ocean sunrise, taken from Lionel's deck. Marlise made no secret of the fact that she was lobbying for Eden to move to Destiny.

So was Iris at Dreamspinner. The two of them had clicked in that special way, like when you sit beside another girl on the first day of school, exchange a few words, and suddenly know you're going to be BFFs. Iris might be shy, but the bookstore's coffee shop was island central, and she was privy to most of the news and gossip, so she kept Eden updated—at least on all the items that were "for public consumption" rather than overheard secrets.

I'm spending more social time emailing with people on Destiny than seeing friends in Ottawa.

She'd lost touch with her friends here, except for having an occasional lunch with Ray. Now, because Navdeep was shouldering more of the workload and her mom was back on her feet, Eden had some free evenings. Maybe she should get in touch with the women she used to hang out with. But on the other hand, what was the point of rebuilding relationships if she ended up moving to Destiny?

More and more, she was seriously considering it. Ottawa seemed a bit oppressive in more ways than just the August weather. What used to strike her as old-fashioned charm now seemed stuffy. Eccentric Azalea hadn't been so wrong in suggesting that it was a city of politicians and bureaucrats, and neither were Eden's favorite people.

Of course it was also the city where Eden's parents

lived, and that was a huge check mark in the Ottawa column.

She glanced at the time. In a couple of hours, she'd Skype Aaron or he'd call her. Until then, maybe she'd read. With the air conditioner buzzing away. On Destiny, she could read on the deck and watch the ocean. Yes, there were lots of check marks in the Destiny column.

When she'd told him that she was warming to the idea of moving, he'd told her he was happy about that, but she'd also read relief in his eyes. He might move to Ottawa, but it would only be because he wanted to be with her, not because he'd really enjoy living here. If that was the case, how could their relationship thrive?

She settled into a chair with her book. She'd become hooked on the thrillers written by Kellan Hawke, the Destiny Island author. Quickly engrossed, she jumped when her phone rang. It was Kelsey, who didn't even say hi. "Eden, you have to come over. Something's going on with Mom."

Eden rose and hurried to grab her purse and put on her sandals. "What do you mean, *going on*?"

"I don't know. She had an appointment with Dr. Wong late this afternoon. Dad went with her. I was out with friends and just came home. She's crying her eyes out and Dad's trying to comfort her, but neither one of them seems up to telling me what's wrong. Just come, okay?"

"I'm on my way." Eden raced out of her apartment and ran for the elevator to go down to the underground parking lot. Dr. Karen Wong was her mom's oncologist. Had she delivered bad news? Surely not; Eden's mom had been feeling so much better.

In her little blue Smart car, she drove the four kilometers to the family home in record time. When she went in the front door, she called, "Hello? Where is everyone?"

Kelsey, in a pretty yellow sundress that contrasted with her worried expression, appeared at the top of the stairs that led to the second floor. "Up here."

After the surgery, they'd converted the downstairs TV room into a bedroom so Eden's mom didn't need to deal with stairs. She'd stayed there through the chemo and radiation, then moved back upstairs.

Eden ran up the stairs and then slowed her pace. She was supposed to be calm and in control; it wouldn't help her mother if she acted panicky. When she entered the bedroom, her parents were both half-sitting, half-lying on top of the duvet. Her dad had his arms around his wife and she was curled into him, her face buried, her body trembling. He was stroking her back, his head bowed so that Eden couldn't see his face either. Her mom's ultrashort hair, which used to be the same shade as Eden's but was growing back silver, was disheveled, the wig a mass of brown curls on the carpet as if she'd flung it away.

Kelsey stood by the bed, her fingers woven tightly together. Eden went to her sister's side, pried one of her hands loose, and gripped it. "Dad? Mom? What happened?"

When neither acknowledged her presence, she bit her lip. It felt almost as if she and Kelsey were intruding. But the four of them were a family. Whatever this was, she and her sister needed to know so they could all pull together to deal with it.

"You went to the doctor today, Mom?" It took an effort to keep her voice steady. After receiving no response, she sharpened her tone, doing her best imitation of her mother's teacher voice. "Mom! Dad! You have to tell us."

The tone worked, at least with her father. He lifted his head, looking as old and shocked as he had when his wife was first diagnosed. "There was a little lump in her armpit." His voice dragged out of his throat, each word sounding painful. "The doctor said it was probably just scar tissue from the surgery. She only did a biopsy to be absolutely sure. That's what she said."

Eden's blood ran cold. She was aware of Kelsey squeezing her hand painfully hard, and she squeezed back. Trying to keep her voice steady, she said, "What did the results show?"

"It's back." Her father's expression was bleak. "The cancer's back."

Eden's heart stopped.

Kelsey made a gulping sound. "Oh God, no."

Eden stared at her, seeing her own horror mirrored in her sister's blue eyes.

Their mom pushed herself out of her husband's arms and shoved herself off the bed. Her legs seemed shaky, barely able to hold her up, but she found the strength to pace over to the window, kicking the wig aside on her way. Turning to face them, she put her hands behind her to brace herself against the sill. "It's not fair!" Her face was tear-swollen and red. "I lost a breast and I agreed to them removing the other one because they said it was safer."

Anger heated her voice. "I did everything they told

me! All the horrible chemo and radiation. I threw up, I lost my hair, and for what? To have the damned cancer come back?"

"It's not fair," Eden agreed. Still linked, she and Kelsey went over to their mother, and the three of them fell into a clumsy hug, Mom's body sagging into the support of her daughters' young, healthy ones. A moment later, Dad's arms encircled them.

"I could die," Helen whispered between sobs. "It's come back and this time it may win."

"It won't win!" Eden said, hearing her father say, "You're not going to die, Helen." Kelsey chimed in with, "You can't talk that way, Mom."

Their attempts to reassure and encourage her only made her cry harder. When the tears finally eased, her husband helped her back to the bed, where she leaned against the pillows, tear-stained and drawn. "I can't face it again," she said bleakly.

"Dad?" Eden turned to him. "What exactly did the doctor say?"

He scrubbed a hand across his face. He wasn't crying. She'd never seen her father cry, but he did look shell-shocked. "It's a recurrence. It seems they didn't get all the cancer cells the first time." Bitterness tinged his voice. "Dr. Wong said it looked really good when she did the surgery, but they can never be sure. Just a couple of cells can be enough. And yes, they can survive chemo and radiation."

"Shit!" Kelsey said, tears slicking her face.

Eden felt like crying, too, but forced back the tears. "What happens now?"

"Dr. Wong wants us to come back tomorrow," he said. "To discuss treatment options."

"All right." Eden took a breath. "Let's try to stay

calm. Maybe it's just a little lump and the treatment will be straightforward." Calm was the last thing she felt inside. Mom was right. It wasn't fair. Not that cancer was ever fair.

Dad nodded slowly. "You're right. We need to talk to the doctor again, and then we'll know what we're dealing with. Your mom and I just heard those dreadful words and . . . well, I guess we overreacted." He gazed at Eden. "You'll come with us, won't you?"

"Of course."

"I want to be there, too," Kelsey said, brushing dampness from her cheeks. "We'll figure this out together."

"I love you all so much," their mom said shakily. "I feel like I've let you down."

They all hurried to hug and reassure her. While Kelsey helped Mom take a sleeping pill and get ready for bed, Eden fixed her dad a stiff drink and took it up to the bedroom.

Leaving their parents alone, she and Kelsey came downstairs and exchanged a long, wordless hug. Then, feeling guilty for leaving her family but knowing she couldn't stay any longer without breaking down, Eden drove home.

Her computer told her she'd missed Aaron's Skype call. She poured herself a glass of wine—the strongest thing she had in the apartment—and called him back.

The moment she saw his face on screen, she began to sob.

"Eden? My God, what's wrong?"

"It's . . ." She pressed her fingers under her eyes, trying to staunch the tears as she struggled to speak. "Mom's cancer is back."

"Oh shit. Jesus, that's awful. I'm so sorry."

"Me too."

"I wish I was there with you."

"I wish you were, too." She took a deep breath, pulling herself back together even as she told him, "I could use a hug."

"I bet. How bad is it, the cancer?"

"It seems there's a recurrence, in her armpit. Mom and Dad were too upset to really take it in. We're all going to the doctor tomorrow to get more information and to talk about treatment."

"That's scary shit. Your mom must be devastated." Despite the limits of technology, she could see the sympathy in his eyes.

"She is. We are. Damn, Aaron, she was feeling so much better." She raised her wineglass to slug back a healthy mouthful. "I feel so powerless. I wish there was something I could do."

"I guess all you can do is be there for her."

"This makes me feel vulnerable," she admitted. "I like situations I can control. If it's like this for me, I hate to think how truly awful it must be for Mom."

"Let me know if there's anything I can do. For you, for her, or for your dad or Kelsey."

"Thank you." As she reached for her wineglass again, she realized her head was pounding. If only she could lay it on Aaron's shoulder and feel his arms around her. "Mom said it's not fair. It truly isn't fair to her. But Aaron, it isn't fair to the rest of us either. Dad's been through so much. Kelsey's trying to be all mature, but she's awfully young to be dealing with something like this. And then there's us." Feeling selfish and petty even as she said it, she went on. "What will this do to us?"

"There you go again, wanting to plan everything

out," he teased gently. "Everyone's going to have to take this a day at a time. Right now, you don't know exactly what your mom will be facing. Of course news like this is a huge shock, but maybe it won't be such a big thing this time. They've been monitoring her closely, so they probably caught it really early."

"I guess. But it can't be good, having cancer again when it's not much more than a year since her surgery."

"Hang in there, Eden, and try not to jump to conclusions."

"You're right." Of course she'd hang in there. Her parents relied on her to do that. And she wouldn't jump to conclusions. She'd use the Internet to research cancer recurrence so she'd be thoroughly prepared to talk to Dr. Wong.

"Does Di know yet?" he asked.

"No. Mom and Dad were in shock. Kelsey and I are the first people they told. Maybe I should tell Aunt Di. Mom's gone to bed now, but I bet she'd appreciate a chance to talk to her sister in the morning."

"Sounds like a good idea to me." He paused. "What could *you* use, Eden? What can I do for you right now?"

Find some way of holding me together because I feel as if I'm going to shatter into pieces. But out of long habit, she said, "I'll be fine."

"Sure you will. But how about letting someone take care of you for just a little while?"

She closed her eyes. Could she surrender control and let herself be looked after? Opening her eyes again, she admitted, "That sounds really nice. If you were here—" She had to break off, to choke back a sob. Why couldn't he be here? "I'd ask you to crawl into bed with me and hold me. To speak in a low voice because I have a headache, and tell me stories about Destiny." Anything to take her mind off the panic that threatened to overtake her. "Tell me about the baby seals, the orcas leaping out of the water, the hummingbirds doing that funny territorial dance."

"Okay, then here's what we're going to do. We'll sign off Skype and you go take a couple of pills for your headache, brush your teeth, and climb into your pj's. Get into bed and give me a call. You can curl up with the cell by your pillow and I'll tell you stories."

The research could wait until morning. This was exactly what she needed right now. She guessed he'd done something similar for Miranda when she was little and feeling scared. He would do the same for his and Eden's children.

If events didn't keep conspiring against them and they did actually manage to build a future together.

Chapter Twenty

Eden had it down to a routine, which was a good thing because she was physically exhausted and emotionally raw on this last Friday of August. She'd flown from Ottawa's international airport to Vancouver's, traveling with only her big purse and a zippered tote bag because she had summer clothes and toiletries at Aaron's.

Her flight had arrived early and she'd climbed into a taxi for the short ride to the public seaplane dock on the Fraser River, getting there in time to see the blue-and-white de Havilland Beaver touch down lightly on the water. She waved as it motored toward her. Aaron would have already picked up his afternoon passengers from the Vancouver Harbor terminal.

When he hopped out and tied up, she waited impatiently and then he was hugging her tight. "So good to see you," he said.

"I know. It's been forever. I'm so sorry you couldn't come to Ottawa in August." They had planned for it, but then the recurrence of her mom's cancer had thrown a monkey wrench into everyone's plans. While

Aaron could still have visited, Eden had been more or less at her parents' beck and call, plus seeing him would have stressed out her mom even further.

It had been tough enough for Eden to get away for this long weekend.

"I wish I didn't have other passengers," he said, "so we could be alone and talk."

"It's okay." He'd warned her it was a busy weekend for Blue Moon Air. His relief pilot wasn't available due to a family wedding, and Aaron and Jillian were both fully booked with multipassenger flights. "We'll have time later," she assured him, but under her breath she added, "I hope." What with his flight schedule and the presence of Miranda and Ariana at his house, who knew when they'd find some private moments?

"I have a surprise." He picked up her tote. "We'll have the house to ourselves."

"Really? What happened? Miranda hasn't moved back to Vancouver, has she?" Eden hoped not, because it would mean Miranda going back to jobs like waitressing and not having the time to pursue her long-term plan of improving her education and job prospects.

"No, she's still sticking with her courses and her job at Blowing Bubbles. But Lionel's staying with Marlise this weekend and my sister and niece are at his house. Lionel left you his car, so when I'm flying you can go into the village, get together with friends, whatever you want. Or you can just stay at the cabin and rest. Laze on the deck or the beach."

An ounce or two of the tension that weighted Eden's shoulders lightened. "I'm grateful to all of them."

Using his hand for support, she climbed into the

Beaver. As she made her way to her usual seat, the
one beside his, she murmured hellos to the passengers: a pair of outdoorsy-looking young women, a
thirtysomething man and woman who were wrapped
up in each other, and a man in business attire, his suit
jacket on his lap and his tie loosened.

Once Aaron had the plane in the air, he said to her,
"We have two for Galiano, one for North Pender, and
the other two are coming to Destiny with us."

That meant no private conversation, but once the
flight ended, they'd have the whole rest of the day—
and night—alone.

Stretching back in the seat, she resolved to stay in
the moment rather than worry about her mom. She
caught drifts of conversation from the pair of women
about campsites and hiking. The madly-in-love couple
spoke only in murmurs, but an occasional female
giggle drifted forward. The businessman was silent
and so was Eden. On another day, she might have
enjoyed talking to the other passengers, but now she
relished the peace.

Aaron had told her that some passengers described
the flight from Vancouver to a more rustic destination
as an easing of pressure, an experience as relaxing as
a massage. She got it. He'd also used the term Zenlike
when he talked about flying and so it was: gazing at
the ever-changing seascape and noting each tug and
log boom, each tanker and container ship, each sailboat with sails unfurled; seeing the waving hands of
people on those boats and wondering about their lives
rather than worrying about her own.

This living-in-the-moment thing was something
Aaron had taught her, not by instruction but by example. She turned her head to smile at him and he

caught the motion in his excellent peripheral vision and glanced at her with a return smile.

They landed at a public dock on Galiano Island to let off the two women. Aaron unloaded intimidatingly large backpacks, which they hitched onto their shoulders without apparent effort.

A great blue heron stood at the line where ocean met rocky beach, elegantly posed on one leg, intent as it waited for fish to come by. When Aaron motored the plane away from the dock, the heron flapped away on giant wings.

The next stop was North Pender, where the businessman deplaned, his jacket on now, tie adjusted, carrying only a briefcase for luggage.

The romantic pair were still whispering sweet nothings in the backseat, seemingly oblivious to the rest of the world. Eden leaned over and touched Aaron's bare forearm. The warmth of his skin, the firmness of his grip on the steering yoke, were like an infusion of vital, healthy blood into her worn-out body and brain.

When he smiled over at her, she whispered her own sweet nothing. "I love you, darling."

"Love you back."

Content in this moment, she released his arm and watched the now-familiar scenery below as they approached Destiny Island.

Once they'd docked and Aaron had dealt with the passengers, he and Eden went to the office. She and Kam chatted while Aaron did his paperwork, and then he left Kam to clean up the Beaver and refuel. Jillian, who was currently out with the Cessna, would be handling another Beaver flight later that afternoon. And Aaron was off work, all Eden's for the rest of the day.

Soon the Jeep, top down, was on the road. She pulled a flyaway lock of hair back into her ponytail and raised her sunglasses to study her bare arms. Despite all the sunscreen she'd applied over the summer, she'd developed a golden-brown tan she quite liked. Here, she was Aaron's girl. A woman who had interesting new friends and activities to add variety to her life. A woman who was loved and who'd discovered within herself a deeper capacity to love.

When she was on Destiny, she could almost believe that everything—her mom's health and her own future with Aaron—was going to work out.

Outside of the village, the Jeep passed an SUV with two kayaks on the roof, a trio of horses sticking their heads over a wood fence, a pair of cyclists with packs on their backs, and the alpaca farm. In the parking lot by the We Got It general store, a truck towing a sleek powerboat sat beside an old Volkswagen van with flower-child paintwork. The sound of a plane's engine made her gaze upward, where a small aircraft approached, almost buzzing them. The wings waggled and she laughed as she and Aaron both raised an arm to wave at Jillian.

Destiny Island. She could be happy here. If only her mom was well and happy herself.

The roads got progressively narrower and the scenery wilder, and then they were in the parking area by Lionel's house, pulling up beside the old Corolla Aaron had bought for his sister. There was no sign of Miranda or Ariana, which suited Eden just fine right then.

She and Aaron took the path to his house and she followed him as he went to the bedroom to drop her bag. She took a quick check down the hall, finding

Miranda and Ariana's room empty and unusually neat. The entire house was spotless, as it always was since Miranda had moved in. Aaron's sister said it was one tiny thing she could do for him.

He came up behind her and Eden turned into his arms. "I love your sister, but it's very nice to think of an entire evening, the two of us alone."

"You love my sister?"

She hadn't thought before speaking, just used a common expression. Now she considered and said, "I do. I love Fairy-ana, of course, because who wouldn't?" She'd adopted his nickname for his niece. "As for Miranda . . . well, she's feeling vulnerable, depressed, and threatened, so she's kind of moody and even bitchy sometimes. But Mom's like that, too, so I understand it." And Aaron hadn't complained, not even once, about her mother's insecurities and demands.

"Your sister's been the closest person in the world to you since she was born," Eden went on. "And I'd love her for that fact alone. But she's worth it on her own merits, too. She's raising a wonderful little girl and always struggling to do her best for Ariana. It's not easy for Miranda, sacrificing her pride, living here, letting you help her." She grinned. "Taking your advice."

He pulled off the clasp that secured her ponytail, stuck it in his pocket, and ran the fingers of both hands through her hair. Each stroke eased tension from her body.

"You're right," he said. "Miranda's special. I'm glad you can see it. But enough about my sister. What do *you* want, Eden? Right now?"

What had she done to deserve such a generous man? "I want you, naked, in bed." Before him, she'd never been bold about stating her needs, but she had learned. "I want to make love slowly and gently, because I'm feeling tired and fragile."

"Your wish, my lady." He hoisted her effortlessly and carried her to the bedroom, where he eased her down to lie atop the navy-colored duvet. "Bed." With careless male efficiency, he stripped off his Blue Moon Air T-shirt, jeans, and boxers, to reveal his mouth-watering body, browner than ever at the end of summer, and a rising erection. "Me naked." He leaned over her and kissed her, an achingly slow and tender caress that, inexplicably, brought moisture to her eyes.

Her emotions were so close to the surface these days. Rather than surrender to the tears and ruin this moment, she said, "I forgot a step. I want me naked, too."

"That goes without saying and we'll get there."

He trailed kisses across one cheek, around the outside of her ear, and then inside the shell, adding flicks with the tip of his tongue. As she shivered with arousal, he kissed his way down her neck, along the flare of her collarbone, into the notch at the base of her throat. Downward he went, to the open collar of her butter-yellow sleeveless shirt. He undid the first button, spread the cotton an inch or so, and planted more kisses.

She propped herself higher on the pillows so she could watch his progress and rested her hand on his head, feeling the springy warmth of his dark hair. Sensations spread through her, a lazy, sensual arousal seeping through her blood.

Moving down one button at a time, he opened the shirt and spread kisses down to her waist. And then he moved up again to undo the front clasp of her bra and spread the cups to reveal her breasts. Her nipples thrust upward in a blatant invitation.

He brushed the tips of his fingers over them, a caress and a tease. Bending, he licked first one and then the other, and after that he used his lips and tongue in combination, sucking them until her entire body trembled with need.

She tugged on his hair. "There's another part of me that could use that sexy mouth."

"I thought you wanted slow."

"I changed my mind. *You* changed my mind, darling. I want to come. Make me come, Aaron, with your mouth and your hands. And then do it all over again, with that lovely big cock of yours." Until him, she'd never spoken the word *cock*, but when she was feeling sexy, saying *penis* just didn't fit the mood.

Besides, when she talked sexy to him, it always got results—whether in person or over the phone. It did again tonight as he not only obeyed her instructions but added a few improvisational flourishes of his own.

By the time he'd finished with her, she was limp, covered in sweat, and utterly satiated.

Aaron raised himself off her. "Hey," he said, "d'you want to sleep or to have dinner?"

"Both," she mumbled. "Can I do both at once?" But she forced herself up. Much as she craved rest, she didn't want to miss out on an evening with Aaron. Besides, she was starving. "Shower. I need a shower. A refreshing one. Alone."

He chuckled. "I'll get dressed and go start dinner."

The shower did refresh her, as did the aroma coming through the open kitchen window. She followed her nose out to the deck to see him at the barbecue. "What smells so good?"

"Cedar-planked sockeye salmon steaks glazed with a mix of maple syrup and balsamic vinegar. I also made a Greek salad. Could you take it out of the fridge and slice some of the French bread that's on the counter?"

"Sure." She went inside and was about to follow his instructions when she saw a box on the counter, wrapped in sunny gold paper with an explosion of multicolored ribbons. Beside it was a folded note with *Eden* written on the outside.

She was reading it for the second time when Aaron came inside. "Did you know about this?" she asked.

"No. Miranda put it there after I left this morning. I didn't read the note. What did she say?"

"It's for my mom. It's one of those bubble kits, with a fancy wand and bubble liquid. Miranda says it's up to me to judge if it's appropriate, but that when you blow rainbow bubbles on a sunny day, it's hard to feel too awful." She smiled up at him. "And here's another reason to love your sister."

"She's got a good heart."

He sliced the bread and they carried it and the salad, plates and cutlery, and a bottle of pinot gris and glasses out to the deck. Eden went back to the bedroom to get her sweater. The air held a nip, warning that September was around the corner.

She rejoined Aaron as he dished out the food. Rather than sit at the table, they both settled into lounge chairs. They'd spent so long making love that the sun had set. The dim light from a nearly full moon and bright stars lent intimacy.

They ate in peaceful silence for a while. Aaron topped up her wineglass but didn't add any more wine to his. She knew he had a morning flight.

"How's your mother holding up?" he asked.

Eden had kept him up to date via Skype. He knew her mom had had a second surgery, to remove a tumor in the lymph nodes in her armpit. She wouldn't be receiving more radiation but was in for another round of chemotherapy—using a different medicine than before—and also antiestrogen hormonal therapy. "Not well," she told him sadly. "She says it's worse than the first time. Then, all the treatments didn't rid her of cancer, and now she has to go through it all again with no assurance that she'll be okay. She's angry, depressed, discouraged."

"I'm so sorry."

She ate a few more bites and then put down her plate and lifted her wineglass. Her right hand shook, so she cupped the bowl of the glass between both hands as she lifted it to her lips. Lowering it, she said, "She's afraid she's going to die. We keep telling her no, she's strong, she'll fight it and come out on the other side. This is a temporary setback."

"I sure hope so."

"I won't let myself think of any other possibility." She took another sip. "I feel guilty for being here."

"You shouldn't—"

She cut him off. "I know. I'm trying not to. But she's so needy right now, Aaron. Kelsey was supposed to leave for McGill this week, but she stayed a few extra days so I could get away. In fact, she said she'd postpone school entirely, but Mom and Dad don't want that. They're afraid she'll never go back and they really want her to get her degree."

Her throat was dry and she raised her glass for another sip. "When I said I was coming to see you, Mom got upset. She said she might be going to die, so how could she bear to lose her daughter? I told her neither thing was going to happen, but she's in no state of mind to listen."

"You know I don't want to come between you. I want you to be happy, Eden."

"I can't be happy as long as she's so sick." She put down her glass and reached across the folding table between them, seeking his hand. When he wove his fingers between hers, she said, "The happiest I am is when I'm with you. I need this time. It'll give me the courage to go back and be strong for Mom and Dad."

Aaron let go of her hand, rose from his chair, and came to sit on the deck beside her chair. He reached for her hand again, and she threaded her fingers through his.

Gazing at the moon rather than at him, she confessed, "When she was diagnosed initially, I was terrified. Panicked. But I don't know how to deal with panic, so I did everything I could to control the situation. I made sure Mom got to all her appointments and took all her meds and I encouraged her to be as positive as possible. Dad did the same, and I know it was because he was terrified, too. But, like me, he never admitted it. I saw him damp-eyed, but I never saw him cry."

She licked her dry lips and swallowed. "Two nights ago, I was at the house for dinner. Mom went to bed and Kelsey was up in her room. Dad and I were alone in the kitchen, talking about Mom's worries about me leaving Ottawa."

She swallowed again. "He broke down. My dad, who's always been a brick, fell apart and cried. He said he couldn't do it without me. Not just to help with appointments and chores; he said he relies on my strength and my positive attitude to help him get through it all."

"That's a lot to put on you, Eden."

"I guess, but it's not like I have a choice. If he's going to fall apart, I can't. Right?"

"You can with me. If it'd help."

The temptation was there, almost tangible in the air of this starlit night. "I don't think it would. If I broke down, how would I gather up the pieces and go on? What does help, though, is being able to talk to you. To be honest. To admit that I'm not always as strong as I pretend to be when I'm with my family. To have you take care of me like you've done today."

Reality struck again, and she took a shuddering breath. "But that's not going to happen after this weekend, or at least not in person. Kelsey will be back at school. I can't leave Mom and Dad again, at least not until Thanksgiving weekend, when Kelsey can come home. As for you visiting Ottawa, that would stress out my parents, which is the last thing we need right now."

"What you need counts, too."

"And so does what you need." She shook her head, a wave of exhaustion and depression hitting her. "I don't see how this is going to work, Aaron."

"Short-term, we'll have to be satisfied with Skype, talking on the phone, email, texts." His voice trailed off and she could hear how *dissatisfying* he found that prospect, as did she. "Long-term, hopefully your mom will get better again and be more open to the idea of you moving. Or, when Miranda's back on her feet, I could move to Ottawa."

"You're gritting your teeth as you say that."

A pause in the darkness, and then he said, "Damn.

Heard that, did you? Sorry. I could be happy in Ottawa with you, really. It's just that before your mom got sick again, it was seeming like maybe you'd move here."

"It was." She sighed and admitted, "I'm discouraged. Mom's right that none of this is fair. It almost makes me want to trade in my life for a different one."

"One without a sick mom?"

She considered. "I'd never trade Mom or Dad or Kelsey, but yes, I'd want a healthy, happy mother. My old one back. That's it. I want to go back two years and change the future so my mom never gets cancer."

"You'd probably still be with Ray. You wouldn't come to Destiny. You wouldn't meet me."

She groaned. "See? Life isn't fair."

"No. But it's what we've got, so it's up to us to figure out what to do with it." He let go of her hand and shifted position on the deck so that he sat with his back against the wall. "This is too hard on you. You're torn in two directions: your family in Ottawa and me here."

"That's exactly it." She left her lounge chair and came to sit beside him on the deck, close but not touching. She didn't reach for his hand.

"It's like a tug-of-war," he said. "I'm afraid that if we pull any harder on your emotions, you're going to break."

Sadly, hating to admit the truth, hating to admit to weakness, hating the implications of her words, she said, "It does feel like that sometimes. I love you all so much, but I'm not seeing a way for those loves to be compatible." Knees up, clasped hands resting on them, she gazed up at the stars. The night sky was so vast and so mysterious. As lovely and as remote as the possibility of a happy ending for her and Aaron.

It was time to face the truth. She had failed again. Right now, she was failing at both being a good daughter and being a good girlfriend. Thank God for Navdeep, carrying more than his fair share, or she'd be failing at work, too.

Her mom had given her life, been the best mother imaginable, and her needs had to come first. It was time to free Aaron so he could get on with his life. She was fighting back tears and trying to find a steady voice to tell him so, when he spoke.

"I don't want to cause you more stress and pain." He gave a ragged laugh. "Hell, what do I know about relationships? I should've known I'd only screw things up."

"No!" She turned to him, alarmed. "Aaron, don't think that. You haven't done anything wrong. My mom's cancer isn't your fault. It's not your fault that Miranda's going through a bad time and has finally admitted she needs your help. It's not your fault that you're an eagle and—"

"An eagle?"

"An eagle," she confirmed. "You need to fly, you need the ocean and open spaces, the wilderness. Those things aren't your fault, Aaron, they're part of who you are. They're among the many reasons I love you so much." Now the tears did slip from her eyes, tracking down her cheeks. No point in brushing them away; more were piling up behind them. Voice breaking, she said, "I have to let you go. We can't keep doing this."

He sucked in a breath but didn't speak. Nor did she. It was so quiet, no breeze to rustle the tree branches, the birds all nestled somewhere for the night. And yet, as she'd learned, it was rarely entirely silent here. Tonight, even though the air was so calm, she could hear the ocean breathing in soft sighs against the rocky shore below. It ebbed and flowed, not pausing for one moment to acknowledge that her heart was breaking.

A rough, "Damn it!" from Aaron broke the stillness.

"I know. I hate the idea of breaking up." But how could they continue like this when they were both in pain?

"I love you too much to give up on us." Tension crackled from his body, but still he didn't touch her. "If it's what you really, truly want—not now when you're exhausted and emotional, but in the cold light of day—then I'll agree. But you'll have to tell me that you see absolutely no hope for us. Because if there's hope, I'm hanging on. And so will you."

"I . . ." Her heart fluttered like the wings of a newborn butterfly. Tentative, wanting to believe that if those wings kept beating, she'd be able to fly. But honestly, how could she? "I want to hope, but I don't think I'm strong enough to do this."

"You're the strongest person I know." He swung around to sit in front of her and cradled her clasped hands in his. "No, that's not expectation or pressure. It doesn't mean you can't show weakness, scream, cry, sleep for two days straight. Whatever you need, Eden. Let me help you. Let me love you and lend you my strength. Your dad leans on you and you can lean on me. We'll get through this somehow, even if it's just a text every now and then throughout the day to keep our connection strong."

She imagined being back home, sitting in the waiting room at her mom's doctor's office, and seeing a text from Aaron: I love you. Hang in there. Yes, that would warm her heart and strengthen her resolve. "Could I give you enough back?" She hadn't, with Ray. "It's so one-sided. You need a real lover, a woman in your bed at night. Someone to kayak with."

He used a finger to wipe tear tracks from her cheeks. "I need a woman who loves me. I need someone I can talk to about Miranda, someone to send photos of Fairy-ana to."

"I love it when you do those things." The pictures always made her smile, and the discussions about his sister made Eden feel trusted, part of his life.

"And then there's the phone sex."

Which was frustratingly inadequate. Yet his tone had lightened, and the wings in her heart were beating more strongly. Had she and Aaron really survived this crisis and come out on the other side? "When Ray and I had problems, we quit rather than try to work out a solution. We didn't love each other enough to try. So is it possible that all these issues that are messing up our lives aren't a sign that we don't belong together but a test of our commitment?"

The starlight reflected in his eyes as he gazed at her. "That makes sense. If our love's strong enough to survive everything that's going on now, we've got a slam dunk on the future."

She smiled a little. "That's a, what, basketball term? I take it that it's a good thing?"

"A very good thing." His teeth gleamed as he smiled back. "To switch to baseball, we're going to knock this one right out of the park."

The butterfly in her heart was flying high now, up

there with Aaron's eagle. "I didn't know you were a sports fan."

"It's a guilty secret I've been hiding from you. Now confess one of yours."

She thought a moment. "Breyers Heavenly Hash ice cream in the middle of the night."

"Damn, even your guilty secrets are fun ones." His smile ebbed to a serious expression, but the glow in his eyes warmed the night. "I'm not going to quit on us, Eden Blaine."

She believed him. He might question his ability to build a healthy long-term relationship but she didn't. He'd hung in there with his sister over the years, even when the going was rough.

"We've been thinking we need to find a perfect solution," she said slowly. "But didn't I once say that people aren't perfect and relationships aren't perfect? We love each other. That's worth everything. I'm not quitting on us either, Aaron Gabriel."

"Good." It was a single word, but his utter sincerity resonated in her heart. "So here's a thought: While I want you to be able to share all your worries about your mom's health, and I still want to whine about Miranda, when it comes to our relationship, let's focus on the positive."

"That sounds like a good idea."

"Like, when we Skype, we won't complain about not being together, we'll be happy for the opportunity to talk."

She gave a soft laugh. "Glass half-full? That makes so much sense. How come you're so smart and I'm so dumb?"

He returned the laugh. "You're overeducated, lawyer lady. It gets in the way of your common sense."

"It probably still will," she warned. "You'll have to remind me on occasion."

"I can do that."

"And we can do this." A full-body shiver of happiness rippled through her, filling her with energy and hope. "Oh, Aaron, I feel so much better. I was on the verge of letting our problems destroy our relationship, when in fact you're the most amazing thing that's ever happened to me. We can do this. We can love our families and honor our bonds to them and still love each other and keep building our relationship. It's going to take work, and also patience and flexibility—which maybe aren't my strongest qualities, though I'm learning—but we have enough love between us to do it."

"I believe that. And now, to focus on the positive, here we are together in an empty cabin with the rest of the night ahead of us. I can think of only one thing that would be even better."

"Let me guess. Being naked together?"

"You read my mind. Come, my love. Let's go to bed."

Chapter Twenty-One

Saturday morning, Aaron woke to a familiar haunting sound and let out a groan before remembering he wasn't alone in bed. When he did remember, he grinned. Some days, fog could be an excellent thing.

Eden, curled on her side with her arm over his chest, stirred and said sleepily, "Aaron?"

He slipped his arm under and around her, pulling her into his embrace. "Hear that?"

"Mmm. That's eerie. What is it?"

"A foghorn. Which means . . ."

"Ah." She yawned. "If it's too foggy, you can't fly."

"Until it clears, which may be too late for passengers who had plans for the day." He squeezed her shoulders, planted a kiss on her forehead, and then shoved himself out of bed. "I have to call Kam and Jillian, check the weather and our flight schedule, and figure out a plan. Go back to sleep, Eden."

"What time is it?" Her voice was still drowsy.

"Five."

"Back to sleep. Going." She rolled over and pulled the covers high on her neck.

"The plus side of fog," he said to her back, "is that if I can't fly for a few hours, we can spend that time together."

"In bed," she muttered.

"You bet." She was so cute when she was half-asleep, that high-speed brain slowed down for once.

Once out of bed, he pulled on a pair of sweatpants and a tee and took his computer into the kitchen so he wouldn't disturb her. He poured himself a glass of orange juice and opened his email program to find a message from Kam, copied to Jillian. A couple of minutes later, Jillian was online, too, all of them wakened by the foghorn. Following their standard procedure, they checked the available weather information from the Vancouver and Victoria terminals and towers as well as the Nanaimo flight service station, and they compared notes with other Gulf Island airlines and seaplane docks.

Everyone agreed that the southern Gulf Islands were likely to be socked in until late morning. Kam would notify their passengers by text and email, so as not to wake those who were still asleep. If he didn't hear back from people within a reasonable time, he'd make phone calls. Some passengers would cancel their flights, others would rebook for another day, and some would still hope to get out today if the weather cleared. Depending on when that clearing occurred, it might or might not be possible to accommodate everyone because the afternoon flights were already almost full. One or more of the seaplane companies located farther north, where the weather was clear enough to fly this morning, might be able to pick up the afternoon overflow.

Grateful for Kam's efficiency and eagerness, and

vowing to give him an extra flight training session this week, Aaron finished his orange juice and went back to the bedroom. Eden lay on her side, her back to the door, exactly as he'd left her. She'd looked so wrung out yesterday, her summer tan not concealing the shadows around her eyes. He loved her so much and was happy about the decisions they'd made last night, but he felt helpless. He wanted to make life easy for her, but, unfortunately, he couldn't solve her problems.

He took off his clothes and, slowly and silently so as not to wake her, slipped into bed. His cell phone, set to vibrate, went on the pillow beside his head. If the forecast changed and flights could get out this morning, Kam would call. For anything nonurgent, he'd text or email.

When Aaron's body brushed Eden's, she stirred, made a small sound, and snuggled into the curve of his body. A soft sigh escaped her lips, but she didn't wake. Aaron, used to being up before dawn, was wide awake, but he lay motionless, enjoying every moment of being with her and glad she was getting some rest.

The foghorn sounded with reassuring regularity, confirming that the fog hadn't lifted.

It was a couple of hours before Eden stirred again, coming awake slowly and then wriggling her butt against him. He responded by rubbing his rising erection against that curvy, warm ass, and they made love like that, him slipping between her legs as he spooned her. There were moans of pleasure and breathless sighs, but neither of them spoke until their bodies had merged in climax.

Still inside her, Aaron kissed her shoulder. "Good morning, my love."

"You're still here. I like fog."

"It has its advantages." Reluctantly, he separated himself from her and got up to dispose of the condom. Returning from the bathroom, he pulled back the curtains. Climbing in beside Eden again, he shoved pillows behind his back so he could sit up and look out. The fog wasn't a thick blanket but crept in smoky fingers through the trees. "Actually, I do like the fog. Even if it wreaks havoc with the flight schedule."

"Aside from getting to stay in bed," she said, shoving herself up to sit beside him, "why do you like it?"

He put his arm around her shoulders, gathering her closer. "There was this poem we had to learn in school, something about the fog creeping on little cat feet."

"I remember that, too. Carl Sandburg, I think. I loved the image of little cat feet. A small, furry gray cat, I always thought."

"When I lived in the city, I didn't pay much attention to the occasional fog. But out here in the forest, I remembered that poem. The cat feet, that's not how I think of the fog myself. It's like"—he broke off— "this is going to sound silly."

She wrapped her arm across his chest, gazing past him out the window. "Tell me."

"You know I'm not a religious guy, or even spiritual, really. Yet fog makes me think of the spirits of all the creatures, the birds and animals, even maybe the trees and flowers that have died out there." He felt kind of stupid saying this, and yet he wanted to share his thoughts with the woman he loved. "Some mornings, those spirits feel kind of . . . not sad, exactly, more like nostalgic. They're in a quiet, soft gray mood and they come back to visit their favorite places. They reach out with their breath, with their fingers, to caress everything they once loved."

She turned her gaze from the window to rest on his face. "Aaron, that's the most beautiful thing I've ever heard."

"Oh. Well . . ."

"You have the soul of a poet."

He laughed in denial. "No way. I just feel closer to nature than I do to a lot of people."

She nodded. "My eagle."

"Yeah sure." Though in his secret heart he was flattered that she saw him that way.

"It's getting late, darling. Aunt Di and Uncle Seal invited me for breakfast at SkySong. What are your plans? Could you come, too?"

He found his phone, where it had tumbled to the floor during their lovemaking. Checking email, he said, "Kam says the earliest it's likely to clear is eleven. Sure, I'd like to come with you."

They showered and dressed and decided to take separate cars. That way, when he later went to Blue Moon Air, Eden could do whatever she wanted.

The parking lot held ten or so cars. Wisps of fog drifted here and there, offering glimpses of the guest cottages and main building, the native trees that had been left on the property and the flowering ones Di and Seal had planted: lilacs, magnolias, camellias, and rhododendrons. Walking silently on the bark-chip path that led to their house, Aaron and Eden passed the deer-fenced organic vegetable and fruit garden. Three gardeners raised hands in greeting and a few quiet *good mornings* were exchanged. Di and

Seal had a plan for the garden, but they left most of the execution to their guests. Many city dwellers found it rewarding, even therapeutic, to tend and harvest produce.

In the butterfly and hummingbird garden, laden with flowering plants designed to attract those winged creatures, only a couple of hardy hummingbirds sipped from honeysuckle blossoms. On a bench, a figure in a gray hoodie and sweatpants sat in lotus position, blending in with the fog, looking almost like a statue.

Di and Seal's house was the original farm-style two-story that had sat on the property for over a century, though they'd done some renovating, including making it as green-powered as possible. The wooden building was on a slight rise, giving them a view over the entire retreat and down to the beach where Aaron and Eden had picnicked and made love for the first time.

After mounting the steps, he paused to enjoy the view. "It's amazing what two former hippies have achieved, isn't it?" The whimsical fog drifted this way and that, revealing a dozen people on the lawn by the ocean, performing the graceful movements of tai chi.

"If Aunt Di's anything like Nana, Mom, and me, I'm not at all surprised. I think there's an organizational gene in our family. Though it may have skipped Kelsey."

"Or maybe she's like Di and needs to find the thing she wants to do. When she does, she may turn out to be like the rest of you Blaine women."

"Maybe so."

Rather than a conventional doorbell or knocker, an

artistically corroded copper bell hung by the front door. Aaron rang it, and a moment later Seal's voice called, "It's open."

The inside of the house, like the outside, wore its age gracefully. The décor was an intriguing mix: bamboo furniture as well as oak; rugs from India and New Mexico; diverse artwork; sculptures made from driftwood and jade. Aaron knew that each piece had a story, though he'd heard only a couple of them.

He and Eden went through to the large kitchen with its white-painted brick walls, white cabinets, brightly colored chairs, and more artwork. Seal, his lanky body clad in faded jeans and a tie-dyed tee, was at the stove. Di, in snug black pants and a colorful woven top that Aaron guessed was Guatemalan, was chopping cilantro.

Everyone exchanged hugs and the usual comments about the weather. In the Pacific Northwest, the changeable weather was always a primary topic of conversation.

The four of them sat down to a breakfast of huevos rancheros, freshly squeezed orange juice, and strong coffee. "A perfect meal for a day like this," Aaron said, enjoying the bite of chili peppers on his tongue.

"That's what we thought," Di said.

As they ate, it seemed to him that Di guided the conversation, keeping it casual and upbeat and avoiding the subject of her sister's cancer. Seeing Eden and her aunt sitting side by side, he could see the physical resemblance. Although the older woman's long hair was streaked liberally with silver, the brown strands were the same walnut as her niece's. Di's eyes were bright blue like Kelsey's while Eden's were amber, yet the shape of their eyes and their jaws was similar. Helen Blaine, he remembered, shared that same firm jaw.

When everyone pronounced themselves full, Di cleared away the breakfast plates and Seal offered refills of juice and coffee. Then he and Di sat down again and exchanged glances. Seal pushed his wire-framed glasses up his nose and gave her a slight nod.

"Eden," Di said, "it's always good to see you and I'm so enjoying getting to know you. But there's another reason I invited you here today. I want to talk about Helen. Her emotional health, especially."

Eden sighed. "I know. She's in a bad state of mind. She keeps saying that she may die. We all tell her it's not going to happen, but she can't seem to believe that."

Di, seated to Eden's right, turned and took her niece's hand in both of hers. "But it's true, my dear, lovely niece. Your mother might die."

Eden's eyes widened. "No. We can't let ourselves think that."

Her aunt gave her a gentle smile. "I know it's hard, but it's reality. We're all going to die one day. An illness as serious as cancer brings that inevitability closer and we need to face it."

Eden shook her head, a stubborn expression on her face. "No, we need to stay positive. So Mom will be positive and she'll fight it."

"That may be what you think *you* need," Di said calmly, "but it's not what Helen needs."

"What do you mean?" Eden's forehead scrunched up.

"I believe that you, your father, and your sister force

yourselves to be optimistic because you can't cope with the alternative, that Helen may die."

Eden tugged her hand free of Di's and clasped both her hands on the table, so tightly that he could see the tension. "Perhaps," she said. "But why should any of us think about that possibility? How can it do any good?"

"Because it's Helen's reality and she needs you to acknowledge it, not brush off her totally genuine concern." Di tucked a tendril of hair behind Eden's ear. "Your mother and I have talked about this at length. When you silence her, it hurts her. She needs to be heard."

Aaron's heart ached at the pain reflected on Eden's tense, shadowy-eyed face. He knew she'd never voluntarily hurt her mom. He glanced at Di, whose gaze was intent on Eden, and then at Seal. The other man, with his nut-brown face, glasses, and ponytailed gray hair, gave him a sympathetic smile. It was obvious the older couple had discussed this beforehand.

Aaron wanted to offer comfort to Eden, to defend her, and yet what Di said made sense to him. If, God forbid, he had some horrible illness, he'd want to be able to discuss it with Eden, not have her deny his reality. Trying to find a middle ground, he said, "Helen has you to talk to, Di. Isn't that enough for her?"

Di turned her warm gaze on him. "She has me and her cancer support group. Believe me, they talk about death a lot. It's a presence in the room. Members of that group have died. Helen's wanted to be able to come home and tell her family about it, to share her grief and the fear that those deaths engender in her. But she knows no one wants to hear about it."

She gathered Eden's hands once again, lifted them to her face and pressed a kiss to them, and then returned the bundle of four hands to rest on the table. "Talking to me and the other cancer survivors helps your mom, but it's not enough. She needs to be able to do it at home, not feel pressured to always put on a brave face and pretend she believes she'll be okay. When she does that, she's deceiving you, Eden. You, your dad, and Kelsey. Deceiving you to protect you. Can you imagine how much energy that takes, at a time when she has none to spare?"

"I guess I can," Eden said quietly. "Because it feels like that for me, as well. Always working hard to put on a cheery face. I've seen how it's affected Dad, too."

"This is part of the reason Helen was so shattered by the news of the recurrence. Just when she was feeling better, feeling hopeful, she learned that she'd have to find all that energy again. Not just to endure treatment and fight the disease but to put that brave face back on. I bet you and Jim and Kelsey felt like that, too."

Eden nodded. "It has to be all that much harder for Mom."

"Exactly." Di nodded firmly. "You want to give your mother what she most needs. That means learning to face the possibility of her death and to discuss it openly with her, as well as helping her to fight against it."

Eden bit her lip.

"You all need to be honest," Di went on. "With yourselves and one another. It won't always be comfortable and I guarantee you'll cry. But isn't it better to cry together than to deceive one another?"

Eden blinked, her lashes damp. "Is it? Aunt Di, I'm lost here. I don't know anything about this."

"But I do. It's part of what Seal and I do here at SkySong. We help people who are going through, or have suffered from, traumas of various sorts. It's a healing place. We felt it the first time we set foot"— she glanced at Seal and grinned—"trespassed, in fact, on this land. It inspired us and helped us find our own lifework."

Seal spoke for the first time since the aunt-niece conversation had begun. "It did." He reached over to rest his hand atop the women's joined ones. "We've helped a lot of people. And we want to help Helen." He nodded his head at Di, a silent invitation.

She took it up. "We want Helen to come here, Eden. Helen and your dad. We want you to be here as often as you can, and Kelsey during every school break."

"But . . ." Eden frowned, looking confused. "But everything's in Ottawa. The oncologist and Mom's other doctors, the hospital, the cancer support group. Dad's job. Their house, Mom's garden, her job when she can go back to it."

"There are excellent oncologists and hospitals in both Victoria and Vancouver, just a hop away by ferry or"—she smiled at Aaron—"by our excellent local airline. There's a wonderful cancer support group right here on Destiny. Seal and I help them from time to time with guided meditations and healing exercises.

"As for the house," Di said, "your parents could rent it out for a while. I know Helen loves to garden and she could do it to her heart's content here. She's already on leave from her job. Your father's job . . . well, maybe he could work something out."

"Dad would do anything for Mom," Eden said slowly.

Di glanced at Seal. "We both truly believe it would help Helen to be here. She'll have our love and support and she'll be part of a healing community. It's also a community of honesty, where she can feel absolutely free to share whatever's on her mind." She fixed her bright blue gaze on Eden's face. "If she and your father come, and you and Kelsey also participate when you can, you have to be honest. There'll be no more pretense, no more denial."

"I . . . I don't know." She tugged her arms back, trying to pull her hands free, but Di and Seal must have tightened their grip because she gave up. "It sounds . . . good, but it would be such a huge change for Mom and Dad. And the honesty part . . . well, I do hear what you're saying. It makes sense. I'm just not sure that we—that I—can do it." She turned troubled eyes to Aaron. "What do you think?"

He smiled. "I think you can do anything you set your mind to. I bet that even if being honest about your emotions is painful, it would bring your family even closer together. You know I'll help in any way I can." He added his hand to the pile on the table, not even feeling strange that it was resting on Seal's. It seemed like the four of them were forming a team.

Another idea struck him, with a force that made him jerk in his chair. "Eden, if your parents did do this, what about you? Would your job be enough to hold you in Ottawa?"

She stared at him blankly, and then realization dawned on her face. "Oh my God." She blinked and then blinked again, and it seemed as if the shadows around her eyes had lifted a little. "No. If you and Mom and Dad, and Aunt Di and Uncle Seal, were all here, I wouldn't stay in Ottawa. Of course I'd move here." She gave Aaron a trembling smile. "I mean, that's not to assume that you and I are, you know, committed for the long haul, but it'd give us a much better chance to find out, wouldn't it?"

"That it would." He was pretty sure he already knew the answer, and so would she once the family pressures eased.

Her mouth straightened. "But Mom and Dad have to make the decision. I can't try to sway them just because it's in my personal interest that they move here."

"I'm convinced that it's in Helen's interest," Di said firmly. "And from what I've learned about Jim, anything that's in her interest is in his as well."

"You're right," Eden said. "Their love is . . . well, it's like yours. It's right. Seeing them, you just know they belong together." She smiled at Aaron. "It's what I think you and I may have one day."

That was exactly what he thought. Now, if only her parents saw the wisdom of Di's proposal.

Chapter Twenty-Two

The next afternoon, when the bell dinged to announce that the plane was safely in the gate at Ottawa airport, Eden rose and gathered her purse and tote. She glanced around to smile at Di who, two rows back, was pulling a woven Guatemalan backpack from the overhead bin.

As soon as they'd shuffled their way off the plane and into the terminal, they joined up. "I can't believe it's been almost half a century since I was last in Ottawa," Di said as they walked side by side. "And since I saw Helen. How did I let that happen?"

"You put the past behind you, Aunt Di."

"I know. Honestly, I'm not dwelling on it or beating myself up. Regrets are a waste of time except for what you learn from them. It's today that counts, and the future."

"Today sure isn't the day I'd thought it would be." Eden had planned to spend the weekend with Aaron and fly back to Ottawa Monday evening. But Saturday's conversation with Di and Seal had turned into a planning session.

Eden's aunt had proved to be as goal-oriented and determined as Eden, all the while never losing her aura of serenity. Di wanted to present her proposal to her sister in person, and she wanted the entire family present. Because Kelsey was returning to university tomorrow, the meeting had to take place today. Eden regretted missing out on time with Aaron, but excitement bubbled inside her at the thought that, if her parents agreed to Di's plan, there would be a whole lot of together time in their future.

She and Di had decided not to call the family to alert them, and Eden only hoped her mom was up to handling the shock of finally seeing her long-lost sister in person.

"You know," Di said, "when I left home, your mom was this bratty, good-girl twelve-year-old. We were enough apart in age and so different in our personalities that we really didn't know each other. Now she's such an amazing woman."

"She's the best mom imaginable, a dedicated and inspiring teacher, and the love of my dad's life. It's hard to imagine her as a bratty preteen. But then, I also have trouble imagining you as a runaway."

Di laughed softly. "People grow up. Thank heavens." She reached out her free arm and hooked it through Eden's. "And thank *you*, for bringing the grown-up Helen and me back together. Now we do truly feel like sisters. And best friends."

They bypassed the luggage carousels because neither had checked a bag and in minutes they were climbing into Eden's Smart car, which she'd left in the airport parking lot. As she drove into the city, each of them was quiet with her own thoughts. Eden was anxious, knowing how stressful and emotional the upcoming discussion was likely to be, and yet she felt a new sense of hope. It wasn't just that things might work out for her and Aaron but that Di's idea could provide greater peace of mind for Eden's mom. Also, it was nice to be able, for a change, to rely on someone else. Her aunt was in charge now and Eden's role was a supporting one.

Di didn't seem worried. She watched the unfolding view with an interested expression, occasionally commenting on something she recognized or that had changed.

As Eden turned into the Glebe, she told Di, "This is the neighborhood where Mom and Dad bought their house, back when they were expecting me."

"It looks friendly. Or at least as friendly as Ottawa's likely to be. I always thought it was a stuffy, old-fashioned city."

"To a hippie teenager, I'm sure it was."

They reached the family home and Di said, "It's a nice house, though all very Ottawa."

As they started up the walk, Di reached for Eden's hand, making her wonder if her aunt was nervous after all. Eden opened the front door and called, "Anyone home?"

"Eden?" Kelsey's voice came from upstairs, faintly, then getting louder as she continued. "What are you doing here? Did you and Aaron—" She appeared at the top of the stairs, summery in shorts and a tank top. When she took in the two women standing in the entrance hall, she let out a whoop. "Aunt Di! Oh my God, you're here!" She flew down the stairs, bare feet thudding on each step.

Di set down her colorful backpack and held out her arms as Kelsey flung herself into them. They embraced for a long time, and then Di pushed Kelsey back to arm's length and said, "Let me look at you. You're even more beautiful in person than on the computer screen. And look, we have the same eyes."

"I can't believe you're here. This is so cool!" Kelsey turned to her sister and said reproachfully, "You didn't tell me."

"It's nice to see you, too," Eden teased.

"Well, I'd have planned something fancy for dinner. It's not fair, taking me by surprise."

"Hey, you're the spontaneous one," Eden said. "Roll with it."

Kelsey laughed. "Okay, you got me."

"Where's Helen?" Di asked.

"Sitting in the backyard with Dad," Kelsey said. "I can't wait to see her face." She grabbed Di's hand and tugged her toward the back door with Eden following. Kelsey flung open the door and called, "Mom, Dad, Eden's home and she brought a surprise." She shoved Di forward and stepped out behind her.

Eden was on their heels, also eager to see her mother's reaction.

Her parents were seated in padded garden chairs on either side of a table that held a pitcher of lemonade and two tall glasses. They'd been facing away from the house, toward a border of purple coneflowers and yellow-green spurge, but at Kelsey's call they both turned.

Her mom rose slowly, nearly bald again and frail in her summer dress, and raised a trembling hand. "Di?" she said in disbelief.

Dad was beside her immediately, putting his arm around her to steady her.

This time it was Di whose steps flew as she rushed across the grass. Eden's father moved aside as Di put her arms around her sister, who returned the embrace. No words were spoken, but tears flowed freely as the two women clung to each other as if they would never let go.

Kelsey gave an excited bounce and Eden's eyes were moist. She wished Aaron could witness the reunion he'd helped facilitate.

Dad walked over to her and Kelsey. "Well." He swiped a hand across his forehead, looking more than a little stunned. "Eden, how did this come about?"

"Aunt Di wanted to meet everyone and this was the only chance before Kelsey goes back to school."

He glanced at his wife and her sister, who showed no signs of separating. "Let's give the two of them some privacy. We need to make up the spare room. And Kelsey, what were we planning for dinner?"

The three of them sprang into action. Twenty minutes later, Kelsey had put fresh sheets and a vase of flowers in the spare room, Eden had a pan of corn bread in the oven, and their dad was draining a big pot of rotini. They'd decided that the warm day called for pasta salad.

The two women came in from the garden arm in arm, blotchy-faced and smiling. "I'm going to show my sister the house," Mom said, "and we both need to freshen up."

Eden and her dad and Kelsey set to work chopping and slicing, assembling the salad with leftover roast chicken, cheeses, veggies, olives, and other goodies. Then, they all sat down at the table—the kitchen table because, as Dad said, Di was family.

From the untroubled look on her mom's face, Eden figured Di had yet to mention her proposal. It seemed dinner wasn't that time; the conversation remained light and the atmosphere was festive. It wasn't until after a dessert of fruit salad and brownies that Di said, "I want to talk to all of you. Let's go into your sitting room."

Leaving the dessert dishes on the table, they went to the front room with its comfortable, well-worn furniture and numerous potted plants. Eden's parents sat side by side on the couch, she took one of the chairs, and Kelsey sat cross-legged on the floor, leaning against her legs. Di waited for them to seat themselves and then chose a straight-backed chair, moving it so she faced the four of them. Despite the formality of the chair, she looked relaxed as she sat down, erect and confident.

"There's a reason I wanted to see all of you together," she said. "Before Kelsey went back to university."

"A reason?" Eden's dad said, his brow furrowing.

"So far tonight," Di went on, "we haven't talked about Helen's cancer, but it's time we did."

"Oh, Di," Eden's mom said, her voice having lost its earlier animation, "let's not. This is so perfect, having you here. Let's not spoil it with talk of illness."

Di smiled sympathetically at her sister. "My intent isn't to spoil it." She glanced around the room at the rest of them, giving Eden a slight nod. "But there's something I need to say, and I'm not big on beating around the bush, so I'm just going to come out with it. It's time you all got rid of the elephant in the room."

Looking puzzled, Eden's dad said, "Elephant?"

Di replied calmly, "I'm referring to the fact that Helen is afraid she might die, and that it's a valid fear."

Eden's mom gave a small gasp and her dad's face hardened. "We don't talk that way in this house."

His wife clutched his arm. "Listen to her, Jim."

"I think it's time you talked that way." Di's tone remained even and nonaccusatory as she told him and Kelsey the same things she'd discussed with Eden the previous morning.

Tears slid down Mom's thin face and Eden was terribly afraid this had been a mistake, but then her mother said, "Thank you, Di. Thank you so much. I didn't know how to say it. I didn't want to let them all down."

"Let us down?" Dad hugged her close to his side. "You could never let us down. We love you."

Kelsey slipped forward to kneel in front of her mother and rest her hands on her knees. "We do. We only want what's best for you. That's what we've been trying to do."

Mom touched her hand. "I know. You've all been trying so hard. I have, too, but sometimes I run out of steam and I get so damned scared. I don't want you to be scared, too, and yet I really want to be able to talk to you about it."

"Mom," Eden said, moving forward to kneel beside Kelsey. Having had more time to process Di's ideas, she hoped she could bring the rest of her family to the same understanding she'd reached. "We can't help being scared any more than you can. I think what Aunt Di says makes sense. Being able to share the fear is better than each of us keeping it locked up inside and trying to deal with it. And failing."

"I know it would be better for me," her mom said. "I hope it would for you."

"It would for me," Kelsey said, blinking teary eyelashes. "Sometimes I feel like a little girl again, scared of monsters. When I was a kid, I could run to my mommy and daddy, but now I cry alone in my bed."

Eden leaned over so her shoulder touched her sister's. "Kelsey, I'm so sorry. I should have known and been there for you. We could have cried together."

"And now you *can* run to your mommy," their mother said, smiling through her own tears. "And your daddy?" She aimed the question at her husband, and before he could answer, she went on. "Jim, even though we're a loving family, in some ways we've all been isolated little islands, holding our misery and fear inside ourselves. I believe Di's right, and if we're honest and share our feelings, share our tears, we'll all be stronger for it."

He drew a ragged breath. "That sounds pretty good to me."

Eden guessed how hard this was for him and her heart filled with pride. And relief.

His shoulders squared, and despite the red rims of his eyes, he already looked stronger than he had in a while. "No more pretending. Not from any of us. Total honesty from now on. Right, girls? Right, Helen?"

"Right," they all echoed.

They would be there for one another, and so would Di and Seal. Eden knew she was extralucky in also having Aaron. She couldn't wait to Skype him, to see the face she loved on her computer screen, and to tell him about her family's new philosophy. She only hoped that, when she did call later tonight, she'd have even more good news.

Her dad turned to Di. "Thank you for coming all this way to knock some sense into our heads."

"You're very welcome, Jim." She beamed at him. "But that's not the only reason I came. I want you and Helen to consider moving to SkySong, at least for the short-term. And I want Eden and Kelsey to visit as often as possible, so we can all work together on Helen's healing."

Kelsey said, "That's brilliant!"

"That's impossible," Dad said. "Our home is here. We can't just pack up and move." He gazed at his wife. "Right, Helen?"

"I suppose not," she said slowly. "I have doctors here, my cancer support group, and my job if . . . when I recover." She turned to Di. "I could retire, I've earned a decent pension, but I enjoy the challenges and rewards of my work. And Jim loves his job, too, and it's here."

"I would never put my work ahead of you," he said firmly.

"That's what I thought," Di said.

"I'm sixty-six," he said. "And look, since our new policy is total truth, here it is: Ever since you were diagnosed, it's made me think about the fragility of life. And how, much as I do love my job, I love you more. I don't know how long I'll have you—or you'll have me, for that matter—and I want to spend more time together. If that's for decades more, I'll be a very happy man. If it's not"—he swallowed hard— "then I want to enjoy the time we do have."

"You never said any of this before," his wife said, sounding confused.

"I was afraid you'd think I was being negative about your chances of surviving the cancer. And I'm not. Absolutely not." He gave her a narrow-eyed stare.

Her lips twitched. "Well. That's telling me, I suppose." She shook her head slightly. "But Jim, you do love your work and you'd be bored out of your mind without it. And I truly hope to get better and go back to teaching. We shouldn't make decisions with the short-term in mind." She gave a small laugh. "And now I'm the one to say we should be positive. See, once I got the fears off my chest, it cleared the way for the optimism."

"You make excellent points," Dad said. "I bet I could stay on as a consultant. Or if not, and I do get bored, I'll find something else."

"Helen," Di said, "if you decide to return to Ottawa, your job will still be here. But you'll also find teaching and counseling opportunities on Destiny, even at SkySong itself. As for doctors, there are great ones in the area, and a wonderful support group."

"You should totally do it," Kelsey said.

"I'm tempted," Mom said slowly. "But it's so much to think about." She gazed down at Eden with troubled eyes. "What do you think? You're the practical one."

"This has to be your decision, Mom. You and Dad. But I will say that Aunt Di and Uncle Seal have built something terrific at SkySong and you'd love it there."

"What about you, Eden?" Dad asked. "Would you stay here in Ottawa? How are things going with you and Aaron?"

Her heart skipped, but she kept her voice even. "My relationship with Aaron shouldn't be a factor in this."

"Total honesty now," he reminded her with a smile.

She took a breath. "Okay, you're right. But I truly don't want to influence you. If you stay here and need me here, Aaron and I will keep seeing each other however we can. I'll want you to support that." She swallowed and told them a truth she hadn't revealed before. "We love each other."

Kelsey broke in with "Yes!" and a fist pump.

"We think we have a future together," Eden continued. "But it doesn't have to be fast."

"And if we move?" Mom asked quietly.

"I love my job, too, but I love you and Dad and Aaron more. I'd give up my job and move as well. I'd look for work on Destiny Island."

"I'm coming, too," Kelsey said. "Don't leave me out of this." She bumped Eden with her shoulder. "I want to see this magical place that turned my sister into a nicer person. Not to mention is home to hotties like Aaron."

Eden rolled her eyes. "You need to finish your degree."

"That's right," their mother said. "You can come visit on holidays."

"Mom," Kelsey said, all seriousness for once, "I love you. You're going through a rough time and I want to be there. I can go to school anytime." She blinked and her voice quavered. "I feel the way Dad does. I d-don't know how long I'll have you. I hope it's forever, but cancer is scary. This recurrence is scary. I can't just go back to school and pretend it's not happening."

"Oh, honey," Mom said, "it's bad enough that this is messing up my life. It shouldn't have to mess up yours."

"But it does," Kelsey said. "We're a family and we're

in this together." Her chin came up. "I'm an adult. I get to make my own decisions. I think you should go to Destiny Island, but that's your decision to make. It's my decision whether to go back to school or to be with you. And I've made that decision. Tomorrow, I won't be going to McGill. If you stay in Ottawa, I'm staying with you. If you move to the island, I'm going." She sniffled. "So there."

Their parents exchanged helpless gazes.

Eden spoke up. "Kelsey's right. She's an adult. She has the right to make this decision."

Her sister shot her a surprised glance. "Thanks, Sis."

Eden smiled back. "Until this summer I wouldn't have said that. I didn't think you were a grown-up. But you've convinced me."

"I think maybe it took this summer for me to grow up," Kelsey admitted.

"Here's a thought," Di said. "Come for a visit. Come for a week to see what you think." She winked at Eden, who well knew the impact a week on the island could have on a person. "You'll soon figure out if it's your destiny." She rose. "And now, you all need to sleep on this. We'll talk again in the morning." She came over to her sister.

Eden and Kelsey moved aside and Di bent down to hug Helen and say, "Good night, my dear sister. I'm going to get ready for bed and phone Seal. Do you know, this is the first night we've been apart in almost fifty years?"

The notion made Eden smile. Decades spent with the man you loved. It was possible. Her mom and her aunt were both doing it, and so had Nana. The track record on her side of the family, together with Aaron's own strong character, would more than compensate for his parents' and grandparents' poor examples.

When Di left the room, the rest of them dispersed quietly. Eden and Kelsey dealt with the dishes while their parents went up to their bedroom. For once, Kelsey wasn't chattering but quiet with her thoughts, as was Eden. When the dishwasher was humming, the sisters parted in the hallway with a hug.

"This is going to be so good," Kelsey said with an air of quiet, tired confidence.

It would be, if their parents agreed. "Sleep well, Sis. Tomorrow's going to be an interesting day."

Eden drove home and walked straight through to the bedroom, where she took her computer from her bag and collapsed on the bed. She Skyped Aaron.

"Hey, sweetheart," he said. "How did it go?"

"Pretty well." She gave him a summary, watching his face as he listened.

"What do you think your parents will decide?"

"Aunt Di was smart, suggesting they visit for a week. They can check out SkySong and Destiny before they make major life decisions. I think they'll agree to a visit."

"If they do, do you think the island will win them over and they'll move here?"

Thinking of her sister's words, Eden smiled. "It's a magical place. Maybe they'll decide it's their destiny. But even if they don't, you and I have our plan. We're going to focus on all the positives and on our love. Right?"

"That's absolutely right."

Chapter Twenty-Three

On this early December afternoon, there wasn't a single taxi waiting outside Vancouver International Airport. Taking her place third in line, Eden sighed impatiently.

It wasn't raining, but the wet ground and the raindrops on passing cars told her it had been. No surprise; she'd learned that on the West Coast, bouts of rain were as predictable in fall and winter as spells of sunshine on summer days.

Finally, she climbed into a cab and told the driver her destination. Though the distance wasn't far, the drive seemed to take forever.

When the cab pulled up at the seaplane dock on the Fraser River, Aaron stood waiting on the side of the road. He was so tall and handsome in jeans and his brown leather bomber jacket, a dramatic figure against the smoke-gray winter sky.

He opened the door for her and she almost tumbled out in her eagerness to be in his arms. They kissed hungrily until a cough broke the spell.

"Lady," the driver said, "you want your stuff or not?"

She'd paid him as they approached the dock but had forgotten about her bags.

Laughing, Aaron pulled them out of the backseat and handed her purse to her, then looped the strap of her giant tote bag over his shoulder. He put his other arm around her and guided her to the ramp that led to the dock. "Fly away with me, Eden Blaine. No, wait, let me change that. Fly *home* with me."

"There's nothing I'd rather do," she said fervently.

"I was beginning to wonder. You're half an hour late."

"There was a headwind and then no taxis."

"Always an excuse," he teased. "I'd almost think you didn't want to see me."

"No, you wouldn't, because you hate being wrong." She wriggled her shoulders, the tension of the past few days dropping away. "It's good to be here. I love you so much, darling."

"Same goes." He squeezed her shoulders. "You got everything packed up?"

"The furniture's all been dealt with, either in storage, to the auction house, or to charity." For the time being, her parents and sister were in a guest cottage at SkySong, planning next spring to buy a house on Destiny. "The cleaners and gardeners did a wonderful job. The new owners are going to love it." She felt a pang at the thought of someone else living in the house that had always been home to her, yet when she'd met the family who'd bought it, she'd had a good feeling about them. "It's someone else's turn to build happy memories there."

She climbed into the Cessna, the only passenger on this special flight. As Aaron went through the now-familiar routine, a light drizzle started to fall. Soon they were motoring through choppy waves. When the little plane separated itself from the river and launched itself into the gray sky, Eden's heart rose with it. The man she loved was flying her home.

"About tonight . . ." he said. "There's good news and bad news."

"Bad news?" Her pulse fluttered, but she took a breath and calmed herself. If anything bad had happened to her mom, he'd never break the news this way.

"The bad news is, you're not going to get to spend the evening alone with me, making mad, passionate love. That'll have to wait for a few hours."

"Damn, and I was counting on it." She was only half-joking. Being away from Aaron for five days had, despite phone sex, left her body and heart aching for him. "And the good news?"

"A family dinner at SkySong, to celebrate tidying up all the details in Ottawa and, uh, how did Di put it? *Turning the page on that chapter of the book and fully committing to the next one.* Something like that."

"A celebration does seem to be in order. Mom feels up to it?"

"You've talked to her on Skype. She's better every day."

"Yes, thank God." Her mom had finished chemo and was on hormonal therapy and also on a diet and exercise regimen prescribed by Di. She participated in a cancer support group on Destiny and, along with Kelsey, had joined a local art club. Her health was still fragile and she had some bad days, but on the whole Destiny Island was agreeing with her. With Eden's dad, as well. He was doing part-time consulting with the charity he used to run and learning to golf.

As for Eden, she was excited about starting her new

job in January. She'd be the lawyer and program director for Arbutus Lodge, where her friend Gertie Montgomery lived.

"I talked to Di before I left Destiny," Aaron said. "Your mom's having a nap, resting up for the fancy dinner, and Miranda and Fairy-ana are with Di and Seal, getting everything ready."

"I love it that they all get along so well. Miranda's doing better, too, isn't she?"

"Seems so. She has her down days, but on the whole she's more confident." He glanced over, a smile crinkling his eyes. "Your mom's hooked on Ariana. Don't be surprised if she starts hinting about wanting a grandchild."

"Oh my! Has she been doing that with you? I'm mortified."

"No, it's cute. I'm just glad she's finally decided I'm a good guy."

"You know it was never about you personally. It was what you represented: the idea that she might lose me."

"I know. And instead, I led her to Di and to Destiny, and I helped bring you here, too. So I'm in her good books."

"Where you deserve to be."

Contentedly, she gazed out the window even though the usually spectacular scenery was partially obscured by the drizzle. As long as Aaron had sufficient visibility to fly, who cared what the weather was like? All the pieces of her world were falling so wonderfully into place.

Except for one niggling question. "Aunt Di and Uncle Seal still won't say anything more about Merlin and Starshine."

"You heard what Marlise said about the cornucopia of drugs at the commune. Some of those drugs fried people's memories."

"There's more to it than that. They're holding back. You're a mystery reader, too. Can't you sense they know something they're not saying?"

"Yeah, maybe. But it's their right. We may have to accept that we'll never know the whole truth."

"I hate it when a book ends like that."

He chuckled. "You and your mom, the romance reader. You want your happy endings."

"That's the truth," she said wholeheartedly. She really hoped she and Aaron were getting theirs and, perhaps even more than that, she hoped her mom won her battle with cancer.

Aaron pointed out the windshield. "There's Blue Moon Harbor."

They were approaching from the south, flying into the bay. The days were so short now that lights shone from every building in the village. "It looks so welcoming," she said. "I love that it's so small that I'm getting to know every business, every owner, every employee." Her friendships with Iris, Marlise, and Gertie continued to grow, as well.

When Aaron had tied up the plane and helped Eden off, she pulled up the hood of her coat against the light rain. She expected him to hoist her tote, but instead, to her surprise, he got down on one knee on the dock. She caught her breath. "Aaron?"

He gazed up at her, his face and hair growing damp from the drizzle. "This would be better in sunshine. Or moonlight. I hadn't planned on rain."

"This?" Her voice quivered. "What's *this*?"

"I love you, Eden. Well, you already know that. And you love me back. We've known each other six months now, and these have been some crazy months. But they've been the best ones of my life. I figure that if we can survive everything we've been through so far, we can do anything together."

She gave a tremulous smile. Was he really doing what she thought he was?

"You told me right at the beginning," he went on, "that what you value most in the world is your family. Well, I dream of us being family. I want to marry you, love you, and raise children with you. I want to be your friend and partner—and lover—for the rest of my life."

He unzipped the pocket of his jacket and produced a small box, which he opened. Inside was a stunning ring, a band woven of gold and silver strands and studded with little diamonds that managed to sparkle even in this gray weather. "What do you say, Eden? Will you share my dream? Share my life?"

She stared into his soulful bluish-gray eyes, the lashes dotted with tiny raindrops almost as dazzling as the diamonds in the ring. "You *are* my dream, Aaron. Yes, I'll marry you, love you, and build a family with you."

Carefully, he took the ring from the box and slipped it onto her finger. Then he rose, giving her the sexy grin she loved so much. "Who'd have guessed, when I first flew you here, that this is how we'd end up?"

She smiled back, showing him all the love in her heart. "I suppose there's no arguing with destiny."

AUTHOR'S NOTE

Welcome to the launch of my new Blue Moon Harbor series! I hope you're as excited about these stories as I am.

It was difficult winding up my Caribou Crossing Romances and I feel a certain sorrow at leaving that wonderful Western community and the characters who populated the eight titles in that series. But at least I know that all my heroines and heroes are living their happily-ever-afters!

In the Blue Moon Harbor books, you'll find the same kinds of contemporary romance stories. My protagonists are intelligent, caring people who deserve love and face significant challenges as they strive to find their happy endings. The setting is close to home for me: a fictional island set among British Columbia's Gulf Islands, not far from Victoria. Tiny Destiny Island is ruggedly scenic and its residents tend to be unconventional—and proud of it! It also happens to be a very romantic spot. When you meet your love on Destiny, life will never be the same.

The island became the perfect home for Aaron Gabriel, who transformed from a delinquent teen to a seaplane pilot who owns his own business. But even Destiny Island couldn't heal the wounds of his dysfunctional childhood. It takes Eden Blaine, an Ottawa lawyer who's pursuing a quest on behalf of her ailing mother, to open Aaron's heart to the realization that love might actually be his destiny. I hope you enjoyed Eden and Aaron's story, as they struggled to find a way to realize their dreams while honoring their deep emotional bonds with their families.

Next in the series is "Blue Moon Harbor Christmas" in *Winter Wishes* (November 2017), a holiday anthology also containing novellas by Fern Michaels, Jules Bennett, and Leah Marie Brown. My heroine is Jillian Summers, the single-parent mom who flies for Aaron's Blue Moon Air. Following that title comes Aaron's sister Miranda's story, *Come Home With Me*, in January 2018. And after that, Iris of Dreamspinner bookstore will get her turn.

I'm grateful to Kensington Publishing for being so supportive of my Caribou Crossing Romances and for committing to the first four titles in the Blue Moon Harbor series. Special thanks at Kensington go to my fabulous editor, Martin Biro, his wonderful assistant, James Abbate, and terrific publicist Jane Nutter. My deep gratitude goes to my agent, Emily Sylvan Kim of Prospect Agency, for her belief in me and my writing, and for always being there. Thanks also to her assistant, Jes Lyons, who isn't a relative, though I wish she were.

I'm also truly appreciative of the feedback I received from my friends and great critiquers: Rosalind Villers, Alaura Ross, and Nazima Ali. Their input always helps me make my manuscripts stronger. Thanks also to John and Bonnie for research assistance.

And last, but most of all, thank you to my readers. It's through your eyes, minds, and hearts that the characters I create truly come to life.

I love sharing my stories with my readers and I love hearing from you. I write under the pen names Susan Fox, Savanna Fox, and Susan Lyons. You can email me at susan@susanlyons.ca or contact me through my website at www.susanfox.ca, where you'll also find excerpts, behind-the-scenes notes, recipes, a monthly contest, the sign-up for my newsletter, and other goodies. You can also find me on Facebook at facebook.com/SusanLyonsFox.

If you enjoyed *Fly Away With Me*,
be sure not to miss the next book in
Susan Fox's Blue Moon Harbor series,

COME HOME WITH ME

*It may be a dot in the Pacific Northwest,
but tiny Blue Moon Harbor always has room for love. . . .*

Miranda Gabriel has finally hit rock-bottom.
As a high-school drop-out, she fled Blue Moon
Harbor and her shattered family life, and chased
after love in all the wrong places. But now, as a
single mom, her priority is her two-year-old
daughter. Her only choice is to swallow her pride
and return to the island she's always hated. At least
between working and studying, she'll be too busy for
romance—especially when the prospect is a nice guy,
exactly the kind she knows she doesn't deserve . . .

The island veterinarian, Luke Chandler is a widower
raising four-year-old twin boys. In high school, he'd
found bad girl Miranda fascinating—and though
life has changed them both, he's still intrigued.
Luke has known true love, and something about
Miranda makes him long to experience it again.
Yet he's wary of opening himself, and his boys,
to hurt. But his heart may not give him a choice.
And together, maybe he and Miranda can give
each other the courage to believe in themselves,
and to embrace a promising new future. . . .

A Zebra mass-market paperback and eBook
on sale January 2018.
Turn the page for a special sneak peek!

"Guess what?" Miranda Gabriel's brother cried, raising his girlfriend's left hand like a boxing referee proclaiming the champ. "We're engaged!"

Diamonds sparkled on Eden's finger, and when Miranda stared from the ring to Aaron's face and his fiancée's, their excitement was no less dazzling.

Miranda's heart sank like a heavy, cold stone.

She had been peeling sweet potatoes in the big kitchen at SkySong when Aaron and Eden burst into the room. Tonight's dinner at the serenity retreat was planned as a celebration of Eden tidying up all the details around the sale of her family's home in Ottawa now that she, her parents, and her sister were becoming Destiny Island residents. Aaron, owner of Blue Moon Air, had flown over to Vancouver in his Cessna seaplane on this chilly, early December day to pick Eden up after her Ottawa flight. Now it seemed the celebration would be a dual-purpose one.

"He proposed on the dock," Eden said, her voice bubbly, neither she nor Aaron seeming to notice that their wet jackets were dripping on the terracotta-tiled floor. "Right there in the middle of Blue Moon Harbor."

She laughed up at him, her amber eyes glowing with happiness and love. "In the rain, and it was the most romantic thing in the world."

Engaged.

Eden's aunt and uncle, Di and Seal SkySong, who owned this rustically lovely retreat on four acres of waterfront, rushed over to the happy couple, offering hugs and congratulations. Miranda's two-year-old daughter remained in her booster chair at the kitchen table, still absorbed in the tea party game she and Di had been playing with one of Ariana's cloth fairy dolls. And Miranda herself stood rooted at the teal-topped kitchen counter, her feet as leaden as her heart.

Of course she'd known where Aaron and Eden's relationship was heading. In truth, the depressed, pessimistic, defeated spot in her soul, the one she hated to surrender to, had known ever since that day back in June. The day when her pride had hit an all-time low. Evicted from her tiny apartment, without the funds to rent another, she'd felt worthless and powerless. For the sake of her precious daughter, she had phoned Aaron and admitted she had no choice but to accept his offer of help. There she'd been, more pathetic than ever before in her life. She'd had no strength left, no option but to leave Vancouver and drag herself and Ariana to Destiny Island, a place she'd always hated, to shelter under her big brother's roof.

But Aaron, the one person who'd always been there for her, was away in Ottawa, visiting a woman he'd just met.

Sight unseen, Miranda—selfish bitch that she was— had hated Eden Blaine for threatening the one bit of stability in her and Ariana's lives. But then she'd met the smart, sensitive, beautiful Eden, seen her with Aaron, listened to what her brother said and didn't say. She'd seen that despite the huge problems the two lovers had faced, Eden made him happy. And Aaron's happiness was the second-most important thing in the world to Miranda. Only the welfare of her daughter ranked higher.

Now, realizing she'd been silent too long, she forced herself to walk across the kitchen, a bright, spacious room. Normally, she found this room so warm and welcoming, with its white-painted wood and brick walls and cabinets, accented by a hodge-podge of vividly colored chairs, kitchen accessories, and artwork. But today her heart was a frozen lump in her chest and it would take a lot more than Di and Seal's cheerful, eclectic décor to warm it.

Throwing her arms around the happy couple, she squeezed both of them, but Aaron a little harder. Her handsome, dark-haired brother, her best and only friend for all their lives, now belonged to someone else. "I'm so happy for you guys."

It wasn't a lie. Honestly, it wasn't. It was just a truth that jostled uneasily side by side with her selfishness and her envy. The guy who'd been so cynical—or, as he called it, realistic—about love had for the very first time had the guts to throw his heart into the ring. And what did he get? A freaking happy ending. As compared to her. She truly did believe in love and she'd been brave enough to go for it, to love and lose and try again, over and over. She'd been doing it ever since she was a tiny child, hoping against hope that one day her mom would love her and be there for her.

And yet here she was, twenty-seven years old and still alone.

So many times, as the children of a cocaine-addicted prostitute, she and Aaron had been the kids left outside, looking in windows at happy families eating together, at stores full of shiny new toys and games, at grocery shelves stocked with more food than anyone could possibly eat in a lifetime. Wanting, always wanting, but not getting.

Now Aaron had crossed over and he was on the inside. And she was left outside, no longer shoulder to shoulder with her big brother but all by herself.

She drew in a long breath, trying to flush the sour gray tang of depression and self-pity from her mind and heart. The fact was, she wasn't alone; she had Ariana. Having a daughter made life so much richer and more wonderful but also created pressures so heavy that a few months back, Miranda had almost cracked under them. Because it was one thing to be strong and resourceful enough to look after yourself. It was quite another when you were responsible for a small, fragile human being who deserved so much more than you'd ever been able to give her.

Miranda went over to the table where her beloved black-haired fairy princess of a daughter had stopped playing with her doll and, it seemed, belatedly come to the realization that everyone's attention was focused elsewhere than on her. Her cute face had gone pouty, a warning that a TTT—terrible two tantrum, as Miranda called them—was threatening to explode, as so often happened when the toddler felt neglected or thwarted.

"Sweetie, this is so exciting," Miranda said, hoisting her mocha-skinned daughter, so unlike her own fair self, into her arms. The familiar weight and warmth, the delicate scent of the baby oil Di made from the petals of wild roses, soothed Miranda's nerves.

Forcing enthusiasm into her voice, she brought the little girl over to the newly engaged couple. "Uncle Aaron is getting married." She glanced at his fiancée, the walnut-haired lawyer who'd given up her entire life in Ottawa to move to Destiny Island. "I guess that's going to make you Aunt Eden?"

Eden beamed, her happiness so vivid that, if Miranda had been a normal woman rather than a seething mess of insecurities, she'd have found it contagious. "I can't think of a bigger honor." She took Ariana's small hand gently in hers. "What do you think, Fairy-ana?" The nickname had been bestowed by Aaron a few months before, when his niece became obsessed with fairies. "Will you let me be your Aunt Eden?"

Now that the attention was back on her, Ariana was happy. "An-te-den?" she ventured.

"That sounds so good," Eden said, turning to put her arm around Aaron, as if she couldn't bear to go more than a moment without touching him.

"It sure does," he said.

Oh God, Miranda's big brother, the guy who'd taught her to shoplift and pick pockets as necessities of survival, had gone all schmaltzy. With a reluctant grin, she had to admit it was actually pretty adorable.

And it was high time she stopped being so freaking pathetic and looked on the bright side. Aaron's happiness proved he'd been wrong to say that love wasn't in the cards for either of them. She was right: They *could* find true love. They could beat their track record of being unloved by their mom, their two dads—because, in truth, she and Aaron were half siblings—and their grandparents.

But right now wasn't the time to muse about love. She had to think about her and Ariana's immediate future. They couldn't keep living in the guest room at Aaron's small log home. That arrangement wasn't fair to him and Eden.

Resting her right hand on her shirtsleeved left forearm, she summoned the power of the tattooed dragon that lay beneath the faded blue cotton. The dragon that symbolized her strength and ability to cope with whatever life tossed her way.

Eden's aunt and uncle got back to the dinner preparations, Seal taking over the sweet potatoes Miranda had abandoned. Eden and Aaron went into the mudroom to take off their jackets and boots, then returned, pulled out chairs at the table, and sat down side by side, hands linked.

Bouncing Ariana gently in her arms, Miranda listened to the conversation with half an ear while she formulated a plan for finding a new home for herself and her daughter.

"Eden, you've told your mom and dad?" Di asked.

"Yes, we stopped at their cabin first." Eden's parents and younger sister were living in one of the eight scenic log cabins at SkySong, though Helen and Jim planned to buy a house on Destiny Island in the spring. "Mom and Dad are thrilled to bits. They'll be over for dinner shortly. Kelsey was out for a run, so she doesn't know yet."

Eden went on, gushing about how she couldn't believe how wonderful the past year had been, finding her long-lost Aunt Di, discovering this wonderful island, and best of all meeting the love of her life.

Helen and Di had been separated since their teens, when Di, the older sister, had run away from their

Ottawa home along with her new, secret boyfriend, a member of the Mi'kmaq First Nation in Nova Scotia, who was also a teen runaway. They'd traveled west, all the way to Destiny Island, where they'd joined the Enchantery commune. Last summer, a long-lost letter had provided a clue that brought Eden here, and the rest was history. A family reunion, not to mention a new love.

Di, who'd been emptying glass canning jars of chopped tomatoes into a large pot on the stove, glanced over her shoulder. "Have you two talked about a wedding date?" The serene woman in her midsixties looked a bit like the hippie she'd once been, wearing one of the woven Guatemalan tops she loved, with her walnut-and-silver hair gathered into a long braid.

"Soon," Aaron said.

"But Aaron," Eden said, "I start my new job at Arbutus Lodge after New Year's. There'll be so much to do, and I need to concentrate on that rather than giving them short shrift."

Yeah, that was Eden. Superresponsible and organized.

"Do *not* tell me we're going to wait a year," Aaron said, sounding a little panicky.

"No, no, of course not. It's just, this is such a surprise. I need to get my head around it, and planning a wedding does take some time and effort."

He groaned, and Miranda gave him a sympathetic smile. Just wait until the poor guy found himself being dragged into discussions about flowers, music, and catering.

The scent of cooking tomatoes and herbs drifted across from the stove, stirring guilt in Miranda. She always tried to pull her weight and really should be helping with the meal. But right now something else was more important. She plunked down on a sky-blue chair across from Aaron and Eden, with her daughter in her lap

Eden, gazing at Aaron, said, "How about the spring? April or May?"

"I guess I can live with that. After all, we'll be living together anyhow."

And there was Miranda's cue. "Ariana and I will clear out of the house as soon as I can find a place." She'd been in denial, should have done this back when Eden decided to move to the island.

Cuddling her daughter, she said, "I'll talk to Iris at Dreamspinner. She and her family know everyone on the island." The Yakimuras' bookstore and coffee shop were the heart of Blue Moon Harbor village. "I bet some of the summer folks would be willing to rent their place at least until May or June, and by then I'll have found—"

"Whoa," Aaron said, casting a quick sideways glance at Eden.

"That's for sure," his fiancée said. "Miranda, Aaron's place is your home, yours and Ariana's, just as much as it's mine. We don't want you to leave."

Even as she appreciated Eden's generosity, Miranda's heart gave a twinge at the *we*. Already, Aaron and Eden were a *we* who made decisions together.

"Besides," Aaron said, "if you pay rent somewhere, you'll have to increase your work hours, and that won't give you as much time for your studies."

For years he'd been urging her to further her education. As an eleventh-grade dropout who'd never done well in school, she'd had no desire to go back to the books. And she'd been busy, what with the wait-ressing and retail jobs she'd held, and her pre-Ariana active life as a young single woman in a dynamic city. But then she'd gotten pregnant and life had changed.

Last summer it had sunk in that, if she was going to give her daughter the kind of life she deserved, she needed higher-paying work. So she'd worked her butt off for the past few months and almost finished her GED online. Turned out, she wasn't all that bad at schoolwork if she applied herself. In the new year, she'd start the online courses to get certified as an early childhood educator. Even if she busted her butt on those, too, which she fully intended to do, it would take her more than a year. "I'll still study," she said grimly.

"Are you sure?" he asked.

She'd have snapped at him for his lack of faith, except he had plenty of reason to doubt her. But now she was committed to building a better future for herself and the precious girl whose weight and stillness now indicated she'd dozed off on her mom's lap. "Yes, I'm sure." Somehow she'd find the time.

"And you guys need privacy," she said firmly. "Stop being so nice and generous and all that good stuff and be realistic." She managed a one-sided grin for her brother. "Isn't that what you've been telling me all these years? To be realistic?"

"Yeah, but—" he started.

"I have an idea." The calm voice was Di's, reminding Miranda that she and her brother had an audience.

Miranda glanced over her shoulder to see that Eden's aunt had turned away from the stove, where a pot of spicy tomato sauce now simmered. "Stay here, Miranda," Di said warmly.

"Here? At SkySong?"

The teen runaways had been together forever now. Never married, they'd rechristened themselves, changing the first names their parents had given them and taking the surname SkySong, and over the years they'd created this retreat by the same name. In addition to the lovely old wooden two-story home where Di and Seal lived, the scenic property included log guest cabins and a huge organic garden.

"We'd be happy to have you," Seal agreed, looking up from spreading something on a loaf of homemade French bread. Garlic and herb butter, from the delicious smell of it. He, like his partner, showed his hippie roots, clad in faded tie-dye and wearing his graying black hair in a ponytail secured by a leather thong. His deep brown eyes were sincere behind wire-framed glasses.

"I can't take your charity."

"It's not charity," Di said firmly. "Nor is having Helen, Jim, and Kelsey in a cabin."

"No, of course it's not, with them," Miranda said. "I mean, they're your family." Not to mention the SkySongs were assisting in Helen's recovery after surgery and treatment for a recurrence of breast cancer.

"You're family, too," Seal said.

"No, I'm not." Aaron and Ariana were her only family.

"Of course you are," Di said, coming over and resting a hand on her shoulder. "Aaron's about to be our . . . uh, nephew-in-law and you're his sister. Besides, you sure can't accuse Seal and me of being sticklers for convention, can you?" Her bright blue eyes danced.

Miranda's lips twitched. "I wouldn't dare."

"For us," Di said, "it's the family of our hearts that counts. You and Ariana most definitely have a place in our hearts."

"It's the truth," Seal said.

Miranda swallowed, trying to clear away the lump that

had formed in her throat. If she could believe them, she might cry. It was more acceptance and support than she'd had from her own grandparents, not to mention the father who hadn't even stuck around to see her born. Or the mom who'd put her next fix or her current boyfriend ahead of her children's welfare.

"We're never full up in winter," Di went on. "You and your sweet girl can have a cabin for the next four or five months at least. You'll have lots of able babysitters, so—"

"It's no problem for me to take Ariana to the store." Blowing Bubbles, where she worked part-time, sold children's toys, furniture, strollers, and so on. Kara, the owner, brought her own little one along with her and encouraged Miranda to do the same. There was a fenced playpen for their toddlers and the kids of customers, and Kara gave the children toys and stuffies to keep them happy. She said the best advertisement was to see a happy child loving one of the store's products. Mind you, since Ariana had turned two at the end of July, the whole happy-child thing wasn't happening as often as it used to.

"You might want to go out in the evenings, though," Di said.

"Going out isn't on my list right now." She hadn't had time to make female friends here. As for dating, her history with men was a succession of screwups: from the musician she'd moved in with when she was fifteen; to the gorgeous African American actor who'd hung around long enough to father Ariana but not to see her born; to the chef she'd fallen for last year before realizing he changed women as often as he changed his special of the week.

Aaron said she looked for love in all the wrong places. Maybe he was right. All she knew now was that this wasn't the time to be looking. And, though she had no affection for Destiny Island, she had to admit it was a good place to be if she wanted to avoid temptation. There weren't many eligible guys, and those she'd seen were way too wholesome and boring for her. "My spare time's for Ariana and for studying."

"Wise priorities," Aaron said.

She sent him an eye roll just as the kitchen door opened again. This time it was Kelsey, Eden's younger sister. She wore damp jogging clothes and with one hand flicked raindrops from her spiky, blond-streaked hair. "Eden, Aaron? Mom and Dad say you have big news."

A grinning Eden held up her left hand.

Kelsey squealed and threw her wet arms around her sister and Aaron. "I'm so happy for you! For all of us!"

The commotion woke Ariana, who let out a demanding screech.

Kelsey said, "Oh, sweetie, are you getting ignored?" She came over to scoop the child from Miranda's arms and made funny faces that worked magic in calming the incipient tantrum.

Eden repeated the proposal-on-the-dock story and then Di said, "Kelsey, Miranda wants to move out of Aaron's house and I've told her she and Ariana should take a cabin here."

"You totally should!" Kelsey said to Miranda, her eyes—the same blue as Di's—sparkling with excitement. "That would be so cool. More additions to our big, happy family!" She gazed down at Ariana again. "You'd like that, wouldn't you? I'd see lots more of you. Mom and Dad would love it, too. They're just crazy about you, you little sugarplum."

Kelsey, at twenty-two, was seven years younger than her sister and almost five years younger than Miranda. She was spontaneous, generous, and optimistic, and she was also completely devoted to her mom. So much so that she'd taken a year off from university at McGill to move here with her parents to help out.

A big, happy family. It was the one thing Miranda and Aaron had always wanted. He was getting it, but she couldn't truly accept that it was being offered to her. Or that she deserved it. She glanced at her brother, who sat with his arm around Eden. His gaze met hers. A quarter of a century ago, the two of them had learned how to communicate without words. Now, she knew he'd read her unspoken question.

Sure enough, he said solemnly, "Eden's right, that our place is yours, too. Never think you need to leave. But if you want to, I think you should accept Di and Seal's generous offer." His tone lightened. "Ariana would love having all these people to spoil her."

Miranda looked around the kitchen. A few minutes ago, everyone's attention had been on Aaron and Eden and now it was on her as they waited for her answer. Her brother knew exactly how to manipulate her. She'd do anything if she believed it was good for her child.

But could she really move to SkySong and be part of all this? The idea was overwhelming. She was so used to living alone with Ariana and had barely gotten adjusted to being in Aaron's house. Could she be a good guest here, pull her weight, ensure that Di and Seal didn't regret having made the offer?

Of course she and Ariana would have a separate cabin. It wasn't like they'd all be living on top of each other. A lot of the time, she and her daughter would have more privacy than they did at Aaron's.

She gazed at her child, so contented in Kelsey's arms. Ariana was her anchor. Her heart.

Slowly, she said, "Di and Seal, if you're really sure, I guess that's what we'll do. But you have to let me at least pay something or cook meals or garden or—"

"Miranda, shut up," Seal said with a smile that deepened the curved lines bracketing his nose and mouth.

In the next moment, Di's arms came around her. Almost like a mother's.

Which was a dangerous way to think, because if there was one thing Miranda knew, it was that she couldn't rely on a mom.